CHASING LIES

Special Agent Ricki James Thriller Book 12

C.R. Chandler

Also by C.R. Chandler

Prologue

"Make sure they're all dead." The man with thinning hair, wire-rimmed glasses, and wearing a black sweat suit along with a dark ski mask, looked down at the body sprawled at his feet. He raised a heavy combat boot and brought it down in a swift, hard stomp on a lifeless hand on the cement floor. The sound of bone shattering echoed in the enormous chamber, but the man attached to the hand crushed beneath the boot didn't even twitch at the brutal contact.

"You don't need to do that, Cap. You blew off half his head. He isn't going anywhere."

Cap looked over at the tall, skinny man staring at him through hollow eyes. "Magpie, you always did have a weak stomach. We can't leave anything to chance. Maybe you don't have the backbone to see this through."

The emaciated man pulled off his mask and took short, shallow breaths. "My backbone is strong enough to do anything for my wife and kids. I'm in for the long haul."

Seeing the sweat lining the other man's brow, Cap doubted

if that haul was going to be very long. Along with the sweat on his face, Magpie's hands were shaking too. Probably a side effect of his chemotherapy treatment. But it made little difference if he was sweating and had the shakes. The hardest part of the operation was done. Now all they had to do was clip off any loose ends before driving off into the sunset and disappearing for good.

If Magpie made it through the seven-year wait they had all agreed on, then the man and his little family would be rich. If the cancer took Magpie before then, well, he'd never let a man down. He would make sure Magpie's wife and kids got his share of the money. Provided the man kept his word and never told the little woman about any of this. Otherwise . . .

With a shrug, Cap let the thought trail off. He'd cross that bridge if he was forced to, but right now he had those loose ends to see to and their payday to collect. And they needed to get to it before the armored car arrived. He looked around. The three dead bodies were lying in their own separate pools of blood. Two more men were still inside the plane and were just as dead.

The big hangar smelled of a mixture of jet fuel and hot oil. A combination that originated from the private corporate jet that had taxied inside fifteen minutes earlier. Cap checked his watch, then frowned. He'd estimated at least a ninety-minute delay for the armored car crew to get the tire changed on their truck, and another fifteen minutes beyond that for it to finish the drive to the hangar. But he wanted to be out of there long before the armored car crew rolled up.

They needed to get a move on it. "Hey, Buzzfeed. Where are you?"

A man strolled out from behind the plane, carrying an M4 semiautomatic rifle with its strap looped over his shoulder, his mask tucked into his belt. He passed Magpie, giving him a friendly slap on the back. Except for a slight difference in their heights, the two men could have passed for twins if you squinted hard enough. At least they could have when Magpie had been healthy. "What's up, Cap?"

"Did you check the cargo hold?"

"Yep. They're in there. Mister Bigshot stashed them exactly where he said he would—tucked away in the back of the hold, underneath a tarp. Just sitting there, side by side, as sweet a sight as I've ever seen—a couple of three-by-three metal boxes with some heavy-duty locks on them." Buzzfeed's eyes gleamed with pleasure. "And now it's all ours."

"It will be if we stick to the plan." Cap looked down at the man Buzzfeed had been talking about. Now Mister Bigshot lay dead at his feet, with a hand crushed flat against the cold cement. *Easy come, easy go,* he thought, then dismissed the rightful owner of all that cash—and the corporate jet—without a twinge of remorse. His planning had been thorough and brilliant. He'd earned that money, and he intended to keep it at any cost.

Buzzfeed followed his gaze. "This one looks dead enough." He shifted his attention to the other two men lying closer to the plane. "What about those two?"

"I'll check on them. You get up into the plane and do a thorough search, including the toilet. Make sure there aren't any other boxes or a briefcase on board. Just in case the boxes in the hold are decoys. Then make sure the pilot and copilot are dead, while Magpie brings the van inside. And use those gloves I gave you to do the search." Buzzfeed gave him a sharp salute before doing a quickstep over to the steep set of stairs leading up to an open door right behind the cockpit. With Buzzfeed gone, Cap glanced over at the skinny man, who looked on the verge of collapsing right there on the pavement. "You go get the van and park next to the other side of the plane. The cargo hold is on that side so it will be easier to load the money boxes there." When Magpie didn't move, Cap snapped his fingers right in front of the man's face. "Hey. Are you with us?"

"I'm here," Magpie rasped, his glazed eyes struggling to focus on Cap. "No problem."

"Okay." With exaggerated patience, Cap slowly repeated his instructions. "Go get the van and park it near the other side of the plane. Then you move your butt to the rear and wait for us. You can even lie down back there if you need to."

Magpie shook his head, his features looking more gaunt than they had even a few minutes before. "I don't need to lie down. I'm okay. My last treatment hasn't worn off yet, that's all."

"Fine. Then get moving." As the sick man slowly shuffled away, Cap checked on the bodyguards, who were as dead as their employer, then approached the jet. Cupping his hands around his mouth, he shouted up to the cockpit. "Buzzfeed? How's it looking?"

The always optimistic Buzzfeed didn't even grimace as he removed his gloves and braced a hand against the back of the leather covering the pilot's seat. Leaning over, he peered into the wide-open but sightless eyes of the man slumped in it, who was only held upright by the seatbelt crossing his chest. Buzzfeed laid two fingers against the pulse point in the neck. A bullet had caught the pilot square in the forehead, execution-style, which made Buzzfeed smile.

"Nice shot on the pilot. You haven't lost your touch, Cap," he yelled to the man below watching him through the cockpit window. Sliding to the side, he repeated the same process on the copilot. Still smiling, he straightened up and raised his voice again. "They're both deader than doornails, Cap. I still have the front of the cabin to search. I found one briefcase and a couple of duffels with nothing but clothes in them in a compartment in the rear." He snapped the latex gloves back onto his hands.

"Finish the search, then get out of there. And bring that briefcase with you." Cap looked at his watch. Sixty minutes left. He wanted to be gone in fifteen. "Make it quick," he yelled up the stairs. "I'll get the money loaded so we can get our tails out of here."

Cap turned his head to watch the van slowly roll across the hangar's floor. He nodded in satisfaction when Magpie stopped right next to the plane. Slipping his arm through the shoulder strap of his gun, he centered it across his back before ducking under the wing and heading to the cargo hold.

Chapter One

"There must be flowers." Marcie put her hands on her broad hips and nodded her head with a snap that was sharp enough to make her short brown curls dance around her head. "A wedding is hardly a wedding without flowers."

Ricki wrinkled her nose up as she shot the middle-aged waitress an exasperated look. She was seated in a corner booth in the Sunny Side Up, the diner she co-owned with Marcie, and Anchorman, the cook. They were not only her business partners, but she also considered them best friends and part of her family. Although right now, Marcie was contending for the title of "difficult older sister" in addition to partner, friend, and former babysitter.

Adding to Ricki's growing exasperation was her fiancé, Police Chief Clay Thomas. He was seated next to her in the booth and doing a great job of pretending not to hear a word about the ongoing flowers-or-no-flowers argument.

She switched her midnight-blue gaze away from Marcie's face and swept it around the room, looking for an excuse to escape. The booths along two walls were filled with customers. A good portion of them were dressed in clothes with designer labels, clearly tagging them as tourists from the nearby resort hotel. Unless one of them suddenly went nuclear and broke a law along the way, she wouldn't be getting any help from that quarter.

Most of the breakfast regulars were sitting at the counter that spanned the back of the diner, or at the tables scattered across the room. The remaining wall up front faced the main street of her hometown of Brewer and sported a long window that drew light into the place. Well, as much light as was possible in the Pacific Northwest, which was deservedly known more for its overcast skies and rain than sunny days.

But being the true Western Washington native that she was, the rain had never bothered Ricki. Like the always circulating gossip, it was part of Brewer. The quaint town with a compact marina running along Main Street, was one of three small burgs that collectively made up the Bay. All three were located along the same highway that separated Dabob Bay from the vast wilderness of Olympic National Park, and just beyond it, the Pacific Ocean.

There were twenty miles between Massey at the northern tip of the bay and Brewer in the south, with the largest town of Edington in between. The highway that linked them snaked its way for fifteen hundred miles up the Pacific coastline, with its northern section passing through the rustic towns on the border of the only natural rainforest in the country.

Having grown up in the shadow of that rainforest, which was enclosed within the boundaries of Olympic National Park, Ricki considered it her personal sliver of paradise. She'd spent her entire life loving the park, and now worked for it, along with the sixty-two other parks in the country, as a special agent for the Investigative Services Branch of the National Park

Service. She loved her job, she loved the parks—especially Olympic—and she loved the diner she'd opened seven years earlier. What she didn't love was dealing with a growing list of wedding plans.

When it came to marriage, this wasn't either her or Clay's first rodeo, and they'd both done the big, elaborate bash the first time around. She really didn't want a repeat performance.

With a reluctant sigh, she turned her attention back to Marcie. "I just don't think waterfalls of flowers hanging down from the rafters will work here. It's going to make the diner look and smell like a funeral parlor."

"I can make the food match that," Anchorman said, the bland look on his face completely out of sync with the amusement in his voice.

The big man with a buzzcut, broad shoulders, and a build as solid as a tree trunk, lounged in the bench seat across from Ricki. He had one arm flung over the back, but even relaxed, he looked every bit the former Marine sniper that he was, and nothing like a cook in a small country diner.

But having grown up in his parents' eatery in New Jersey, he'd learned to man the stove at an early age. Even his twenty-year stint in the military hadn't dulled his genius at preparing the comfort foods loved by everyone in the Bay. "We need to get the menu settled so I can get back to my kitchen. Sam's been in there all by himself holding down the breakfast shift, and if we don't wrap this up, he'll have to deal with the lunch crowd, too."

Sam was Marcie's older brother, and the relief cook for the diner. At Anchorman's statement, the waitress took three steps backwards and looked through the large cut-out window between the kitchen and the dining room. "He's fine," she declared with a sniff before returning to her former position and crossing her arms over her chest. "First we need to agree on the flowers, and then we'll get to the food."

Anchorman glanced at Ricki. Lifting his wrist, he pointedly tapped the face of his watch. "This needs to be wrapped up. We've already been sitting here for over thirty minutes."

Marcie gaped at him. "So? Did you expect us to plan a whole wedding in thirty stingy minutes?" She threw her arms into the air. "You've been married three times. You should know more about weddings than that."

The big Marine shrugged his shoulders. "I got married at a courthouse all three times, so I don't know anything about weddings. But I do know we all need to get some actual work done."

Silently agreeing with that, Ricki crossed her long legs beneath the table while she slowly drummed her fingertips on its top. Deciding it took two to make a wedding—and why should she be the only one making all the decisions?—she turned her head and met the steady gaze of her fiancé. Gray eyes, set in a face that could easily be featured on a Hollywood screen, returned her long look before crinkling at the corners in answer to the frown she was directing at him. "Okay, Mister Police Chief. You're the law around here. Flowers or no flowers?"

"It's not a law," Marcie piped up. "It's a fact. Weddings have to have flowers."

"And a minister" came floating over from the table closest to Ricki's booth.

Recognizing the thin, crusty voice of Pete, the keeper and distributor of all gossip in the Bay, Ricki gritted her teeth at the old man's blatant eavesdropping, then forced herself to relax before leaning over to peek around Clay. "That won't be a problem," she assured the elderly man who had recently passed his eightieth birthday and was a regular early-morning patron of the Sunny Side Up.

Clay reached over and took one of her hands, tucking it into his own as he smiled at Pete. "I've taken care of that. But I appreciate the reminder, Pete." He lifted Ricki's hand to his lips and placed a quick kiss on the back of her knuckles. "There's no legal precedent that I know of for flowers at a wedding. But maybe just a few at the front door, and something simple on the tables."

"Okay." Ricki nodded at Marcie. "That sounds fine. A couple of smaller vases at the front door, and maybe some daisies, or something like that, on the tables."

"And roses all along the back counter," Marcie added. "Just a single row of them," she put in when Ricki opened her mouth to protest.

Giving in, Ricki slumped back against her seat and tucked a strand of her long, dark hair behind one ear. "Fine. A few roses on the back counter." She gave Anchorman a hopeful look. "How do you feel about burgers and fries?" She barely kept from wincing when Marcie snorted loudly.

"You can't seriously be thinking . . ."

Marcie's new tirade was cut short by a loud yell, followed by a violent curse that was cut short by the sound of a gunshot coming from the back. Three bodies were out of the booth in a flash, knocking Marcie off her feet. She lost her balance and toppled right into a startled Pete's lap.

Clay was first to reach the double door leading into the kitchen. The firearm he carried on his hip was already drawn as he skidded to a stop. Anchorman crouched on the opposite side as Ricki slid over the customer counter on one hip, scattering several coffee cups before landing right under the open cutout.

She stayed still for a moment, mentally berating herself for not wearing her shoulder harness. She rarely did on a day off, and her plans were to work at the diner, not confront an active shooter. The only weapon available was one of her rifles, along with one of Anchorman's, stored in a closet in the kitchen. Which meant that only Clay was armed.

She drew in a breath and called out to the relief cook. "Sam? Are you all right?" When no answer came, she straightened up just enough that the top of her head was barely below the lower sill of the cutout. The murmurs and movement of bodies in the dining room had her looking over at Anchorman. He was staring at her as she pointed to the crowd behind them and ran a single finger across her throat.

The Marine nodded and cupped his hands to his mouth. "Everyone be quiet. Get down flat and don't move."

The noise completely cut off, as if a switch had been flipped off. Satisfied, Ricki again put her whole concentration into listening, but all she heard was the banging sound of a door opening and then shutting in a steady, repetitive rhythm.

Clay had moved to squat alongside one of the double doors. He was peering through a crack between them when she called out to Sam again, and again there was no answer. If he was hurt, the last thing she wanted was for him to bleed out on the kitchen floor. They needed to get to him. And fast. She looked over at Clay, who shook his head, then frowned when she cautiously straightened up another few inches and peered over the edge of the cutout. If there was anyone in the kitchen, he was crouching lower than the prep table that stretched down the center of the room. And if there was someone there, at least he hadn't blown her head off.

Her eyes darted to the door leading into the back alley. It was open and banging against the frame as if someone had left in a hurry. Her gaze shifted to the small closet on the far wall of the kitchen where the rifles were stored. That door was still shut, so the odds were good that the guns were still in there.

She carefully controlled the sound of her breath as she tried to get a feeling for the space on the other side of the cutout.

There wasn't a sound coming from the kitchen, and her gut told her it was empty. From her vantage point, there was no sign of Sam. Praying he wasn't lying dead on the floor, she hunched over and quick-walked back to where Clay and Anchorman were waiting.

"Nothing. I didn't see anyone, including Sam. He might be hiding in the freezer, or he could be unconscious on the floor. Either way, we need to get in there. It looks like the back door is open, so I'm thinking whoever fired that shot is gone."

Clay nodded. "Me too. He probably shot off that round, then hightailed it through the back alley. I'll go in first and head for the rear door. You look for Sam in the kitchen."

Ricki shook her head. "He might be wounded. Anchorman is better with that." She pointed at the Marine. "You find Sam and help him. I'll get the rifles and back up Clay." When the Marine nodded, she tapped her fiancé on the shoulder. "Let's go."

Without hesitation, the chief flung open the door, reared back and waited half a beat for any fire coming their way, then plunged through the opening. Before the double door swung back into place, Ricki slapped a hand on it to keep it open and Anchorman slid into the kitchen behind Clay with her close behind.

Clay rounded the corner of the center prep table and pointed at the floor before continuing to the back door. "Sam's over here, next to the stove."

Anchorman sprang in that direction while Ricki ran to the closet and threw it open. She grabbed her rifle and with an expertise derived from hours upon hours of practice, she loaded it from a box of shells kept with the two guns. After also loading Anchorman's rifle and dropping extra shells into one pocket of her cargo pants, she trotted back into the kitchen and laid the former Marine's rifle near his feet.

"It's not good," he growled at her. "I'm keeping pressure on the wound. Make sure someone has called for the ambulance." They both looked over their shoulders when the sound of a siren split the air just as Marcie came running into the kitchen, with Pete and a whole crowd close behind.

"We heard Clay yell Sam was lying by the stove, so we called for help. How is he?" She took one frantic look at Sam, whose blood was seeping through the cloth Anchorman was holding to his chest, and went as white as chalk. Her hands flew to her mouth as she stared at her brother lying on his back, arms straight out from his sides, his blood sliding slowly along the tiles. "Oh my god, oh my god!"

Pete laid a bony hand on her shoulder and gave it a gentle squeeze. "Now don't you worry. Sam is tough. Didn't you tell me he finished two combat tours? Anchorman knows how to take care of him."

Bill Langly, the commander of the local Veterans of Foreign Wars post, shoved people aside. "Everyone, get back to the dining room and stand against a wall so the ambulance guys can get through." He turned to face the room and raised his voice to a shout. "Now. Do it now." As the crowd moved, with the people in front forcing the ones behind them to back up and return to the main room, Bill spun around again and gestured at the rifle in Ricki's hand. "You get after Clay. I'll stay with Anchorman and Sam."

Grateful for his help, Ricki fled through the door and into the alley. Clay was nowhere to be seen, so she sprinted down the narrow opening between two brick buildings. When she burst out onto the sidewalk, there was a startled scream from a tourist standing in front of the Sunny Side Up. "Get back inside," she ordered just before spotting Clay coming out of the shop next door.

"This one's clear. I'll go north," he shouted.

Nodding, Ricki turned in the opposite direction and sprinted down the sidewalk, away from the diner, just as the ambulance pulled up.

"Gunshot wound to the chest," she yelled to the young EMT who was only a handful of years older than her own son. "He's in the kitchen. In back." She didn't wait for a response but ducked into a shop that sold souvenirs of Olympic Park to the tourists. "I'm here, Ricki," the owner called before standing up behind the cashier's counter in back. "What's going on?"

She took a quick glance around the store. "Are you alone?" At the owner's nod, Ricki pointed to the front door. "Lock that and stay inside."

"How long for? What's going on?" The man leaned over the counter to look out his front window, panic written all over his face.

"Shooting. Lock the door and stay low," Ricki said before heading back to the sidewalk and to the next shop on the street. Five minutes later she had just stepped out of the fourth shop along the row, when she heard Clay call her name. Switching directions, she met him halfway down the block. "Nothing," she said by way of a greeting. "How about you?"

"Same." He gave a hard stare at the shops along the opposite side of the street. "Jules and Ryan just pulled up to the diner." He made a gesture in that direction where the only cruiser owned by the joint police department of the three towns in the Bay was double-parked amid a flurry of activity. "They're helping load Sam into the ambulance, then I'm going to set Ryan on crowd control while Jules helps me search the other side of the street." He huffed a short breath as he ran an agitated hand through his hair. "The shooter is probably long gone, but we need to be sure."

Ricki started to nod but was distracted by the ring of her cell phone. She dug it out of her back pocket and seeing "Anchorman" displayed on the caller ID, immediately held it to her ear.

"How's Sam?" She listened for a few moments, slowly closing her eyes as a deep cold crept up her arms and down her spine.

"Not good. You need to get here now," Anchorman stated in a flat voice. "Marcie is going to need you."

Chapter Two

L ocated just north of Brewer on a side street directly off the main highway, the clinic also served as a four-bed hospital when necessary. By the time Ricki made the turn onto the road, the generous two lanes had turned into a very narrow single lane, with both sides of the street lined with cars and trucks right up to the clinic's parking lot and past it as far as she could see.

A crowd of people was jammed into the small space in front of the one-story structure and spilled out onto the road. With nowhere to park, Ricki left her jeep in the middle of the street and shouldered her way up to the short sidewalk leading to the front of the clinic.

The entrance was guarded by Pete, who stood on the top step, his thin, bony arms crossed over a sunken chest as he scowled at the wall of people milling around in front of him. Just behind him was Mike, who'd lived full time in the Bay ever since he'd retired twenty years earlier and was Pete's faithful sidekick. Unlike Pete, who looked as mean as an old bear who'd had his meal stolen right from under him, Mike had too kind a soul to manage even a glare. His worried gaze flooded with relief when he spotted Ricki.

"Hey there." He flung his arms wildly out in front of him. "Let Ricki get by, now. She's the law. Everyone just let her get by."

Ricki wove her way through the last few feet to the steps, climbing them and turning to face a sea of expectant faces. It wouldn't do any good to tell them to go home. A few people were sitting on small camp stools, clearly intending to stay put until they got word on Sam.

No one threw questions at her because they didn't have to. Everyone who lived in the Bay would have heard by now what had happened at the Sunny Side Up, and that Clay and his deputies were searching the town for whoever had shot Sam. That was old news. Now they were gathering on the other side of town at the clinic to keep vigil, waiting to hear what was going on inside. In the Bay, and especially in a place the size of Brewer, this was a family affair.

"I'm not the law," she stated in a clear, steady voice just as the mayor and three councilmen popped out of a car that had stopped right behind her jeep. "Chief Thomas is. And right now, he and his deputies are turning the town inside out looking for the person who did this to Sam." She waited for the wave of murmurs and whispered comments to pass through the crowd. "And you all know Clay. He won't stop until he finds him." She paused and stared down a small group of men giving her a skeptical look. "You can count on it."

One man shuffled his feet and stuck his hands into the back pockets of his well-worn jeans. "Will you and Anchorman be helping him?"

Behind Ricki, Pete snorted in response. "Now that's a stupid question, Maury." He glared at the man who crossed his arms over a massive chest and glared right back at him. "And you'd better know, whoever shot Sam is going to regret having Clay, Ricki, and Anchorman all on his tail." Pete's chin jutted out. "Who here doesn't believe that?"

Another more enthusiastic murmur spread through the group as Ricki turned and headed for the doors leading into the clinic. She gave a brief nod to each of the two younger men standing behind Pete and Mike, and a quick smile to the woman in her mid-forties who was standing next to them, looking every bit as fierce.

Patricia Forker rarely went by the name her parents had given her. Like Anchorman, she preferred the handle bestowed by her fellow Army Rangers.

"Merlin," Ricki acknowledged. "Thanks for the help out here."

The woman's spine straightened, bringing her solid build a full inch over Ricki's leaner, athletic five-foot-eight-inch frame. "Glad to help." Her tone and gaze softened. "Anchorman is inside with Marcie."

Nodding her thanks, Ricki walked into the clinic, letting the heavy door automatically close behind her, effectively shutting out the steady, underlying current of noise from the crowd outside.

The lobby was the size of a large living room, with cushioned chairs and low tables scattered around the circular counter in the center. Every five years, like clockwork, the walls were painted a different color, with the latest selection being a light desert tan.

Marcie and Anchorman were sitting in two chairs pushed close together. He had an arm around her shoulders and was holding her hand. Her head rested against his chest, her eyes closed and her lips trembling. At the sound of Ricki's footsteps, her eyes flew open and she was out of her seat in a flash. She ran full tilt toward Ricki, almost knocking her down as she locked her arms around her employer and partner.

Ricki staggered back a step before regaining her footing. Returning the fierce hug, she ran a gentle hand up and down Marcie's back to soothe the sudden flood of tears.

"Who would do this?" Marcie choked out between sobs. "Who would do this to Sam?"

Good question, Ricki thought as she looked over her friend's head toward Anchorman. His expression was grim as he shook his head. Digging her teeth into her lower lip to keep from adding her tears to Marcie's, Ricki slowly led the waitress back to the chair she'd just vacated then urged her to sit down. Once Marcie was slumped in the seat, Ricki knelt down in front of her, laying a hand on a denim-covered knee.

"I'm staying right here with you. Whatever comes, we're going to face it together." She looked up at Anchorman. "Have you called Dan?" Dan Wilkes was Marcie's boyfriend. A former CIA researcher, who had jumped from the black-ops agency over to the National Park Service, Dan was comfortably into middle age like Marcie. The two most solid, steady, and predictable people Ricki had ever known fit each other like a hand and glove. Although Dan worked in Seattle five days a week, he spent every weekend, and any days off, hanging out in the Bay.

"I called him," Anchorman said quietly. "And since it's Saturday, he was just getting off the Seattle Ferry." He glanced at his watch. "He should be here in another ten minutes or so, provided he keeps it down to only twice the speed limit."

The double doors on the far side of the lobby swung open, giving a brief glimpse of the long hallway beyond them. Bill Langly stepped into view. He hesitated when he saw Ricki, then quickly crossed the distance between them. The VFW post commander was in his mid-fifties, with a long, carefully trimmed beard reaching past his chin and a bald head that reflected the lights built into the ceiling. He was wearing jeans and a plaid wool shirt along with a pair of standard hiking boots rather than the combat variety still preferred by many of his fellow vets.

"I was just on my way to check on Pete and some of the other guys."

Ricki reached into the front pocket of her jeans and held her car keys out to Bill. "I'd appreciate it if you would move my ride. I left it in the middle of the road."

He smiled and took the keys. "I can do that. Although if you're still driving that lime-green jeep of yours, I doubt if anyone would dare hit it."

She doubted it too, but only shrugged in response. "Who's in with Sam?" she asked, deliberately avoiding any question about her relief cook's condition. Not with Marcie sitting just a foot away.

"Dr. Torres and TK," Bill said, which had Ricki lifting her eyebrows.

TK was Dr. Richard Evans, who had set up his practice in the Bay over forty years ago. He'd built the clinic, and still owned a good piece of it, having sold the rest of the interest to Dr. Luca Torres, who worked there full time, and his partner, who came in two days a week.

The long-time doctor still filled in occasionally and had even served as the Bay's medical examiner until recently, when he'd also retired from that role. Now he spent all his free time fishing out on Dabob Bay. Which was how he'd earned his nickname of TK, for Trout King. While Ricki had all the confidence in the world in the much younger Dr. Torres, she blew out a soft breath of relief that TK was watching over Sam. Like a good number of the Bay's residents, Sam had been one of TK's patients since he was a young boy.

"He was still getting his gear together when he got the call about Sam," Bill offered. "I guess he got here just as the ambulance was pulling in. At least that's what Nancy said."

Nancy was the only nurse at the clinic and had stayed on with Dr. Torres after TK had retired. And if Bill had his way, Nancy would officially be his girlfriend in the very near future. Which was why the VFW commander spent more time hanging around the clinic than TK did.

"That's good." Ricki twisted around to look over her shoulder as the front doors to the clinic burst open, briefly filling the room with the sounds from the mushrooming crowd gathered outside.

Dan rushed into the room, his gaze immediately zeroing in on Marcie before he ran over to where the small group was gathered. Ricki had just enough time to jump to her feet and step out of the way as the former CIA researcher sank into a squat in front of the waitress. "Honey, are you all right?"

Marcie stared at him for a long moment, her eyes wide and swimming in tears. "Oh, Dan. It's horrible. I can't even think," she wailed, then clamped her arms around his neck so tightly that he made a small choking sound even as his own arms came around her.

Stepping back to give them a bit of privacy, Ricki turned to face Bill. "It would be great if you could keep an eye on the crowd and make sure they stay outside. I saw the mayor arrive a few minutes ago. I'm sure he wouldn't mind saying a few words."

Beneath his beard, Bill's mouth curved into a grin. "Yeah. I'm sure that can be arranged."

As the VFW Commander headed for the door, Ricki glanced at Anchorman and jerked her head toward the opposite side of the room. The big Marine stood, carefully stepping around Dan and Marcie before following her.

Keeping one eye on the couple clinging together as Marcie continue to sob against Dan's shoulder, Ricki's lips pressed into a thin line. "What do you think?"

"It's not good," the Marine said in a low voice. "It's a damn miracle he didn't die right there on the kitchen floor." His jaw hardened to stone. "What's the sitrep on the search?" he asked, using the military shorthand for situation report.

"Nothing yet," Ricki replied, matching her soft tone to his. "Clay and I got through one side of Main Street. He and Jules were about to search the other when I left to come here."

"The bastard's gone," Anchorman stated in a flat voice, all the more scary for its complete lack of emotion.

Ricki pushed away the stray lock of hair that always escaped the long ponytail she'd anchored at the nape of her neck with an elastic band. "That's what Clay thinks, too."

Anchorman gave her a direct, penetrating look. "And you, Special Agent Ricki James? What do *you* think?"

"Maybe," she said, then winced when her cook's gaze sharpened on her face. He knew what her "maybe" meant, and his question cracked out a second later.

"So you think he's hiding somewhere close to the diner?" Anchorman's whole body tensed, ready to spring into action.

She sighed as her boot started tapping against the tile floor. "I don't know. Right now, I'm having a hard time with Marcie's question." She glanced over at the waitress, who was quiet now as she listened to whatever Dan was saying to her. "She wanted to know why Sam was shot?" Ricki's gaze narrowed on Anchorman's suddenly blank expression. "So do I. Or maybe he was collateral damage, and it shouldn't have been Sam at all."

The Marine ran a big hand across the top of his short, military-style buzz cut. "I don't know. But if you're thinking it was me the guy was after, he would have been smarter to come around during the dinner shift. Sam was filling in for me this morning, but I'm usually about fifty-fifty on the breakfast crowd. However, I almost always cook the dinner. The asshole's chances would have been better if he'd waited a few hours." He lowered his hand and stared back at Ricki. "That is *if* I'm the one he wanted to shoot."

She frowned. He had a good point. If the shooter had been watching long enough to know how to get into the kitchen through the back door, and knew how to get clean away within minutes, then the odds were good he would have also known what time of day Anchorman was most likely to be in the kitchen.

The double doors leading into the back of the clinic opened, distracting her from her thoughts. Nancy, dressed in jeans with a white coat over a blue shirt peeking along the neckline, appeared in the opening. She did a quick scan of the room before her gaze latched on to Ricki. Lifting a hand, she waved her over.

Feeling as if there was lead in her boots, Ricki cast a quick glance toward Marcie. The older woman was slumped in Dan's arms, her face hidden against his shoulder. Not wanting to draw her attention, Ricki tiptoed her way to the double doors where Nancy was waiting. The nurse stepped back, holding the door open enough for Ricki to slip through, then letting it close softly behind them.

"TK wants to talk to you," Nancy said. She lifted her red-rimmed eyes to meet Ricki's gaze. With a slight shake of her head, she pointed down the hallway. "He's in Exam Room One. It's that first door on the right." She bit her lip before adding in a subdued voice. "Just go right in."

The walk to the exam room seemed to go in slow motion. Ricki forced herself to take one step and then another, each forward movement adding to the ball of dread mixed with sorrow building up inside her. When she reached the first door on the right, she put her hand on the knob and closed her eyes. Taking a deep breath, and then two, she slowly opened her eyes while she turned the knob and stepped inside.

"Come in," TK said quietly. He was standing on the opposite side of a long table that held a body with a white sheet draped over it.

Ricki's mind went blank and her breath grew shallow as she stared at the figure outlined underneath the sheet. "Anchorman said Sam should have died on the kitchen floor." Having no idea why that was the first thing out of her mouth, Ricki clamped her lips together and fell silent.

"Instead, he died here." TK held up a hand when Ricki's head snapped up, meeting her stricken stare with a calm look. "He never regained consciousness according to the ambulance crew. And was barely breathing when they brought the gurney off the rig. By the time he reached the exam room, he was gone." He paused and lightly rubbed his hands together. "I'm sorry, Ricki. Sorry this happened at the Sunny Side Up, and even sorrier for what I have to tell you." He walked around the exam table. Standing directly next to the body, right at the hip, he gathered up the side of the sheet with both hands, then turned his head and nodded at Ricki. "You need to come closer and take a look at this."

It wasn't the first time she'd seen a bullet wound on someone she cared about, and probably wouldn't be her last either. But that didn't make any real difference because nothing ever made it easier to bear. But at the insistence in TK's voice, she walked forward. "I need to look at what? I've seen bullet wounds before, TK."

"It's not the bullet wound I'm talking about. That's in his chest, and will be for the Bay's new ME to explain to you." He lifted the sheet higher, exposing a small section of the abdomen.

25

"See this?" He pointed to a spot close to the hip and ran his finger in a straight line across the skin right below the stomach.

Not seeing anything, Ricki leaned forward. TK's finger was on top of a thin white line that looked like an old scar. "Okay," she said, straightening up. "It's a scar."

TK dropped the sheet and crossed his arms over his chest as he turned to face Ricki, his craggy features set into stern lines. "Yes, it is. A scar. Or more specifically, a scar from an appendectomy." When Ricki cocked an eyebrow at him, he took a wider stance and lifted his own shaggy eyebrows as he stared back at her. "Sam never had an appendectomy." He broke the staring contest long enough to glance down at the body on the table. "I don't know who this is, but I do know that he isn't Samuel Parkman."

Chapter Three

Ricki stared at TK in disbelief, looking for any signs that the elderly doctor had snapped under the strain of seeing a long-time patient of his shot to death.

"I'm thinking as clearly as you are," TK cracked out. "And given that idiotic look on your face, maybe a damn sight clearer." He stepped back and pointed at the sheet-covered body. "That poor soul died from a bullet straight to his chest, but he is not Marcie's brother, Sam."

Lifting her hands to her face, Ricki scrubbed her cheeks hard before closing her eyes and taking a deep breath. "Okay, okay. Let's just back up here a second." She gave the body a quick glance then settled her gaze on TK. "Sam was gone a long time. First when he was in the army, and then afterward when he disappeared for all that time and didn't come home or contact his family. Not even once. At least, that's what Marcie said. It caused her and her parents a lot of grief."

"I know that. I talked to Marcie's parents many times about their son. Right up until they both passed away." TK huffed an annoyed sound, then stalked over to the corner and pulled out a

27

low wheeled stool. Rolling it closer to Ricki, he stared up at her. "But you're wrong about Sam never coming home. He did. Once. Right after he left the army, and before he pulled that disappearing act of his twenty-five years ago. He was only here for a few days, but he made a point of dropping by my old office and asking for a physical." His chin jutted out into a stubborn line. "And I'm telling you, that boy did not have any appendectomy scar."

"All right." Ricki's boot tapped on the shiny tile floor. "Like you said, he disappeared from the Bay, and then he was gone over two decades. He could have had an appendectomy during that time."

"Of course. But he didn't have this one," TK stated flatly. "Or whoever is lying on that table didn't. That scar is at least thirty years old."

Ricki couldn't help the skeptical look she shot at him. "Thirty years? How do you know that?"

TK's expression turned smug as he rolled his eyes at her. "You might be a brilliant investigator and a crack shot, Ricki James, but you do not have any medical training beyond basic first aid." He unfolded his arms and waved one hand toward the body. "That's a surgical scar. And surgically removing an appendix went out of style at least thirty years ago when a laparoscopy became the standard procedure. And it does not leave a scar like that."

Ricki blinked, casting another swift glance at the body while she did the calculations in her head. "I'm not sure," she mumbled, more to herself than TK, before she continued to stare at the body with a frown. "Sam's been back in the Bay for three years now, I think. But I'm not sure when he got out of the service."

"I am," TK stated. "I've been that boy's doctor since the first day he started school. He enlisted when he was nineteen.

Then spent twelve years in the army. He was thirty-one when he came home that last time and had his physical, and he's fifty-six now. You do the math. He was gone twenty-five years, not the thirty when that appendix was removed." TK held out a hand and let Ricki help him from the stool. "I'm telling you, this man is not Sam Parkman."

Ricki held on to TK's hand until she was sure he was steady on his feet. When he nodded his thanks and released his hold, she paced the five steps she could take in the exam room before hitting a wall, then turned around and paced back. "Are you sure?"

"I am," TK said. "Now, I need to talk to Marcie. Is she still out in the lobby?" When Ricki nodded, the old doctor heaved a heavy sigh. "I'm going to join Dr. Torres in his office at the end of the hall. You go on and bring Marcie back, and then after she's heard the news and asked her questions, you can take her home."

"No." Ricki was shaking her head before TK had finished talking, sending her long fall of dark hair sliding across her back. "I'll have Dan bring her back here to speak with you and Dr. Torres, and then he can take her home."

The old doctor studied the determined set of her face for a long moment. "You be careful looking for the answers to this riddle, Ricki. It takes a lot of brass to step into someone else's shoes for three years, and in that person's hometown to boot. Whatever this man was hiding from, it can't be good."

"Good or bad, TK, I am going to find those answers," Ricki stated baldly. With a last look at the shrouded figure on the table, she headed out the door and down the hallway. Once she reached the lobby, she walked over to where Marcie was sitting.

The waitress watched her approach with wide, tear-soaked eyes. Her teeth dug into her lower lip when Ricki pulled over a chair and sat down next to her,. "You have a weird look on your face, Ricki." She cast a fearful glance toward the closed double doors. "Is it Sam? Is he going to be okay?"

Not sure how to answer that question, Ricki went for the truth. "I don't know. But TK needs to talk to you." She looked over Marcie's head at Dan. "You take her on back. TK's in the office at the end of the hall. When Marcie's done talking with him, take her home." She leaned over and gave her longtime friend and waitress a quick hug, then leaned back and looked her in the eyes. "I'll be by later to check on you and we can talk then, I promise."

Marcie's lips trembled as her gaze darted between Ricki and the closed double doors. "What's going on? Did Sam die? If he died, you tell me right now." The older woman's tone ended on a high squeak.

Ricki laid a hand on Marcie's arm and gave it a gentle, soothing rub. "I don't know how Sam is." *Or where he is*, she added silently. "TK can explain, and we'll talk soon. I promise," she repeated. Getting to her feet again, she nodded at Dan, watching as he drew Marcie out of her chair and led her across the lobby. As soon as the doors closed behind them, Ricki did a quick spin around to face Anchorman. "We need to get out of here and find Clay. Bill still has the keys to my jeep. Is your truck here?"

"Yeah. But it's parked out front and we'll have to break it loose from the mob."

"Fine," she said and started for the door but was stopped by Anchorman's hand, latching around her forearm.

"Hang on there. Is Sam dead?"

"Yes, and no."

He scowled and tightened his hold on her arm as she tried to pull it away. "Yes and no? What the hell does that mean?"

She glared back at him. "It means we have to find Clay and I'll fill you in on the way there. Now come on. Get the lead out." When he let go, she shook her arm, then marched through the front door and right down to the end of the sidewalk. She joined Bill Langly, who was standing with his feet in a wide stance, his eyes on the crowded parking lot, with Pete, Mike, and Merlin fanned out on either side of him. When Ricki appeared beside them, the entire crowd in front, as well as those lined up along the road, went silent.

Anchorman's black pickup truck was parked right at the end of the parking lot, and without any hesitation, Ricki walked the short distance, then climbed over the tailgate and faced the crowd. She stared at them, most of them people she'd known all her life. "I have some bad news," she started slowly, choosing her words carefully. "The person who was shot at the Sunny Side Up this morning has passed away." She paused as the gasp rose from the crowd, waiting for it to settle down before continuing. "Everyone needs to go home now and let Marcie have the time and privacy she'll need to deal with this. We'll talk about a memorial service in a few days when we all get over this first shock." She clapped her hands together to keep their attention on her. "I'd appreciate it if you would step to the side and make a path so we can back this truck out of here. Dan and the doctors are with Marcie right now, and Anchorman and I are needed at the Sunny Side Up."

"To help the chief find the bastard who murdered Sam?" was yelled from somewhere in the crowd.

Ricki nodded, setting off a round of applause that had her taking a step closer to the tailgate. Placing her hand on top for leverage, she sat, swung her legs over, and jumped to the ground.

Behind her Bill Langly came to life and let out a shrill whistle. "Okay. Everyone back up. Make a hole, people." He and Merlin strode over to the truck, gesturing for bodies to move to either side, clearing a pathway out of the parking lot. Neither

Anchorman nor Ricki wasted any time climbing into the truck's cab.

As Anchorman slowly and carefully backed the truck up toward the road, Ricki rolled down the window and waved at Bill. "Thanks for the help. Do you have the keys to my jeep?"

"Yep." He patted the front pocket of his shirt. "Got them right here. I'll make sure it gets back to the Sunny Side Up and leave the keys under the mat on the rear stoop in the alley."

Ricki smiled. "Thanks again. That will be a big help." She gave him a last wave, then rolled the window back up.

Once they were on the highway back to the center of Brewer, Anchorman glanced over at her. "We'll be at the diner in a few minutes. Fill me in."

"Sam isn't Sam," Ricki said bluntly.

He rolled his eyes. "Uh-huh. First Sam is dead and not dead, and now he's Sam and not Sam. What's going on?"

She quickly recounted TK's discovery of the scar from an appendectomy that Sam never had, and ended with the bombshell that the long-time physician was absolutely sure the man lying dead in his clinic was not Sam Parkman.

Anchorman let out a whistling breath through clenched teeth. "Great. That's just great. Then who the hell was that guy we had working in our diner for the last few years?" He shot a glare at Ricki. "And why didn't Marcie know he wasn't Sam? She didn't recognize her own brother?"

"She was still young when Sam enlisted, and she hardly saw him after that," Ricki said in defense of her friend. "And according to TK, Sam only came home once after he was discharged, and then only for a few days. At least that's what TK says, and when it comes to his patients, the man has the memory of an elephant. Marcie was already married with kids of her own at that point. I don't know if she even saw Sam again before he left town twenty-five years ago.."

Anchorman fell silent, his gaze locked on the road and his mouth turned down at the corners. When he pulled up in front of the diner, he stayed in his seat with the engine idling. "Sam and I weren't every-weekend drinking buddies or anything like that, but we were friends," he finally said.

Ricki took her hand off the door handle and half turned in her seat. Anchorman clearly had something to say, and she was going to wait until he was ready to say it.

Rubbing a wide, large hand across the back of his neck, it took a few more moments for him to look over and meet Ricki's gaze. "No matter who he was, we were friends. And he didn't deserve to get mowed down like that when all he was doing was cooking some bacon and eggs." He turned his head and looked out the front windshield. "He didn't have a weapon on him. There was no way he could have defended himself. It was plain, cold-blooded murder. And I can't sit here and do nothing. I'm going to catch this bastard."

"*We*," Ricki corrected, reaching over and putting a hand on his shoulder. "*We* are going to catch him. Or rather we're going to help Clay catch him. This is his case, and he's going to put this guy behind bars." When Anchorman shot her a sideways glance, she nodded. "We're going to be there every step of the way to have his back."

The Marine reached out and turned off the ignition, then straightened in his seat. "Okay. That's fair." He opened the driver's side door before looking over his shoulder at Ricki. "Let's find that fiancé of yours and get started."

Chapter Four

"My dead body isn't Sam Parkman?" Clay frowned and drew up to his full height of six feet one inch as he crossed his arms over his chest and stared down at Ricki.

She'd sent him a text, asking him to meet her at the Sunny Side Up. He must have been close by because he was waiting at the front door when she and Anchorman arrived. Once inside, Ricki hadn't bothered finding a seat. Closing the door to keep out any curious onlookers, she'd simply turned to face him and delivered the shocking news. Now she studied his face, only half surprised Clay looked more annoyed than shocked. *It's those ten years he spent as a homicide cop in Los Angeles*, she thought.

"*Our* dead body," Anchorman insisted, his gaze narrowing just a fraction when Clay glanced at him and lifted an eyebrow.

Ricki's boot tapped against the wooden floor of the dining area. "Clay's dead body," she immediately corrected her cook. "We've already talked about this." She nodded when Clay shifted his attention back to her. "But the three of us work well as a team, and we'd like to help." When Anchorman scowled, she sighed. "All right. We intend to help. But it is definitely your case."

"We do work well together." A ghost of a smile flitted across Clay's lips. "You're law enforcement, so it shouldn't be a problem."

Anchorman's jaw set into a stubborn line. "And I'm a trained sniper. I'd call that a pretty handy skill to track down a killer."

Clay shot the big Marine an exasperated look. "You aren't going to go out and shoot this guy on sight."

"I will if I have to." Anchorman shifted his legs into a wider stance as his mouth flattened into a straight line. "He murdered my friend."

The chief matched his stance, accompanying it with a hard stare. "Not your friend, according to what Ricki just said."

Taking a step closer, Anchorman put his nose a bare six inches from Clay's. "It doesn't make any difference what name he went by. He was my friend."

"Hey." Recognizing the signs of the two men being frustrated, and on unusually short fuses because of it, Ricki managed to get her hand in the small space between them. She waved it up and down right in front of their noses before slapping it onto Clay's chest and pushing as hard as she could. It only bought her a couple more inches' separation, but that was enough. "We're all upset. He was our friend and a part of our inner circle and that made him family." When both men breathed out simultaneously before turning their heads and looking at her, she took a step back and frowned at them. "Family," she repeated. "Who was murdered fifty feet away, and we didn't protect him or even catch the guy? And we're all going to have to live with that." She watched two male faces wash in red, which she knew was a dose of embarrassed pride mixed with a lot of anger. "Add that to finding out that Sam isn't who we thought he was, and this whole mess is going to force us all to hold our tempers."

Clay's shoulders relaxed as he rubbed a hand across the back of his neck. "Having to track down who Sam really was is going to put us behind in finding the asshole who killed him." He sent Ricki a crooked smile. "Which gives us the entire country to search."

When Ricki nodded, Anchorman's gaze bounced from one to the other. "Why are we behind? We've searched for guys before. Let's get out there and turn over every rock. We'll find him."

Ricki reached out and wrapped a hand around the thick bicep of the Marine's upper arm. "You need to cool down and think." Her grasp turned to a soft pat. "He could be halfway to Seattle by now. And from there? Maybe an airport. Especially if his only reason to be in Brewer was to kill Sam." She dropped her hand and sighed. "Or kill an impostor, if he didn't know his victim wasn't the real Sam Parkman. We don't know enough about the real Sam to search for someone who was out to kill him. And as far as the victim is concerned, we don't even know his name, much less a motive for why anyone would want to kill *him*. So, yeah. I'd say we're a lot of steps behind the killer."

"Which is going to make it very difficult to know where to look as we don't have any kind of who, much less a why, to hang our hats on," Clay put in.

"Well, shit." The diner's head cook, who'd been Sam's mentor and boss, stalked over to the wide front window and stared out onto Main Street, keeping his back to the room.

Clay glanced at Ricki, who shook her head. Anchorman had a bone-deep loyalty to anyone he considered family. He would need time to accept Sam's death, no matter who he was. Unfortunately, the one thing they didn't have was time. "Did you and the deputies finish the search down the other side of Main Street?" she asked, directing the question at Clay even as she kept an eye on Anchorman's back.

"We did. No one saw anything. But most of the people we talked to were inside tending their shops at the time of the shooting." Clay rocked back on his heels as his forehead furrowed in thought. "So the odds are that the shooter got to his car and simply drove off with no one the wiser. There were just enough tourists meandering around to make it look like the normal, off-season morning crowd in town, and no one noticed any particular face or any odd behavior." He shook his head at the question in her eyes. "Or saw anyone with a gun, or who slipped into the back alley behind the diner. So right now, we have nothing." He shrugged. "Or almost nothing. We know that the real Sam Parkman was in the military, which gives us at least half a step forward in finding the shooter."

Anchorman did a slow about-face. "How do you figure that? This guy wasn't Sam."

"Which we're going to confirm with fingerprints off the military records," Ricki said, taking up the narrative. "And if it's confirmed he wasn't Sam, we'll run those prints against the army's entire database. But the only way we can do any of that is through the FBI."

"Why?" Anchorman demanded. "I thought all the fingerprints, including the military records, got entered into the same national database. Whatever it's called."

"AFIS," Ricki supplied. "And you're right. The FBI enters them into the AFIS system, but Sam enlisted in the military over thirty years ago. There was no AFIS when he went through the enlistment process, and not every base took fingerprints back then, so they might not be on file at all. And there's only one way to check records that go back that far. By a manual search."

The former Marine looked at Clay. "Which means bringing in the FBI. Is that what you're saying?" He shook his head. "Do you really want to alert the Feds and risk them walking in and taking over this case? What if it turns out that Sam, or this guy who was pretending to be him, was actually a deserter?"

Now a smile tugged at the corners of Ricki's mouth as she exchanged a look with Clay. "Well, that's a possibility," she said slowly. "But there's bringing in the FBI, and then there's just using their access to military records."

Anchorman looked blank for a moment, but when he finally smiled, his gaze was lit up with understanding. "You're talking about Finn," he said, pursing his lips as he thought it over. "Great idea. He'll help without bringing the entire Bureau to our doorstep."

"He will if he can," Ricki replied.

"And we also have our own secret weapon." Clay nodded at the Marine. "You."

Anchorman's mouth opened, but it was a long moment before he said anything. "Me? Are we back to talking about the sniper training? Which, I have to say, I've already pointed out."

"You're still not going around and shooting anyone," Clay repeated in a firm tone. "I mean the fact that you spent twenty years in the Corps. Who can spot a vet faster than you?"

While Anchorman took that in, Ricki tilted her head to the side. "Well? Do you think the impostor was a vet, or will we be spinning our wheels by checking the military database?"

"Yeah. Sam was a vet," Anchorman said without hesitation. "He didn't talk about his time in the service much, but I figured he must have spent at least one tour in a combat zone."

"The same reason you don't talk about it much either," Ricki said softly.

He slowly nodded. "It's the same reason a lot of guys don't

talk about it. Anyway, once we were working late, doing the prep for the expected large holiday crowd the next day, and we both got into a talkative mood. I told him about some tight spot Kelly got into with a prank of his, and Sam gave up a story about training at Fort Riley." When Clay and Ricki gave him a blank look, he smiled. "It's a big training base, and home to the 1st Infantry Division. Fort Riley is in Kansas, and as it so happens, I've been on that base. From the way Sam was telling his story, I'm positive that he'd been on that base too. I'd bet my military pension on it."

"Could he have been a civilian working there?" Clay asked.

Anchorman crossed his arms over his broad chest and shook his head. "Nope. That story was straight out of the barracks. Whoever this Sam really is, he once was a grunt in the army, living on base."

"Good," Clay said. "Now all we have to do is wait for Cheron to get us those prints."

There was a solid knock on the locked front door. Before Ricki could get to the window to check who it was, Cheron's face appeared, pressed against the glass as she squinted behind her thick-framed glasses to see inside.

The big Marine strode over to the door and unlocked it, a smile of pure pleasure on his face. "Hey, honey." When Cheron appeared in the open doorway, he drew her inside, then shoved the door closed with his boot heel as he drew her into his arms and gave her a quick kiss. "We were just talking about you."

"Oh?" The renowned forensic pathologist adjusted the glasses on her nose, then turned her slight frame to face Ricki and Clay with one of Anchorman's arms still wrapped firmly around her shoulders. "I called Dr. Torres to offer any assistance as soon as I heard about the shooting, and he told me he'd let me know if they needed an extra pair of hands." She blinked up at Anchorman. "I didn't immediately race over here because I was assured by Pete, who called me right away, that it wasn't you. And I knew you'd go with Sam to the clinic, so I've been waiting to hear any news."

Anchorman's face fell as he placed a softer kiss on her forehead. "I'm sorry. I should have called. My mind's been a blank."

She patted a thin hand against his chest. "You shouldn't feel bad about that. The shock of seeing someone who had been killed like that would have muddled up anyone." Completely oblivious to Anchorman's stunned look, Cheron's gaze slid away from him and back to Ricki. "This whole thing is awful. Just awful. Then TK called and told me I'd need to do an autopsy, because the man who'd been shot had died, and he wasn't Sam Parkman." Her eyes widened, magnified by the lenses of her glasses. "Is that true?"

"TK thinks it is," Ricki confirmed. "And he's known the real Sam most of his life, so I'm inclined to believe him." She paused and lifted an eyebrow at the doctor. "But we won't know for sure until we run his fingerprints through AFIS."

Cheron frowned. "How long ago was Sam in the military? I believe Marcie told me he left the army at least twenty years ago?"

"We need to run them through AFIS and send them to the FBI to check the older records," Ricki amended. "Or at least send them to an agent in the FBI."

Cheron's nose wrinkled before her expression cleared into a big smile. "You mean Finn? You want me to send them to Finn?" She glanced at Clay for confirmation. "This is your case, Chief," she said, automatically slipping into her professional mode. "Is that okay with you?"

"It would be a big help," Clay said. "Thanks."

Cheron clasped her hands together in front of her. "All

right. I'll do that first thing. I'll call Agent Sullivan," she agreed, using Finn's FBI title, "and ask him where he wants them sent. I assume, Chief, you would also like the fingerprints sent to you?"

Clay nodded. "Yes, and again, thanks."

"No problem," the doctor chirped. "I'll be on my way and have the fingerprints to you in no time. I'll also look for any broken bones that might have needed a rod or some other implant placed inside the body. They'd have serial numbers stamped on them that can be traced back to the manufacturer and the records of who received the implant." With answering nods from both Ricki and Clay, the doctor beamed. "All right then. I'll be on my way."

"I'll drive you," Anchorman declared.

With a patient sigh, Cheron shook her head, sending her plain brown hair that was cut into a straight line beneath a scraggly row of bangs, brushing over the top of her shoulders. "Of course you won't. You can't hang around the clinic for hours while I do a preliminary work up on the body for an autopsy in the morning. So how will you get back here?"

He gave her a bemused look. "In my truck."

"If we ride over to the clinic in your truck, how will I get back to my lab?"

Anchorman's gaze turned cautious as he stared at her. "You'll call me when you're done and I'll come pick you up."

She shoved a bony shoulder against his chest and broke free of his hold. "Why? I have a perfectly good car outside."

Ricki bit her lip on hearing that. As far as descriptions went, that one was a real stretch. Cheron's car was a decades-old compact Toyota, with fading paint and doors that would barely shut.

"There's a guy running around shooting people," Anchorman said. "So I'm going to drive you."

Cheron took a comically long step back. "Shooting at me? Pete told me that Sam was standing by the stove when he was killed. That's the very spot you usually occupy, so don't think for one moment, Norman Beal, that I am unaware that Sam might have been mistaken for you."

"Me?" The clear amusement in Anchorman's tone had Cheron's mouth forming into a rare scowl. "Sam was five inches shorter than me, and thin as a stick. There is no way anyone would get the two of us mixed up."

The doctor looked taken aback for a moment, then waved a dismissive hand in the air. "You can't possibly know that. Besides, although I'm absolutely not a target, you might be." Her gaze darted around the empty dining room. "But you should be all right here at the Sunny Side Up with Ricki and Clay." While he stood with a stunned look on his face for the second time, she smiled and made a break for the front door. "I'll be in touch as soon as I can," she called over her shoulder before bolting out onto the street.

When Anchorman's jaw dropped to his chest in a confused reaction as if he'd somehow been ambushed, Ricki had to choke back a laugh.

The big Marine pointed at the spot where the love of his life had disappeared out the door. "Did she just say I needed a babysitter?"

A wicked gleam crept into Ricki's eyes. "Why not? You think I need one often enough."

He shook his head as if he hadn't heard her. "Oh. The good doctor and I are going to have to have a talk about who is responsible for protecting who around here."

"Yeah, well, good luck with that," Clay said. When Anchorman took a step toward the door, Clay's unexpectedly sharp tone stopped him in his tracks. "Unless you want to be barred from her life, I wouldn't do that." When Anchorman glared at him, he crossed his arms over his chest. "Cheron just told you she needed some space, and you'd better give it to her. In the meantime, we have to come up with next steps. The first person we need to talk to is Marcie, to find out all we can about both the real and the fake Sam."

"Agreed," Ricki said. "Whoever is lying in the clinic had to have known Sam well enough to be able to impersonate him in his own hometown."

"He must also have known he could get away with it because Sam hadn't been here for several decades, and there was no chance that he'd show up in the Bay again," Clay said. "Which all points to him and Sam having crossed paths long enough for him to gain all that information."

"During the real Sam's stint in the military would be a great place to start." Ricki hesitated while her teeth lightly gnawed her lower lip. "But there's a problem. TK said that Sam served for twelve years. He would have run into hundreds if not thousands of guys in that time frame."

"Yeah." Clay shoved a hand through his dark blond hair, pushing it away from his face. "Let's hope we get a hit off AFIS, or Finn gets one from the old military records." He moved closer to Ricki and laid a hand on her shoulder. "You'd be the best one to talk to Marcie."

"I know." She wasn't happy about that. Intruding on Marcie's shock and grief over having no idea if the real Sam was dead or alive, was not a welcome task. But as Clay had said, it was a necessary one. "I told her I'd stop by. I'll see how she's doing, and if she needs more time before she feels like answering questions, I'll go back to her place tomorrow."

"That works," Clay said. "I'm going to get my deputies started on interviewing everyone who was at the Sunny Side Up this morning. Maybe someone saw or heard something we can use."

"Fine. You all do that," Anchorman said. He jerked his thumb toward the kitchen. "I'm going to clean up. The stove is going to need a good scrubbing, and so are the floor and the prep table." He stared at the double doors at the back of the room. "And who knows what else before we can open again. I should have a better idea in a couple of hours." He was silent for a moment, then loudly cleared his throat. "Look. When I'm done, I'll bring some food over to your place and cook dinner for all of us." He rolled his eyes to the ceiling. "Including Cheron when she's finished at the clinic and drives herself over to your cabin."

"Sounds good," Clay said. He glanced at his watch. "I should be there in three hours or so, if that works."

"Fine with me," Anchorman said.

"Me too." Ricki sighed and straightened her shoulders under her jacket. "Hopefully Marcie can give us something to go on." She looked at Anchorman and held her hand out, opening it so it was flat with the palm up. "My jeep is still at the clinic, so I'll need to borrow your truck."

Chapter Five

Ricki turned on to a quiet street at the northern end of Brewer. The houses were spread along the road with enough distance between them to afford each a comfortable amount of privacy. It was deep enough into spring to bring the wildflowers to life, dotting the sides of the road with vibrant splashes of color that continued from the street to straggle along the border of walkways and porches.

Halfway down the block, Ricki slowed the truck, letting it roll to a stop in front of a sturdy house with brown-shingled siding and an inviting front porch. It had once belonged to Marcie's parents, and she had grown up there.

Dan's car was parked behind Marcie's in the narrow driveway that led to the detached garage out back. Since there was enough space to also accommodate Anchorman's big truck, Ricki pulled in behind the other two cars. After shutting off the engine, she didn't move from the driver's seat, but stayed in the truck. Staring blindly at the empty vehicles in front of her, she steeled herself to face Marcie and what was sure to be a deep pool of misery.

She finally climbed out of the truck and did a slow walk to the steps, then up to the covered porch, where an old wooden swing hung from sturdy hooks at one end, and a row of potted plants were lined up on the other. Ricki had known Marcie and her brood of six for so long that she didn't bother to knock, and wasn't surprised when the knob turned easily in her hand. This was Brewer, not some giant city where everyone was anonymous, and no one knew their neighbors. Everywhere in the Bay, locked doors were far rarer than unlocked ones.

Pushing the door open, Ricki stuck her head inside the house and called out. "Hello. It's just me."

Dan appeared in the open doorway leading into the kitchen. "Hi. We're back here."

When he vanished from view, she followed him into a spacious area that was easily the largest room in the house. A long rectangular table, with eight chairs placed around it, took up one side of the open space, leaving a wide gap between it and the opposite wall. A counter spanned the wall's length and was broken up at intervals by a sink and a stove, with the dishwasher between the two built-in underneath it.

There was a large refrigerator anchoring the far end of the counter, and another one on the back porch was visible through the window. A necessity Marcie had bought years before when the three-bedroom house had been bursting with a mob of hungry kids. They might have been short on bedrooms, but never on food.

Marcie had married young, had six children within a dozen years, and then divorced when most of them were still living at home. Now they were grown and scattered all over the West Coast, with even her youngest two daughters recently deciding to leave the Bay. Although each of them regularly popped up in town whenever they came to visit their mom. Until that morning, it had been just Marcie and her brother, Sam, living in the house, along with Dan who took up residence every weekend.

The short, stocky waitress with wide hips and a big heart sat at the kitchen table looking small and lost. Despite the misery on her face, her red-rimmed eyes still crinkled at the corners as her mouth struggled into a smile when she spotted Ricki. "I'm so glad you're here. I was just telling Dan that I know you'll do it. I just know it."

Not sure what Marcie was talking about, Ricki walked over and pulled out a chair next to her. Folding her hands on the table, she returned Marcie's smile. "Do what?"

"Straighten out this whole mess." Marcie bobbed her head up and down as she reached over and laid one of her hands on top of Ricki's. "You'll catch whoever killed that poor man, and find out where Sam really is."

Seeing the hope in Marcie's eyes had Ricki's stomach twisting into a knot. She sent up a silent prayer that TK was right and it wasn't Sam lying on that table in the clinic. *Or in a grave somewhere else*, she thought as the knot tightened even more inside her stomach. But with a complete stranger so openly taking up Sam's life, as much as she wished he were alive, there was a much better chance he was dead. But she wanted proof of that before she brought it up to Marcie.

"It's Clay's case to solve," Ricki said quietly. "But Anchorman and I will help all we can. Do you feel like answering some questions? I don't want to push you. If you don't want to talk about it right now, we'll just sit here together for a while and get to the questions tomorrow, after you've had some rest."

Marcie sighed. "I don't think I'll be resting for a good long while. That man looked so much like Sam, and he was lying on the kitchen floor, as white as a ghost and bleeding everywhere." Her body visibly shivered. "It's not a picture I'll soon forget."

"Probably not." Ricki looked down at their hands stacked together on the table. "Did any of the tourists who came into the diner this morning stand out to you?" she asked, wanting to get Marcie's mind onto something besides Sam. At least for a few moments.

"I didn't notice anyone carrying a gun, if that's what you mean," Marcie said. "It's still early in the season, so there weren't that many strangers in for breakfast. At least not like there are in the summer. Most of the guests up at the St. Armand hotel eat there in the mornings and come in for one of Anchorman's hamburgers for lunch or dinner." She paused to give Dan a nod of thanks when he set a fresh cup of tea in front of her.

"Knowing how superior Anchorman's coffee is, I thought I'd stick with tea," he said as he set a second cup in front of Ricki, then retreated to the stove where the kettle was still whistling.

Marcie aimlessly stirred her tea as she stared down into the cup. "Lulu from the Quick Pie over in Edington was helping out this morning. Since nobody wants pizza for breakfast they open late on weekdays, and she likes to have the extra work. Most of the tourists who came into the Sunny Side Up this morning were sitting at her station in the booths along the wall, so you should ask her. She might remember someone acting funny."

"Okay. How about the last few days?" Ricki persisted. "Did you see a stranger more than once in the diner, or maybe the same rental car parked nearby that's been somewhere on the street for the last two or maybe even three days?"

"Not really." The waitress shook her head. "Nothing much at all out of the ordinary has gone on since you got back from your last case in Maine." She trailed off and lifted her gaze to look out the kitchen window. Beyond the screened-in back porch that held the extra refrigerator, was a short expanse of cleared-off space that was mostly dirt and ended at a wall of trees. "Sam loved the forest and especially the park. I was really surprised when he didn't come home for so long." She drew in a ragged breath as she slowly turned her head to meet Ricki's gaze. "Surprised and hurt. Then when he showed up on my doorstep again, it was like a prayer come true, even if he was different." At Ricki's questioning look, she pursed her lips. "Nothing you wouldn't expect. He was just quieter, and didn't smile as much as he did before he joined the army. And I remember Sam being so neat, and he never forgot anything. But since he's been home, he hasn't been as neat and his memory wasn't as good." She sniffled out a watery laugh. "I had to make a copy of the work schedule every week for him to carry around so he wouldn't forget to show up for his shift in the kitchen." She wrapped her hands around the teacup and shrugged. "But those were all little things. I know everyone is going to ask why in the world I didn't realize that the man standing on my front porch with his hat in his hand wasn't really Sam. But I was so young when he left. I knew he'd changed some, but only those little things. And they could easily be explained by a twenty-five-year absence and all of us getting older." She reached up and patted her short brown curls shot through with strands of gray. "Lord knows I certainly don't look the same, so why would he?"

"There are many people in town who knew Sam when he was growing up here," Ricki pointed out. "And they didn't question if he was the real Sam either."

"Mostly because I didn't question it," Marcie countered. "But it had been so long," she repeated. "And I barely saw him when he came home after he left the army. He was only here for a few days and then he disappeared. Mom and Dad were really upset, and then sad after he left. I certainly remember that. And it always stayed with them, so I thought maybe Sam knew he wasn't coming back again, and he'd only come home to tell them goodbye." She stared out the window over the sink as a single tear trickled down her cheek. "I guess he didn't feel the need to say anything about that to me."

Ricki slowly turned one hand over and gave Marcie's a gentle squeeze. "Maybe he couldn't bring himself to say goodbye to his little sister." She paused to let Marcie dab at her eyes with the Kleenex Dan held out to her. "Your parents never told you why Sam left like that?"

"No. But they never told me anything that they felt might be a burden to me. Since both grandma and grandpa had passed by then, if Mom talked to anyone about Sam, it would have been one of her friends."

"One of her friends," Ricki echoed with a frown. Like a best friend. She gave a mental sigh. Dorothy Parkman's closest friend had been Ricki's own mom, Miriam McCormick. She leaned back in her chair. It was more than possible that Dorothy had talked over her son's prolonged absence with her mom. The two women had been close, right up until the car accident that had claimed the life of both Marcie's parents.

But years had passed since then, and today Miriam McCormick was in the advanced stages of Alzheimer's and living in a full-time care facility in Tacoma. Since the disease had advanced enough that she no longer recognized her own daughter, there was no chance she would recall a conversation from several decades earlier. "What did Sam do in the army?" Ricki asked, changing direction. "He must have liked it to stay in for twelve years."

"At first he did," Marcie said. "The army trained him to be some kind of big-engine mechanic. You know, like on those huge troop carriers, or tanks, and stuff like that. He used to write me letters, saying how much he enjoyed doing the work.

Even when he went to Europe, he wrote to me almost every week." She sniffed as a tear trickled down her cheek. "But when he got back to the States, suddenly there were no more letters. They just stopped." She looked at Ricki through watery eyes. "I asked Mom about it, and all she said was that he was going through a difficult time, and he'd start writing to me again once he'd worked it all out. But he never did. Then he was discharged and came home. He barely said a word to me before he took off again, and like I said, not a thing about never coming back. One morning I called Mom and she said that Sam had left and that was that. I never saw or heard from him again until he, or at least the guy who said he was Sam, showed up here in Brewer three years ago." She bent her head. "Well, almost three years, actually. It's been closer to two and a half, I guess."

When Marcie withdrew her hand to place it in her lap, Ricki settled more deeply into her chair, watching her quietly. Behind the waitress, Dan lifted his hand, and using his thumb and index finger to form the universal sign for small, indicated that Marcie wouldn't be able to hold on for much longer. Giving a brief nod to show that she understood, Ricki kept her voice low and calm. "You said that Sam wrote to you every week when he first went into the army. Do you remember where he was stationed?"

Marcie's nose wrinkled as her teeth chewed her lower lip. "I was ten years old when Sam enlisted, Ricki. Barely more than a child." Her eyebrows drew together. "Besides, I never got a letter just to me," she said slowly. "Sam always included it with the one he sent to my parents. He used to use a bit of tape to keep it shut, but Sam was Sam." She let out a short laugh that ended on a sigh. "He was always kind of thrifty, I'd guess you could say. I remember our dad teasing him about folding up paper bags and reusing them, and he mostly took leftovers for his school lunch so they wouldn't go to waste. And he scavenged up things to fix so we wouldn't have to buy it new. He would never have spent money on two envelopes and two stamps. Not when one would do." Her eyes had a vague look when she glanced at Ricki. "Now, how did we get off on that topic?"

"I was wondering if you knew where Sam had been stationed when he was in the army?" Ricki repeated.

"When he was here in the States? I'm not sure. He always referred to it as 'the fort' in his letters. When he went overseas, Mom told me he'd been sent to Kosovo. I remember because I didn't know where that was, so I looked it up on a map. Then it started showing up in the news because there was some war going on over there." Her gaze came back into focus. "I was scared. Then Sam came back and I thought it would be better, but it wasn't." Her bottom lip trembled. "He was back here, safe in the States, but he never came to the Bay. Mom kept saying that he was safe, and that was the most important thing, and I thought maybe he couldn't get a leave to come home. But he didn't write to me anymore either. By that time I had a family of my own, and Sam only came back that once." She gave a defeated shrug. "He didn't even ask to meet my kids. Mom was planning a big family dinner, but he left before she could get us all together."

Marcie clamped her mouth shut and stared out the kitchen window. The silence drew out as Ricki waited and Dan kept a worried eye on Marcie. A full minute passed before she shifted in her chair, her gaze still fixed on a point somewhere on the other side of the window.

"Wheat fields," she said softly. She drew in a deep breath, then straightened her shoulders as her gaze refocused on Ricki. "I was so mad at him for leaving like that that I threw his letters out. But I remember him always making a joke about how flat it was all around him compared to the mountains here. And lots of wheat fields. He always wrote a comment that there were wheat fields as far as the eye could see." Tears streamed down her face. "I shouldn't have tossed away his letters. I shouldn't have done it."

Ricki leaned over the table until she caught Marcie's eye. "You were mad, and he acted like a prick."

Marcie blinked at her as her hand flew up to cover her mouth. "Ricki James. When did you start using that word? And don't say that about Sam. I'm sure he had something going on that he didn't want to talk about."

Satisfied that she'd managed to distract Marcie from sinking into a big hole of self-blame, Ricki deliberately crossed her arms over her chest and lifted her shoulders into a dismissive shrug. "And you didn't have things going on? A whole gaggle of kids, with another probably on the way, and a household to keep together. Not to mention a husband who didn't believe in helping out much."

"No he didn't." Marcie raised a chubby finger and wagged it at the woman sitting across from her. "But we aren't talking about him. It's Sam I'm concerned about. Where do you think he is?"

Hopefully living his life and breathing just fine, Ricki thought, but she only shrugged again. "I don't know. But I'm going to do my best to find him, since he probably knows the real identity of the impostor."

Marcie's mouth turned down at the corners. "Do you think so?" Her frown deepened. "Well, of course he did. That man showed up here knowing my name, and even the names of some of my kids. And he knew Mom and Dad had passed away, even though he didn't come to their funeral. He said they were already buried by the time he got word about the car accident. He also knew about you, and Anchorman, and Clay, and asked about some of our neighbors and what they were doing." Her frown stayed in place as she bobbed her head up and down. "He had to have heard all that from Sam."

"Makes sense." Ricki looked around the old-fashioned kitchen with its family table and long counter. "This was your parents' house, wasn't it?"

"That's right. They left it to me, and thank god they did. Me and the kids had a place to go after the divorce."

"Did they leave you a picture of Sam as a grown man?"

"Yes." Marcie lifted her eyes to the ceiling. "There was one that they kept out all the time. It's actually Sam and me, taken on the only day I saw him when he came home after being discharged. I got a neighbor to watch the kids for an hour so I could come here and at least give my brother a welcome-home hug." Her shoulders slumped again. "The last one I ever gave him."

"Where's that picture now?" Ricki asked.

Marcie's gaze drifted to the ceiling again. "Upstairs. In Sam's room. He asked if he could put it on his dresser, and I said it was fine by me."

"Marcie," Ricki said, her voice barely above a whisper. "I'm sorry. But I'll need to search Sam's room."

When her longtime friend's shoulders slumped over even farther, Ricki's gaze turned miserable. She really, really did not want to intrude like that, but it had to be done.

Dan, who had been standing guard behind Marcie's chair the whole time, laid a hand on her shoulder. "Once Marcie is resting, I'll search Sam's room." When Marcie remained silent, Dan gave her shoulder a gentle squeeze. "But honey, first I want you to lie down for a while." He stepped to the side and leaned over to capture one of her hands. "I'll take you to our room and then get the picture for Ricki." He gently drew Marcie out of the chair and put a protective arm around her shoulders when she slumped heavily against him. "Come on now." Dan shot Ricki a look over Marcie's head. "I'll be right back."

Worried at how pale Marcie had suddenly become, Ricki nodded, then watched helplessly as Marcie shuffled out of the kitchen with Dan by her side.

Chapter Six

Ricki turned onto Main Street and parked Anchorman's truck in a rare empty spot right in front of the Sunny Side Up. Another reminder that it wasn't open today.

When she'd come home with her young son, Eddie, to lick her wounds from the divorce and then murder of her best friend, she'd immediately started the work to change what had been an incense and scented candle shop into a rustic café. And for the first time since then, she didn't want to go inside. She'd poured a good piece of her life, not to mention sweat and money, into the Sunny Side Up, and now all she wanted to do was turn her back on it and drive home.

Giving herself a stern reminder that she had work to do, and that a lot of people she loved were counting on her to do that work, she forced her reluctant feet into motion. Crossing the sidewalk, she let her hand rest on the front door handle for a long moment before giving it a firm twist and stepping inside.

The absolute silence of the room was only magnified by the soft tinkling of the bell that hung over the door. On a normal day, you could barely hear it above the clink of dishes and the voices of her customers waiting for their food. But today, the tiny bell sounded like a fire alarm, echoing through the empty room. She almost winced before she caught herself, and stiffening her spine, she put her hands on her hips and cocked her head to one side. The faint but inventive curse that drifted through the cut-out window between the kitchen and dining room had her shoulders relaxing. The single, aggravated voice of Anchorman floating out from the back of the diner breathed life into the place.

Ricki grinned when a second, louder curse came from the kitchen. "Anchorman? I brought your truck back."

A moment later, the big Marine strode through the double doors. An apron with a huge wet spot coating most of the front was tied around his waist, and he was wiping his hands on a dishtowel as he crossed the room, a scowl on his face. "Thanks. Langly stopped by and left the keys to the jeep. Your lime atrocity is parked in the alley. He was going to leave the keys under the mat on the back stoop, but since I was here, he came in and left them on the counter."

"Great."

When he pulled out a chair from the nearest table and took a seat by straddling it, she walked to the opposite side of the table and sat down as well. Facing him, she leaned back and studied his face. It was only the second time she could remember seeing him look tired. The first was when his closest friend, Kelly, had been killed on their annual camping trip together in the Great Smoky Mountains National Park. When he met her gaze, she shook her head. "You aren't responsible for what happened."

"I was right here." He looked down at his arms stacked on the back of the chair. "It's getting to be a habit. Having a friend shot while I just stand by."

Exasperated, Ricki's boot beat a quick tap against the floor. "You weren't standing by, so don't use that to fuel some kind of misplaced guilt complex. When Kelly was shot, you were drugged, and this morning you weren't even in the kitchen during the attack." She leaned forward and tapped a finger against the tabletop. "You had no way of stopping someone from coming in through the alley. Sam, or whatever his name was, would have had to have kept that back door locked."

"It doesn't make any difference what his name was," Anchorman countered. "He was a friend."

Since she'd had the very same thought, Ricki nodded. "Yeah. I know."

He sighed, even as the line of his jaw hardened. "Did you know that Sam and Marcie drove in together this morning? She was working the shift this morning, too. If we hadn't been out here in the dining room having that idiotic discussion about flowers, she could have easily been in that kitchen and ended up dead on the floor, just like Sam." His gaze was troubled as he stared back at her. "Or you could have been back there doing something."

"I could say the same about you," she replied evenly. "There was a bigger chance that you would have been in that kitchen helping Sam out with the breakfast crowd. You weren't on the schedule this morning, but that wouldn't have stopped you from lending him a hand. You coming in every morning is common knowledge, and you usually spend it in the kitchen. Besides you and me, only Sam, Marcie, and Clay knew about that last-minute wedding planning session. Which makes it just as probable that the actual target was you."

"I wish I had been at the stove instead of Sam."

Ricki had been pushing the idea away all morning, and now to have it voiced out loud made her blood run cold. Sam was a friend, and considered part of her family, but Anchorman was as much her older brother as if they'd been tied together by blood. It was selfish to be grateful he hadn't been in the kitchen that morning, but she couldn't imagine losing him, any more than she could imagine losing Clay or Eddie.

Taking a deep breath to combat the ice settling along her spine, she pressed her lips together until she could talk without a tremor in her voice. "What would you have done?" she asked quietly. "You don't even own a handgun, and I don't think you've taken to hiding a rifle under your apron."

The Marine's chin jutted out at a stubborn angle. "I would have gotten to him before he got a shot off."

"That's ridiculous, and you know it," she fired back. Anchorman was good, and he was fast, but he wasn't Superman. If he'd been in that kitchen, he would be as dead as Sam, and that was that. Wanting to drop what could easily escalate into a full-blown argument, she tilted her head toward the back of the dining room. "How's the cleanup going?"

Effectively distracted, Anchorman's nose wrinkled in distaste. "I think I got most of the blood, but it sprayed all over the damn place. I don't know if we can cook in there or not."

Ricki reached into her shirt pocket and pulled out her cell phone. "I'll call a biohazard cleanup outfit I've worked with before in Tacoma and see if they can get up here sometime tomorrow. Once they give me a firm date and time, you can call the power company and have the gas turned off for a day or two."

Anchorman's whole body immediately perked up. "That's a great idea. I wish we'd thought of it before I spent a couple of hours on my hands and knees scrubbing the floor."

"My fault," Ricki said. "I should have mentioned it back at the clinic, but I was too focused on what needed to be done to kick off the investigation."

"Yeah." He rubbed a hand against his cheek. "So, did you

talk to Marcie?" When Ricki nodded, he cocked his head to the side. "Find out anything?"

"Something. And then there's this." She reached into her coat pocket and drew out the picture Dan had given her and held it up in front of Anchorman. "That was taken just before Sam disappeared from the Bay. Notice anything?"

Anchorman leaned forward and studied the photo for a long moment. When he straightened up again, he was frowning. "He's taller than the Sam who's been working at the diner the past couple of years."

Yeah, I think so too." Ricki tucked the picture back into her coat pocket. "Which supports what TK said. They're two different men. We can talk it over at dinner. Are you still bringing the food out to my place?"

"Roger that." Anchorman stood up and flipped the chair around before shoving it back under the table. "Clay came by for some coffee to take to his deputies and wanted me to let you know that he'd meet us there around five." He glanced at the clock hanging above the front door. "That gives me about an hour to throw something together and check on Cheron."

"Hang on. I got a text from her that I haven't had a chance to read yet." Since her phone was still in her hand, Ricki tapped the messages icon and pulled up the latest from Cheron. She skimmed through it, then hesitated.

When she didn't say anything, Anchorman frowned. "Well?"

It would have been nice if the doctor had delivered the message to her boyfriend herself, but it looked like Ricki was stuck giving Anchorman the news. "Um. She's letting me know she talked to Finn and sent the fingerprints to him and confirmed that she will be doing the full autopsy tomorrow."

"And?" Anchorman prompted. "I can tell by the look on your face that Cheron said something else."

"And that she'll be working late at her lab so won't be joining us for dinner." She took a quick breath before getting the rest out in a rush. "And that she isn't alone. Dr. Torres is there with her and will be her escort out to her car, so I should let you know there's no reason for you to rush out there."

The Marine crossed his arms over his chest as his eyes narrowed. "Dr. Torres. Is that so?"

Since it was exactly the reaction Ricki had expected, she rolled her eyes. Standing up, she said, "Yes. And I'm betting TK is there as well, so you can just shake off the green beast and start getting some dinner together while I make that call to the biohazard company."

"I'm not jealous," Anchorman growled. "Just concerned. We don't know much about this Dr. Torres."

Ricki grinned. "Oh? You mean the guy you and Bear went camping with last week?"

"Hey, that was purely by accident. I promised your ex-husband a couple of months ago that we'd go camping in Olympic Park. I didn't know he and Torres had gotten so chummy that he'd invited the guy along too."

She shrugged at the cautious look in his eyes. "I don't care who you go camping with. Even if it's my ex. I'm just pointing out that you had two days to talk to the doctor over a campfire and beer, so you must have gotten to know something about him."

Anchorman responded to that by huffing and waving a big hand in the air. "Whatever. I need to see to the dinner arrangements. Let me know what day to ask the gas company to shut everything down." He marched across the room, pointing to a set of car keys lying on the back counter. "There're your keys."

Ricki followed him, scooping up the keys as she passed the bar and headed to the double doors leading into the kitchen. By the time she got there, her cook was already rummaging around in the back pantry. Leaving him to that, along with his suddenly grumpy mood, Ricki walked to the rear door, pausing long enough to study the floor where a man had died.

It looked spotless after Anchorman's diligent scrubbing, but that didn't keep her from looking up the number of the biohazard cleanup company as she made her way out the door and down the three steps leading into the alley. It only took a few moments to slide behind the wheel of her jeep and call the company. With arrangements made for them to come first thing in the morning, Ricki sent a quick text to Anchorman before putting her phone away and heading home.

One of the nicer things about living in a small town was the five-minute commute to reach the driveway of the cabin she'd rented after she'd returned to the Bay. The compact but cozy house had two bedrooms upstairs and a large room downstairs, equally divided between a kitchen on one side and a living space on the other.

The two areas were separated by an island that gave her additional storage. Its bar top featured an overhanging lip with plenty of room for tall stools to be pushed underneath. With nowhere to put a table, it had provided her small family with a comfortable place to sit and eat together, rather than using the couch or retreating upstairs to their separate bedrooms.

Eddie, who was now a full-fledged teenager, occupied one of the upper rooms on the weekends he was home from his boarding school for gifted kids, while the other one was hers, now shared with her soon-to-be husband. After much discussion, Clay had given up his more spacious cabin so Eddie wouldn't have any extra adjustments to make on top of his decision to attend the prestigious school on the far side of Seattle.

But while Ricki's cabin had been a great sanctuary for her to recover from the sting of a divorce, it was definitely too small for the three of them, even if Eddie was only home on the weekends. So they'd already contacted Minnie Cuthry, the only real estate agent in the Bay, to be on the lookout for a bigger place once they got through the wedding. That was, if they ever managed enough free time to actually have a wedding.

But as much as she might have wished otherwise, that free time would not be today. Murder was always a major roadblock to wedding plans, not to mention that the person who had happily commandeered responsibility for the bulk of the planning was tucked away at home, paralyzed with a mixture of hope that her brother was still alive out there somewhere, and grief that it was just as possible he was already dead.

The sound of the jeep's engine as it rounded the last curve in the long gravel drive leading up to the cabin set off a frenzied round of barking from Corby. The seventy-pound boxer mix had wandered up to the cabin four years earlier and promptly adopted Ricki and her son.

Smiling, she pulled into the enlarged space that served as a parking area directly in front of the cabin. Two seconds later, the big dog with a light brown coat and white markings on his face and chest burst through the trees at a dead run. He skidded to a stop right in front of the jeep and plopped his butt down on the gravel. Now that he'd alerted the empty cabin and surrounding woods of her arrival, he sat quietly in the driveway, waiting with a patience that was unique to hunting and guard dogs everywhere.

Once Ricki had exited the jeep, Corby stood again and came trotting over to where she was standing. He bumped his head solidly against her legs, waited for the expected head scratch, then loped over to the cabin, climbing onto the small front porch to take up a position next to the door.

The minute Ricki opened it, Corby walked straight over to his food dish, latched on to one side, and carried it to the corner where she kept a large bag of dog food. When he turned his head to look back at her, she laughed, even as she held out her hand and wagged a finger back and forth.

"You know very good and well that dinner isn't for another two hours." Ignoring his soulful look, she filled his water dish at the sink, set it down in front of him, then walked over to the refrigerator. She gave the beer a good look, but opted for a can of soda instead. Clay might have some work for them to do that night, and she wanted to keep a clear head.

She was sitting at the island, keying notes into her laptop, when she heard the deep rumble of a large vehicle coming up the drive. It sounded like Clay's SUV, which was confirmed when Corby didn't move a muscle away from his favorite spot underneath the large picture window adjacent to the front door. It was only a minute before heavy boots clomped across the wood planking on the porch.

Clay closed the door behind him, then walked over to where Ricki was sitting and placed a slow, lazy kiss on her mouth. When he lifted his head, he smiled into her eyes. "Hi there."

She smiled back as he stepped away and shrugged out of his jacket. "Hi there yourself. How'd the search go?"

After hanging his jacket on a hook near the door, Clay headed for the refrigerator. "As expected." He glanced at her over his shoulder. "It was a replay of this morning. No one saw or heard anything unusual." He grabbed a can of the same brand of soda pop she was sipping. "Oh, and Minnie called. She has a place that she swears is just perfect."

"That's great. We'll put that on our to-do list, right after 'catch a killer'." When he snorted in response, Ricki pointed at her cell phone lying on the counter. "I got a text from Cheron. She sent the fingerprints off to Finn. We should know if there's a hit within the next twenty-four hours."

Pulling out a stool next to hers, Clay took a seat and slowly lowered the soda can that he'd been holding up to his mouth. "Cheron also mentioned that she'd talked to Finn. Did she happen to tell you if he was at Quantico when he got those prints?"

Ricki looked away from her laptop screen to frown at him. "As opposed to where?" When he didn't answer, her eyes narrowed. "As opposed to being in Miami with Kate?" When he gave her a sour look, she jabbed a finger against his arm. "Clay Thomas. You have got to be kidding me. Both your sister and Finn are adults."

Clay shrugged. "Kate is. The jury is still out on Finn."

"Funny," Ricki responded in a dust-dry tone. "Does your sister give you grief about living here with me?"

"That's different. We're engaged."

She batted her eyes in an exaggerated blink. "Oh really? So, you'd feel better if they were engaged, because I'd be happy to pass that along to Finn."

"Nope," he said quickly. "And don't give Finn any ideas."

Shaking her head, Ricki's gaze went back to her computer screen. "I would take that to mean you don't like Finn, but I'm positive you'd say the same thing about any guy who made a move on your sister." When Clay frowned, she shrugged. "At least that explains why she chose to live on the other side of the country."

"Now who's being funny?" he groused. Leaning in, he read her screen over her shoulder. "Those are the notes from your talk with Marcie?"

"Yes. She's shaken up about the man who's been living in her house not actually being her brother, and wondering where Sam is." Ricki's fingers began a rhythmic drum against the counter. "She didn't keep all the letters Sam wrote to her when he was in the service, and couldn't remember him ever mentioning the name of his base. But he did say the surrounding area was flat. With wheat fields." Her forehead furrowed in thought. She tapped the keyboard then turned her screen so Clay could see the list of army bases by state that she'd pulled up from the Internet.

"A lot of Texas is pretty flat," Clay observed. "But no wheat fields."

"So is a sizeable piece of the Midwest, and lots of wheat fields," she countered. "Including Fort Riley. The base the fake Sam mentioned to Anchorman." Ricki swiveled the top of the stool around until she was facing him. "Marcie also mentioned a few other things that stood out. The one that struck me is that she was sure on his last trip home, Sam knew he wouldn't be back. But the man who showed up and passed himself off as Sam knew about all her kids, even though some hadn't been born before he disappeared, and Anchorman, and you. And just like those younger kids, neither you nor Anchorman had made any kind of appearance in the Bay before the real Sam left. It's possible Marcie's brother was keeping tabs on his hometown from a distance, and then passed the information along. It's either that, or the impostor did some great research before he showed up in the Bay."

Clay nodded as he took another sip of his soda. "That is interesting. And you're right. I'd never met the man until he showed up here."

"Neither had Anchorman," she said. "Marcie also mentioned that her brother was a scavenger and very thrifty. As in the kind of thrifty where he would include his letters to her in the same envelope as the ones to their parents because he wouldn't buy two stamps when one would do."

"Huh. There's thrifty and there's cheap."

"Very true," Ricki agreed. "But I wouldn't have pinned either description on the Sam who's been here the last few years. Whoever he was, Anchorman is positive he was in the military, and knew Fort Riley pretty well." She pointed at the list still on display on her computer. "Which happens to be in the very flat state of Kansas. At least it's flat compared to here, which is exactly how the real Sam described his base to his little sister."

"I wonder if our dead Sam had anything else to say about his time in the service," Clay mused. "Maybe to one of the other vets who lives in town."

"We could wander over to the VFW after dinner and ask around," Ricki suggested, grinning when a growling noise came from the vicinity of Clay's stomach.

"Good idea," he said. "Exactly what time did Anchorman say he'd be here with dinner?"

Chapter Seven

Ricki stepped out of Clay's SUV and onto the sidewalk in front of the local VFW post. The single-story house with the wooden sign out front was on a quiet side street several short blocks from the center of Brewer. Tucking her hands into the deep pockets of her lined brown leather jacket, she peered through the dark, straining to identify the faces belonging to all five people lingering on the porch, as well as the three sitting on the front steps. When her name was called out, she recognized the voice of another neighbor, and raised a hand in a friendly greeting just as Clay came up beside her.

Since she'd left the passenger side window of the vehicle down, Clay stuck his head halfway through it to peer into the interior. "Come on. Make yourself useful while you're giving Cheron her space."

The mumbled response from the backseat had Ricki joining Clay at the window. "Stop pouting," she said distinctly enough that it drew the attention of the men sitting on the steps. That got the SUV's door flying open and a clearly disgruntled Anchorman stepping out.

"I don't pout," he stated with a glare, then lowered his voice so it didn't carry beyond the three of them. "I just not in the mood to listen to old war stories."

"Well, you only have to listen long enough to figure out if any of these vets were ever based at Fort Riley," Ricki told him. "They're more likely to open up to another vet than to two civilians. And after we're done here, we'll drop you back at your truck and you can drive over and pester Cheron to your heart's content."

Anchorman stretched out his long leg then stuck his hands in the pockets of his cargo pants and shrugged. "I don't feel like doing that either."

Silently wishing Cheron was there to deal with the big man's bad mood since she was the one who'd caused it, Ricki put her hands on her hips as her boot tapped against the sidewalk. "Well? What *do* you want to do?"

"Go home, have a beer, and put my feet up. It's been a lousy day."

Since a man had died in the part of the diner that Anchorman considered his domain, Ricki bit off a sour reply. He could probably use a beer and a sympathetic ear, but with a killer on the loose, that was going to have to wait. Latching on to his arm instead, she pulled him toward the house. "You're in luck, then. You can do one of those right here. Two, if there's an empty chair to prop your feet on."

Clay gave the Marine a friendly slap on the back. "We've got to look for answers somewhere, and this is as good a place to start as any."

"Yeah, yeah," Anchorman mumbled as he gave in and stalked up the short walkway leading to the front porch.

The men lounging on the steps quickly scooted to the side, making a narrow path for them. Ricki followed her cook, smiling a greeting to everyone crowded onto the small porch before stepping over the threshold and into a long hallway. It first led to a compact area that had formerly functioned as a dining room, and continued to the larger great room in the back of the house. Tables surrounded by chairs took up most of the floor space, creating a maze that had to be navigated in order to get to the bar that stretched along the back.

The walls were jam-packed with pictures from every branch of the service. Most were informal photos of men and women, dressed in fatigues and posing with friends—some at bases and others clearly taken in a war zone. Just as she always did when she walked into the VFW, Ricki glanced over at the photo of Anchorman, standing with his best friend Kelly, somewhere in the countryside of Afghanistan. She smiled at the familiar shot of the two men, then slowly shifted her gaze to take in the mob scene her Marine-vet-turned-cook was trying to wade through.

The place was humming with a standing-room-only crowd, which was exactly what she had expected. When something major happened in the Bay, everyone in town headed for their favorite gathering place to go over all the details and tap into the latest gossip making the rounds.

And a murder at the Sunny Side Up, with a federal agent, chief of police, and a trained sniper present, was definitely a major event.

When Anchorman finally powered his way to the bar, he waved several men to move down to make room for Ricki and Clay. Ricki slid into the skinny spot and waved at Bill Langly.

The post commander was at his usual place behind the bar, expertly filling an ice-cold mug with even colder beer from a tap. He smiled and nodded at Ricki before picking up two foaming glasses and carrying them to the far end of the bar. He raised his index finger to let her know he'd be with her in a minute, so she left him to the chore of working his way back down to her and turned around to watch the crowd.

Pete and Mike were holding court at their usual corner table, while Merlin sat with a mixed group of army and air force vets. Clay stepped up beside Ricki and leaned against the bar as Anchorman deserted them to leisurely wind his way around the room. The former Marine sniper was welcomed with huge smiles at every table. In this room he was a hero, and among these men and women, that was saying a lot.

Next to her, Clay chuckled softly. "He doesn't even know how much everyone here admires him." When Ricki turned her head to look at him, he smiled. "Your cook thinks of everyone who served, male or female, as just one of the guys. Like him."

"Yeah, he does," she said. "That's why we love him." Her mouth widened into a grin. "Even when he's pouting." She wiggled her eyebrows at Clay's laugh before her gaze grew sober. Somewhere in this friendly chaos there had to be someone who could shed light on the real identity of the fake Sam. Or at least a little more of his background.

"If we stand here long enough, maybe someone will volunteer a tidbit or two of information," Clay said close to her ear so she could hear him over the crowd. "And hopefully we'll get something concrete tomorrow from Finn about those fingerprints."

"Hang on," Ricki said, her gaze fixed on the woman weaving her way in between the crowded tables. "We might get lucky. Merlin is on her way here, and she's got Rory in tow."

Clay turned his body enough that he could watch the progress of the two clearly heading their way. "Rory Greyson? The guy who works for the utility company?"

"That's right," she confirmed. "He spends a lot of time traveling to jobs out of town, but he grew up here. We were in the same class all the way through school."

"Good to know," Clay said. "Who's the third guy trailing after them?"

Ricki stretched her neck as she tried to see who was following the tall, lanky Rory. "That's Curt Tandoon. He served in the army, most of it overseas, as I recall. Or at least according to Pete."

"Our local town crier who knows just about everything about everyone," Clay said.

She smiled. "Yes, Pete certainly does. Anyway, Curt moved here after his enlistment was up. That was about ten years ago, I think." She looked up at Clay and rolled her eyes to the ceiling. "I'd have to check that out with Pete to be sure."

"Uh-huh." Clay straightened up and smiled at Merlin as she came to a halt in front of him, then leaned slightly to the side to look around the former Army Ranger and nod at the man behind her. "Rory. How are you doing?"

"He's doing about the same as you, Chief." Merlin spoke up as Rory's gaze dropped to study his feet. She glanced at Ricki. "Or more like you, I guess. The chief here has a murder on his hands, and Rory lost a friend. Even if he wasn't Sam Parkman. And before he gets into all that, I wanted to ask you about that memorial service you mentioned at the clinic this afternoon. I'd like to help with that in any way I can. Do you think it's all right to call Marcie and let her know? Or maybe drop her a note?"

"I'm sure she'd appreciate it," Ricki said, ignoring Merlin's speculative look after her announcement that the man shot at the Sunny Side Up was not the real Sam Parkman. "Just give her another day to get steady on her feet again, and there won't be much planning until after the autopsy."

"Autopsy?" Merlin's gaze went from Ricki to Clay. "Why is there going to be an autopsy? It's pretty obvious the man died from a bullet wound, isn't it?"

"There's always an autopsy when murder is involved," Clay explained. "This one won't be any exception."

"But . . ." Merlin's protest was cut off by Bill, who had silently made his way back up the bar and was now standing opposite the small group, wiping his hands with a dishtowel.

"Okay. The chief has explained it enough. We don't need to hear more than that." The post commander shook his head, ending on a long sigh. "Knowing it, though, isn't going to make it any easier on anyone, especially Marcie." He quickly glanced around the room. "I'm sure the VFW can help out. How long before Marcie will want to start making the arrangements?"

"Not long. After Dr. Garrison performs the autopsy tomorrow morning, the body can be released," Clay said.

"What if Marcie doesn't want to make the arrangements at all?" Merlin blurted out. "I mean, since this Sam isn't her brother."

"There will be a service for him." Ricki frowned, then looked at Rory, waiting patiently as he slowly lifted his gaze to hers. "I'm sorry you lost a friend and want you to know that we feel the same way. The man who died this morning was our friend, too." She switched her attention back to Merlin. "That's the second time you've sated that the victim is not Marcie's brother. What makes you think he wasn't Sam Parkman?"

Merlin jerked her head toward the corner table. "Pete. He said he had it on the best authority that TK stated the dead man wasn't Marcie's brother, Sam." Her gaze darted to Clay. "Is that the truth, Chief?"

"I don't know. That hasn't been confirmed yet one way or the other." Clay took a small step to the side so he could directly face Rory, without having to talk over Merlin's head. "Did you know Sam well?"

Rory's thin face contorted into a grimace. "Well enough to feel a hole with his loss." Shoulders with their bones clearly outlined by the loose T-shirt the utility man was wearing, lifted into a shrug. "We hung out some. Every few weeks we'd stop by that bar near Anchorman's place and have a drink. Maybe play a couple of games of darts." His brown eyes drooped at the corners. "And we used to swap stories over a meal. Mostly about our days in the service. We were friends."

"What the hell, Rory."

At the angry voice behind them, the small group turned in unison to stare at a red-faced Bill Langly. He clutched at the towel he'd been holding between his hands, slowly twisting it as if it were Rory's neck. At the hard look from both Clay and Ricki, he took an involuntary step back. "Sorry. I'm sorry." He loosened his grip on the towel long enough to lift a hand in a casual wave at Rory. "I apologize to you, too. But good lord, man. Everyone in here has been racking their brains to come up with some information about the guy who got shot this morning, and you're just now getting around to saying you two were friends?" He leaned his forearms against the bar top and shook his head, sending first Ricki and then Clay a rueful smile. "Before you get around to questioning me about Sam, or whoever he was, I hardly knew the guy. But it wasn't from lack of trying. I'd heard he was a vet, but whenever the opportunity came up to talk to him about his time in the service, he'd just shake me off and walk away. I thought he might be interested in meeting other vets, but as far as I know, he never came in here at all."

"Sam didn't like crowds," Rory volunteered. "We only went to the bar sometimes, and usually in the middle of the afternoon when it wasn't busy." Rory's gaze wandered over to Ricki.

"Mostly we got a pizza or something and took it back to my place and sat around watching a game on TV."

"Well, that's a lot more than I ever did with Sam Parkman," Bill declared. "And I would bet everyone in this room would say the same thing." He straightened up and wagged a finger at Rory. "It's good that you spoke up. Do you know where the guy was based, or even what branch of the service he was in?"

"The army, like me," Rory said, then clamped his mouth shut and once again dropped his gaze to the floor.

Merlin laid a hand on Rory's arm before turning an annoyed gaze on the post commander standing behind the bar. "Come on, Bill. There's no reason to yell at Rory. Maybe he didn't get very talkative right on your cue, but he got around to speaking up, didn't he?" She frowned and lifted a hand to rub across the back of her neck. Abruptly whirling into an about-face, she reached out and gave the man who had been standing behind her a light shove. "Geez, Curt. Back off. You're breathing all over me." She jerked a thumb toward the far side of the bar. "Why don't you find someplace else to drink your beer?"

Curt's mouth curled into a crooked smile. "I like this spot." Beside his odd smile, there wasn't much that stood out about Curt. He had brown hair and brown eyes, and stood at Ricki's height, which put him a good inch shorter than Merlin, who was still glaring at him.

"Suit yourself," she said. "But find somewhere else to breathe."

Curt rolled his eyes to the ceiling. "Sure. Whatever you say."

"I'll tell you what." Clay's deep voice cut across the challenging huffs Merlin was directing at Curt. "You both can have my spot and Ricki's too so you don't have to go looking for an open place at the bar." He looked over and nodded at Rory. "And we can go find a quieter place to talk."

Bill eyed the revved-up crowd and shook his head. "This would have been a good time to hike into the forest and pitch a tent, if I liked that kind of thing,"

Ricki smiled but didn't take her eyes off of Rory. "You don't like to go camping?"

"I stick to fishing. I did enough hiking and living out of a tent when I was in the Army. Haven't done it since." He frowned at the crowd standing three deep in front of the bar. "I can clear out a space at one end of the bar if you want a place to talk. It won't take long."

"It's a nice night," Ricki put in. "We can take a walk outside and leave the bar to the vets who come in to have a social drink." She turned her back on Bill and smiled at Rory. "What do you say? Does going outside to talk sound like a good idea?"

Rory gave her a long look before he finally bobbed his head up and down. "I guess I can do that."

Clay stepped up and gently shouldered several people out of their way. "The sooner the better. Let's start digging our way out of here and find a quieter spot outside."

At Clay's subtle nod, Ricki took up a position behind Rory. "Okay, Rory. You help clear a path and I'll be right behind you." As they wound their way through the crowd, Ricki caught Anchorman's eye. He was sitting at a table with three other men, and when he glanced her way, she inclined her head toward Rory's back. The Marine frowned but gave a quick thumbs-up before returning to the serious-looking conversation with his fellow vets.

Once outside, Clay kept walking until the jumbled roar of voices pouring through the open front door of the VFW Post was reduced to a steady background noise. When he stopped by an old pine tree, Rory did too. Ricki stuck her hands into her jacket pockets and stepped around him, drawing in a deep breath. The night air was clean, fresh, and just cool enough to enjoy but not to make you shiver. A smile ghosted across her mouth as she also felt the slight hint of rain. It was how she always recognized her hometown that sat next to a rainforest. There was that constant touch of moisture in the air.

"So, Rory." Clay's deep voice cut into her musing about the night air, bringing her back to the reality of murder. "What can you tell us about Sam Parkman?"

Rory lifted a hand and used his long fingers to lightly scratch down his cheek. "I'm not sure what you want to know, Chief. He was a guy like a lot of guys I served with. Maybe a little more wound up than most, but he was all right." Rory's face lit up with a smile. "Sam really liked football. He's a big fan of the Chiefs. I mean the football team." The smile faded and he awkwardly shuffled his feet. "He was. I meant to say he was a fan of the Chiefs."

Clay leaned against the trunk of the tree at his back. "That's okay. I got your meaning." His mouth scrunched up. "The Chiefs. That's an East Coast team, isn't it?"

Ricki carefully kept her expression blank. Her fiancé was an avid football fan himself, and he knew damn good and well what city the Chiefs played in. And it wasn't on the East Coast.

It only took a second for Rory's smile to come back as he shook his head. "Nah. They're straight out of the Midwest. The Chiefs play in Kansas City. I thought everyone knew that."

Clay only smiled. "Did Sam ever mention how he became a fan? I imagine everyone in town knew that he wasn't from Kansas."

Rory's eyebrows drew together as he thought that over. "I don't know. Sam never talked about himself. I don't know much about those years he was gone, but I know he trained at Fort Riley, and that's in Kansas. Maybe he started following the

Chiefs when he was stationed there. He said the team was a pretty big deal around the base."

"I'll bet." Clay kept his voice casual. "Did he ever mention any family? Besides his sister, Marcie, I mean? They should be told what happened here."

Rory gave him a puzzled look. "You said you didn't know if he was Marcie's brother or not. If he is, wouldn't she do that?"

Ricki watched Clay's poker face, knowing he was silently weighing his options of how honest to be with Rory. When he glanced at her, she nodded back. From what they'd heard from Merlin, the whole town most likely knew by now that according to TK, the man shot that morning wasn't the real Sam Parkman.

"She would," Clay said slowly. "If that was in fact her brother who died this morning." When Rory didn't have any reaction to that announcement, Clay lifted an eyebrow. "You didn't say anything when Merlin asked about it, but I'm guessing you already heard there's some question about who the man really was?"

The scarecrow-thin man turned his head to look off into the distance. "Yeah. I heard that. Merlin told me, but I didn't believe her." He turned back to squarely face Clay. "Is there any truth to it?"

"When I said we don't know yet, that was the truth," Clay replied. "But we're working on it. Which is why it's important for you to tell me anything you know about Sam."

"It isn't much." Engaging in his go-to habit of dropping his gaze to his feet, Rory scuffed the toe of his heavy working boot in the dirt. "Sam and I never talked about the past much. I already told you he liked football, and he didn't like crowds."

"You also said he did some training at Fort Riley," Ricki said. "Isn't that right?"

He glanced at her from the corner of his eye. "Yeah. That's right."

"Did he ever mention what kind of training he did there?" she asked.

The question had Rory's gaze snapping up to hers. "Yeah, yeah. He did. It was some kind of communication work. Not sure what." His chin jutted out slightly, and he shifted his legs into a wider, more defiant stance. "Sam was a smart guy. He never acted like it much, but he was. He knew how to tap into people's phones and computers without them ever knowing about it. I don't know how he did it, but he said he could." Rory shrugged. "We'd had a few drinks at my place, and I guess he felt like bragging a little."

"Did he brag about anything else?"

Rory rubbed a tired hand across his forehead. "He mentioned he had a ham radio setup somewhere in Massey, but later he said he was just kidding. Other than that, I don't know. I'll have to think about it." He looked over his shoulder at the building behind him. The post was lit up like a candle in the night sky. "I'd like to get back if that's all right. The guys are celebrating knowing Sam, and I'd like to be there with them."

"No problem," Clay said. "Can you let Anchorman know we're waiting for him out here? We need to give him a ride back to his truck."

"Will do." Lifting his hand in a brief salute to Clay, Rory nodded at Ricki with a smile, then did a quick about-face and headed toward the Post.

Clay crossed his arms over his chest as he watched the utility man disappear inside the house-turned-into-VFW Post. "What do you think?"

"I think Anchorman is right and the victim was in the service," Ricki said. "And TK is right, too. He wasn't Sam Parkman. Marcie told me Sam trained as a big engine mechanic, not in communications the way he bragged to Rory. But if our dead guy was in the army during the same time as the real Sam Parkman, then it was too long ago for him to be in any facial recognition database."

Unwinding his arms, Clay wrapped one around Ricki's shoulders. "I have to agree there. Right now our best hope is that Finn will come up with something."

Chapter Eight

Ricki lifted her head and looked over Clay's broad shoulder at the clock on the small table next to the bed. Another hour had passed since the last time she'd looked at it. The good news was that she must have slept for most of that hour. But that was about all the sleep she'd managed since she'd gone to bed.

There had been too many lows, and no highs at all, in the previous twenty-four hours for her to get any solid sleep. The picture of a man, no matter who he was, bleeding to death on the kitchen floor of her diner kept playing in a constant loop in her mind. She heard the sound of a gunshot, followed by her own voice calling out to Sam and getting no answer, then saw the gruesome image of him sprawled on his back, blood covering the front of his shirt and pooling on the floor next to his chest. Everything was in slow motion until that image of Sam came into focus, and there it seemed to get stuck. The surreal scene stayed with her until she finally was forced to open her eyes and concentrate on putting it away, only to have the whole loop play on repeat when exhaustion drew her into sleep again.

Feeling helpless, and annoyed with the frustration building inside her, she finally gave up and carefully swung her legs over the side of the bed. Moving quietly so she wouldn't disturb Clay, she slipped on a pair of sweatpants to go with the oversized T-shirt she'd slept in. She scooped up a pair of heavy socks, with the intention of sitting at the top of the stairs to put them on so she wouldn't bother Clay.

Tiptoeing down the short hallway, she made a point of stepping over the squeaky board near the top of the stairs, then suddenly froze. Lifting her nose, she took a deep breath, then exhaled it slowly. Coffee. There was no mistaking the smell of freshly brewed coffee.

Wondering if Eddie had heard about the shooting and high-tailed it home very late the night before, she stood on the top step and bent over to look into the great room on the bottom floor. The tall, muscular figure sitting on one of the stools next to the kitchen island was definitely not her son. Eddie was getting to that height, but the build of her visitor was more like that of a tree trunk than a long-distance runner. She would know that build anywhere.

Exasperated at the early morning caller, though thankfully seeing who it was meant her son had not managed to find a ride home in the dead of night after all, she plopped down on the top step and pulled her socks over her feet before heading downstairs.

"Good morning," Anchorman called out without turning around. He didn't sound any more happy to be up and about at this hour than she did.

Moving across the room, she made a beeline for the coffeepot that was steaming away on the stove. She didn't say a word, or even turn around to acknowledge him, until she'd poured herself a large mug of the brew and had taken several healthy sips. Feeling a little less groggy, she carried the mug to the island and sat down on one of the vacant stools. She glanced at the picture window where Corby always slept. His favorite spot was empty, and so was his food dish.

"Where's Corby?"

Anchorman lifted his mug toward the deep forest beyond the front window. "He greeted me at the door this morning with his food dish in his mouth. So I fed him, and he's now out scouting his kingdom, probably for something else to supplement his breakfast."

Not doubting that one bit, Ricki settled more comfortably on her stool. "What are you doing here? The sun isn't even up yet."

Anchorman took another glance out the big window. "It will be in a few minutes, and I might ask you the same thing."

"Couldn't sleep," she admitted. "Sam's murder was on a continual replay all night."

"PTSD. If it doesn't wear off in a week or two, you'll need to find some help. Lydia could probably steer you in the right direction for that."

"She probably could," Ricki agreed. Lydia Hudson was the wife of the District Attorney in Seattle, and was a well-respected psychiatrist with a thriving practice. "So, why are you up so early?"

"I'm always up early."

Ricki lifted her coffee mug and eyed him over the rim. "Not this early. What gives?"

His mouth pulled down at the corners as he stared into his coffee mug. "I think Cheron blew me off last night."

One of Ricki's eyebrows shot halfway up her forehead. "You think?"

His shoulders moved in a half-hearted shrug. "She's not

very good at that kind of thing. My first wife was a master at it, but Cheron? Not so much."

"Which is probably one of the reasons you were so attracted to her from the start. She's nothing like your first wife."

"That's for sure," Anchorman grumbled.

When he fell silent, Ricki nudged his calf with her sock-covered toe. "So what did Cheron say to you? Or more importantly, what did you say to her that made her blow you off?"

He shot her an annoyed look. "Nothing. I called her up and offered to bring some dinner over to the lab, and she said she was already home. So I said I'd bring the food over there, and then she tells me that she's tired, and is going to bed because she has to be up early tomorrow morning. Which would be this morning." His slight frown turned into a full-blown scowl. "Funny thing, though. I drove by her place on my way here, and her car was still in the driveway."

Ricki snorted a laugh. "It's not even 5:30 in the morning. I doubt if she meant she had to get up this early."

"Early means early," Anchorman maintained, a stubborn note creeping into his voice.

"Only if you're a bird out hunting for the first worm of the day," she said with a grin. "And how did you happen to drive by Cheron's on your way here? She lives on the opposite side of town."

He slowly took a sip of his coffee as he pointedly ignored her.

This man, who could get any squad he was in safely back home through a barrage of enemy fire, was entirely clueless when it came to one wispy-thin, completely nerdy Cheron Garrison. With an effort, Ricki choked back the laughter bubbling up in her throat. "Okay. I'll let that one pass. So what did you say when she clearly did not invite you to come over and go to bed early with her?"

"I said okay, and then hung up." When Ricki gave him a bug-eyed stare, the Marine held up one hand in defense. "I was giving her some space."

"And you did that by hanging up on her?"

"No," Anchorman ground out. "I said, 'okay', and *then* I hung up."

"Did you throw an 'I love you' somewhere in there?"

"There's no need. She knows that."

Ricki's mouth dropped open, but nothing came out as she slapped an open palm against her forehead.

"What's going on down here?" Clay's voice cracked out.

When Ricki and Anchorman swiveled around on their stools, they were met with a bleary-eyed Clay, standing at the base of the stairs in his boxers and a T-shirt, his arms crossed over his chest.

Ricki hopped off her stool and rounded the island as she headed for the stove. "I found Anchorman sitting here, having a cup of coffee. Since I couldn't sleep, I decided to join him."

"And suck me into a relationship discussion before the sun is even up," Anchorman said, drawing a glare from Ricki as she carried a mug of coffee over to Clay.

Clay's eyes closed as he took a long sip of the hot brew. When he opened them again, he lasered his gaze right at Anchorman. "Whose relationship? Yours or mine?"

"Mine," Anchorman groused. "Look. I came over to talk about what I found out last night. Do you want to hear it or not?"

"Sure. But I'm going to sit down first."

"Maybe you should put on some pants first," Anchorman pointed out, which had Clay literally growling at him.

"I'm going to sit down to hear what you found out over at

the VFW, and then I'd like to know how you got in here. I know I locked that door last night."

"He has a key," Ricki supplied. "In case of an emergency."

"Great." Clay tromped over to the island and took a stool next to Ricki's. "Okay, I'm sitting." He paused, waiting while Ricki settled back on her seat. "Let's hear it."

"It's not much," Anchorman admitted. "But at this point, I'm guessing something is better than nothing at all. One of the guys I bumped into told me there was another vet who spent time at Fort Riley."

"Who?" Ricki prompted.

"Curt Tandoon. It turns out he trained to be a radio operator there. My guy told me Curt has a pretty elaborate ham radio setup in his house."

"Is that so?" Clay leaned against the high back of his stool. "It might be worth paying him a visit."

"Maybe." Ricki did a quick calculation in her head. "Curt's quite a bit younger than Sam. I'm not sure they would have been at Fort Riley at the same time."

Anchorman rolled his shoulders back and forth, trying to work out the early-morning kinks. "I've never warmed up to Curt. He always seems to skulk about, listening in on things that aren't any of his business. He might have overheard something we'd be interested in knowing. That alone, along with his connection to Fort Riley, should be enough to justify a visit."

"Maybe." Ricki cut her words off as a riot of noise exploded outside. Framed in the picture window, Corby rushed out of the trees to stand at alert in the middle of the driveway, his whole body rigid, barking loud enough to wake the dead.

"Corby doesn't recognize the engine of whatever is coming down the driveway," Ricki said over the noise.

Anchorman immediately headed for the gun locker underneath the staircase while Clay reached over and grabbed the service revolver he'd left on the kitchen counter the night before. Ricki's shoulder holster with her Glock was on a hook next to the front door, and she grabbed it before following Clay out onto the small porch.

A black Infiniti sedan rolled around the last corner. The plates declared it a rental car, and the heavily tinted windows kept her from seeing who was driving it. Apparently Corby didn't have the same problem. His barking came to an abrupt halt as he plopped his butt down on the gravel and waited. The minute the car stopped and the door opened, the big dog trotted over to the driver's side, his stub of a tail wagging in a friendly welcome.

It took Ricki a second to realize it was none other than Special Agent Fionn Sullivan who had crouched down to give Corby a good head scratch. He said something to the person still inside the car, just before his passenger opened the door and stepped out.

"Well, shit," Clay said under his breath as Ricki grinned.

She hurried down the steps and past the vehicles already parked in the crowded space. Stepping around her green jeep, she walked over to greet the tall woman with a sun-kissed complexion and gray eyes that were an exact mirror of Clay's with a warm hug. "What are you doing here?" she whispered.

Clay's sister, Kate, laughed and took a half step backwards. "Finn said he had to come, so I thought I'd tag along in case you needed some help with the wedding plans." Her face sobered as she met Ricki's gaze. "He also told me what happened to Sam. I'm so sorry. How's Marcie doing?"

"All right, everything considered," Ricki replied. "Why did Finn say he had to come here?"

Kate made a face. "I don't know. He clammed up about that. And he wasn't too happy about me coming along, but since there wasn't any way he could stop me, he very ungraciously gave in about it."

Her description of Finn's reaction had Ricki smiling.

When Clay came up and tapped his sister on the shoulder, Kate turned around and gave him a hug before stepping back and raising one finely arched eyebrow. She slowly looked over his boxers and bare legs before lifting her gaze to his. "Interesting fashion choice, but I doubt if it will catch on."

"We can talk about my attire later. What are you doing here?" His lips pressed into a thin line. "And with Finn?"

"Oh," she said, feigning surprise. "Haven't you heard? We're dating. And *I* came to help with the wedding plans." She waved a hand in Finn's direction. "I have no idea why *he's* here. He's still learning how to share."

"Finn told your sister he had to come," Ricki interjected. "But didn't tell her why, and he isn't all that happy she came along, so I'm guessing it isn't great news."

Clay's eyes narrowed on the FBI Agent who was talking quietly with Anchorman. "Well then, I guess we'd better hear it and get it over with." He raised his voice, directing it at the two men. "Finn. Anchorman. Let's go into the house and put on some more coffee."

"No argument there," Finn called back. As Anchorman made a straight line toward the house, Finn walked over to where Ricki, Kate, and Clay were standing. He took Clay's outstretched hand and gave it a firm shake. "I've got some news about those fingerprints Cheron sent me," he said without preamble. "And you aren't going to like it."

"I haven't liked much about the last twenty-four hours, so that's no surprise." Clay snaked an arm around his sister's shoulders. "Let's go inside. Maybe you can go upstairs and lie down for a bit while Finn and I talk. You've got to be tired."

"Not a chance, Clay." Clearly exasperated, Kate shook off

his arm, then walked up to Finn and took one of his hands in hers. "But I will have a cup of Anchorman's famous coffee."

Finn tucked her hand into the crook of his arm. "We can both do that."

Clay watched them walk off, glancing at Ricki when she moved to stand next to him and ran one hand lightly over his back. "You do realize that you're standing out here in your boxers, don't you? Maybe you'd like to put on some sweatpants before you hear what Finn has to say."

Her fiancé continued to stare after his sister. "Maybe he'd like to keep his hands off of Kate."

"Maybe we could do Chief Clay right now, and big brother Clay later on?" she countered. "Their relationship is their business, and I'd like to hear what Finn has to say before you decide whether or not you're going to shoot him for dating your completely grown-up sister." She stopped rubbing his back and gave it a gentle slap instead. "I've heard enough of that from Anchorman. Don't you start too."

Clay looked genuinely puzzled as he stared at her. "Heard enough of what? Anchorman doesn't even have a sister."

"I know you're being deliberately dense," Ricki called over her shoulder as she started walking toward the cabin. "And put on some pants."

She walked through the door with Corby trailing after her, and went straight for the refrigerator while the boxer mix headed for his food dish. Opening the door to the fridge, she bent over and peered inside. Half a loaf of bread, two eggs in an otherwise empty carton, and a couple of slices of leftover pizza were the only things she was positive were still edible.

She frowned, sure that she'd made a grocery run just a week earlier. Or maybe it was the week before that. One of the perks of being part owner in a diner was that she never had to cook a meal, unless she really wanted to. And that was a rare occurrence. Why would she eat her own bad cooking when she could have something really excellent made by Anchorman, or Sam, or just about anyone else on the planet?

Anchorman was standing at the sink, refilling the coffee pot. "I've already looked in there and told them the bad news. There's nothing to eat here, and right at the moment I can't send for something from the Sunny Side Up." He glanced at the large watch on his wrist. "Nothing else will be open for another couple of hours."

"I'm sure the café at the hotel will be serving by the time we get there," Kate said. "And that will be fine."

Clay walked in just in time to hear what Kate had said. His eyes narrowed on Finn before he caught sight of Ricki, standing in front of the open refrigerator door, shaking her head at him. Her gaze held steady as he hesitated, then he lifted his palms in the air in surrender. "You're staying at the St. Armand?"

Ricki smiled. While Clay's tone wasn't exactly friendly, at least he didn't voice an objection.

Kate looped her arm around Finn's. "I don't want to take Eddie's room, and Finn is allergic to sleeping on couches." Ignoring the long look exchanged between the two men, Kate leaned over and scratched Corby's head. The boxer was sitting right in front of her, his food dish in his mouth and a hopeful look in his liquid-brown eyes. "I think poor Corby here is ready for his breakfast."

"Which he's already had," Ricki said. "So ignore him." Belatedly closing the door to the fridge, she walked over to the island and faced Kate and Finn, who were standing on the other side. "Have a seat. We'll pour the coffee." She paused to glance at Clay. "While you find some pants, and then Finn can fill us in on whatever had him flying all night to get here."

Clay headed for the stairs while Anchorman set out two more

mugs for the unexpected visitors. By the time Clay reappeared, fully dressed to start his day, Ricki was carrying steaming mugs over to Kate and Finn. After setting them on the counter, she headed back to the stove and picked up Clay's topped-off mug as well as her own before returning to her spot on the kitchen side of the island. Clay walked over to stand next to her, while Anchorman followed with his own coffee and took up a spot on her other side.

"Before you start," Clay said. "If this has to do with my murder case, I'm not sure Kate should be hearing it."

"Why not?" his sister asked. "If you're going to say because I'm a civilian, I'd like to point out that so is Anchorman. And besides, Finn wouldn't tell me exactly what this was about, but he did say that it's public information."

"Most of it," Finn amended for her. "I said most of it had been published in the newspapers."

Kate smiled as she unbuttoned her coat. "I'll cover my ears when you get to the secret part."

Clay shook his head at his sister before nodding at Finn. "Fine. Let's hear it then."

Finn helped Kate with her coat, laying it carefully across the back of the couch behind them. He took a manila envelope out of an inside pocket of his calf-length, very upscale leather jacket, before shrugging out of the coat and tossing it next to Kate's. Claiming a stool, he took a seat and scooted it a few inches closer to Kate's before resting his forearms on the counter. When he wrapped large hands around the steaming mug, his face was set into sober lines as he looked from Clay to Ricki, and then to Anchorman.

The FBI agent was as tall as Clay, with the same type of build, but that was where the similarities between the two men ended. Finn had dark hair that set off green eyes, leaving no doubt of the heritage passed down through his Irish ancestors.

Which also included a bad-boy kind of charm as a balance for his quick temper.

"The good news is that we know who those prints belong to," Finn said, his voice the only sound in the quiet room. "The bad news is that your victim was a wanted man. We think he was part of a trio who orchestrated a heist of two million dollars cash, left five bodies behind in the process, and shot up an armored car while they were making their escape."

Chapter Nine

The silence deepened. Ricki finally moved, turning her head to exchange a glance with Clay as they both took a deep breath.

"Were any of the armored car crew hurt?" Clay asked quietly. He slowly breathed out when Finn shook his head.

"No. They were late getting to the pickup point because of a flat tire. In a twist of good luck for us, and not so good for the robbers, the company happened to have a spare truck available and got it to them in record time, so they were only an hour late to the drop-off. If it hadn't been for that, we wouldn't have any witnesses to what went down. When they came upon the scene, a white van was pulling out of the hangar where the robbery took place. From that point, it turned into chaos.

"The next thing the guard and his partner sitting up front knew was that two people in the van opened up on them. One from the passenger seat, and another through the side door. The armored car guys didn't have time to get a shot off before the van was gone, and the driver swore to us it didn't have any plates. His partner backed him up on that, and the third guy in the back of the car didn't see a damn thing."

"And they got away with two million?" Clay frowned as he waited for the FBI agent's confirming nod. "I don't remember a bank robbery that big. When did this happen?"

"Seven years ago." Finn drummed long fingers against the countertop. "And it wasn't a bank heist. They took the money off a private jet, and left two pilots, two bodyguards, and the guy who owned both the money and the jet dead on the ground." With two fingers he shoved the manila envelope he'd set on the counter closer to Clay. "A picture of your guy, plus the crime scene photos."

Clay opened the envelope with an apologetic look toward Kate, who had her gaze carefully fixed on Corby. Reaching into the envelope, he removed a handful of photos and fanned them out along the counter.

Ricki leaned to the side and studied the one showing a head-and-shoulder shot of a man in military uniform. She drew in a sharp breath. A much younger version of the man she'd known as Sam Parkman was staring back at her. She pushed the photo over toward Anchorman, who swore viciously under his breath. Raising her gaze to Finn's, she pointed at the picture. "Was that for his military ID?"

"Yep. Army. 1st Infantry Division. He was an SPC—that's a specialist—at the time he was discharged. I've got a basic fact sheet that I'll email you when I get to the hotel." He hunched his shoulders as if he was expecting to take a punch. "Blake is sending it to me later this morning." He visibly braced himself against the suddenly steely looks from three pairs of eyes. "I needed some help, and he's the one who could deliver it."

"Help?" Anchorman demanded. "What kind of help?"

"To keep the FBI off our backs," Clay said. He braced his arms against the counter and leaned forward. "For how long?"

"He has a wide reach," Finn said. "That's the reason I went to him." He stretched an arm over the counter and tapped a finger on Sam's photo. "I knew the minute those fingerprints came back on a guy the Bureau has been looking for for seven years, red flags would be raised everywhere." He looked over at Clay. "I didn't think you'd appreciate an entire task force dropping onto your front porch, and the only way I could see to stop it was to have Blake intervene. He's the top profiler in the country, and his reputation is gold in the Bureau. Especially since that Critical Crime Unit he started up has been kicking ass."

Despite her annoyance at hearing about Blake's latest intrusion into their lives, Ricki smiled. "The Critical Crime Unit? Is that the one Gin is part of?" Gin Reilly was a highly skilled FBI agent Ricki had gotten to know through several of her prior cases. She'd not only been a big help, but had become a friend. She knew Gin had been assigned to Blake's new unit, but she hadn't heard from her friend in a while so wasn't sure if the new appointment had actually gone through.

"That's right."

Finn's slight grimace didn't escape Ricki's notice. She narrowed her eyes and watched a streak of color spread across the agent's cheeks. "Is there something you want to tell me?"

"Well, nothing that should come as a surprise. You know by now that any favor from Blake has a price tag attached to it."

"Which is?" Ricki asked as both Clay and Anchorman crossed their arms over their chests.

The FBI agent glanced down at his watch. "I'm sure you'll get the call as soon as it's a decent hour, but Blake is going to get in touch with Hamilton and have you loaned to the Critical Crimes Unit, as a local area expert, to help solve the riddle of Preston Malone, aka Sam Parkman."

Ricki's boot started tapping the floor. Hamilton was the senior agent in charge of the district ISB office in Seattle.

Which made him her boss. It wouldn't be the first time she'd been loaned to the FBI as a local area expert. The last time she hadn't minded since she'd been trying to clear Anchorman of murder in a case that was not only a joint effort with the FBI, but also out of her assigned district. This time she wasn't feeling the same need.

The victim had been discharged from the Army, so technically, his murder was no longer the concern of the federal government. The case belonged to Clay, and she didn't need the FBI's permission to work on the case. Clay's nod of approval was all she needed.

"Investigating a two-million-dollar robbery that didn't happen in a national park isn't in my wheelhouse, Finn." She shot him a suspicious look. "It didn't happen in a park, did it?"

Finn shook his head. "No. About six miles northwest of Dallas, at Love Field." He ran an agitated hand through his dark hair. "Look. I know you don't want to work for Blake, or be reassigned, even temporarily, without any kind of say in it. And we all know how much Blake would like to recruit you into his Critical Crimes Unit. But this way, the FBI can officially cite having a team assigned to look into this new information about Specialist Malone, and we'll just have to make sure we never get to the second step of the protocol."

"What would that be?" Anchorman demanded.

"A task force."

Skeptical about Finn's explanation, Ricki pinned him with a direct stare. "And the FBI would be satisfied with a team of one agent?"

"Technically, it's a team of two." Finn nodded at her before pointing a thumb at his own chest. "You and me." His mouth twisted into a semblance of a smile. "If it's any consolation, I've been loaned to Blake's new unit too." Ricki choked out a laugh. "We're supposed to be partners?" She shook her head, dislodging a strand of dark hair from the ponytail she'd hastily made before coming downstairs that morning. "I don't work with a partner, and neither do you."

"I've been assigned one from time to time," Finn said before lifting his hand and shifting an index finger from Clay to Anchorman. "And what do you call those two?"

"Friends," she stated flatly. "Friends who have my back, and I have theirs."

Anchorman grinned. "Well, technically, we are partners."

"And not so technically, we're going to be," Clay put in, leaning down to kiss her cheek before returning his attention to the FBI agent. "I'm not thrilled with the idea of Blake getting his hooks into her, but I can see the benefit." He shifted his gaze back to Ricki. "What do you think? This arrangement is up to you."

She loved that he asked, but it was a done deal. There was no way she would bring a whole FBI task force down on top of them. In her mind, that was a sure way to delay anything getting done. "Fine. When Hamilton calls, I'll act thrilled with the idea."

Clay laughed. "I think a 'yes', with a little pushback, might be more convincing."

Ricki waved a hand in the air. "Whatever." She put both hands on her hips and tilted her head to one side. "Okay, partner. Tell us what's on that fact sheet about one Preston Malone."

Finn settled more comfortably on his seat and lifted his coffee mug. Indulging in a long sip, he set it down again and shrugged his shoulders. "Not a lot, to be honest. He's fifty-eight, which makes him two years older than the real Sam Parkman." Finn reached across the island and plucked a picture from the bottom of the pile that Clay had left. He slid it across the counter's smooth surface so Ricki could get a clear view of it. "This is the real Sam Parkman's ID picture."

Moving the photo of Preston Malone next to the one of Sam, Ricki carefully studied the faces of the two men. "Close, but definitely not twins," she murmured. "But add thirty years, and being absent all that time, and yeah, I can see how they could pass as each other." She looked up at Finn. "But we already knew that, and that Malone was at Fort Riley. We're pretty sure that Sam was too." When surprise passed over Finn's features, Ricki sighed. "Marcie couldn't remember if the exact name of the base was ever mentioned. Just a general description which fit the base in Kansas."

"Sam was there," Finn confirmed. "And so was Preston Malone. I compared their military records, and Fort Riley was the only posting where their paths would have crossed. I haven't narrowed down exactly when or how yet. They were both specialists, but in entirely different fields, so they wouldn't have been in the same training classes."

"Because Sam trained as a large engine mechanic, and Malone was in some kind of radio or communications field." When Finn stared at her, she grinned. "He was bragging about being some kind of communications genius to a friend of his here in Brewer. Word has it that he might have had quite a ham radio setup somewhere out in Massey."

"I was going to check that out today," Clay stated. "Ricki is having Malone's room at Marcie's house thoroughly searched. Hopefully it will turn up a key."

"That's good." Finn nodded his head and smiled in satisfaction. "I've got both their military records printed out in the car, and Blake is running a search on the current whereabouts of Sam Parkman. It seems he disappeared in more ways than one twenty-five years ago, so it's going to take some serious digging."

Ricki blinked. *Disappeared? Not just from Brewer, but altogether?* "He hasn't surfaced anywhere?"

"Not that we could find easily. No use of his credit cards

from back then, or his social security number. His fingerprints haven't been submitted from any law enforcement agency, so if he has any kind of record, it hasn't shown up in AFIS. And I doubt if there's anyone left at Fort Riley who remembers him. His last assignment was doing a six-month recruiting stint up in Omaha."

"What about Malone?" Clay asked. "When was he discharged?"

"Ten years ago," Finn said. "Three years before the robbery."

Ricki silently did a quick calculation. "And fifteen years after Sam disappeared. Hard to see a connection between them. Where did Malone spend his time after he was discharged?"

Finn stood up and rolled his shoulders back, stretching out muscles that had cramped from sitting on a plane for seven hours. "It's a long way from Miami to Seattle," he commented absently. "Malone was honorably discharged from Fort Campbell in Kentucky, which was where he served his last posting." He took out his cell phone and tapped the screen several times. "Blake has asked for a report on his movements since then from the old case file, but I haven't seen it yet."

Clay shifted his weight from one foot to the other. "Has any of the money surfaced? Two million dollars is a lot of cash."

"We don't know," the big Irishman said. "It couldn't be traced."

Dumbfounded, Ricki stared at him. "Why not? Did this very rich guy just fly around with two million dollars on his plane? He must have gotten it from some bank."

"Probably more than one," Finn said. "The very rich guy was John Hanover, the founder of Hanover Industries. They're a big private contractor that works on projects on our military bases overseas. Often in not so friendly territory. We think the two million was his slush fund for bribes his employees used at one of our, shall we say unpublicized, bases in a hot zone. They were told to evacuate, and according to one Mr. Kroker, the chief operating officer at his company, Hanover made a personal trip there to collect the cash. He got as far as Dallas. Another ten miles and he would have been home."

"Who else knew he was making the trip?" Ricki asked.

Finn scrubbed his hands over his face, then looked at her with tired eyes. "Too many people, and it took us years to check them all out. But we came up blank."

"Except for Malone," she said slowly, her boot tapping a steady rhythm against the kitchen floor. "You said Malone was part of the crew who robbed and killed Hanover. How do you know he was there?"

"Fingerprints," Finn said, stifling a yawn. "We finger-printed everything inside that plane along with the entire cargo hold, which is where we think the money was stored during the flight home. At least that's what the armored car crew was told when Hanover's staff made arrangements for the money to be picked up. We eliminated all the prints, though, except a thumbprint we found on the back of the pilot's seat. That one belonged to Malone. The only person out of all those prints who had no business being on that plane."

Clay rolled his eyes toward the ceiling. "Are you telling me that the FBI tracked down and eliminated the owners of every single print on that plane except for Malone's?"

"No. I'm telling you that out of the ones we did positively identify, Malone is the only hit we got of someone who had no reason to be on that plane."

"Since you haven't mentioned Sam's prints, I'm guessing his weren't anywhere on the plane," Ricki said.

"No," Finn replied. "They weren't. But that doesn't mean he wasn't there. Remember, two of the armored car crew said they saw three men. One was driving and the other two were shooting. And there must be some link present since Malone was passing himself off as Sam."

"That's pretty flimsy to accuse a man of a robbery and multiple murders." Picking up her mug, Ricki walked over to the stove and poured herself another cup of coffee. "They were both at Fort Riley, but training in different specialties." She carried the full mug back to the island. "Did their time at Fort Riley overlap at all?"

"About six months of it," Finn said. "So they could have met from just walking around the base, noticed how much they resembled each other and got talking. Who knows? What I can tell you for certain is that it took us three years to get that print. A cold case team was going through the old evidence about four years ago and came up with the idea of running the prints in the cockpit. The original investigators figured the robbers must have been on the ground waiting for the plane since everyone on the passenger manifest was dead, including the pilots who were shot through the plane's windshield. And the flat tire that kept the armored car from arriving on time was due to a bullet."

Ricki froze with her coffee mug halfway to her mouth. "Four years? And you said the robbery was seven years ago?"

Finn gave her a crooked smile. "Almost. And isn't it a coincidence that Malone shows up here, pretending to be Sam Parkman, just about the same time we found those prints and started tracking him down?"

"And you tracked him down to where?" Clay asked.

"Like I said, I haven't seen that piece of the old case file yet. But I expect I'll have it later today. Hopefully after we get some food and a nap." He ran a hand lightly down Kate's back. "Are you ready to head to the hotel? I'll flash my badge and get us an early check-in."

"Must be nice," Kate said dryly as she slid off the stool in a single graceful movement.

Corby, who'd been lying near her feet, suddenly sprang up and dashed to the window, his whole body quivering as he let out a series of low growls.

The sound of a car engine sputtering and coughing had Anchorman stepping around Ricki and Clay as he headed toward the window. "That sounds like Cheron's car."

A moment later he was lunging for the front door and yanking it open just as the grating screech of metal sliding on metal echoed through the trees. Everyone else poured out of the cabin right on his heels as a startled-looking Cheron emerged from her battered Toyota.

"I guess I was going faster than I thought," she said to no one in particular. She let out a squeak of surprise when Anchorman came racing across the gravel and scooped her up in his arms.

"Are you hurt?" When she shook her head, he looked at her car. "What happened?"

"I must have been going too fast," she repeated. "I wasn't expecting to see so many cars parked here and couldn't quite avoid that one." She pointed to Finn's rental car. "Who drives an Infiniti?"

The FBI agent closed his eyes before walking over to his car to view the damage. "It looks like you took a lot of paint off this side." He turned and crossed his arms over his chest as he glared at Cheron.

Anchorman carefully set her on her feet as he returned Finn's glare. "Don't yell at her. She had a good reason for coming down the driveway like that." He put an arm around Cheron's thin shoulders. "Didn't you, honey?" When she gave him a blank stare, he smoothed her hair away from her face. "Are you sure you're all right?"

"I'm fine. But I need to talk to Chief Thomas right now. Something horrible has happened." She looked wildly around until her gaze latched on to Clay. "I'm sorry, Chief. So very sorry. I don't know how this happened."

Clay gave an annoyed Finn a warning look before stepping in front of the doctor, who was wringing her hands as she watched him from behind the thick lenses of her glasses. "Whatever it is, Cheron, I'm sure we can deal with it."

"You need to get all the deputies out there," the doctor insisted. She turned a pleading look to Anchorman. "And maybe some volunteers from the VFW. I'm sure they would help."

"Help to do what?" Anchorman asked in a calm, low voice. "Tell me what happened, honey. I'll fix it."

Cheron wrapped her arms around her waist, then shook her head. "Not fix. Nothing needs to be fixed. We need to find it." She bit her lower lip as she looked at Clay. "It's gone. The body of the murder victim is gone."

Chapter Ten

C heron kept nodding her head and wringing her hands as the entire group gaped at her. "It was there in the clinic when we, that is Dr. Torres and I, left last night. I saw it on the exam table, fully draped with a sheet, before I turned out the lights and closed the door. But this morning, it was gone."

"Gone?" Clay's eyebrows winged upward. "You mean it isn't where you left it?"

"That's right." Cheron leaned back against Anchorman as if all the energy had suddenly left her body. "You know I'm also the part-time medical examiner for Jefferson County? Well, I went to the clinic this morning to get the body ready for transport to the ME facility in Port Townsend, and it was gone. Someone stole the body."

"Did you search the clinic?" Clay asked.

The doctor unwound her arms, then adjusted her glasses, staring at Clay as if he'd lost his mind. "Are you thinking the dead body got up and changed rooms?"

"No. But it's possible it was stashed somewhere else in the

clinic to be retrieved at a later time. It's an avenue that needs to be tied off," Clay said.

"Not too much later because the smell alone would tell us where the body was hidden," Cheron said in her best teacher-to-student lecture voice.

Clay politely nodded. "Okay. I'll keep that in mind. Is there anyone at the clinic now? Did you call anyone before you came here?"

"I called TK. And of course I contacted Dr. Torres since he runs the clinic. I waited until TK got there before I left to come here and notify you."

Over Cheron's head, Ricki caught Anchorman's wince. She knew how he felt. TK was long past the age where he'd be an effective guard for anything, much less someone determined to retrieve a stashed body. Hopefully the younger, and in-much-better-shape Dr. Torres, was already there with him.

Cheron's shoulders slumped forward. "I don't even know if it's illegal to steal a body no one has claimed." She looked off into the distance. "Although how can anyone claim the poor man since we don't know who he is?" Her hand flew to her mouth as her eyes opened wide in horror. "Oh no. We only suspect he isn't Sam Parkman, but what if he is? Who's going to tell Marcie that her brother's body was stolen?"

Anchorman placed a kiss on top of her head. "No one needs to tell anyone anything yet." He looked at Clay. "Isn't that right, Chief?"

Immediately nodding, Clay took out his phone. "I'm going to call in a deputy to stand guard at the clinic until we get there." When Cheron audibly sniffed, Clay gave her a reassuring smile. "It's just a precaution. We're still dealing with an unsolved murder, even if we don't have a body at the moment."

Ricki waited for Clay to take a few steps to the side to make his phone call before walking over to Cheron and patting her gently on the shoulder. "Do you know who the last person to leave the clinic yesterday was?"

"Me, I guess," Cheron said in a small voice. "Well, along with Dr. Torres. TK left earlier, and so did Nancy and Bill."

"Bill was there after all the crowds went home?"

"Yes. He was waiting for Nancy, but he stayed outside. I only saw him because I walked out for a few minutes with TK to finish discussing the arrangements to transport the body this morning. Nancy went with him, and TK drove off in his own car. That old station wagon he likes to drive."

"I know the one," Ricki said. TK used to use the ancient vehicle with wood paneling on the side to pick up bodies when he'd been the town ME before Cheron had arrived in the Bay. The long-time doctor had really enjoyed sending the town council a bill for gas and maintenance on his ancient station wagon. He'd pinned each invoice on a corkboard in his office. "And you said you were the last person to leave, along with Dr. Torres?" Ricki asked. "Did you walk out together?"

Cheron's eyes gleamed with signs of tears as she slowly nodded. "Yes. He walked me to my car, and I went home. I'm not sure if Luca drove to his house or somewhere else."

Anchorman looked down at the top of her head and frowned. "Luca?"

She turned her face up to his. "It's his name. I thought you knew that?"

Seeing the tears in her eyes, the big Marine quickly settled his expression into pleasant lines. "Oh yeah. That's right, honey. It slipped my mind."

Ricki shot him an "oh sure" look, which he ignored. The last time Anchorman had forgotten anything, he'd been heavily drugged. "Did you see Luca drive out of the parking lot?" she asked, giving an encouraging nod when Cheron's gaze came back to her.

"No. I drove off first. But I'm sure he left right behind me." Her forehead wrinkled in confusion. "What else would he have done? We'd already locked up, and he'd given me his key so I could get into the clinic this morning to prepare the body for transport." Her confused look turned into a startled one. "He said he'd come in and assist me with that, but he didn't think he could get in so early because he was planning on a late night." She chewed her lower lip as she thought that over. "Yes. That's what he said. He was planning on a late night. But that could have been to catch up on medical journals." She shifted in Anchorman's arms when he snorted sharply. "I stay up late reading medical journals all the time."

"And I'm sure Dr. Torres does too," Ricki quickly put in, nodding at Clay as he took up a position beside her.

"Don't worry about it, Cheron. We'll sort everything out." Clay held out his phone and wiggled it in the air. "I talked to Jules. He's headed over to the clinic now to keep out any stray curiosity seekers until we get there."

Noticing he hadn't included any desperate killers in that announcement, Ricki turned to ask Finn a question and caught both him and Kate stifling yawns. Thinking she wouldn't ask him if he wanted to come along on the round of morning interviews she was sure Clay had planned, she nudged the chief in the side instead. "I think we can handle the first steps in the investigation." She tilted her head toward Clay's sister and Finn who were leaning heavily against each other.

"Finn?" Clay said. "Why don't you and Kate head over to the hotel and get something to eat and then take a nap?"

The exhausted Finn didn't even pretend to argue with the suggestion. "Sounds good." He directed a weak smile at Ricki. "My partner can cover for me." When she made a face at him, he managed a grin. "Call me later and we'll meet up this afternoon."

"Will do," Ricki said.

He eyed the damage to the rental. "I think I can back out of here without losing any more paint."

"I'm so sorry," Cheron almost wailed. "I was just so focused on reporting the body being stolen to the chief that I didn't notice your car."

Ricki saw Kate dig her fingers into Finn's arm hard enough that he gave her a pained look. "Don't worry about it," she said. "It's insured, so it will all work out." She steered a flabbergasted Finn toward the damaged car. He had to crawl into the driver's seat from the passenger side, which had him scowling and Kate laughing, but the two of them finally maneuvered around Cheron's car and headed down the driveway.

Anchorman shifted Cheron to his side, keeping an arm firmly around her shoulders. "Do you need to ask Cheron anything else? Because I have to get to the diner to let the biohazard guys in, and Cheron is going to stay with me."

"Maybe I should go back to the clinic with the chief and Ricki," Cheron said. "I could help search for the body."

Anchorman shook his head. "Then I'd have to go to the clinic, too, and that isn't going to work. Besides, we have a freezer and a walk-in cooler at the diner. You can look for the body there and save them a trip."

When Cheron slapped a hand against his broad chest, he chuckled. "I think you'd be more help supervising the biohazard team. This cleanup has to be done right or we won't be able to open the Sunny Side Up any time soon. Think of the impact that would have on the social life of the community. Not to mention Marcie and Ricki's income."

Ricki suppressed a smile. Since her paycheck from the National Park Service showed up in her bank account every two weeks, she wasn't worried about income. And Anchorman had his military pension. But he did have an excellent point about Marcie. The Sunny Side Up was the waitress's only source of income, and Ricki knew Marcie would never take a dime, much less a whole paycheck, from the diner until it was open and running again.

"He's dead-on about Marcie," she said, putting her thoughts into words. "The job needs to be done properly, and we need to get open again." When Cheron still didn't look certain, Ricki added more weight to her argument. "You know Anchorman won't get a good night's sleep until he helps us catch this guy. And he can't do that until he gets the diner and Marcie all squared away."

That made up Cheron's mind. Ricki could see it in her face. As much as Anchorman's overly protective nature exasperated her, the brilliant forensic pathologist was in love with the rough-and-tumble Marine.

"All right," Cheron said. "I can help with the biohazard team." She adjusted her glasses as she glanced up at Anchorman. "But don't think for one minute I'm going to be checking your freezer for a dead body."

"No problem," Anchorman said as he ushered her over to his truck. "I'll do it."

She gave him an aggrieved look, then dug her heels in as she glanced over her shoulder at her dilapidated car. "What about my Toyota? I need to call someone to get it fixed."

"I'll call the junkyard to get it towed," Anchorman said to get her moving again. He listened to her protests the whole time he was settling her into his truck. When he finally slammed the door, he scooted around to the driver's side, giving Ricki and Clay a thumbs-up before climbing behind the wheel. Executing a neat U-turn, he headed down the driveway with Cheron's arm frantically waving goodbye out the window.

Clay shook his head. "I don't know why those two make sense, but they do." He tucked his cell phone back into his pocket. "Jules sent me a text. He's at the clinic, so we'd better make an appearance there too. Let's get our jackets and gear from the house and head out."

It only took a minute to grab what they needed and walk back outside. Correctly sensing their intent to leave, Corby had already disappeared into the trees before they'd even crossed the small gravel drive and, in silent agreement, got into Clay's black SUV. Once they reached the main highway, Ricki half turned in her seat to look at Clay. "So why take the body?"

"To keep us from identifying the victim," he said. "Because it's all over town that the guy who was shot wasn't Sam Parkman after all."

"It got out almost as soon as TK said it," Ricki said in a dry tone. "And it leans toward the shooter being a local since he heard the gossip. It was big news yesterday, literally the talk of the town. So all he would have had to do was drop in at any store or the only bar in town and he could have overheard it."

"And the minute he did, he would have known there would be an autopsy, even in a place as small as the Bay," Clay said.

"Especially with a former homicide cop as the chief of police," Ricki added, then frowned in concentration. "Okay. He steals the body so we can't do the autopsy. But we've already identified the body through the fingerprints Cheron took." She glanced at Clay. His mouth opened slightly as he caught on to her train of thought. "That means he didn't know about the fingerprints, or why else go to the trouble of stealing the body? The damage, so to speak, was already done."

"We need to keep it that way," Clay stated. "The fewer people who know we've identified the victim, the better. So who knew?"

"Cheron and Anchorman." Ricki retrieved her phone from her back pocket. "I'm sending them a text right now not to mention it to anyone."

"Besides Finn, Blake, and probably a good chunk of the FBI, who else knows?"

Ricki smiled. "Fortunately for us, Blake and that chunk of the FBI don't pay regular visits to the Bay, so we can pass them off to Finn. That leaves Kate, TK, and whoever else saw Cheron take the prints at the clinic." She immediately tapped Cheron's contact number. A few minutes later she hung up and placed her phone in the console between the seats. "Cheron said that only TK was there at the time. Dr. Torres was in his office, and Nancy was out front in the lobby, standing guard in front of the doors with Bill."

"Did Cheron tell anyone else about the prints?" Clay asked.

"She said she didn't. And she scanned and emailed them to Finn from her home office instead of her lab, so no one there knew about them either."

"Good." Clay nodded his head in satisfaction. "That might give us a leg up on Malone's killer."

Ricki shifted in her seat again, keeping her gaze on the road ahead. "Have you got any ideas about who that might be?" When he remained silent, she couldn't help sighing loudly. "Does that mean you're thinking it might have been the real Sam Parkman?"

"Or the third guy in that heist, whoever he was," Clay said evenly. "But I'd bet my badge that the reason Malone was in the Bay was to hide from someone. The question is whether he was ducking the FBI, his partners in crime, or both."

"But you think one of those partners was Sam," Ricki persisted.

Clay glanced at her from the corner of his eye. "He was using Sam's identity, so that's a strong possibility."

"Maybe he and Sam were friends, and when he needed to disappear, Malone thought Sam's former life was the perfect way to do it, and he either killed Sam to get it, or Sam doesn't even know his buddy is here impersonating him." She rubbed the bridge of her nose. That explanation sounded like an impossible stretch, even to her. Except for the part where Malone killed Sam to steal his identity. And if Malone knew the FBI was close to tracking him down for the robbery, why would he take on the identity of one of his partners?

When Clay shrugged and said "I don't know," Ricki winced. Most of her life she'd had the habit of speaking her thoughts out loud without knowing it. But even after all this time, she still didn't like it.

"It doesn't make sense," she said. "If he knew the FBI was onto him, he would have had to have assumed they were also on to his partners, so why hide behind one of their identities?"

"I still don't know." Clay made the turn into the clinic's parking lot and took a space next to TK's battered station wagon.

Jules trotted down the steps and waited for them on the narrow walkway. "Everything is quiet here, Chief. TK is inside with Dr. Torres. I haven't seen anyone else. TK said Nancy had the day off, so she hasn't been by."

"That's good," Clay told his deputy as they walked back up the steps. "Why don't you hang around here for a while, and then I'll have some work for you and Ryan to do."

"Will do," Jules said before leaning to the side with a smile. "Hi, Ricki. Are you doing okay? How about Marcie?" His smile vanished and his eyes drooped. "This must be real hard on both of you."

Jules had been with the Bay's police department since Ricki was a teenager. The deputy was beanpole thin, with long arms and legs that gave him the appearance of a spider, but he had a soft heart, which made him a favorite with her. "We're both hanging in there," she said. "Anchorman too."

The deputy immediately perked up again. "He's a good man and will take great care of you." He blinked and shot a quick look at his boss. "Just like the chief. You can count on him."

Clay chuckled. "Thanks for the endorsement, Deputy Tucker." He opened the front door and held it for Ricki. "I'll be back in a few minutes."

Once they were inside with the doors closed securely behind them, Ricki smiled. "Don't be offended. You know that Anchorman's a local hero. Most people don't have a former sniper living in their town, and everyone in the Bay is positive that he can do anything."

"Him *and* the Hulk." The underlying amusement in Clay's tone made her laugh. "All right very Special Agent Ricki James. Let's start eliminating suspects."

Chapter Eleven

"This is the most outrageous thing I've ever heard." TK jabbed a finger in the air with each word. His cheeks were a fiery red as he puffed them in and out. "You're the chief of police around here." He switched directions and pointed an accusatory finger at Clay. "What are you going to do about this?"

Clay stood calmly with his arms at his sides as he listened to the country doctor's livid tirade. "I have men out looking for the missing body."

"What the hell for?" TK demanded. He surged to his feet and teetered just enough to have Clay reaching out a steadying hand that the elderly doctor quickly shook off. "I'm fine. I'm not going to topple over like a drunken fool. And if those deputies are beating the bushes trying to find that body, they're wasting their time. It's buried somewhere in the forest where it will never be found, or it's been weighted down and tossed into the bay. Take your pick. There has to be at least a dozen places to get rid of a body around here where it will never be found."

"Not a very comforting thought." Dr. Torres was standing

next to the exam table where he and Cheron had left the body the night before.

The small room was crowded with four adults squeezing into a space designed for a single doctor to move around in. TK had commandeered the only chair in the room, while Ricki leaned against the counter with its built-in drawers that ran along one wall.

"No. It isn't," TK snapped at his colleague. "And not a thought I'd ever had until I got Dr. Garrison's call this morning." He glowered at Torres. "And how the hell did anyone get in here? Are you sure you locked up last night?"

"I'm sure." The doctor answered in a pleasant voice, but his gaze was cooler than it had been the moment before TK had tossed the suspicious-sounding question at him. Reaching into the oversized pocket of his lab coat, Torres pulled out a piece of paper and held it out to Clay. "Here's a list of people who have keys to the clinic."

"My name had better not be on there," TK warned. "Because I'm not being put on any most-wanted list."

"You have a key, so your name is on there. Mine is too." Torres dropped his hand to his side when Clay took the list. "I've included the private cell number of my partner since he also has a key. I contacted him this morning, appraising him of this latest event and alerting him to expect a call from you."

"Thank you." Clay quickly scanned the short list, then looked back at Torres. "There's a number two by your name. Does that mean you have two keys?"

Torres nodded, his dark brown eyes crinkling slightly at the corners. "That's right. I keep a spare in case someone forgot, or perhaps misplaced, his key." He smiled when TK stuttered a sound of protest. "However, any misplaced key has been found, so all the keys are accounted for."

"And you have both of yours, Luca?" Ricki cut in. "I assume you have one with you and the other is at your house?"

Torres visibly relaxed when Ricki dropped the formality and used his given name. "No. I gave my key to Dr. Garrison after I locked up last night." He glanced at TK. "Which is how I know I locked the door. As soon as it was secured, I turned and handed my key to Cheron." He smiled when TK acknowledged that with a nod. "I brought the spare key with me this morning."

TK crossed his arms over his sunken chest. "All right. The keys are now all accounted for. What's next?"

Clay took a step back and leaned against the counter next to Ricki, crossing his boots at the ankles. His grey eyes showed a hint of amusement. "First, I need to know if you have the victim's personal effects, or did you give those to Cheron?"

"I have them," Dr. Torres said, answering Clay's question. "We thought it was best to lock them up, and there is a small safe in my office. Do you want me to get them for you, or should I wait for Dr. Garrison to pick them up?"

"I'll take them, thanks." As Torres left the room, Clay smiled at TK. "Now I get to ask you what all cops want to know. Where were you last night?"

TK dropped his arms as he blinked at Clay. After a moment, he lifted one hand and tapped a finger against his chest. "Me? You want to know where I was last night?"

"Uh-huh," Clay said, his mouth twitching with a smile.

"The same place I am most nights. Eating out. I left here and went up to the St. Armand to have dinner."

"I see. And do you usually go to the resort for dinner?" Clay asked.

"Didn't I just say so? My wife did the cooking. Now that's she gone, I go out to eat. Most nights I go to the Sunny Side Up, but that wasn't an option last night, was it? So I drove up to the hotel."

Clay gave a solemn shake of his head. "Did anyone see you at the St. Armand?"

TK's eyes narrowed for a moment before he glared at Clay. "Of course they did. It's a damn hotel. And I know you're pulling my leg."

The chief broke into a grin. "Yeah. I am."

When Dr. Torres came back into the room carrying a paper bag, Clay took it with a nod of thanks as the doctor returned to stand in his spot near the exam table. "How about you, Luca? Where were you last night?"

"I went home for dinner," Luca said then hesitated for a brief moment. "But after I ate my sandwich, I went over to the VFW for a drink." His mouth curled into a faint smile. "I heard that both of you were there earlier in the evening."

Ricki, who'd been quietly listening to the exchange, frowned. "I didn't know you were a vet, Luca."

"I'm not," the doctor said with a sheepish look. "Patricia invited me to meet her at the VFW post."

"Patricia?" Clay looked at Ricki. "Is she a local?"

"Oh yeah." She grinned at him. "Patricia Forker. Better known to everyone besides Luca as Merlin."

Understanding dawned on Clay's face. "Ah. Merlin. So I assume she can vouch for your whereabouts last night?"

Torres shuffled his feet and then shrugged. "Up until midnight. Then we both went home. Alone."

"Now that's a cryin' shame," TK said. "I like Merlin. You could do a lot worse. And I'll bet she can cook. Those military types are pretty good in the kitchen. Just look at Anchorman."

Clay cut him off. "That's fine, Luca. I understand Nancy left the clinic with Bill Langly?"

"Yes," Torres confirmed, looking relieved at not being asked anything else about his personal life. "But that isn't unusual. He picks her up two or three times a week after the clinic closes." He looked around the crowded room. "But she won't be coming in today. I told her to take the day off, and that TK and I would manage."

TK carefully sat down in the chair again, resting his hands on his knees. "I don't want you bothering the poor woman today. She had nothing to do with that body disappearing and was very upset about Sam's death." He sighed and ran a finger through his thinning hair. "Or who she thought was Sam. I didn't tell her any different, but somehow, the word got out." He made a quick sound of disgust. "I heard all about it last night while I was at dinner. It was the only thing the staff at the hotel was talking about."

"I'll speak to Nancy another day," Clay promised. "But I need to know if either of you told anyone about Cheron taking fingerprints yesterday?"

When both doctors shook their heads, Clay smiled. "That's good. I'm asking you to keep that to yourselves. And neither of you mentioned it to Nancy either?"

"No. I didn't think to," TK said. "I just assumed Cheron was getting a jump on her autopsy, and Nancy doesn't get involved with that."

"I didn't talk with Nancy about it either," Torres said. "Or with anyone else," he added in a pointed voice. "I didn't even mention it to my partner when I spoke to him this morning."

"All right. Then the last thing we need to do is make a thorough search of the clinic." Clay quickly held up his hand, palm out, to stop the protest from TK. "I know it's a long shot, but we need to look, just in case this whole thing is a prank and the thief hid it close by."

"A prank?" TK pushed himself out of the chair, his outrage

back in full force. "It had better not be, or I'm going to be peeling the skin off the back of whoever did such a fool thing."

"You'll need to stand in line," Torres declared before marching out of the room.

It only took fifteen minutes to search the entire clinic. There weren't too many places to stash a full-grown male. Even the dumpster out back was thankfully empty, since the garbage had been collected the day before, prior to the body disappearing.

After retrieving the paper bag he'd left in the examination room, Clay thanked the two men for their help and cooperation. Ricki smiled at Torres and told TK to get some rest before she walked to the SUV. Climbing into the passenger seat, she rummaged through the paper bag while Clay talked to his deputy. A few minutes later he jogged over to the SUV and stepped into the driver's side, settling behind the wheel.

Ricki held up a plastic evidence bag containing a small key ring and another key fob. "Look what I found."

"I'm betting you were looking for the key to the fake Sam's place up in Massey."

"Good guess," Ricki said. Keeping hold of the keys, she set the paper bag with the rest of Sam's belongings on the floor. "Since Marcie never once mentioned it, I'm assuming he kept it secret from her and hopefully carried the key to the place with him." She held up the evidence bag and peered at the contents. She dismissed the key fob as belonging to his car. The remaining ring held two keys. She studied them, a frown on her face. With a sigh, she passed the bag to Clay. "Besides his car key, there are only two others on a separate ring. That oversized one belongs to the diner. And the second one is probably to Marcie's house."

"Which leaves us without a key for his little secret spot in

Massey," Clay finished for her. "If one actually exists. If it does, all we have to do is find it."

"That might not be as hard as it sounds." Ricki took out her cell phone and scrolled through her contact list. "One of the benefits of small-town life is that there is only one real estate agent in the area. And she handles almost all the rentals." She tapped a number and lifted the phone to her ear. Minnie Cuthry answered on the second ring.

"Ricki James. I was just thinking about calling you."

"I have a quick question," Ricki said, wanting to cut the woman off from launching into a discussion on finding a new place for her and Clay. "I'm in a hurry, Minnie. I was wondering if you rented a place up in Massey to Sam Parkman?"

"You mean the impostor?" Minnie gasped. "Of course not. And why would he need a place in Massey anyway? He was living at Marcie's house. Can you imagine anything more horrible? All this time they've been living there together, just the two of them, when they weren't actually related at all."

"A fact Marcie didn't know," Ricki stated firmly. "Remember, she was very young when he left home, and hadn't seen him in decades. I can think of a lot of other people in town who were closer to his age and had known him all their lives and didn't know Sam wasn't who he said he was." She waited a beat before adding. "Come to think of it, weren't you and Sam in the same class at school?"

"No. He was a whole year ahead of me." Minnie's tone dropped into the arctic zone. "And I never knew him all that well."

Refraining from pointing out that there were less than a hundred kids in the entire high school, Ricki settled for repeating her question. "About that place? Are you certain he didn't rent anything up near Massey?"

"Of course I am," Minnie insisted. "Why are you asking?"

"Just a shot in the dark," Ricki said in an offhand voice. "And it sounds like it isn't a very good one."

"Well, if there's nothing else, I need to get back to work." And even though it was obvious she was still miffed, Minnie couldn't help adding, "Now remember, you and Clay need to get out and see this place I found for you. Don't wait too long, either, or some other buyer will snatch it right up."

Ricki frowned as she hung up. *Buyer?* Ahe gave Clay a speculative look. "Minnie said that she didn't rent anything to Sam."

"Great. Maybe the victim was just bragging to Rory and doesn't have a ham radio set-up at all."

"Uh-huh. There's another thing Minnie did mention."

"What's that?" Clay asked without taking his eyes off the road winding in front of them.

"Are you buying a house?"

He was silent for a moment. Draping one arm casually over the steering wheel, he looked at her. "Since anyplace we live will require your approval, then I'd say that *we* are buying a house."

Ricki pursed her lips as she thought that over, then slowly shook her head. "Us buying a house implies that I'm putting up my share of the down payment, and all that. Which I don't happen to have at the moment."

"But I do. Enough to cover both our shares if you want to look at it that way." He gave her a bland look. "You know my grandparents left a pile of money to me. And to Kate as well. So who puts up the cash to buy a house is not a big deal." He drummed a finger against the steering wheel. "We really aren't going to fight over money, are we?"

Ricki's temper had started to flare, but it quickly subsided. She didn't like thinking she wasn't pulling her weight in their relationship, but when it came to money, there was no way she could keep up with Clay's inheritance. It was all she could do to stay even with the bills for the nursing facility where her mother was being taken care of. Fortunately, Bear was putting up most of the money for the tuition at Eddie's school that wasn't covered by his partial scholarship.

If we end up divorced, I'll have to be sure Clay gets the house, she thought, then sighed at the ludicrous thought. There was no way she was going to go through another divorce. And she couldn't imagine going through one with Clay.

She sighed again, ignoring his sideways glance, and looked out the passenger window. "No. I don't want to start a fight over money. But you putting in the whole amount for a house and me putting in nothing makes me feel weird."

"Don't worry about it." Apparently deciding the house discussion was over, he tapped a finger against the steering wheel. "Since we don't know if the victim really did have a place up in Massey, it isn't worth making the trip up there."

Ricki sighed in frustration. "Probably not. Maybe we should head back to the police department and take a closer look at everything else in that paper bag before you lock it up. I can also call Dan and let him know where we're headed. He might have found something from his search of Sam's room. I'm surprised I haven't heard from him by now about that."

When her cell phone rang, she plucked it from the center console, half expecting to see Dan's name on the caller ID. But it was Hamilton's that floated across the screen. She held the phone up so Clay could see it before answering her boss's call.

"Hi. You'll be happy to know that Special Agent Sullivan showed up here this morning."

"I heard." The senior agent didn't sound too happy about it. "I'm assuming that Finn told you I got a call from Blake, asking that we loan out your services to help find the person who killed Preston Malone?"

"He mentioned it," Ricki said. "I'm not too happy about it, but he had a good reason."

"That I'd like to hear. I told Blake I would get back to him this afternoon. After I talked to you. He wasn't thrilled with the idea, but there wasn't much he could do about it either." Hamilton's voice took on a note of satisfaction. "It's a good day when I don't have to hand Jonathan Blake everything he wants. But he's the one who told me that the guy you thought was Sam Parkman is really Preston Malone—a suspect the Bureau has been after for a while for an armed robbery."

"He used to be in the military, but not anymore, so that makes Malone's murder Clay's case, not the FBI's." Ricki shrugged when Clay rolled his eyes at her. "But the last thing he needs right now is for the FBI to send a task force snooping around. You know how they are."

"Yes, I do," Hamilton said. "But they're still a federal agency and so are we. Unless you come up with an objection I can hang my hat on, it seems that Blake is going to have his way."

"Nothing new there."

"All right. Then it's settled. You're on temporary loan to the FBI. Is there anything I can do from here to speed this investigation up and keep this loan period as short as possible?" the senior agent asked.

"We're just starting out, and right now aren't sure where to look," Ricki admitted. "But if something does come up, you'll be the first person I call."

Chapter Twelve

The police station was located in Edington, the largest of the three towns in the Bay. Sitting on a side road, the sprawling single-story building, made with an abundance of glass windows set against log siding, fit in perfectly with its surroundings of tall trees and large boulders. Just down the street was the conveniently located Quick Pie, the favorite pizza parlor within a fifty-mile radius, and only a quarter mile beyond that was the multi-purpose building that served as City Hall, recreational gym, and a catered event venue.

When Clay pulled the SUV into the station's parking lot, Ricki was disappointed that her Uncle Cy's truck wasn't in its usual spot. The building housing the police department was much too large for a three-man force, so the city council leased out most of it to the National Park Service, as a base for the eastern side of the massive Olympic National Park.

Cyrus McCormick was her dad's younger brother, and the only uncle she had on either side of the family. Like her parents, he'd made a home in the Bay, and worked for the

National Park Service's law enforcement unit. When her dad had passed away, Cy had taken his only niece under his wing and taught her how to hunt, fish, and shoot a rifle. And he'd never failed to express his pride in her, whether it was for her career with the ISB, or when she'd temporarily quit law enforcement and started up a small diner in their hometown.

"Cy must be out catching bad guys," Clay remarked as he turned off the engine.

Ricki picked up the brown paper bag containing Preston Malone's personal effects before grinning at Clay. "Or giving out speeding tickets to the tourists racing up the hill to take in the spectacular views from Hurricane Ridge." She stepped out of the SUV and headed for the steps leading up to the double glass doors into the building. As soon as she stepped inside, Ricki stopped dead in her tracks. Sitting at the lobby desk, chatting away on the phone, was Pete.

When he spotted Ricki and Clay, he hastily hung up and pushed himself to his feet. "Good morning. You're getting an early start today."

"So are you." Clay looked pointedly at the phone on the desk in front of Pete. "I thought those phones were forwarded to the officer on call for the night."

Pete lifted a paper off the desk and held it up. "I see that was you, Chief."

Clay didn't even glance at the paper. "Yes, it was."

The elderly man smiled. "These phones aren't that hard to figure out. And there're instructions right here in the top drawer. I know you haven't found anyone to take over this desk since Ray passed."

"Ray didn't pass," Clay said. "He's in prison for murder."

Pete scrunched up his face. "Well, he's passed out of the Bay. Anyway, some of us were talking and thought you could use some help. So I came right down here this morning to sit for a couple of hours."

When he swayed slightly, Clay pointed to the chair. "Why don't you sit now?" He sighed and rubbed a hand across the back of his neck. "I appreciate the help, Pete. How long were you planning on staying?"

Pete smiled. "I can only help out until noon. Then I've got to get on back to Brewer."

"And just for today?" Clay prompted. When Pete started to protest, Clay's voice dropped half a notch on the friendliness scale. "It's a big help this morning, Pete. But I think that will be all we need."

The elderly man's face drooped in disappointment. "But not much is coming in yet. Mostly just people wanting to hash over old gossip."

Ricki quickly lifted a hand to cover her smile and had to give major points to Clay for keeping a straight face. The newest gossip was Pete's specialty.

"Calls from the public are important," Clay stated in an acceptably grave tone. "But I understand that you have other obligations and can't sit here all day, every day, the way Ray used to."

"Oh good heavens, no." Pete looked horrified at the idea, then quickly busied himself with rearranging the row of pencils on the desk. "Just until noon today."

Clay stepped forward and held open the small gate separating the lobby from the back hallway. "That will be fine. Thank you."

"Pete," Ricki acknowledged with a nod as she sailed past him toward Clay's office. She didn't let herself grin until she'd stopped in front of the door. Since it was rarely locked, she gave the knob a twist. When she stepped inside, she was still smiling. Quickly crossing to the desk, she dropped the bag on top of it before plopping down in one of the two visitor chairs. "You handled that really well."

Clay shrugged. "Pete isn't going to change, and the last thing I need is for him to be listening in on our phones."

Ricki shook her head. "I don't think he'd do that, but he'd sure jot down every person who called, and try to get a reason for their call out of them."

"Yeah. I saw the running log he was keeping." Clay sat in his desk chair and leaned back until the leather squeaked in protest. "Let's see what's in that bag."

Without a word Ricki scooted her chair closer to the edge of the desk, then reached for the paper bag. Upending it, she carefully arranged the few scattered evidence bags into a straight line.

Clay leaned forward and separated out the bag holding the keys. "We've already seen this one. What else have we got?"

Ricki plucked up a bag holding a mixture of coins and bills. "Money." She laid it back down on the desk. "It looks like twelve dollars and thirty-five cents."

"That's a far cry from two million." Clay reached over and picked up another evidence bag. "Cell phone. This might help, provided he doesn't have a password on it." Opening a desk drawer, he took out a pair of latex gloves and pulled them on with a hard snap at his wrist. "Let's see what we've got." He hit a key and the phone lit up. "It needs a password," he muttered. Setting it aside, he gestured at the remaining bag. "Is that his wallet?"

"Yep." Ricki slid the bag across the desk, watching silently as Clay opened it and thumbed through the ragged-looking wallet.

"Two credit cards and a driver's license. All in the name of Preston Malone." Clay slipped the wallet back into the evidence bag and resealed it. "That's risky. He would have had to use only cash in the Bay. I guess he couldn't get an ID in Sam's name." He peeled off his gloves and tossed them back into the desk drawer. "Too bad he didn't ask me. I could have given him the names of a couple of guys in Seattle who sell fake IDs."

"I guess he didn't have any contacts in that black market. Which is just another piece of the puzzle," Ricki said.

"Yeah. You'd think a guy who stole two million dollars and killed five people in the process would be better connected in the criminal world."

"Hmm." Ricki frowned at the evidence bags randomly lying across the desk. She pulled the paper bag closer and peered into its depths before turning it over and giving it several shakes.

"Lose something?" Clay asked.

"I don't know." She took out her phone and tapped a contact number. Cheron answered on the first ring. "Hi. Things are coming along smoothly here. Norman is already accepting deliveries and thinks you'll be able to open tomorrow morning."

"Which will make Pete ecstatic," Ricki said.

"What?"

"Never mind. I'm calling to ask about the personal effects you bagged up from Preston Malone's body."

"Who?"

"Never mind," Ricki said. "Sam. From Sam's body."

"Oh, yes. Preston," Cheron replied. "Norman told me that was Sam's real name. But you wanted to know something about his personal effects?"

"Uh-huh. I'm looking at them now and I see a wallet, keys, money, and a cell phone. Was there anything else?"

"No," Cheron said. "Just the four things. I have them

written down in my log, but it's back at my lab. Do you need me to get it for you?"

"Not if you're sure that's all you found on the body?"

"I'm sure."

Ricki nodded. "Okay. Thanks. And thank you for helping out with the biohazard crew."

"I'm sure Norman would have managed just fine, but I'm happy to help."

After Cheron delivered a quick update on the progress of the crew, Ricki said goodbye and hung up the phone.

"So, what do you think is missing?" Clay asked.

"A schedule," she said in a clipped voice. "Marcie said the fake Sam didn't have as good a memory as the real Sam and had to carry a copy of the weekly schedule around with him, so he'd know when to show up for work."

"Maybe he left it in his room that morning," Clay suggested.

"Maybe," Ricki said, but her gut was telling her no. It was a habit, and Sam, aka Preston Malone, always carried the schedule with him. *Which means what?* she wondered. *That he gave it to someone? And why would he do that?* Having no answer, she tucked the question away for the time being and asked another one out loud. "Why now? The robbery was seven years ago, and he's been here for the last three. What made him a target now?"

Clay straightened up in his chair and leaned his elbows against the desk. "The usual reason is that he pissed someone off. Which could be completely unrelated to the robbery. Or . . ."

"He'd become a liability," Ricki finished for him. "To one or both of his partners."

"Depending on how many of them are still alive." Clay shrugged. "The motive could be as simple as greed. If there's only one surviving partner, he might have decided all of two million is better than half. Even if both are still alive, that's still an extra three hundred thousand a piece."

Ricki drummed her fingers against the desk. "Which assumes that the whole two million is still available. Or a partner ran through his share and wanted Malone's." Her eyes narrowed in thought. She picked up the evidence bag with the cash and bills in it. "Which Malone certainly wasn't flashing around town."

"I'll run a check on his local bank account, and on those credit cards," Clay said. "Aside from that, we'll need to read the FBI's case file and try to pick up where they left off in tracing Malone's movements. If we can trail him, we're going to run into one and maybe both of his partners in crime somewhere along that line."

"Then you think one of them tracked Malone here and shot him?" Ricki asked.

"It's the most likely scenario, but I'm open to other possibilities."

A knock at the door had them both turning in that direction. "It's not locked," Clay called out.

"Good morning, Chief. Ricki." Dan stepped over the threshold, carrying a cardboard box. He closed the door with the back of his heel and walked over to the desk. Setting the box in front of Ricki, he took a seat in the only other visitor's chair. "What I found in Sam's room, and it isn't much."

Ricki stood and leaned over to look into the box. As Clay scooped up the personal effects and transferred them to a large manila envelope he retrieved from a desk drawer, Ricki carefully laid out Dan's search results.

"He had about three changes of clothes and a stack of underwear and socks, and that was about it," Dan said. "No jewelry, or even a watch, unless he was wearing one." When

Ricki shook her head, he shrugged. She held up a baggie with a scrap of paper in it, and he nodded at her. "Now that was the second most interesting thing I found. It was tucked under that stack of underwear in his dresser drawer."

"Looks like a phone number," Ricki said, studying the numbers scrawled in pen across the paper. "Where's area code two-seven-o?" She glanced at Dan, certain that he'd already looked it up.

"Southwest Kentucky," he said without missing a beat. "And that prefix of numbers puts it in the vicinity of Hopkinsville. Nice little town that's about an hour north of Nashville, and just thirty minutes from Fort Campbell."

"Where Malone was discharged." Ricki set the last of the items from the box on the desk. "I guess you talked to Hamilton."

"I did," Dan acknowledged. "But all he told me was that Sam's real name is Preston Malone, that he was involved in a robbery that ended up with five dead people, and that he used to be in the military." He pointed at the scrap of paper in the baggie that Ricki was holding. "So our guy was discharged from Fort Campbell over near Hopkinsville?"

"That's right," Ricki confirmed. "You didn't happen to call this number, did you?"

Dan smiled. "I did. It's disconnected. Hamilton has put in a request to the phone company to find out who has been assigned that phone number over the last seven years. I found out it was a landline, if that's any help."

"I don't know if it is or not."

Dan shifted in his chair and cleared his throat. "I also found out through the local grapevine that there's an FBI agent in town. I'm guessing that it's Finn?"

Ricki nodded. "Yeah. He showed up this morning. Right before Cheron told us that Malone's body had gone missing."

The former CIA researcher's eyes widened as he gaped at Ricki. "You're kidding? The gossip mill hadn't spit out that one yet, and Marcie's phone has been ringing all morning. I unplugged her landline and set her cell phone on silent when I left so she could get some rest. She didn't sleep much last night."

"Neither did I," Ricki said.

"It didn't help that Anchorman showed up on our doorstep before dawn," Clay drawled. He reached over and picked up a cheap white ball cap with the name of a hardware store stamped across the front. "What's this?"

Dan sorted through the other items on the desk and selected two of them. "I guess I'd call it an anomaly. Sam didn't have many personal things in his room, but I found that cap on a hook in his closet, and these in the bottom drawer of his dresser."

Ricki frowned and picked up both items Dan had singled out. "A key chain." She glanced at the hat that Clay was holding. "The tag on it has the name of that same hardware store." She held up a stick that was flat on one end and rounded at the top. "So does this paint stir stick." She shifted her gaze between the three objects. "Now why would he drag a cheap hat, key chain, and a stir stick from a place called Bernie's Hardware all the way across the country?"

"The only reason a man does that is if they belonged to his dad, or someone close to him. Usually a woman," Clay said.

"Meaning guys don't keep souvenirs from other guys?" Ricki's dry tone had Clay chuckling.

"Not unless he's in love with him." Clay tapped a long finger against his lips. "Some random stuff all from the same place, and a scrap of paper with a disconnected number on it. I'm guessing this all has to do with a woman."

"Who has something to do with this hardware store in

Hopkinsville, Kentucky." Dan shook his head. "That's not much to go on. That could just be the place where Malone met her." He turned toward Ricki. "Hamilton mentioned that you're going to be partnering up with Finn, and that Blake was going to send him the FBI case file." When Ricki nodded, so did he. "Would you mind if I took a peek at it, too? I'm going to try getting a more detailed copy of Sam's and Malone's military records through a backdoor connection I have."

"That's a good idea," Ricki said. "Finn already has the FBI reports scanned and will send me a copy as soon as he wakes up. I'll shoot you his email with the FBI's case file attached after he coughs it up."

"Thanks." Dan drew in a long breath and then let it out slowly. "I need something to keep me busy. And it will make Marcie feel better to know that we're all pitching in to find the real Sam, along with the fake Sam's killer." He looked down at his hands. "I'd like to know what you think the odds are that the real Sam is still alive and that he was involved in that robbery seven years ago."

"It depends on who you ask," Ricki said. "Clay thinks it's almost one hundred percent that he was involved in the robbery and isn't alive."

"What about you?" Dan asked quietly. "What do you think?"

Ricki chewed her lower lip, not sure how to answer her fellow agent. "I don't know," she finally said. "There's nothing concrete to tie him to the robbery, but I'm leaning in that direction. And it's hard for me to believe that the real Sam would send someone like Malone to his sister's doorstep if he were still alive."

Dan let out the breath he was holding. "Yeah. From what Marcie has been telling me about her brother, that's the way I read it too." He stood up. "One more thing. Marcie wants to talk to you. She wants to help, and I think that would do her some good." He glanced at the institutional clock hung over the door. "She'll probably be awake by the time I get back. She doesn't get more than an hour or two of sleep at a time. And I'd like to have an excuse to get her out of the house for a while."

"Not to the Sunny Side Up," Ricki said, smiling when both Clay and Dan nodded their agreement. "How about our place? I'll call Anchorman and let him know so he can bring us some food when he's done with the biohazard team."

"And I'll call Finn," Clay said. "Kate can keep resting at the hotel, but Finn has had enough sleep. It's time he got to work."

Chapter Thirteen

J ust as Dan was leaving the office, Jules appeared on the other side of the doorway. The two men greeted each other before Dan moved out of sight and Jules stepped into the room.

He held his hat in his hands as he dipped his head in Ricki's direction. "Morning, Ricki."

"Hi, Jules." Ricki smiled as she placed several items from Malone's room back into the cardboard box. "I hope everything is quiet at the clinic?"

The deputy's gaze traveled to Clay. "That's what I came to report. Not much activity when I first got there, but it picked up a lot in the last hour. When Ryan stopped by so I could go out and get some coffee, I thought I should leave him there to guard the front door and come on over here for that coffee so I could give you a report. Wanted to kill two birds with one stone, Chief."

"An excellent idea." Clay leaned back in his chair and gestured toward the empty one next to Ricki. "Have a seat. What kind of activity?"

Jules nodded his thanks before slowly lowering himself into the chair. He carefully balanced his hat on one knee before giving Clay an earnest look. "Lots of cars driving by, mostly. Mike came by in that ancient Ford truck of his." A light suddenly dawned in his eyes and he jerked a thumb toward the door. "Say. Did you know Pete is answering the phones out in the lobby?"

"He's leaving at noon, and I'll make sure that he does," Clay said. "Besides increased traffic on the road, was there anything else you needed to report?"

"Well, I took a walk out to the edge of the parking lot. I thought being more visible would discourage anyone who didn't need to be there from pulling in. I waved and was friendly and all, but everyone got the message and kept on driving. Then when I saw Mike coming down the street for the fourth or fifth time, I flagged him down and asked him what was going on, because he sure as hell wasn't lost." He immediately turned and gave Ricki a sheepish look. "Sorry. Didn't mean to lose my temper like that."

Ricki smiled. If the whole world had the same way of getting angry as Jules Tucker did, they'd all be a lot better off. "You don't have a temper, Jules. So what did Mike say?"

"He apologized first, for causing me some worry. Mike's a nice guy." Jules bobbed his head up and down. "Then he said that Pete had thought it would be a good idea for him to come out that way and sort of help keep an eye on the clinic on account of all the activity this morning." Jules paused for breath. "So I asked him what activity. And he said someone told Pete that Dr. Garrison drove through town this morning like a cat with its tail on fire, and she turned off on the road to your place. Then he got a call from someone else who works up at the St. Armand." The deputy shook his head hard enough his hat was in danger of falling off his knee. "But Mike didn't know who that was."

"I'll look into that later," Clay said. "In the meantime, what did this anonymous source of Pete's have to say?"

"That two FBI agents checked into the hotel. One male, and one female. And the male agent was Fionn Sullivan." His eyes widened as he stared at his boss. "Lots of people can recognize Special Agent Sullivan, because he's been here a couple of times before. So I thought I should get back here right away and let you know the FBI is in town." He leaned forward, his voice dropping to a loud whisper. "You should also know that those two agents are real cozy together."

While Ricki had a sudden coughing fit, Clay closed his eyes and dragged a hand down his face. Heaving a sigh, he ignored Ricki's wide grin and focused on his deputy. "That's good work, Jules. I'll go pay him a visit as soon as we're finished with the evidence here."

Jules blinked and looked down at the items still on the desk. "Evidence? Where'd it come from?"

Clay laid a hand on the manila envelope. "Everything in here the victim had on him at the time he was killed, and the rest of this is from his room over at Marcie's."

Jules' entire face turned down with concern, deepening the lines etched along his cheeks and forehead. "How's she doing? Lots of folks are worried about her."

"Dan is keeping her company and looking out for her," Ricki said. "And she's coming over to my place for lunch." She glanced up at the clock. "Which reminds me, we'd better get moving. I still haven't told Anchorman he needs to put together something to bring on over or for us to pick up."

"Pizza place is right down the street. I can call them for you, if that would help," Jules offered.

"I'll tell you what," Clay said. "Why don't you take a quick look at the evidence, take some photos of it, then go ahead and lock up the manila envelope and return the rest of the items to Dan over at Marcie's house. We'll meet up tomorrow and go over your conclusions."

Jules's jaw dropped to his chest. "Me? You want me to look over the evidence?"

Clay nodded as he stood up. "Why not? You're the senior deputy. Meanwhile, I'll have a talk with Special Agent Sullivan." His lips pressed together. "And the other agent he's so cozy with."

"Yeah." Jules didn't actually smirk since that wasn't in his nature, but he came close to it. "Guess you don't have to sneak around when you're this far from Quantico. But I know you two are friends, so you might want to warn him that people are noticing."

"I think giving him a warning is a good idea." Clay walked around the edge of his desk and waited for an amused Ricki to join him. "I'll call you later."

"Don't say a word," he warned Ricki when they were halfway down the hall leading back to the lobby.

"Small town, people talk," Ricki said.

"Yes it is, and they certainly do." Clay clammed up as they walked into the lobby. He nodded at Pete, then lifted his hand and tapped a finger on the face of his wristwatch.

"Just another hour, Chief," Pete called out. "And then I have an appointment up at the St. Armand that I must keep."

Ricki could hear Clay's teeth grinding together and thought it might be prudent to keep her mouth shut as they walked out to the parking lot.

"I'm the chief of police, and have a reputation to protect," he muttered once he'd started up the SUV.

Ricki bit her tongue for a whole three seconds before she couldn't hold back any more. "Oh? So it's okay for the chief to be cozy with someone, but not his sister who, I should point out, doesn't even live in the Bay?"

"That's different. The whole town was taking bets on when we'd get together."

Since that was true enough, Ricki laughed. "Not the whole town. I think Corby refrained from putting any money into the pool."

He shot her an annoyed look from the corner of his eye. "Not funny. All Kate and Finn are creating is gossip about how they're violating a professional standard."

"Which they are not," Ricki stated as she pulled out her cell phone. "Since Kate is not an FBI agent, no matter what the gossips think."

"I wouldn't be surprised if one of those busybodies got it into his head to call Quantico and let them know what's going on," Clay groused.

"Which would give his boss a good laugh at Finn's expense." Ricki put her phone to her ear. "What do you want Anchorman to throw together for lunch that doesn't take any electricity or gas to produce?"

"Sandwiches are fine," Clay said, still sounding put out. "And maybe some of that coleslaw he always serves with his meatloaf, if there's any left over from meatloaf night. As a matter of fact, if he has any leftover meatloaf, that would be good, too, along with the sandwiches. We can heat it up at our place. Maybe some chips in case someone doesn't like coleslaw, and one of those pies he keeps on hand."

Ricki shook her head as she relayed Clay's list to Cheron, who had answered Anchorman's cell.

"Good heavens," Cheron muttered.

"You've seen the guys eat," Ricki laughed. "And Finn isn't any different from the other two."

"Norman does tend to consume rather large meals," Cheron replied. "I'll let him know."

"When can we pick it up in case you have to stay late at the diner?"

There was a muffled conversation on the other end of the phone before Cheron's voice returned. "He said we're almost done here, so we'll bring it all over."

"Great. See you soon." Ricki disconnected her phone and lowered it to her lap before glancing at Clay. "Gossip has never bothered you before. You just don't like the idea of Finn and Kate canoodling together."

Clay let out a snort. "Canoodling? What kind of word is that?"

"A much politer one than several others you'd undoubtedly recognize," she stated. "Anchorman is going to bring the food by our place." She lifted her phone to her ear again. "I'll let Finn know not to loiter around the lobby."

"Yeah, that, and he needs to be out of the hotel and on his way to our place before noon. The last thing I want to deal with is Pete's questions about Finn's ethics."

Shaking her head at him, Ricki got hold of her new, temporary partner and relayed the message just as they were passing the outskirts of Brewer. A few minutes later they were turning into their driveway. Corby came out of the trees as the SUV pulled to a stop right behind Dan's dark blue sedan.

"I suppose Marcie also has a key to our place?" Clay asked as they walked together to the cabin with Corby by their side.

"Sure. And who else had a key to your old place?" Ricki asked.

Clay shrugged and took her hand in his. "Just you and me. Who else needed one?"

"So, you gave out one key in the six or seven years you've been here. I've lived in the Bay all my life. You do the math."

He chuckled and swung their hands back and forth between them. "Flawed logic, James. You haven't lived in this cabin your whole life."

"That's big-city thinking, Thomas," she said with a smug grin. "Out here, the same number of people expect a key to your place no matter where you live."

He halted in his tracks, pulling her to a stop. "So you're telling me half the town will have keys to our new place, too?"

Ricki put her tongue in her cheek and pretended to consider the matter. "Not half, Chief, but close to it." She tugged his hand. "Come on. Stop stressing over nothing and let's see how Marcie is doing."

They didn't have a long wait because the waitress stepped out onto the small porch. "Get in here, you two." She looked up at the overcast skies. "I think it's going to rain any minute, and from the looks of it, we're going to get a good soak."

Ricki dropped Clay's hand to jump up on the porch and put an arm around her friend's shoulders. "How are you doing? Did you get any sleep?"

"Some," Marcie said as they walked into the house together, leaving Clay to close the door behind a trailing Corby. "I only wish Dan wouldn't worry so much about me. It will take some time, but I'm going to be all right."

"Dan doesn't mind worrying about you," the agent said from his place on the couch.

Marcie smiled at him. "I know. I just wish you didn't have to." When Corby bounced up from his place underneath the window and stared outside, his body on full alert, Marcie let her gaze drift in that direction. "That doesn't look like Anchorman's truck." She glanced at Ricki. "Dan said he'd be bringing some lunch over here."

"He'll be along pretty soon," Ricki said. "That's probably Finn and Kate."

Marcie's eyes lit up with pleasure. "Kate? Really?" She pretended to give Dan a shaming look. "You didn't tell me that Clay's sister was in town."

"I didn't know she was." Dan got to his feet and walked over to stand next to Marcie. "That's certainly Finn." He walked closer to the window and peered out with a slight squint. "What happened to his car?"

"Cheron." Clay nodded at Dan's puzzled look. "She didn't see Finn's car when she came around the corner at the speed of lightning. And I wouldn't mention it to him."

Dan's lips twitched. "Ah. Got it."

Ricki shook her head at both of them and stepped over to open the front door. Corby shot past her before she could grab his collar and greeted the new guests with unbridled enthusiasm.

"Always nice to be welcome," Kate said, bending down to give the dog's head a solid scratch. When she looked up, her gaze slid right past Ricki and latched on to Marcie. "Hi. I'm so glad to see you." She walked over and gave the waitress a warm hug before holding her at arm's length to look into her face. "How are you doing?"

"Better," Marcie answered with a nod. "Especially since I'm seeing you again. Clay never said a word about you paying a visit."

"He didn't exactly know about it, because I didn't tell him." Kate wrapped an arm around Marcie's waist and wiggled her eyebrows at her brother, who was staring at her with his arms across his chest. "He doesn't approve of Finn and me being together. In any way at all, but especially not in *that* way."

Marcie frowned at Clay. "Really? What's wrong with Finn? I thought you liked him?"

"He does," Finn interjected, shrugging out of his coat and hanging it on a hook next to the front door. "Just not as a partner for his sister." He winked at Marcie. "I think he wants to take me to the woodshed out back and have a serious talk." He grinned. "Which around here is a literal thing since there really is a woodshed out back."

"What I'd like to have a serious talk about is the case." Clay sent the FBI agent a pointed look. "We can discuss a visit to the woodshed later." He pulled out one of the stools and smiled at Marcie. "While we're waiting on Anchorman and the food, why don't you tell us what you wanted to talk about?"

"I'll make some coffee," Ricki volunteered, then skidded to a halt when Dan raced over and cut off her path to the kitchen.

"Not a chance," he declared. "I've had that sludge you call coffee, and there's too many of us to use the new single-cup machine that Clay bought. I'll make the coffee, and put on a kettle for tea, if you have any."

"Top right cupboard," Ricki said with a shrug before settling on the stool next to Marcie's. "So, what's going on?"

The older woman sighed as she looked around at the expectant faces watching her. "That's what I need to know. What's going on? Dan said that you know the real name of the man who pretended to be Sam, but he thought I should ask you about it." When she saw the hesitation in Ricki's eyes, she doggedly plowed on. "I know I'm not some kind of agent, but I'm part of this family, too, and feel I have a right to know. That man lived in my house for almost three years. He ate at my table, talked to my kids. And he knew about us." She glanced around the group. "All of us. How did he find out so much? You could look some of it up on the Internet, I guess, but not everything he knew. So I'm involved in this case too, because he stepped deep enough into my life that it feels like I've been violated somehow."

"Preston Malone," Ricki said quietly. "And that needs to stay in this room."

Marcie's back went stiff as she lifted a hand and wagged a finger at her business partner. "You don't need to tell me that, Ricki James. Of course it will stay between us. But why did he pretend to be Sam? I know it was more than just needing a place to live, so I figure he was hiding from someone." She studied Ricki's face for a long moment, then smiled. "Aha. I'm right, aren't I? I can see it in your face. What did this Preston Malone do?" Her hand flew to her mouth. "Oh. Please don't tell me he was a serial killer. I introduced him to all my kids."

"He stole a lot of money," Ricki said, leaving out the part about the five dead bodies the man and his two cohorts had left in their wake. "The FBI has been searching for him for years."

Marcie glanced at Finn. "So now they've found him, but he's dead. Does that mean he hid a lot of money somewhere around here? Because it certainly isn't in my house."

"We don't know where the money is," Finn admitted. "Or who his partners were." When Ricki glared at him, he shook his head. "I have to agree with Marcie. She has a right to know."

Ricki grimaced. Marcie deserved to hear the truth. Or at least the part of it they'd already uncovered. She just didn't want to be the one to tell her. It would be better coming from her than Finn, though, so she took a deep breath. "Malone had two partners who were in on the robbery. We don't know who they are, but we do know about Malone. He was former military—in the army."

"Like Sam was," Marcie said slowly. "Did they know each other?"

"For a short period of time they were at the same base together," Ricki confirmed. "But they were training in different disciplines."

"It's possible, then, isn't it?" Marcie looked from Ricki to Finn. "Could they have known each other?"

"Fort Riley is a very large base," Finn said. "And it was a

long time ago. We do know they weren't in the same barracks."
He nodded at Ricki's sharp glance. "I went over the military
records last night."

"Where is it?" Marcie asked. "Where is Fort Riley? Is it in
Kentucky?"

"No. Kansas," Ricki said. "Why did you think it was in
Kentucky?"

Marcie clasped her hands together and rested them on the
counter. "That's the other reason I wanted to see you. Sam, or
Preston Malone, or whatever his name was, never talked about
his past, even the part when we were growing up together in
the same house. But I remembered that one day he asked me
for a stamp. He had a letter in his hand, which surprised me
because I'd never seen him write to anyone before." Her lips
curved into a wistful smile. "My brother used to write letters all
the time. He liked to get them, too. But this Malone person
never got any mail, or sent any either, as far as I know."

"What about the letter?" Ricki asked to get her back on
track and off what was bound to be a painful trip down
memory lane. "Did you get a look at the address?"

"Not all of it," Marcie said. "But I saw a KY and a zip code.
I don't remember the zip code, but figured that KY had to mean
Kentucky." She blinked, then looked down at Ricki's boot,
tapping against the wood floor. "Is that a help?"

Ricki slowly nodded. "Yes. Yes, it is."

"Good," Marcie responded. "And since I told *you* something, now it's your turn. Did Preston Malone kill anyone?"

Chapter Fourteen

Ricki closed her eyes. She should have known Marcie wouldn't let it go until she had the whole story. Opening her eyes again, she squarely met Marcie's troubled gaze. "We don't know for sure, but five people were killed during the robbery.

"Was Sam one of the dead people?" Marcie's voice was even but her eyes misted over.

"No. They all worked for the man who was robbed. He was also killed," Ricki said. "The FBI believe that all three men who were in on the robbery got away unharmed."

"And you think Sam was one of the three men who did that?" Marcie shook her head and kept shaking it. "Not the Sam I knew. He would never have done something like that." She bowed her head as her chin trembled and a single tear escaped to slowly trickle down her cheek. "But then, he wasn't the same brother I knew when he came home for the few days after he was discharged. I only saw him for maybe an hour, but he was sad, and angry, and distant. He'd never been like that before." She lifted her gaze back to Ricki's. The tears that had threatened to spill a moment earlier were now rapidly receding. "I didn't know him that day, and even less twenty-five years later when he showed up on my doorstep."

Dan moved to stand behind her, placing his hands on her shoulders. She reached up and laid one of her hands on top of his.

The silence in the room was broken by a deep voice. "What happened to my welcoming committee?" Anchorman demanded. "I thought you'd all dropped dead from starvation." When no one moved, he glanced at Corby. "Okay. What about you? Are you hungry?" When the big dog only yawned, Anchorman shrugged. "Fine. You can starve too." He marched over to the kitchen island and set down the large cardboard box he was carrying.

Cheron stepped in after him, clutching a paper shopping bag in one hand. "Hello, everyone." Her gaze went around the room, stopping when she spotted Marcie. "How are you doing?"

"Better." Marcie gestured toward Ricki, and then Clay and Finn. "Our three super agents told me about the robbery, and I just heard that Sam might have been a part of it." She slid off the stool, patted Dan's hand, then pivoted around him. She marched to the front door and retrieved her coat off one of the hooks before turning to smile at Cheron. "All those agents, along with your boyfriend, who has appointed himself their back-up, will want to talk over details of the case. Since I don't want to hear any more, I'm going to go back to the Sunny Side Up and do some prep work so we can open again." She looked at Anchorman. "Dan said you had a biohazard team cleaning up our place this morning. How is that going?"

"They're all done." Anchorman said. "We might open tomorrow if I can get everything ready."

"You stay here," Marcie insisted. "You're part of this team.

I'll get the diner ready. Did you fill out order sheets for any deliveries, or should I surprise you?" At his frown, a tiny spark of amusement bloomed on her face. "You know, like those cooking shows where the chefs never know what they're going to make until just before they have to make it?"

"I'll help you," Kate piped up before Anchorman had a chance to say anything. "Finn doesn't want me to hear even a whisper about the case, and helping to straighten up and plan a surprise cook for Anchorman sounds like a lot more fun." She walked over and grabbed Cheron's hand, pulling the startled doctor away from her equally surprised protector. "Why don't we all go? A girls' trip with a purpose."

Cheron opened her mouth, and then closed it again as she seriously considered the suggestion. "It would be easier if Norman wasn't around to tell us what we should be doing. He's like that when it comes to his kitchen." She gave Kate a big smile. "And I think I'd enjoy surprising him. Maybe we could stop by my lab first? I need to check in on the staff, and Norman won't let me go by myself." She lowered her voice to a rare, dramatic whisper. "He thinks there might be a body snatcher in the closet."

"He watches too many zombie apocalypse movies," Kate stated with a wave of her hand. "They all do." She hooked an arm through Cheron's and grinned at Marcie. "How about it? You lead, and we will follow."

For the first time in forty-eight hours, Marcie laughed. "Great." She looked at Ricki and then Anchorman, peering down her nose at both of them. "I never get to be the boss. And that means I should drive." She walked over to a small table between the front door and window and scooped up a set of keys from the small basket on top of it. "Let's take the limecicle. It will give the whole town something else to gossip about when they see me driving it instead of Ricki."

When Marcie jangled the keys in front of her, Ricki only grinned. "Have a good time." When the three women exited, laughing at something Kate whispered to them, Ricki swiveled back around in her seat only to come face-to-face with a clearly annoyed Finn and Anchorman. She shrugged in response to their glares. "They needed a ride."

"I'm toast if those two give Cheron advice about our relationship," Anchorman said.

"And I'm in for a major third degree if the three of them get to comparing notes," Finn complained.

"Your track record with women was bound to come back and haunt you one day. It always does." Dan pretended to shiver when Finn shot him a hot glare. "Don't shoot the messenger. I'm not the one who will be talking about your past conquests."

"Marcie is in on those discussions, too," Finn growled. "Which means that you'll be a topic on the table, just like the rest of us."

"Strangely enough, I'm not worried about it." Dan walked over to the stove and lifted the coffeepot. "I only boiled water for tea for Marcie this morning. I was going to put on more hot water and make a pot of coffee, if anyone is interested?"

Anchorman stalked to the sink. "I'll make it. And maybe you should worry."

"I wouldn't get worked up about the women talking either," Clay stated. "It's a good healing step for Marcie. What I *am* worried about is this case." He looked at Finn. "We've uncovered a couple of things, but you start. You said you went over the military records?"

"And didn't find much except that one short overlap of the time Malone and Parkman spent at Fort Riley. That and one odd thing on Parkman's record," Finn said. "He got a reprimand for not signing up any recruits during his six-month stint in Omaha."

Anchorman turned away from the stove, the coffeepot in this hand. "Not any? As in, not even one?"

The Irishman nodded. "That's right. And it was a pretty active station, so that was very unusual."

"Marcie said the last time she saw Sam, he was angry and distant, and that was right after his discharge." Ricki's eyes narrowed as she thought it over.

"Maybe he was pissed about that ding on his record," Anchorman said with a glance at Finn. "Unless there were other dings on his record?"

"Nope. Excellent work reviews by his commanding officers, and otherwise nothing that stood out." Finn frowned at Ricki. "Angry and distant? He could have been mad at the army in general. Maybe mad enough to talk anyone coming into the recruiting station out of enlisting, and mad enough to take part in that robbery, since it was contractor money being used to build and maintain military bases. That's the bulk of Hanover's business. They mostly supply the military, and more specifically the army."

Anchorman grunted and went back to measuring out coffee grounds. "He wouldn't be the first guy to become disillusioned with the service."

"Follow the money is always a good starting point," Dan said. "How did that robbery crew know the day and time that money was coming? Hamilton mentioned the job was pulled off at Love Field, outside of Dallas. How did they know it would be there?"

"A lot of people knew," Finn answered. "And we checked them all out, but most of the people Stateside only knew it was coming back at some point, and only had one day's notice of the exact date and time. The Hanover people made up a much smaller group. Just Hanover's secretary, who kept his schedule, and his chief operating officer, who arranged for the armored car pick-up and knew about the thirty-day notice of the base shutting down. And according to those two, even Hanover's wife didn't know the precise date he was coming home."

"What about the armored car crew?" Clay asked, frowning when Finn immediately shook his head.

"They all checked out, too," the FBI agent said. "That was kept in a very tight circle in-house."

"Malone was a communications expert," Ricki said. "Would that include hacking skills?"

"It might," Dan said. "Especially as the field went more and more electronic. He could have kept up."

"There's nothing in the military record to verify that," Finn stated. "But that's not to say he didn't develop them on the side, or in the three years between the time he was discharged and when the robbery occurred."

Ricki's eyebrows drew together. "Hacking skills. So he could have listened in on a phone conversation or got into their computer?"

"It's possible," Dan nodded. "But that can take a pretty high level of sophistication. It's not easy to listen in on a cell phone conversation unless you're on the same Internet network. Same with hacking into a computer. It depends on how complicated the security protocols are. It would be a lot easier to get close enough to clone the apps on the cell phone." He paused and smiled.

"Like a personal calendar. That he's synced with his one at work."

"Which might list a time and date to book an armored car." Ricki's boot started tapping. "I wonder if Preston Malone ever made a trip to Dallas just before the robbery?" She looked down and pretended to study her nails. "It would be very handy if we knew someone who could check out the commercial flights between the time that evacuation order for the base went out to Hanover, and when the robbery took place."

"I'll get on that." Finn took out his phone and tapped in a note.

"How does that get you back to Malone's killer?" Dan asked.

Clay accepted a steaming mug of coffee from Anchorman and passed it over to Ricki before being handed a second one for himself. "Assuming one of the other partners in the robbery killed Malone, we have to figure out who that is and where they crossed paths. If all three spent time together in Dallas before the robbery, they'll be easier to track down."

"If they're smart, they came in separately and stayed separate," Finn pointed out. "And used burner cells to communicate. But I'll have the flights checked out. If we find him, we'll start looking at the hotels near Love Field and the Hanover offices. It will be a lot easier if we have specific dates to look at, and placing them on a commercial flight would make that a lot easier."

"Let's assume they somehow got wind of the thirty-day shut down and got to Dallas as quick as they could to lock down the details," Clay said.

"And the only way they could have known about that money in the first place was through the active military on the base, or through employees of Hanover. And most of them are former military," Finn said.

"Money that wasn't traceable." Dan drew out each syllable. "Why is that? With that much pure cash on hand, I would think Hanover would have been concerned about theft, both internal and external, and would have recorded the serial numbers."

"All I was told was that we couldn't track the money," Finn

stated. "And anything beyond that is above my pay grade." He ran an agitated hand through his dark hair. "I don't know. Rumor has it that the money was used mostly for bribes to the local officials and buying protection from the rebels in the area. That sort of thing. And off the record, I'm assuming Hanover didn't record the serial numbers because the money wasn't theirs. They got it from another source."

"Like the CIA?" Dan inquired politely with a crooked smile. "Bribing the locals and paying off the rebels sounds about right. But here's the deal. You can bet the CIA recorded those numbers, and they wouldn't take kindly to having two million in slush fund money disappear."

"Are you suggesting they might have already taken care of this problem and just didn't bother to let the FBI know?" The hand Finn had rested on the countertop formed into a fist. "They would have had to do that on U.S. soil, and they aren't supposed to do any kind of op inside our domestic boundaries."

"That's what their charter says," Dan agreed in a bland voice. "If you think Sam Parkland was part of that crew, and he's dead too, then I guess you'll have your answer."

"Maybe they didn't know who really owned that money, and put a CIA target on their backs when they stole it." Ricki stood up and paced a few feet away, making Corby lift his head and carefully watch her. When she turned around and paced away from his food dish, he laid back down again. "But what if they did know and stole it anyway, because they had a plan to lie low until the heat died down?" She stopped in front of Dan. "How much money can you transfer out of the country without raising red flags?"

"Ten thousand," her fellow ISB agent said. "If you moved that out steadily, say nine thousand a month, it would take you. . ." He paused, but his lips kept moving as he did the math in his head. "About eighteen years to get it all moved."

"If you made three separate transfers, to three separate bank accounts, then that would be six years," Clay said. "Close to the time that has passed since the robbery, and when Malone was conveniently killed."

"Your idea about greed seems to fit the timeline," Ricki said with a nod. "So Malone was either hiding from the CIA, or from one or both of his partners. But if this is where he came to hide out, why was it four years after the fact? He couldn't have been too worried about the CIA tracking him down if it took him that long after the robbery to take on a secret identity."

"Either that or he heard Sam was dead and decided they'd never go looking for a Sam Parkman after that, so he took advantage of them looking alike and came here to the perfect hiding spot," Clay said. "Which would leave the third man as his killer, and probably Sam's too."

"Maybe," Ricki said.

"But?" Anchorman put in for everyone else.

She sighed, struggling to put her thoughts in order so she could make a logical case. "Lying low in order to slowly move the money out of the country makes sense. And something definitely spooked him to come to the Bay and hide. But I don't think the CIA would leave all that money behind. If they'd already recovered it, why not leave the problem of tracking down the thieves to the FBI with a few well-placed, anonymous tips? And if they are still looking for the money, or at least Malone's share of it, why kill him before they knew where it was?"

"Yeah." Clay's mouth flattened into a thin line. "There was no time to interrogate him. Whoever killed Malone just walked into the kitchen and shot him."

Dan blinked and then frowned. "Which isn't very CIA-like," he said. "Those operatives would have made Malone disappear and taken him somewhere to question him about the money, and the leak who told him about it in the first place, if they didn't already know. They wouldn't shoot him in broad daylight. Especially not when no one would question Sam Parkman, or someone they thought was Sam Parkman, suddenly disappearing since he'd done it before." He looked over at Finn. "And what about Malone's background? If he was secretly keeping in touch with family, maybe in Kentucky, where he sent that letter, would anyone miss him if letters stopped coming and he simply vanished?"

"No family was listed in his military records. Not even an emergency contact. The background check done on him after his prints were identified came back pretty thin. Mom OD'd on heroin. No dad listed on the birth certificate. He mostly grew up in a series of foster homes until he was eighteen and joined the army."

"Which became his family," Ricki said softly. "A family he was discharged from ten years ago from a base in Kentucky." She sat back down and tapped a finger against the counter. "Besides the discharge, did he have any other ties to Kentucky?"

Finn shrugged. "He grew up in Arkansas, and until the army sent him to Fort Campbell, he'd never been to Kentucky as far as we knew. But he did hang around the area until three years ago. The FBI reports on the search for him showed he left the army and then spent some time in St. Louis. Our guys went there. He was living under a fake name, but same birth date, which is pretty typical, doing handyman work for a local company. But he left there, and we managed to track him down back to Kentucky and another fake name. He did handyman work again, and we were told he had a girlfriend who no one had actually met, and who supposedly worked at some bar no one could remember the name of. Malone himself poofed into thin air just a few weeks after we caught on to him, and the trail went cold in Hopkinsville, Kentucky. We couldn't pick it up after that. Until you sent us those prints."

"A girlfriend in Kentucky." Ricki exchanged a quick glance with Clay. "Where he sent a letter ten years after he was discharged."

Clay grinned. "I told you it was a woman. What do you think of a field trip to Kentucky to check out Bernie's Hardware Store?"

"Sounds like a plan," Ricki said.

Anchorman lifted a large package of hamburger wrapped in cellophane from the cardboard box he'd set on the counter. "Since I've been tagged as your official backup, I'm in. Now, who's hungry?"

"Make mine medium rare," Finn said before scowling at Ricki. "I don't care if Blake finds out what we're up to, and I should warn you that the agent in charge of the search didn't believe the whole girlfriend fairytale. If he ever did happen to hear her name, he didn't bother to put it into his report. But if you're determined to dive down that rabbit hole, then I'm going too. Like a good partner should. And what the hell is a Bernie's Hardware Store?"

Chapter Fifteen

"Do you think Dan will sniff out any more information from those files I sent?" Finn's question was met with a shrug from Clay and a smile from Ricki.

"If anyone can get more from those files, it will be Dan," she said. "I looked them over on the plane and didn't see anything useful besides what you'd already told us. But Dan has a special talent for interpreting data, so we'll just have to wait and see."

She readjusted the strap of her backpack, so it didn't interfere with her shoulder harness. Despite her annoyance with Dr. Blake and his high-handed tactics, he did have his uses. Like getting permits in record time to carry firearms on the plane. He'd even secured one for Clay, who had managed a grudging thanks for Finn to pass along to the profiler.

"Welcome to Nashville," Anchorman said through gritted teeth. "The car rental's down that way." He stomped past the other three, who had stopped to read the signs.

Finn stared after him. "He has a problem with Nashville?"

"Tennessee in general," Ricki said. "Bad memories. He used to fly in here every year to go camping with Kelly."

Understanding mixed with sympathy passed over the FBI agent's face. "Ah. His best friend who was murdered last year." He walked beside Ricki and Clay as they trailed after the big Marine. "I was truly sorry to be tied up on a case so I couldn't help out."

"The NCIS guy they sent was a big help," Clay said. "Nice guy. Good investigator. He used to be a navy rescue pilot, flying helicopters before he joined NCIS."

"He helped us on my last case too," Ricki put in. "But by then he'd jumped ship to the FBI."

Finn nodded. "Yeah. Trey Robard. I've heard good things. He's got some legendary rescues under his belt, and by all accounts seemed to really like his work, so there are a lot of rumors going around about why he left the navy." He strained his neck to see over the crowd. "Where did our grumpy backup guy disappear to?"

"He'll find us at the rental counter. Let's just keep heading that way," Clay said. "It's on the ground floor, if I remember correctly from our last trip here."

"Agent James."

Ricki turned at the sound of her name, looking through the shifting crowd, trying to pinpoint its source.

"Agent James."

She zeroed in on the location, then almost rubbed her eyes in disbelief. A man with the shape of an enlarged pear sat on a bench placed along the wide hallway. Christopher Young was the most sought-after attorney in the South and looked the same way he had the last time she'd set eyes on him. A bulging stomach hung over his knees and blue eyes sparkled at her from beneath white hair and a matching set of bushy eyebrows.

Despite his large girth, the man still brought to mind one of the more famous Southern figures who'd made a fortune selling chicken.

While Christopher certainly had a fortune of his own, he'd made it in a courtroom, wearing an expensive three-piece suit with a gold chain across the vest just like the one he currently had on. Ricki had decided during their last encounter that he must have a closet full of expensive suits with matching vests, since that was all she'd ever seen him wear. Her lips stretched into a wide grin when he lifted his hand in a royal gesture and beckoned her forward, exactly the way he had the first time she'd met him.

"Who's that?" Finn asked.

"The best damn lawyer in the South," Clay said with a laugh. He took Ricki's hand in his and smiled down at her. "I guess we've been summoned. Again."

She added her laughter to his. "So it would seem."

They threaded their way through the shifting crowd, with Finn right behind them. When they reached Christopher, Ricki leaned down and gave him a hug. "What are you doing here?"

"Meeting a former client of mine, pretty lady." He winked at her, then held out his hand to Clay. "How are you doing, Chief Thomas?"

"I'm fine, Christopher. How have you been?"

"Can't complain, can't complain. When I got the call, I couldn't resist coming down myself to see some of my favorite people. Especially since you wrote me a satisfyingly large check that didn't bounce." He looked around Clay to squint at Finn. "And who is this?"

"This is Special Agent Fionn Sullivan, with the FBI," Ricki said. "We're working a case together."

"FBI?" The attorney's heavy eyebrows winged upward.

"My. You do seem to collect quite a number of federal agents, don't you? What happened to that nice young man from the Naval Investigative Service? Trey, wasn't it?" He smiled. "No need to confirm that. I never forget a face or a name."

Ricki grinned as Christopher pushed his rotund body off the bench with the help of a walking cane. It was topped by the flat, silver-headed image of a mockingbird. Seeing Ricki's interest, he held it up so she could get a closer look. "Not only was Atticus Finch the hero of *To Kill a Mockingbird*, he was also a lawyer, and one of the greatest characters to ever breathe life from the pages of a book. The mockingbird is also the state bird of this very great state of Tennessee." He looked past Ricki, then lifted the cane up high and waved it above her head. "There he is now. Mr. Beal? It's good to see you again."

Anchorman strode up, a smile on his face. "Mr. Young. The feeling is mutual." He gave his former attorney a firm handshake. "I wasn't expecting to have you deliver it personally."

Ricki's eyes narrowed on Anchorman's face. "It? What 'it' are you talking about?"

"This, my dear." Christopher tapped his cane on a metal box lying next to a paper bag close to the spot he had occupied on the bench. "Mr. Beal here called me and asked if he could borrow a handgun. Specifically, a Beretta M9. Which I have brought with me."

"A Beretta?" Ricki put her hands on her hips and stared at Anchorman. "You asked your former lawyer to bring you a handgun?"

"Well, I'm not going to tote a rifle around in the city, and while it's not my choice for a weapon, I took the mandatory training on a pistol." He leaned over and opened the metal box to reveal the deadly-looking Beretta with its inky black finish. "I know you and Clay prefer your Glocks, but I thought this would be best for me since it's what I trained on." He lifted the gun out of its case and held it flat in his hand, testing its weight.

Clay shook his head. "Look. I know you don't like being unarmed when you're helping out on a case, but are you sure about this?"

"I'm sure," Anchorman said. "I would have picked one up in Washington but didn't have time because of the ten-day wait period to buy one, and then it would have taken more time to get a license for a concealed carry. And I'm sure that Blake wouldn't have been willing to extend that expedited permit he got for you to me as well."

"That's a fact," Finn said. "But neither Tennessee nor Kentucky require a license to carry a concealed weapon, or to own one, for that matter, so you wouldn't have needed one from Blake."

The former Marine nodded. "That's right. But Washington does, so picking one up here didn't put Ricki or Clay in the position of walking a very fine legal tightrope for me."

Since she had never seen Anchorman fire a pistol, Ricki looked over the gun with a skeptical eye. "Are you sure you know how to use one of these? It's been a while." She shrugged at the bland look from the former Marine.

Christopher waited a beat, then politely cleared his throat. "I also brought you that belt you asked for. It's in that bag."

"Great." Anchorman unzipped the duffel he was carrying and stuffed the paper bag and gun into it, along with the box it came in, then closed them securely inside. "Thanks. I appreciate this."

"No problem. No problem at all." Christopher reached into his suit jacket and pulled an envelope from an inner pocket. "I also got one of these for you." He chuckled at Anchorman's puzzled look. "It's an official permit to carry that gun home on the plane. You will have to keep the weapon in whatever you are using for luggage, of course, but this will spare you the problem of returning it. Consider it my gift as a thank-you for your service. I don't believe I had an opportunity to do that in our prior meetings."

"Not letting me rot in a jail cell for murdering Kelly was thanks enough," Anchorman said, a quiet sincerity coating every word.

"No, no. While that was also my pleasure, I was paid for that, my boy. This is a gift." Leaning heavily on his cane, Christopher took a step toward the exit, then stopped to wave them on. "You all be on your way now. I'm sure there are bad men out there who need catching." He nodded at Finn. "It was nice to meet you, Special Agent Fionn Sullivan. You keep my friends there safe, and I'm sure they'll do the same for you."

"Yes, sir," Finn said as Christopher turned and slowly ambled away. The agent looked over at Anchorman, a slightly stunned look on his face. "He was your lawyer?"

"Yeah." Anchorman pointed in the opposite direction from the way Christopher had gone. "I got the car all squared away while the rest of you were loitering in the hall here. It's an hour and fifteen to Hopkinsville. Straight up the twenty-four, and then we cut over once we hit the town's outer limits."

He led the way to the rental car, tossing his canvas overnight bag into the trunk of the large sedan, leaving the rest of the group to do the same as he took up a position behind the wheel.

"I don't think I've ever seen you drive anything except a truck," Ricki observed as she took a seat in back with Clay, so Finn could sit up front.

"I didn't have anything to do with picking out our transportation," Anchorman said as he started the engine and pulled into the traffic exiting the airport. "Mister FBI Agent arranged for the fancy car."

"It's a four-door sedan," Finn said in a dry voice. "It probably cost less than that truck of yours with all its detailing on the side."

"One very thin red stripe isn't any kind of detailing," Anchorman maintained. "And I don't want to debate it for the next hour either."

As the former Marine expertly maneuvered onto the highway that would take them north, over the border and into Kentucky, Ricki scrolled through the same FBI file that she'd sent to Dan the day before, reading it again for any detail she might have missed. Halfway through, she yawned. The early morning flight from Seattle, on top of the events of the last few days, had sapped her energy until all she really wanted at the moment was a good nap. She yawned again, then checked her watch. It would be another twenty minutes before they reached Hopkinsville. Leaning forward, she reached an arm over the front seat and tapped Finn on the shoulder. "You also made our hotel arrangements, partner. Do you know where it is?"

Finn lifted his phone that he'd set on the center console and jiggled it in front of her. "I put the address into my GPS and have already told our designated driver what turnoff to take." When his phone let out a beep, he tapped the screen. "Email from Blake." The agent frowned. "I sent him my progress report last night, so he can't be complaining about me not keeping in touch."

Wondering what the man wanted from Finn, Ricki settled back into her seat and waited while he pulled up his email.

"I don't know," Finn muttered. "Blake must have some kind of bug up his ass." He passed his phone with the open email on display back to Ricki. "What do you think of that?"

She held the device up so Clay could also see the screen.

"Blake says there will be someone waiting for us at the hotel," she read out loud for Anchorman's benefit. "He'll be in the restaurant when we arrive, and we need to talk to him." She handed the phone back to Finn. "But he doesn't say who this guy is. Any ideas?"

Finn shrugged as he set his phone back in the cup holder. "Since I'm here, and he manipulated you into being on the official team, I don't think it's another agent. Which makes your guess as good as mine."

Ricki glanced at Clay, who rolled his eyes in obvious disgust.

"Since Blake sent him, the odds are we aren't going to like whatever this guy has to tell us." Clay crossed his arms over his chest and stared out the side window.

"Not every message Blake sends is bad news, you know. The man did help you sort out that mess with your brother," Finn casually pointed out.

Clay didn't look away from the view out the window. "He also helped cause that mess with my brother."

Knowing that Clay's feelings about Blake would not change anytime soon, Ricki let the silence descend and went back to reading the FBI file on the efforts to find Preston Malone.

The actual reports didn't add much more information to Finn's succinct summary of the search, and she didn't notice anything she'd missed the last time she'd read it. They had tracked Malone to St. Louis and then back to Hopkinsville. They'd even come up with the alias he'd used once he'd returned to Kentucky. Patrick Murray. And Finn had been right about the birthdate. Malone had used his real one, along with the fake name. "Same initials, too. P.M.," she muttered to herself. "Not very original."

She'd just finished the file when Anchorman turned off the interstate highway. Less than ten minutes later he was pulling into the parking lot of a two-story rectangular building sporting a sign out front for a large hotel chain. Between the flight, the time difference, and the drive from Nashville to Hopkinsville, it was late afternoon by the time they walked into the hotel lobby. Ricki looked around and spotted the restaurant off to the left. "Why don't you give the reservation info to Clay and Anchorman, and they can get us checked in while we find Blake's messenger?" she said to Finn.

"Good idea." He brought the information up on his phone, then handed the device to Clay. "There you go. Hopefully this won't take long."

Clay glanced at the wide opening leading into the restaurant. "If it does, Blake's mouthpiece is going to get some additional company. You might want to let him know to keep that in mind, along with the fact that we're both armed, and that should make it quick."

Finn wiggled his eyebrows above a wide grin. "I'll be sure to mention it."

Giving Clay a light kiss on the cheek, simply because she thought he needed it, Ricki crossed the lobby with Finn. They walked side by side through the open archway at the front of the restaurant, stopping a few feet beyond it to look around. The space was well lit by large windows across the front and was crowded with tables set closely together. Since it was late for lunch and still early for dinner, there were only a handful of customers spread about the dining room. Ricki's gaze zeroed in on a lone man, sitting in the back, who had stood when they'd entered the room. Finn spotted him as well and raised a hand in greeting.

When the man followed suit, Finn nodded. "He must be our guy."

As Ricki threaded her way through the maze of tables and chairs, she kept her gaze steady on the stranger. He had sun-bleached hair and a ramrod-straight posture inside a dark suit. His matching dark necktie stood out in stark contrast to the white of his collared shirt. "Looks like one of you," she said in a low voice, smiling at Finn's disgruntled snort.

"I don't know anyone in the Bureau who dresses like that anymore. The black suit, white shirt, dark tie thing went out in the seventies." As they approached the unsmiling man, Finn stretched out a hand. "I'm Special Agent Fionn Sullivan, and this is my partner, Special Agent Ricki James."

The man gave Finn's hand a brief shake as he nodded at Ricki. "I'm sorry to have to ask, but can I see your credentials?" When they both held them out, he leaned closer to get a better look at Ricki's. Once he'd straightened up again, he gave her a long stare. "This says you're with the National Park Service."

"She's moonlighting," Finn cut in. "You can see plainly enough that I'm with the FBI, and Agent James has been assigned as my partner at the Bureau's request." When the man reluctantly nodded, Finn gave him a skeptical look. "Now then, I'm sorry to ask," he said, using the man's own words. "But I'm assuming you also have credentials?"

The other man hesitated as he did a quick scan of the room before reaching into an inner pocket and bringing out a black case. Flipping it open, he held it up for Finn and then Ricki to see and then tucked it away out of sight.

"Aaron Reynolds. CIA. Well, what a surprise." A touch of sarcasm coated Finn's voice. "And Blake sent you?"

"Yes, he did." Reynolds gestured to the table behind him. "Do you mind if we sit?" He didn't wait for an answer but took his seat again and politely waited as Ricki and Finn did the same. There was already a pot of coffee as well as three empty cups on the table. Reynolds lifted the pot and hovered it over the cups. "Would you like some coffee?" When his two reluctant companions shook their heads, he poured one cup, took a quick sip, then set it to the side.

"All right," Finn said. "What can we do for you?"

"Nothing, actually." Reynolds leaned forward, resting his forearms on the tabletop before clasping his hands together. "It's what I can do for you. Blake sent me so you wouldn't be spinning your wheels about the Hanover Industries heist that took place seven years ago."

Finn looked at Ricki and shrugged before settling back in his seat and staring at Reynolds. "Fine. Let's hear it."

"The short version is that Hanover is one of our civilian contractors who deals with the locals in locations all over the world."

"Which includes making any necessary payoffs," Finn said.

Except for a slight tightening along his jaw, Reynolds' expression didn't change. "If it ensures the safety of American lives, the IC considers it a justified expense."

"IC?" Ricki questioned.

"Intelligence Community," Reynolds replied in a clipped tone. "That money stolen from Hanover belonged to us. Hanover was simply the distributor." He paused to take another sip of his coffee. "Blake wanted us to assure you that as far as the robbery goes, we have always considered it the FBI's case."

Underneath the table, Ricki's boot began to tap. "And you don't mind losing two million dollars?"

"What we minded more, Agent James, is how those three men who pulled off the heist got their information in the first place."

Ricki's gaze remained on the CIA agent as she tilted her head to the side. "Funny you should say that. We were wondering the same thing. And how Preston Malone knew enough to get out of Kentucky right ahead of the FBI."

"Especially when he'd been sitting here for two years after he left St. Louis," Finn said, taking up the narrative. "Then we show up and just like that," he snapped his fingers together, "poof, he's gone."

Reynolds shook his head. "He wasn't tipped off by us. You'll need to look to your own people, Agent Sullivan. Or inside Hanover. But we were told every one of their employees was cleared of any involvement by the FBI."

"It's a puzzle." Ricki studied the CIA operative for a long moment. "So what you're telling us is that the CIA didn't shoot Malone?"

"We did not," Reynolds confirmed. "We didn't even know where he was until this morning when my boss got a call from Dr. Blake." Reynolds took one more sip of coffee and then pushed his chair away from the table and stood. "You'll have to look for your shooter elsewhere, Agent James." A hint of a smile pulled at the corners of his mouth. "And to ensure full disclosure of all the facts, we lost one million dollars. As the contractor responsible for management of the funds, Hanover absorbed the rest of the loss. I am also authorized to let you know that none of that money has surfaced or been recovered."

Finn's face suddenly flushed red as his eyes shot hot daggers toward Reynolds. "So you had the serial numbers all along and just didn't bother to pass them along to us?"

The CIA operative reached for his outer coat. "It was a pleasure meeting you. If you have any other questions, please direct them to Dr. Blake." He gave them both a brief nod then walked off toward the archway separating the restaurant from the hotel's lobby.

Ricki watched him go, a thoughtful look in her eyes. "Do you believe him?"

Still annoyed, Finn stuck his hands in his pant pockets then leaned back in his chair. "An operative from the CIA? Not usually. But I think I'll need to make an exception for this one. So I'd have to say yes, even though saying no would be a helluva a lot more satisfying."

Ricki slowly nodded her agreement. "Yeah. And I believe him too."

Chapter Sixteen

The next morning, Ricki and Clay strolled into the lobby and nodded to the desk clerk before heading outside. Anchorman and Finn were already standing next to the rental sedan, sipping from cardboard cups of coffee. Anchorman greeted them by pointing at a takeout carrier perched on the roof of the car with two more steaming cups nestled in it.

"Brought yours along." He stepped to the side so Clay could retrieve the coffee. "Finn here told me that Blake sent a CIA agent."

"Apparently they're case officers, not agents. I would have told you about him last night, but you disappeared early," Ricki said.

"I ordered room service since the FBI is paying for this and spent the evening making calls back home." He leaned against the car. "Marcie had a lot of questions about the reopening, which we can talk about if you want to, but only after you tell me what the spook had to say."

Ricki lifted an eyebrow at Finn. "You didn't tell him?"

Finn shrugged. "Didn't have much of a chance, and I wanted to hear if you still believed Case Officer Reynolds now that you've had a night to sleep on it."

Surprised by the question, Ricki shot Finn a curious look. "I'm still inclined to believe him. How about you? Have you changed your mind?"

"Nope. But not because I didn't think I should. I just couldn't come up with a good reason. I can't see the CIA risk getting caught shooting someone on domestic soil. Even if he was a very bad guy. And not for a million dollars. That would be chump change to them."

"The contracting company had to eat the other million," Clay said in an aside to Anchorman before the Marine could ask about it.

"Which eliminates that theory. And since the FBI never caught up with Preston Malone, the only suspects we have left are his old partners. One, or both of them, probably shot Malone, and we don't have a solid lead on either of them." Ricki looked off into the distance, silently weighing the possibilities. "Somehow, at least one of those partners tracked him down in the Bay."

Clay took a long sip of his coffee, then opened the passenger side door. "Well, we won't figure it out by standing around here. I thought we should start where the Feds left off, and that would be with The Last Nail Handyman Services, according to Dan's email. I have the address, so I'll drive." When Anchorman tossed him the key fob, Clay waited until Ricki took the shotgun seat before crossing to the opposite side of the car and slipping behind the wheel.

"How far away is this place?" Finn asked as he buckled his seatbelt.

"About five miles," Clay said. "I've already called one Mr.

Fred Brightwood, who owns the business. He said they're in a residential neighborhood."

"Sounds like a mom-and-pop shop." Finn smiled. "Although from the name it could be just Pop who is running it."

The GPS on Clay's phone got them to the address listed in the FBI file without a hitch. It turned out to be a duplex, with a midsize car parked in the driveway on one side, and a battered old utility van on the other. There was a plank with a home-made sign nailed to a short post stuck in a patch of dirt. Crooked letters in bright red, spelling out THE LAST NAIL, were painted on one side of the flat board.

"Looks like they're still in business," Anchorman remarked before exiting the car.

More or less, Ricki thought as she, too, stepped out of the sedan.

Clay was the first to reach the door, painted in the same red as the sign. Since there wasn't a doorbell anywhere in sight, he gave the solid wood a loud rap with the back of his knuckles. An older man, with steel-gray hair and dressed in dark blue overalls, opened the door. He peered out at the group through wire-rimmed spectacles.

"Are you Chief Thomas?" When Clay nodded, the man adjusted his glasses and took another long look at the three people standing behind the chief. "Then who are all these people?"

"Colleagues," Clay said. "Are you Mr. Brightwood?"

"Sure am," the man confirmed. "Are any of these colleagues of yours with the FBI? Because I already talked to them about Patrick Murray until I was blue in the face, and I don't intend to do it again."

"Just one." Clay pointed at Finn. "And I promise he won't say a word."

Fred Brightwood frowned for a moment before finally stepping to one side. "Fine, fine. Come on in." He led the way into a cluttered space that had once been the duplex's living room. "Just set whatever is on the couch and chairs on the floor and have a seat." He pulled out a folding chair tucked under an old desk that had seen better days. Resting his hands on his knees, he stared at Clay. "Now what is it you wanted to know about Patrick?"

"He worked for you for two years. Do I have that right?" Clay asked.

"You certainly do, son. Patrick was a good man and a hard worker. Knew a lot about fixing things and even knew how to set up those DIY security systems that everyone is buying these days. We made some very good money off that business. I was sorry to see him go." He looked at Ricki and smiled. "Now tell me who your friends are." He pointed at Ricki. "You can start with her."

"This is Special Agent Ricki James with the National Park Service," Clay said, then gestured toward Anchorman. "And this is Anchorman, our backup."

"Uh-huh. Backup is it?" Fred Brightwood pursed his lips as he gave the big Marine a slow once-over. "Are you in the military, son?"

Anchorman smiled. "Retired, sir. From the Marines."

"My son was in the Marines. I was too. Family tradition." He adjusted his spectacles again. "And I'm thinking you're pretty good with a rifle."

The former Marine's smile slowly faded. "Good enough."

Fred nodded before centering his attention on Ricki. "How about you, young lady? How are you with a rifle?"

Ricki cocked an eyebrow at him before echoing Anchorman. "Good enough."

The old man chuckled. "Pretty and deadly, is that it?" He

didn't wait for an answer, but turned his body in the chair until he was facing Clay. "Those two and an FBI agent? That's a lot of firepower, son. Exactly what is it you think Patrick did? The FBI never would tell me. Did he shoot someone?"

"We're not sure," Clay said. "What we do know for sure is that the man you knew as Patrick Murray was shot dead three days ago."

What little color there was in Fred's cheeks drained away. "Shot dead? Are you sure we're talking about the same man?"

Clay reached into his jacket pocket and took out an FBI photo of Preston Malone. "Is this the man who called himself Patrick Murray?"

Fred stared at the photo, then slowly took off his glasses and rubbed his eyes. "That's him. What happened?"

"He was killed in northwestern Washington, near Olympic National Park." Clay tucked the picture back into his pocket. "That's in my jurisdiction, which is why we're here. We're looking for the person who shot him."

"Olympic National Park?" Fred echoed. "That's somewhere near Seattle, isn't it? Patrick mentioned it once." He glanced at Ricki. "Is that why you're here? Was Patrick killed in the park?"

Ricki's whole body went on full alert, and sitting next to her, she could see Finn reacting the same way. "No, Mr. Brightwood. Not in the park."

Clay shifted slightly in his chair, his expression staying friendly. "Did he say anything specific about Olympic?"

"Not really." Fred lifted a hand and rubbed it across his cheek. "Patrick never talked about his life much, past or present. I think I mentioned how nice it is to live so close to the Great Smoky Mountains Park, and he mentioned having a friend who lived near this Olympic Park out in Washington, near Seattle."

"A friend," Clay repeated while Ricki held her breath. "Did he mention this friend's name?"

Fred's face wrinkled as he thought it over. "No. Not that I recall. Just called him an army buddy." He shrugged. "Like I said, he tossed that out once and never talked about it again. And I didn't ask him about it either. I figured he must have put in some serious combat time because he didn't like to talk about the service. I thought if there was something he wanted me to know, he'd tell me." He settled his glasses back onto his nose. "Patrick was a nice guy. I had no reason to pry or poke at him." In a sudden change of mood, the old handyman slapped a palm against one knee. "Except, of course, about that supposed girl-friend of his. I was always needling him about her."

Clay shot a sideways glance at Ricki before turning a puzzled look on Fred. "Supposed? Do you mean she didn't look at him that same way?"

Fred chuckled. "I mean I think he made her up. Two years that boy worked for me, and this Heather person never once came around. So I never met her. I was even over at his place more than a couple of times, and there was nothing in his apart-ment that said a woman was living there. Patrick liked working extra hours, which was kind of odd for someone who had a pretty woman waiting for him. That's how he described her. Pretty, with that white-blond hair like Marilyn Monroe, and blue eyes. Kind of petite, with big knockers, if you get my drift. She was supposed to have worked in a bar somewhere around here, but I never did catch the name of the place." Fred shook his head. "Yeah. I'd say Patrick had quite a fantasy going on over Heather."

"Is that what you told the FBI when they came around with questions about Patrick?" Clay asked.

"Sure. I talked with an agent for quite a while about it." Fred scratched his chin. "Now, what was his name?"

"Special Agent Drake?" Finn supplied helpfully.

Fred pointed a gnarled finger at the Irishman. "Yep. That was his name. Agent Drake. After we'd talked a bit, I think he agreed with me that Heather was a figment of Patrick's imagination. Especially since he mentioned checking every bar in a ten-mile radius and never finding a Heather working at any of them."

Since Agent Drake had never mentioned Heather's name in any of the daily reports he'd filed on the search for Preston Malone, Ricki silently agreed with Fred's conclusion. The agent had searched, couldn't verify the girlfriend story, so hadn't believed that Heather had actually existed.

"Patrick didn't live far from here. I can dig up the address if you'd like, but don't know what good it's going to do. He hasn't been there for three years."

"I have the address, Mr. Brightwood. Thank you. Is there anything else at all you can tell us about your former employee?"

Fred contemplated the question for a moment before shaking his head. "Not that I haven't already told the FBI. Like I kept saying to them, and now again to you, the man I knew was a nice guy. Quiet and steady. A good worker. Not the best dresser, maybe. Always looked like he bought his clothes at a thrift shop. But he sure had a top-notch set of tools. He never had to borrow any of mine, which really helped get our jobs done a lot faster. Yep. I'd say what he didn't spend on fancy clothes he invested in his tools." Fred got to his feet and held out a hand when Clay also stood. "I've got to get going, Chief Thomas. I have a job scheduled in thirty minutes, and it's on the other side of town." He dropped Clay's hand and nodded at Ricki and Anchorman, ignoring Finn. "It was good to meet you all. I hope you catch this guy so Patrick can truly rest in peace."

"Thank you for your time, Mr. Brightwood." Clay handed

him a small rectangular card. "If you think of anything else, I'd appreciate a call."

Fred tucked the card inside the top pocket of his overalls. "I'll do that."

Ricki walked out of the duplex right in front of Clay. No one in the group said a word until they were back in the car.

"Where to now?" Anchorman asked from his position in the back seat.

"Bernie's Hardware. It sounds like Malone spent a lot of time there buying tools," Ricki answered as she tapped the screen of her cell phone. "I looked the address up last night."

Finn smiled. "Are you still thinking there was some kind of romantic encounter in the paint brush aisle? Brightwood sounded convinced that the whole girlfriend thing never happened. That Malone just made it up. He certainly had Special Agent Drake thinking along those same lines."

"We need to check it out," Clay stated as Ricki's GPS chirped out the first set of streets to get to the hardware store. "Heather might not have been real, but the tools Malone carried certainly were, and you get those at a hardware store. So like Ricki said, it sounds like he spent a good chunk of his time there."

"Fine. Bernie's Hardware it is." Finn settled back in his seat and checked his email, while Anchorman and Ricki watched the buildings and trees move past their windows.

The little hardware store was made of red brick and was located at the end of a small strip of stores fronting a busy road. Clay found a parking space right in front. They all sat for a moment, studying another hand-painted sign. This one was more professionally done than the one at The Last Nail, and was hung over the door by a set of thick chains rather than on a short post stuck into the ground.

"Another mom-and-pop shop," Finn observed. "I'm not

sure it's a good idea for all of us to descend on the place." He grinned at Ricki. "Want to do a round of rock, paper, scissors to see who goes inside?"

Ricki turned in her seat to look at him. "As opposed to . . .?"

"Hitting up that ice cream store two doors down." Finn poked Anchorman with his elbows. "You definitely need to get some ice cream or stay in the car. Apparently you intimidate people."

Anchorman's mouth turned down into a scowl. "I do not."

While Finn laughed, Ricki unbuckled her seat belt. "Clay and I will go in. You two hit the ice cream shop." She opened the door. "I'll take two scoops of chocolate. With sprinkles if they have them." She smiled at Clay. "How about you?"

"Root beer float." When Finn's eyebrows lifted in surprise, Clay shrugged. "Don't blame me, blame Anchorman. He's the one who got me hooked on them."

"Who doesn't like a root beer float?" Anchorman asked as Ricki and Clay exited the car.

"Let's hope Mom or Pop is in the store today," Clay said just before he pushed open the glass door to Bernie's Hardware.

A bell tinkled softly when the door opened, reminding Ricki of the one at the Sunny Side Up. A middle-aged man with long sideburns and a mustache looked up from his seat behind the counter.

He smiled and bobbed his head in a quick nod. "Morning, folks. Can I help you with anything?"

"Good morning." Clay returned the smile as he walked over to the counter and laid his police ID on it. "I'm Chief Clay Thomas from the Bay in the state of Washington, and this is Special Agent Ricki James with the National Park Service." Once Ricki had set her ID next to his, Clay politely waited as the man behind the counter carefully studied them.

When he finally looked up, he was no longer smiling. "I'm not sure why a police chief from Washington, or an agent with the National Park Service, is standing in my store, but I'll be happy to help you if I can."

Clay nodded his thanks as he scooped up both ID's and handed Ricki's back to her. "I appreciate that. Are you Bernie?"

The man's smile was back as he shook his head. "Nope. I'm Christian. Bernie was my dad. He started this place forty-some years ago, and when I took over, I didn't see any need to change the name." He leaned his elbows on the counter as his expression sobered again. "Now, what's this all about?"

"You had a regular customer a few years ago who we're hoping you'll remember. He might have gone by the name of Patrick Murray?" Clay asked. "He worked for a handyman service here in town called The Last Nail."

Christian straightened up and his gaze hardened as he looked from Clay to Ricki. "Why do you want to know? Did he steal something from a gift shop at one of the parks?"

Used to the question, Ricki's smile didn't dim one bit as she shook her head. "No."

"He was shot and killed," Clay said. "And we're trying to trace his movements, to catch the person who murdered him."

Christian's eyes flew open in shock. "Murdered? Where?" His gaze dropped to the pocket where Clay had tucked away his ID. "In Washington? Is that where he's been for the last three years?"

Ricki's smile widened a fraction of an inch. "So you do know Patrick Murray?"

The store owner ran an agitated hand through his thick, dark hair. "Yeah. I knew him. But like I said, he hasn't been around here for three years, maybe a little longer. I don't recall exactly when he stopped coming, but Hailey quit her job here sometime after that."

"Hailey?" Ricki's boot tapped against the floor and her smile faded like mist in the sun.

"She was Patrick Murray's girlfriend."

"His girlfriend?" Ricki mentally rolled her eyes. Hailey, not Heather. Preston Malone wasn't very good at disguising names.

"Yeah. Hailey Dickson. They were a thing." Christian used his foot to roll his stool closer, then sat down. "She was pretty pissed when he just took off like that. After a few months had passed and he hadn't even bothered to call her, she decided to make some changes in her life."

"Such as?" Ricki prompted.

"Well for one, she quit her job here to work full time at The Whistle Stop. She had been here during the day, and over there at night. But she didn't make any secret of the fact she made more money over there, and she was saving up to go to New York and be an actress or some wild idea like that."

Ricki's hopes dropped. It was hard to question someone if they'd moved to New York City without a forwarding address. "How long ago did she leave for New York?"

Now Christian laughed. "She never did. Or at least she hasn't yet. She's still working at The Whistle Stop, and even got herself a new boyfriend. As a matter of fact, she should be opening the place up today. I drop in now and then to say hi. Went over there yesterday for my lunch break."

"Okay." Ricki's shoulders relaxed and her smile was back. "Can you tell me where The Whistle Stop is located?"

Christian winked at her, completely ignoring Clay. "Sure can. It's not far from here. Just a couple of miles away, over by the CSX train tracks. I'll draw you a map."

"Thanks." She produced a card from her pocket and handed it to him. "If you think of anything else, give me a call, and I've written the name of the hotel where we're staying on the back of the card. We'll be there until tomorrow."

"Really? Your hotel, huh?" Christian's gaze took on a speculative look. "The Whistle Stop opens at noon, but if you wait a while, maybe I'll see you over there. The store closes at six."

Ricki winked back at him. "Maybe."

When she turned and left, Clay lingered a moment to lean over the counter. "When she said that we are staying there, she meant both of us." He smiled when Christian's grin disappeared. "I just wanted to clarify that for you."

Chapter Seventeen

"How did it go in there?" This time Finn slid into the back seat of the car before handing Ricki a cup with two generous scoops of chocolate ice cream in it.

"Thanks. Extremely well," Ricki said, also taking the root beer float that Anchorman handed her and passing it to Clay.

"There was even the bonus of the owner trying to hit on Ricki." Clay shrugged at Anchorman's sudden, sharp stare.

"With you standing right there? What did you do?" Anchorman demanded.

Ricki glanced at her watch before twisting around in her seat and pointing her plastic spoon at the Marine. "Since I don't wear a sign around my neck saying 'hey, I belong to him' he didn't do anything, but politely waited to make sure I would take care of it. Which I did."

"Okay. What did *you* do?" Anchorman asked.

When Ricki ignored him, Finn leaned forward. "I'd like to know. Maybe I can pass a tip or two along to Kate."

"Kate doesn't need any tips," Ricki said. She closed her eyes and took another bite of ice cream, savoring the smooth, rich flavor as it slid down her throat.

"After we got the information we needed, the guy asked Ricki to meet him at The Whistle Stop," Clay supplied as he checked his watch. "That's a bar next to some train tracks. And she said maybe."

Anchorman laughed. "Which means 'no way' in Ricki speak."

Finn sent Ricki a skeptical look. "Okay. But how's the guy in the store supposed to know that?"

"He doesn't have to. As long as Clay does."

When she looked at her watch again, Finn's eyes narrowed. "Do you two have someplace else to be, or are you going to fill us in on what the bozo inside had to say?"

"The bozo inside's name is Christian." Ricki took a last bite of her ice cream, then dropped the plastic spoon into the empty cup. "And he told us about The Whistle Stop. The bar that Clay mentioned. Besides being one of his regular watering holes, he also goes in there to see a former employee of his named Hailey Dickson." When Finn gave her an "and so?" stare, she smiled. "The woman Malone used to talk to Fred Brightwood about."

Light dawned in Finn's eyes. "Heather? Hailey Dickson is the made-up girlfriend?" He relaxed back into his seat. "So she really does exist?"

"Alive, well, and working at The Whistle Stop," Clay said. "Which opens its doors at noon." He started the sedan. "We passed a place on the way here where we can get some coffee and real food while we wait."

As Clay pulled onto the street, Finn opened his phone and scrolled through a document. "This Patrick Malone is hard to get a handle on," he said to no one in particular. "He's not so good at covering his tracks, but then he ups and vanishes into thin air. It's like he's got a split personality."

"Yes, it is." Ricki absently set her empty ice cream cup on the dashboard as she silently considered her victim's behavior.

It wasn't long before the small restaurant came up on the right. It looked like an old-time café, with a neon sign in the shape of a pastry hanging in the window. There was plenty of parking available along the curb, so it didn't take long for the three men to step out of the SUV, with a quick slamming of car doors following. Still mulling things over, Ricki was barely aware of Clay taking her hand and pulling her from her seat and out onto the sidewalk, where they fell into line behind Anchorman and Finn.

The FBI agent cheerfully greeted the young waitress doing double duty as the hostess, his green eyes crinkling at the corners as she stared up at him, clearly dazzled. Until she got a look at Clay. Laughing at being so obviously dumped, Finn gave Anchorman a friendly slap on the back and headed for a table near the back, leaving the chief to deal with the awestruck young woman.

Ricki ignored the good-natured ribbing her fiancé was enduring, her mind still on the puzzle of one Preston Malone. Finn was right. He wasn't any good at hiding in plain sight. Once the FBI had his identity from those fingerprints, they had tracked him to St. Louis, and then Hopkinsville easily enough. Why would anyone stay near their last base, which would also be their last known location? Especially if they had stolen money that belonged to the CIA.

Putting that aside for the moment, she went back to concentrating on Malone's movements. He'd hopped from being discharged from a base on the Kentucky–Tennessee border, to St Louis, which couldn't be more than what? She visualized a map of the Midwest. St. Louis wasn't more than five hours from the base. And then back to Hopkinsville, which was only thirty minutes from the base. If he thought he was hiding, he was doing a damn poor job of it. Until the FBI started tracking him down. Then suddenly he completely vanished. Not even the Bureau could find him, until he showed up in the Bay. Halfway across the country.

"Are you done with your toast?"

Clay's voice cut into Ricki's reverie, making her blink up at him. She rubbed her hands against the side of her face to help clear her head, finally noticing three pairs of eyes staring at her. "I'm done." When Clay lifted a skeptical eyebrow, she looked down at the small plate in front of her containing two slices of uneaten toast. "I'm not hungry."

He sighed but took her hand as they both stood up. "What are you thinking so hard about?"

"Two sides of the same coin." When he frowned, she shook her head then checked her watch. It read ten minutes past noon. Time to visit a bar.

They all piled back into the sedan, with Clay once more behind the wheel and the GPS on Ricki's phone chirping out directions.

A minute later, Finn leaned forward and tapped Clay on the shoulder. "You missed a turn. You were supposed to go right back there."

"Didn't miss it," Clay said with a steady look in the rearview mirror. "I don't want to lead the car that's following us to Hailey."

"What?" Finn slid over on the back seat and angled his body enough that he could look in the side-view mirror, with Anchorman doing the same on the opposite side of the car.

"Which one?" Ricki asked as she also studied the sparse traffic behind them reflected in the side mirror.

"That black SUV," Finn stated, then waited for Clay's confirming nod.

"Pretty common car," Anchorman observed as he scooted farther down in the seat to get a better angle on the mirror.

"Cars are common, license plates are not. That one has a ZBR on it," Clay said.

Ricki spotted it in the mirror. The heavily tinted windows didn't give much away, but she was sure there was a passenger sitting next to the driver.

"At least two, maybe three or four in there, depending on who might be occupying the back seat," Anchorman said. He switched his gaze to the front windshield. "Find a corner you can get around without them being able to turn right behind you and let me out. I'll keep up."

"We'll keep up," Finn said. "Drive like you don't notice them until you find a place to box them in."

"There was a two-level parking garage a couple of blocks down. We went by it on the way to the restaurant. I'll keep it slow so you have time to get there. Wait for us on the second level."

"Roger that," Anchorman said.

Silence descended on the car, broken only by the muffled sound of the engine. Clay turned a corner onto a narrow street, then quickly made another right. Anchorman leaped out of the car with Finn immediately behind him. They both landed on their feet and took two running steps before diving behind one of a dozen cars parked in a solid line stretching down the entire block. Ricki had already rolled down her window, her body half hanging out of it. She shoved the rear passenger side door, slamming it shut and ducking back inside the car just as the black SUV rounded the corner behind them. Clay drove on and made another right back onto the main street.

"They're bound to notice we've lost a couple of passengers," Ricki said, her eyes glued to the side mirror.

"If they're any good at their jobs they will," Clay agreed. "I noticed them when we left Bernie's Hardware, so they probably picked us up at the hotel. I'm betting if they sat there most of the night waiting for us to make an appearance this morning, they'll stick with us now."

They drove at a leisurely pace along the street, occasionally slowing down even more as if they were looking for an address. Luckily, there wasn't enough traffic to make their lagging progress stand out like a neon light.

A minute later, Clay pointed to a sign up ahead. "There's the garage."

He pulled in, slowing as he turned onto the ramp leading up to the second floor.

"The SUV came in behind us," Ricki announced. She unbuttoned her jacket and withdrew the Glock from her shoulder holster.

"Do you see Anchorman and Finn anywhere?" Clay asked.

She shook her head but wasn't concerned. "They're here."

Clay held on to the wheel with one hand and withdrew his own Glock before backing into a parking space on the empty side of the upper floor. "Okay. Here we go."

Ricki nodded. "And here they come."

The SUV's driver executed a quick turn, stopping the heavy vehicle at a right angle behind the sedan, blocking it in. At Clay's nod, Ricki stepped out of the car, using the door as a shield, Clay doing the same thing on the driver's side. Her gun was up and aimed at the SUV's windshield, moving slightly when the passenger side door opened, tracking the man who stepped out. He also had a gun in his hand but was keeping it down by his side.

When the second man appeared, Clay called out. "Something we can do for you gentlemen?"

The driver, who had a short buzz cut and wore a leather bomber jacket, smiled at Clay. "We just want to talk."

"You could have done that back at the restaurant," Clay said in a mild, pleasant voice. "You didn't have to follow us all over town."

The man looked away for a moment. "Yeah. Well, sorry about that." He took another step away from the car. "I'm Mark, Chief Thomas." He didn't move his hands as he tilted his head to the side. "And that's my partner, Ron."

"Nice to meet you, Mark and Ron. Can't say I'm too surprised you knew my name."

"Yes, sir," Mark said. "But I'm not acquainted with your friend pointing that Glock at my partner."

"No problem. This is *my* partner, Special Agent James. Is that all you wanted to talk about?"

Mark did a double take. "Special Agent? Are you with the FBI?"

"Not usually," Ricki said politely. "Are you?"

"No, ma'am." Mark made a show of leaning slightly to the side. "Where are the other two guys who were with you?"

"Right behind you."

Mark froze at the sound of Finn's voice.

"Just so we're all clear on the matter, I'm also a special agent," Finn said in a voice bordering on cheerful. "My name's Sullivan, and I *am* with the FBI. My other friend here is not a special agent. As a matter of fact, he doesn't have a fancy title at all. But he was a Marine sniper, so I'm pretty sure if you move a muscle, he'll shoot you dead."

"Roger that," Anchorman said.

"Shit," Mark said under his breath, just loud enough to be

heard. He carefully lifted his hands until they were in plain view. "I'm going to put my gun away."

"You're going to put it on the ground," Clay corrected, his smile gone. "Slowly." His gaze shifted to the other man Ricki and Finn were watching. "You too."

Mark nodded and slowly bent over. "Put it down, Ron."

When both men complied, Ricki and Clay moved forward, kicking the guns out of reach and having the men turn around and put their hands on the hood of the car. Clay did a quick pat down for other weapons while Anchorman searched their SUV and Finn moved forward to help Ricki keep a close eye on the pair.

"Okay," Clay said when he was finished. "Lace your fingers behind your heads, then turn around."

"Is that really necessary, Chief? We only want to talk," Mark complained.

Anchorman lifted an amused brow. "I'm guessing your hearing is fine."

Without another word, both men laced their fingers together across the backs of their necks and turned to face Clay.

"So, gentlemen." Since there were three other guns still trained on the two men, Clay reholstered his Glock. He stood with his feet apart and arms crossed over his chest as he sighed theatrically. "We have a busy afternoon ahead of us. What did you want to talk about?"

"The two million dollars that went missing," Mark said. "We'd like to get it back."

Clay stroked a hand along his chin. "Do you two work for the CIA, by any chance? Or one of the other alphabet agencies in the federal government?"

Mark shook his head. "No, sir. We work for Hanover Industries. Mr. Kroker sent us."

"Hanover?" Clay's hand dropped back to his side. "The company that lost the two million in a robbery?"

"Yeah. The money, our CEO, and some good friends." The bitter note in Mark's voice was as clear as day.

Finn stepped around Ricki to confront the two men. "Sounds like you have a real beef with the guys who did that. Which wasn't us. So I'm confused. Is this little visit of yours personal or business?"

"Like I said, Mr. Kroker sent us."

"Hanover's chief operating officer," Ricki said, connecting the name to one of the FBI reports that Blake had sent. "The man who arranged for the armored car to meet Mr. Hanover at the airport."

"Mr. Kroker is the acting CEO until Hanover's son can take over the firm." Ron spoke for the first time. He was shorter than his more talkative partner and had a slight hook at the end of his nose, but still the same buzz cut and identical bomber jacket as Mark. "Those guys sabotaged the armored car, slaughtered our people, and stole our money. That's the short version. The longer one isn't as pretty."

"We've seen the pictures, and I get that you'd like your money back," Clay said. "But I still haven't heard how you knew we were here."

"The team in Washington told us." At the flash of anger on Clay's face, Mark wet his lips and slowly looked around the group. "The FBI informed us they'd received a request to identify Malone's prints, and they were sending an agent out to some place called Brewer in Washington to check it out. But right after we got that intel, our source dried up. He said the entire operation was under a lockdown on orders from way up the command chain. So Mr. Kroker thought we should have our own set of eyes and ears on scene to find out what was going on. They got there just as you were leaving and couldn't find out much of anything, then we got word that you were headed out to find Malone. We figured you were on your way here, so we came up from Dallas and waited." He glanced around again. "They didn't mention anyone else coming with you."

"Well, isn't that a shame." Clay's face hardened into stony lines. "I hate to disappoint you, but we aren't going to share any of that intel you're after, so it looks like your trip here was a waste of time. And if you try to follow us again, I'll see that you're locked up."

"We're in Kentucky," Mark snorted. "You can't do that here."

"No, *I* can't." Clay jerked a finger toward Finn. "But Mister FBI over here can."

Finn's lips stretched out into a wide smile. "I'd be glad to."

Mark didn't look at all happy even as he nodded. "Fine, fine. We'll head back to Dallas. But Mr. Kroker wanted us to relay a message when we got the chance." He gave a short laugh. "And this appears to be the only chance we're going to get." At Clay's patient stare, he sucked in a breath. "Mr. Kroker would like to talk to you."

Clay shrugged, reached into his jacket pocket and pulled out his card. Taking a few steps forward, he tucked it into the pocket of Mark's jacket. "I'm busy right now, but tell him to try me next week." He stepped back again. "Now why don't the two of you get back into that nice car of yours and take off? It's a long way back to Dallas."

Both men slowly lowered their hands, then walked to their SUV. Ron didn't say a word as he climbed into the passenger seat, loudly slamming the door behind him, which made Anchorman smile.

Mark hesitated before he got behind the wheel, looking back at Clay over the top of the open door. "It isn't just the money for any of us, Chief Thomas. Those men killed our friends when they didn't have to. No one was going to start a firefight over CIA money. So if you've found any of them, and are looking for the others, we'd be more than willing to help." He looked over his shoulder at Anchorman. "It looks like you've got at least one civilian on your team. A couple more wouldn't hurt."

Clay nodded. "I'll keep that in mind. Have a safe trip home. And tell Mr. Kroker, if he wants any cooperation from us, he'll remove his spies from my town." He made a sweeping gesture with his arm to include Ricki, Finn, and Anchorman. "If they're still hanging around when we get back, I can guarantee we'll find them."

Chapter Eighteen

The Whistle Stop looked like any other bar in the slightly run-down part of town. The train tracks that had supposedly inspired its name were a good quarter mile away, but on a clear, quiet night, it might still be possible to hear the faint grind of wheels rolling along steel tracks. Clay drove the sedan into the mostly deserted parking area next to the drab-looking building. Ricki counted three cars in the dirt-and-gravel lot and hoped one of them belonged to the elusive Hailey.

"So, how should we play this?" Finn asked from the back seat. "Do we go for the less-threatening female trying to coax information out of Hailey, or should we send in gorgeous Clay to dazzle her into telling him everything?"

"I'm kind of inclined to go with the second option," Anchorman said. "I've never seen a female fail to turn into complete mush around our chief of police." He grinned. "Except Ricki. Word has it she didn't notice him at all when he first showed up." He tapped a finger against his lips. "Come to think of it, Cheron didn't seem to notice him either."

"That's because our brilliant doctor prefers ugly," Clay said without turning around. "It's more interesting from a forensic viewpoint." Now he did turn his head to look at the two grinning men in the back seat. "I'll conduct the interview because it's my case. You two are just along for ballast, and because Ricki likes having you here. You're the entertainment."

Having already checked that her weapon was secured, and the small case with her ID, credit card, and folded bills was tucked away in her jacket pocket along with her badge, Ricki opened the car door. "I'm going inside. You three come along whenever you're through taking jabs at each other." She shut the car door with a firm snap, leaving her fiancé, surrogate brother, and temporary FBI partner to stare after her.

The place was as drab inside as it was out, with the only bow to the trains of a long-gone era being a gaudy replica of an old-fashioned steam whistle sitting on the counter in back of the bar, surrounded by liquor bottles. A beefy man with thick arms and dark hair hanging down to his shoulders stood behind the bar, reading a newspaper. The lone patron at the moment was seated on a stool at the middle of the counter. He had his hand on a long-necked bottle of beer and his eyes glued to the TV hanging in the corner.

Ricki's gaze slowly quartered the room. When she didn't see another female anywhere in the large square space, she walked over to one of the smaller tables near the center of the room. Unwinding the scarf from her neck, she draped it over the back of one of the two chairs, then sat down in the other. She'd barely had time to make herself comfortable when the rest of the team walked in.

Clay took a seat at a larger table, in between Ricki and the door, while Anchorman and Finn split up and headed for stools at opposite ends of the bar. The man who'd been watching TV glanced at Anchorman, who simply stared back at him. The lone patron then slowly rotated his head to meet Finn's steady gaze.

He carefully slid off his stool and dropped a bill on the counter. "I'll see you later, Frank." He didn't wait for the bartender's nod before making a beeline to the door.

Frank watched him flee, then set his newspaper aside and got to his feet. "Get out here, Hailey. You've got customers," he yelled as he walked over to stand in front of Finn. "What can I get you?"

The FBI agent pointed at the bottle abandoned by the customer on his hasty exit. "I'll have one of those."

The bartender bent over and plucked a bottle from a tub of ice underneath the counter. He opened it, then set it down in front of Finn. "You look like a cop."

Finn lifted the bottle and took a deep sip. "Good guess, but no prize." He jerked his head toward Clay. "He's the cop."

"Huh," Frank grunted, then pointed at Anchorman. "Well, I know he's either military or ex-military." He shifted his hand around to point at Ricki. "And she's just fine." His mouth split open to reveal a row of badly yellowed teeth.

A door set into the side wall opened and a middle aged woman with platinum-blond hair and heavy makeup around her eyes walked into the room, still tying a red apron around her waist. She stopped and blinked at the four people scattered around the open area before making her way to the bar and scooping up a small tray. Frank pointed at Clay and mouthed "cop", which had her making an annoyed face back at him before heading toward Ricki.

"What can I get for you?" Her voice was smooth, with a hint of the South in it, as she politely looked at Ricki with light blue eyes.

"Whatever beer you have on tap," Ricki said, deciding to

risk one of the bar's glasses, hoping it was cleaner than the table which had a slightly sticky residue coating its top.

"Lager or an ale?"

"Lager, thank you," she told the waitress. "And the same for the gentleman at the table behind me."

Hailey glanced at Clay. "Are the two of you together, or are you buying him a beer because you hope to be?" She cocked her head to the side and gave Clay a good once-over. "He definitely looks like he'd be worth taking a run at." She shrugged and took a firmer grip on her tray. "I'll be back in a minute."

Ricki kept an eye on Hailey, pulling her cell phone from her pocket as she did. She tapped the record icon and set the phone on the table, covering it with her folded scarf. While the waitress retrieved a bottled beer for Anchorman, then filled two tall glasses from a tap behind the bar, Ricki took out her small wallet and covered it with one hand as she pretended to look around. She caught Frank staring but ignored both him and the naked leer in his eyes. When Hailey returned, giving Clay his beer first and then swinging by her table, Ricki smiled. "It's quiet here. That's nice."

Hailey shrugged. "Easy on the nerves, but hard on my bank account."

"I imagine." Ricki opened the wallet and took out three twenty-dollar bills. She laid them side by side on the table then looked up at Hailey. "Maybe I can help you with that."

The waitress stared, open-mouthed, at the money, before slowly raising her gaze to meet Ricki's. "Why? Are you my long-lost sister or something?"

Since they couldn't have looked more different, Ricki laughed. "No, nothing like that. I just want to buy a little conversation." She pointed at the empty chair on the opposite side of the small table. "Have a seat. This won't take long." From the corner of her eye, she saw Frank scowl and open his mouth, only to close it again when Finn leaned over the bar top and said a few quiet words.

Hailey saw the exchange, too, and with a smug look, pulled out the chair and sat down. She swept up the twenty-dollar bills and neatly folded them before tucking them into the large pocket on the front of her apron. Clasping her hands together and resting them on the table, she smiled at Ricki. "Okay. What did you want to talk about?"

"A mutual acquaintance."

"You must live around here," Hailey said, "because I've never been anywhere much outside of Hopkinsville. But I don't remember seeing you before."

"I've never been here before. I live in a town called Brewer. That's in Washington," Ricki said.

"DC or the state?"

Ricki smiled. "The state."

"Well then, I doubt if we have, what did you call it? A mutual acquaintance?"

Ricki pulled her badge out and set it on the table. "Preston Malone."

Hailey's eyes almost popped out of her head at the gold glint of the badge, even in the dim light inside the bar. "Geez, geez. Are you with the FBI or something?"

"For the moment," Ricki said.

The waitress peeked over at Clay. "Are all of you cops? Because I don't know any Preston Malone. I mean, if he came in here one or two times to have a drink, I don't remember him." She held up her right hand with the palm out. "Honest."

"You might know him better as Patrick Murray. Medium height, lanky build with dark blond hair and brown eyes. Ring any bells?"

Hailey's mouth dropped open and her eyes widened, this time with shock. "Patrick? You're here about Patrick? What about him? He left three years ago with barely a word, and I haven't seen him since." Her gaze dropped to Ricki's left hand. "Are you two a thing and going to get married?" The shock drained from her voice, only to be replaced by anger. "Did he send you here to apologize for just taking off that way and leaving me high and dry when we were about to move in together? He left me stuck with the lease on the place we'd just rented, and boy, did I have so much fun wiggling out of that. Getting a ring out of him is a lot more than I got, so congratulations to you."

Ricki let her go on with her list of injuries that the big jerk, Patrick Murray, had inflicted on her. When she wound down, Ricki leaned forward. "We're not engaged, and I'm not here to apologize for him. I need to know if you've heard from Patrick at all since he walked out on you."

"Oh sure." Sarcasm fairly dripped from Hailey's mouth. "Two whole letters in three years. I got the last one about a year ago, and not a peep since. Not even a postcard. All he said in that last letter was that I should hold tight, and that in a year we'd be sitting in sun and sand, just like he promised. Sun and sand, that's what he said, as if there's a lot of that up in Wash—" She clamped her mouth shut, cutting off her words. Her eyes narrowed into a suspicious look. "You said you're from Washington?"

Ricki nodded. "That's right. And apparently you knew Patrick was living there too. Did he tell you that?"

"Of course not," Hailey snapped. "Didn't I just say he never wrote anything solid in either of those letters? It was on the postmark. He couldn't control what the US Post Office stamped on the envelope, now could he?"

"And he told you something was going to happen in the next year?" Underneath the table, Ricki's boot began to tap.

"Sun and sand," Hailey repeated, her voice turning bitter.

"But I'd heard that tune before. Just you wait, babe. We'll be living it up where there's lots of sun and sand. He'd say that all the time." She looked off into the distance. "And stupid me. I believed him. Then one day, I walked into his place unannounced. I thought we'd go out and celebrate signing that new lease, and maybe I'd help him start packing up for the move." She looked at Ricki again as her hands clenched into fists on the table. "Oh, he was packing all right. He had that ratty old duffel from his army days open on the bed, and he was stuffing clothes into it like he was late catching a plane or something. I thought he was running out on me. When I asked him what was going on, he said he had to get out of town, but he'd be back as soon as he could. He told me he had to go see a sick friend who wasn't going to last much longer. And I knew, just knew, that was a line of bull and he wasn't coming back. So I begged him to stay." Her lips curled into a sneer. "Begged, mind you. But he just closed that crappy duffel bag and walked out the door. Let me tell you, I went to bed crying every single night for six months until that first letter came. But I never cried again after I read it." She opened one of her fisted hands and slapped a palm against the table. "He said he was so sorry, but he'd gotten word that there was a glitch, and he couldn't come back for a while." She slapped the tabletop again. "A glitch. What was that supposed to mean? And then he said he'd lost a magpie. Now what kind of glitch involves a magpie? That's a bird. He's never had a bird, so how could he lose one?"

"Those are the exact words that he wrote?" Ricki interrupted. "I lost a magpie?"

Hailey's nose and mouth scrunched up. "I don't know. I think so. It was something about losing one. I couldn't figure it out." She subsided a little as she sank into her chair. "Don't get me wrong. I'm not some stone-cold bitch or anything. I'm real sorry if he did have a sick friend and all, but how long was I supposed to wait?"

"It doesn't sound like Patrick Murray treated you fairly at all," Ricki said with a sympathetic smile as she filed the name "Magpie" away. "And you didn't hear from him again until that second letter about a year ago?"

"That's right. But by then it was too late for him. I had a new guy. Lenny is the nice and steady kind. You know the type? Not much to look at, maybe, but a big heart, and he treats me really well. He might never get out of Hopkinsville, but he won't run out on me either, and that counts for a lot. He's even mentioned marriage a couple of times, which is more than Patrick ever did."

Despite Hailey's defiant tone, there was still vulnerability and hurt in her eyes. *Hasn't been able to put Patrick completely behind her yet*, Ricki thought. A part of Hailey Dickson would probably be waiting for Patrick Murray for the rest of her life. Unless she was convinced there was no chance he'd ever be coming back.

Ricki leaned forward and kept her voice low. "Hailey? That man behind me is a police chief, and he used to be a homicide cop. We aren't looking for Patrick. We're here searching for a lead on the man who shot him."

Hailey's gaze jumped to Clay. "Homicide? Like in murder?" Her eyes slowly returned to Ricki. "Patrick is dead?" What little color she had faded away, leaving her face a chalky white. "What happened? Did Patrick rob a bank or something?" She stared at Ricki for a horrified moment. "He did, didn't he? I thought he'd made that up to impress me. And he was really drunk at the time, so I didn't believe him. Now you're saying he really did?"

"We believe he was involved in a robbery that left five people dead."

"Oh good lord," Hailey gasped, even as both hands covered her mouth. "Patrick killed five people?"

"We aren't sure who pulled the trigger, but he was definitely part of the robbery. They got away with two million dollars."

"Two million?" Now the waitress gasped. She looked wildly around the room, looking for an escape. "If you're here about that money, I don't know anything about it. If Patrick Murray had millions of dollars, he sure never shared any of it with me." Fear settled on her whole body like a blanket and her hands shook.

Ricki reached out and grabbed one of them, holding on and giving it a squeeze hard enough that Hailey tried to jerk it away. "We don't think you had anything to do with the robbery, or hiding the money for Patrick." Ricki gave Hailey's hand another squeeze. "Do you hear me? You aren't in any trouble."

The other woman blinked several times and then slowly nodded. When her body visibly relaxed, Ricki released her hand. "We're here searching for the man who killed Patrick. Finding stolen money is the FBI's job."

Hailey shook her head. "I thought you were the FBI."

Great, Ricki thought. "Another branch of the FBI," she amended. "Is there anything else you can tell me about Patrick Murray? Any idea where he went after he left Hopkinsville?"

The waitress let out a tired sigh. "I told you. He said he had to go see a sick friend." She frowned. "An old army friend." She looked at Ricki and nodded. "Yeah. He said it was an old army friend." She hung her head as she pushed away from the table and slowly stood up. "I don't remember anything else. I'm sorry." She mumbled the last words before turning on her heel and running toward the door in the side wall. She opened it with a hard jerk, stepped across the threshold, and slammed the door behind her.

Ricki turned and looked at Clay, shrugging before picking up her scarf with her phone buried in the folds and getting to her feet. Stuffing the scarf and phone into her pocket, she headed for the door with Clay right behind her. It only took a minute for all four of them to get back into the car and be on their way to the hotel.

"From the look on Hailey's face, I'm guessing you broke the news about Malone being shot to death," Clay said.

"And we all heard her say she had nothing to do with the money," Finn added.

"It seems Malone ran out on her three years ago. She doesn't know where he went, except he claimed he had to visit a sick friend. An old army buddy. And from the way Hailey described it, it sounds like this buddy of his was dying."

"Did she have any idea where he was taking his last breath?" Finn asked.

"Nope. But she did get a couple of letters from Malone. In the first one he mentioned a magpie, and a warning about some kind of glitch. The postmark on the last one was from Washington."

Finn let out a snort. "A glitch? Interesting way to look at a half dozen FBI agents hot on your trail." He ran a distracted hand through his hair. "We suspected there was a leak somewhere. The robber's information was too good."

"A magpie?" Clay shook his head. "Isn't that a bird?"

"Yep." Ricki reached into her pocket and withdrew the scarf. Unwrapping her cell phone, she held it up. "I recorded our conversation. You can all hear it when we get back to the hotel." She stared out the front windshield without really noticing anything as she silently went back over the conversation with Hailey. "If we assume this old army buddy was one of the three men who ambushed the guys from Hanover, then there's a high probability that the third guy was also in the army with them at some point."

"That wouldn't be a big leap," Clay agreed. "So, what are you thinking?"

"I'm thinking that Dan is an expert at this kind of research. I already sent him Sam Parkman's and Preston Malone's military files from Blake, and he said he put in a request to a friend of his to get a more detailed record. Let's tell him what Hailey said and set him loose to find the army connection between the two men, and look for any mention of a possible third."

"Sounds good." Clay made the turn into the hotel parking lot. "In the meantime, we have a flight back to Seattle at seven tomorrow morning. And an hour's drive to get to the airport in Nashville in order to catch it. I say we have an early dinner and get some rest."

Ricki smiled. "And I say that also sounds good."

Chapter Nineteen

Ricki was still yawning when she and Clay entered the hotel lobby at a few minutes past five the next morning. It was dark outside, and rain was drizzling down the panes of the front windows. The drive to Nashville was going to be wet. She pulled out her phone and sent a quick text to Anchorman and Finn while Clay walked over to the front desk and dropped their room key into the open slot in the desk's top that was designated for early checkouts.

When the lobby doors opened, Ricki glanced in their direction, staring in surprise. Hailey's blue eyes peeked out from underneath the hood of a bright orange plastic rain poncho. She took two steps into the lobby then stopped, chewing her bottom lip as rainwater steadily dripped from her poncho onto the tiled floor.

When the waitress didn't move any closer, Ricki took several steps forward until she was standing directly in front of Hailey. "Hi. I'm surprised to see you here." She glanced at her watch. "Especially at this hour of the morning."

"Yeah. I'm kind of surprised to be here." Hailey lowered the hood of her poncho and looked back over her shoulder. "I can't stay long. Lenny's in the car waiting for me." She returned her gaze to Ricki. "Christian came into the bar yesterday and told me where you were staying. He also kept pestering me to tell him what we talked about."

"Did you tell him?" Ricki asked.

"No." Hailey smiled. "I've been brushing him and his hands off for years. But he got me to thinking. With Patrick dead and all, there wasn't any reason to hold on to that part of my past. So last night, while Lenny was out on a late towing job, I got out all the pictures and little gifts Patrick gave me. You know, that stuff you keep as a kind of memento? Anyway, I had most of it in an old shoe box, but now it's all in the trash." She flipped up the edge of her poncho and reached into the back pocket of her jeans to pull out a folded envelope. "Except this." She stared down at it. "I was so angry I ripped up that last letter he sent me and tossed it into the garbage bin at the Circle K down on Main Street. But I never got rid of the first one he sent, after he'd been gone for six months." She looked up again and nodded at Ricki. "Do you remember I told you about that?"

Ricki returned the nod. "I remember."

"Okay." Hailey shuffled her feet. "I was sure you'd be leaving early, because that's when a lot of the planes going west head out of Nashville. And that's the closest airport that has the big jets going all over." She huffed out a quick laugh. "I used to look up all kinds of airline schedules whenever I was planning my escape from Hopkinsville. But I don't think I'll be doing that anymore." She held out the envelope. "So here."

Ricki took the neatly folded square and tucked it into her jacket pocket. "Thank you. I appreciate this very much."

Hailey shrugged then flipped the hood of her poncho back over her head. "If it isn't any help to you, then just throw it away. I don't want it back." She made a half turn before looking back at Ricki, a smile on her face. "I have to go. Lenny's waiting for me."

"I'm glad he is." Ricki returned the waitress's smile. "Have a good life, Hailey."

Hailey laughed. "Thanks. Now that I have my head on straight, I intend to."

As the young woman slipped through the front doors and back out into the rain, Clay came up to Ricki. "What was that all about?"

"Something that might be a big help in tracking down Marcie's brother." Ricki patted her pocket. "She gave me the first letter Malone sent her after he left Hopkinsville to visit his sick army friend."

"Who could have been the real Sam," Clay said. "The second letter had a postmark on it. Are you hoping the first one will too?"

"Yeah. And that it doesn't say something like New York City." She spotted Finn and Anchorman exiting the elevator, each carrying a duffel bag. "I'll take a look at it once we're on our way."

The next few minutes were spent loading the car in the increasingly heavy rain. Dripping wet, Ricki climbed into the back seat, along with Clay, while Anchorman took the wheel. As soon as they reached the interstate highway, Ricki pulled out the envelope from Hailey. She gently unfolded it, careful to hold it away from her damp jacket, and smiled in satisfaction when she spotted the postmark stamped across the upper right-hand corner. Both Finn in the front seat and Clay sitting next to her were watching as her smile spread across her face.

"Well?" Clay leaned over and squinted at the envelope. "Is that an NE?"

"It sure is. Nebraska. Omaha, to be more specific." Ricki removed the letter inside, then handed the envelope to Clay.

"Omaha?" Finn's voice rose a notch in surprise. "That was Sam Parkman's last posting. To the recruiting station there. And you're saying he was still in Omaha just three years ago?" He pretended to slap an open palm against his forehead. "With an entire country to pick from, Malone hangs around the town closest to his last posting, and so does Parkman. These guys sure don't believe in traveling too far." He leaned back in his seat and stretched his long legs out. "Unless they plan on stealing a couple million dollars. It seems they were willing to travel for that."

Clay handed the empty envelope back to Ricki. "Anything useful in the letter?"

"Not really." Ricki folded it up again and slid it back into the envelope. "It's pretty much the way Hailey related it to me back in the bar. He talks about a magpie, then a glitch, and goes on to promise her sun and sand." She tapped a finger against the armrest built into the door. "I wonder exactly where he had in mind to enjoy all that sun and sand he kept talking about."

"The Caymans would be my first guess," Finn said. "It's a good place to park money you don't want to be asked any questions about. There's plenty of sun and sand there. And if you move the money in small increments, like we talked about, he would have increased his odds of flying under the federal radar. All he'd need is the cover of some shell or bogus company if he's doing a wire transfer." He paused. "Or if you're worried about any bills in a cash deposit being traced, you could smuggle out the actual cash by boat or a small plane."

Ricki's interest immediately perked up. "How hard would that be?"

"If you aren't too obvious about it, not that hard, I suppose. But it's not a cakewalk either." The FBI agent frowned. "The coast guard patrols two hundred miles out, and they intercept a fair amount of smugglers off the Florida and Gulf coasts." Now he shrugged. "Even though it's not like the big oceans, there's still a lot of water out there in the Caribbean. If you're careful, plan well, and up your odds with some decent intel on the locations of the coast guard ships, you could move the cash."

"Then why do it in chunks of less than ten grand apiece?" Anchorman asked. "Why wouldn't they have smuggled the whole thing at once?"

"To keep the people they're bribing and paying off to help from getting too greedy themselves," Finn stated with a nod. "I think we've already talked about there being no honor among thieves."

"We know they're careful and plan well," Ricki said, going back to the list that Finn had recited. "And since they knew about the money, and when it would be arriving back in the States, not to mention knowing when to tip Malone off about the FBI heading his way, I'd say they have a pretty solid inside track somewhere.

"They might be using multiple methods to get the money out of the country," Finn said. "And stagger the routines over a year. Rinse and repeat for seven years, and presto. The money is offshore and no one is the wiser."

"No might about it," Clay said. "However they're doing it, they have gotten away with it. And the timing of Malone's murder is making sense. It's coming up on that seven-year mark, and it's looking like one of the other partners is getting greedy."

"Yeah." Ricki leaned back in her seat and closed her eyes. "That sounds about right." *But the* how *does matter*, she thought before dropping into sleep.

The next thing she knew, someone was gently shaking her shoulder. She opened one bleary eye and focused it on the person's face.

"Ricki. We need to get going."

Clay's voice was close enough to stir the fine strands of hair next to her ear. "Okay. I'm awake." She yawned and sat up.

The sun was definitely shining, and the rain had disappeared. The sedan was cruising along the roadway approaching the airport. Anchorman followed the signs to the car rental return, parking in the spot the lot attendant was pointing at.

Clay stepped out of the sedan and moved to the trunk. As soon as the lid popped open, he reached in and pulled out canvas overnight bags, tossing them on the ground. Ricki stretched her back as she walked over and joined the others crowded around the back of the car. She reached down to pick up her bag, but Anchorman beat her to it.

"I've got it. You concentrate on what's bugging your fiancé. He got a phone call while you were asleep and has been simmering about something ever since," he said in a low voice before moving off.

Ricki immediately frowned. What was Anchorman talking about? Walking next to Clay, she slipped her hand into his and then deliberately dragged her feet, putting some extra distance between the two of them and the others. When she gauged them to be out of earshot, she looked at Clay. His expression was like stone, and he hadn't said a word since he'd prodded her awake. Anchorman was right. Something was definitely bugging him.

"You got a phone call while I was asleep?" she ventured.

"Did one of our helpful sidekicks tell you that?" he asked, without looking at her.

"Something you don't want me to know about?"

"No." He snapped his mouth shut, then let out a large breath. "I meant I don't have a problem with you knowing about the call," he said in a much milder tone. "I just haven't figured it out." When she silently waited, he shrugged. "The call was from Jules, and something is going on back home. I just don't know what."

A niggle of alarm shot through Ricki's stomach. "Is everyone okay? Marcie?"

"She's fine, and I specifically asked," Clay said. "Along with asking about Ryan, TK, and even Bear. Jules said everyone is okay."

Puzzled, Ricki shook her head. "Then why do you think something is wrong?" She waited for an answer while he ushered her into the security line. They breezed right through, despite having to show paperwork for their weapons. When they were on the concourse, headed for their gate, Ricki repeated her question. "What set your cop warning signal off?"

Clay smiled, but the smile quickly faded. "The fact my senior deputy called and wanted to know when we'd be back. And he sounded damned relieved when I said we were on our way and would be home before noon."

"Maybe it makes him nervous to be in charge," Ricki said, thinking of the very easygoing Jules Tucker. The job of chief had come up twice since he'd joined the force, and not once had the lanky deputy ever expressed an interest in it. She might have been in her teens and not paying all that close attention the first time, but she remembered when Clay had been hired. Jules had been the former homicide cop's number one backer to the city council.

"He's been in charge before," Clay replied. "And I've never gotten a call like that. Not in that voice. He sounded close to panic and practically hung up on me when I asked him about it." He guided her toward an empty section in the waiting area, where they both took a seat. "Whatever the problem is, I need to get there and sort it out."

Since she couldn't argue with that, Ricki nodded, then settled back to wait for their flight to be called.

It was another thirty minutes before they were on the plane and lumbering down the taxiway toward the takeoff point. Once they were in the air, Ricki pulled up a book on her phone and read, letting Clay brood for a while. About halfway home, she thought he'd had enough time to think things over. "What are the next steps on our case? We have a lot of bits and pieces we need to pull together."

Shifting in his seat, Clay took her hand in his and gave it a gentle squeeze. "Are you trying to distract me?"

"Yes." She smiled. "And it was either the case, or a discussion about wedding plans."

He lifted their joined hands and placed a kiss on the back of her knuckles. "Honey, I really don't care what there is to eat, the number of people we invite, or if there are any flowers at all."

Ricki sighed. The truth of the matter was, she didn't care about any of that either. She'd already done it up big the first time around. Simple and meaningful sounded better now, and more suited to both of them. The problem was getting Marcie, and the rest of the town for that matter, to buy into the idea. Even her son had said he was looking forward to a big party. Shaking the problem of the wedding off, she turned to one that was more urgent.

"Okay. Then let's talk murder. Who killed Preston Malone?"

"Since no one in Hopkinsville mentioned he was having trouble with something, or had a big gambling debt or some other run-in with someone who might want to bump him off, I'm going to have to go with one of his partners in crime."

"And we're back to no honor among thieves," Ricki quipped. "So if we interpret Malone's comment to mean he only needed another year before he'd be set up to enjoy life where there's sun and sand, then we have to assume the bulk of the money has already been moved to an untraceable, offshore account."

"Since we know the CIA can trace that money, and something tells me they can do it on American soil without any help from the FBI, then it seems the bad guys have been sitting on that pile of cash for almost seven years," Clay said. "Moving it out of the country slowly would explain why they were still hanging around. They can buy help to make the transfers to the Caymans, but who could they trust to manage the bulk of the cash sitting on this end? If I were a careful man, I'd stick around and do it myself."

"Which brings up an interesting question." At Clay's raised eyebrow, Ricki shrugged. "Who set up that elaborate money transfer scheme?

Clay's eyebrows drew together when he frowned. "Who indeed? Because if the fake Sam is anything like the real Sam, and given the fact that no one in town, including his own sister, could tell them apart, then I have some serious doubts that either of them could have cooked up that scheme."

"Or the one for the robbery," Ricki pointed out. "Which means we're still missing the leader." She sighed and stared out the portal that served as a window. "And if Sam was dying three years ago, the way Malone implied to Hailey, unless that glitch he talked about was some kind of miraculous recovery, then the leader is also the last man standing."

"And now the entire two million is his." Clay pressed his lips into a thin line. "At least it will be once the whole amount is moved, if it hasn't been already."

"So all we have to do is figure out who and where he is."

Clay leaned his head back and closed his eyes. "That's about the gist of it."

Ricki returned to looking out the window, watching the clouds below the aircraft move off to the east, creating a picture of white cotton candy in slow motion. "Wonderful," she muttered. "We're searching for a needle in a haystack with a ticking clock behind us." Her shoulders tensed, and she had to work at keeping her boot from doing its staccato tap against the floor of the plane. But there wasn't anything she could do to change the cold, hard fact that when the clock ran out, their killer would be gone for good.

Chapter Twenty

Ricki waved goodbye to Clay, watching until his SUV disappeared around the bend in her driveway. Mentally crossing her fingers that he could untangle whatever it was that Jules was wrestling with, she picked up her duffel and headed for the house. Having done his usual loud and frenzied greeting, Corby trotted along beside her as she walked past the small blue sedan parked behind her jeep. If Dan and his car were here, that meant Marcie was as well. She smiled to herself. It was nice to have a welcoming committee when you returned from a trip. Even if you were only gone for one day.

She was about to climb the two steps up to the porch when the door was opened by one of the two members of her ad hoc welcoming committee. "Hey, Dan." When he held out his arm, she handed over her travel bag. "I'm glad you're here. I want to talk to you about some research."

"Not a problem."

When he slowed his pace to a crawl, Ricki sent him a

puzzled glance. "Is there something you want to talk to me about?"

"Yeah. Marcie. She's inside and needs to talk to you." At Ricki's resigned look, he smiled. "Not about the wedding. We came over to your place because she needed to hide out."

Ricki stopped and put her hands on her hips. "Hide out? From who?" Her eyes narrowed as she studied Dan's face. "Did she get a threat of some kind?"

Dan shifted her bag from one hand to the other as he shook his head. "Not exactly."

"Then what, *exactly*, is going on?" Ricki's boot started tapping. "First Jules calls, making it clear that Clay needed to come back to the Bay, but he wouldn't say why, and now Marcie feels the need to hide out? What's going on, Dan?"

Her fellow ISB agent sighed. "If I were back in the spy business, I'd say it was a flood of misinformation designed to rile people up."

"What?" Ricki stared at him as if he was speaking an alien language. "I have no idea what you're talking about."

"Talking is the problem." Dan started walking toward the cabin where Corby was already sitting by the front door, patiently waiting for the lagging humans. "Marcie can explain it to you," he said over his shoulder, then climbed the porch steps.

Ricki followed him, her gaze shooting straight to Marcie as soon as she'd stepped into the cabin. The waitress was sitting at the kitchen island, sipping from a mug with steam rolling off the top. Without any hesitation, Ricki walked over and sat down on the stool next to her. Marcie watched her with a gaze that looked more annoyed than troubled, which was a relief. At least whatever was going on here wasn't scaring the older woman. "What's up?" Ricki asked in an even voice.

"This town." Marcie's voice was flat. "It's enough to make a body move into Seattle with her underhanded lover."

Momentarily speechless, Ricki's mouth dropped open and she blinked in surprise. "Is . . ." She trailed off and shot a sideways look at Dan, then cleared her throat. "Um, would that be Dan?"

Marcie bounced her head in a hard nod. "Oh yes. Beside committing the very scandalous sin of staying at my house every weekend, with only a murderer for a sometimes chaperon, it's clear he's using me as a smokescreen so he can spy on the whole town and run interference for you and Clay. And oh, did I mention that there is absolutely no possible way that a former homicide cop would not have known that Sam was a murderer? I mean, heavens." Marcie paused to make an exaggerated show of batting her eyes. "It must be so horrible to be told your own brother, who really wasn't your brother at all but some kind of impostor, had killed so many people. But even worse to know that your best friends had raced all the way to Kentucky to gather evidence on him, which will probably be destroyed. Or maybe stored away in Dr. Garrison's lab with the rest of it, so you can all decide together how to dispose of it." She made a face, and Ricki could almost see the steam coming out of her ears. "Because all of you are in on covering up for a murderer. Why, that completely explains Anchorman's weird attraction to the very plain Cheron. It's all an act to cover up your conspiracy."

Ricki sucked in a quick breath, her thoughts swirling like a whirlpool, and disappearing down a drain just as fast. In sheer self-defense she held up both hands. "Hang on a minute. Just hang on. Who was saying all this crap to you?"

Marcie's upper lip curled in disgust. "Crap is the right word for it. And my phone hasn't stopped ringing since the three of you left. Almost every caller wanted to know what I knew about you, Clay, and Cheron concocting a smokescreen, along with the FBI, of course, to keep everyone from knowing the truth about my murderous brother." She slapped a palm on the island's counter. "Even the vultures I ran into at the market were very sure about you three, and Finn to boot, but the opinion was split on Anchorman. Some of them were so, so sure that he'd been tricked into going along with all this because of his loyalty to you." When Ricki gawked at her, she nodded again. "That's right. You're all in on it. And it was also made very clear, in the most sympathetic voices, of course, that you weren't entirely to blame since Clay used his amazing good looks to seduce you into being part of the whole cover-up, just like Dan seduced me so he could keep me under control and I'd not go snooping around."

Ricki turned her head and lifted a disbelieving eyebrow at Dan, who answered with a shrug.

"Yeah. That's what I thought too. I've never been known as the seductive type. But I guess there's a first for everything," he said.

His practical tone, seasoned with just a sprinkling of sarcasm, was like a mental slap, snapping Ricki out of her daze. She reached over and grabbed both of Marcie's hands, holding them firmly in her own. "Just stop." When Marcie cut off in mid-sentence and stared at her, Ricki gave her friend's trembling hands a squeeze. "I want to hear this slowly. Can you do that?" She waited while Marcie drew in several long breaths, blowing them out and then sucking more air in until her breathing evened out and her cheeks lost most of the bright red that had created streaks across her broad face. "Okay," Ricki said in a low voice. "Let's start at the beginning. Clay, Anchorman, Finn, and I left, and you started getting these phone calls about us and a conspiracy?"

"That's right. You should have heard—" Marcie's words

were cut off again when Ricki clamped down on her hands like a vise.

"Slowly," she reminded the waitress. "When did the calls start coming?"

Marcie's expression changed in a blink from angry to confused. "When? I'm not sure what you mean?"

"How soon after we left did you get the first caller wanting to gossip?"

The waitress jerked back, snatching her hands away. "This wasn't just gossip, Ricki James. It worked itself into a lynch mob. Even some woman up in Massey that I barely say hello to in church called and wanted to know if it was true that my brother wasn't the only killer being harbored in the Bay. That's when I turned off my cell phone, unplugged my landline, and escaped over here just in case the crazies started dropping by when they couldn't get me on the phone."

As much as she didn't feel like it, Ricki tried a smile. "I'm surprised there wasn't a warning sign posted at the end of my driveway." When Marcie only flopped back in her seat, Ricki looked over at Dan. "Were you with Marcie when the first call came in?"

"Yes, and it was no more than a couple of hours after you left." Dan looked down at his hands as if he suddenly realized he was still holding Ricki's bag. He walked over to the stairs and set it on the bottom step. Returning to the kitchen island, he stood behind Marcie, his hands on her shoulders. "One call came in, and then another. By yesterday afternoon it had built into a tsunami, with each wave getting more absurd, carrying just enough specific tidbits here and there to raise alarm bells all over town."

Ricki thought that over for a moment before nodding and turning back to Marcie. "Did more than one person call the fake Sam your murderous brother?" When Marcie dismissed the question with a wave, Ricki shot her a stern look. "Marcie, this is important. Think. Did more than one person claim he was a murderer?"

Marcie's eyebrows slowly drew together. "Yes. I heard it at least five, maybe six times. I can't be sure."

"How about his name?" Ricki pressed. "Did anyone call the impostor Preston Malone?"

Marcie looked taken aback. "No, of course not. You swore us all to secrecy, and I'm sure none of us would have blabbed that around town."

Ricki nodded. "Okay. Then you're sure the only other way anyone referred to Sam was as the impostor, and never by his real name?"

"I'm sure."

"And who said that we had run off to Kentucky to look for evidence?" Ricki asked. When Marcie's eyes reflected her misery, Ricki softened her tone. "Did you hear that more than one time?"

The waitress chewed her lower lip for a long moment. "Yes. At least a couple of times. I remember Merlin mentioning it, but not in a mean way. She just asked if I knew how long you'd be in Kentucky. Someone else said that you'd run off to collect evidence there that you intended to get rid of, because the FBI didn't want anyone to know who the fake Sam really was."

When Marcie rubbed two fingers against her temple, Ricki slid off her stool and went over to a cabinet next to the refrigerator. She retrieved a bottle of aspirin, then filled a glass with water and carried both back to Marcie. "Here. Take a couple of these, then go upstairs and lie down for a while. Dan and I will track down what's going on here and calm everything down. You just concentrate on getting some rest."

Her friend and business partner didn't put up a word of argument, but let Dan help her off the stool and then walked with him to the stairs. When they were out of earshot, Ricki grabbed her phone and called Clay.

He answered on the second ring, his voice snapping out, "Is it important? I have a mess I'm trying to untangle here."

"If it has to do with wild rumors going around town, then I've been listening to the same mess for the last thirty minutes."

"From who?"

"Marcie," Ricki said in a clipped tone. "And in all the bull-shit dumped on her, there were some interesting facts that no one should have known. And knowing Dan, I'm sure he has a theory about all this."

"Really?" There was a drawn-out silence before Clay sighed. "I have a stack full of complaints, with a big chunk of them bordering on accusations, but nothing I would call a fact. So I'd like to hear those, along with any theory that Dan might have. Give me twenty minutes to get my deputies squared away here and I'll join you. Are you still at the cabin?"

"Yeah. I'll call Anchorman and Finn and find out if they've been hit with the same rumors."

"Good idea. I'd like to hear about that too. See you in twen-ty," Clay repeated, then hung up.

Ricki did the same and called Anchorman and Finn, who both promised to head her way. She finished her calls just as Dan came back down the stairs.

"Marcie fell asleep the minute her head hit the pillow." Dan smiled with relief as he walked over and sat on a stool next to Ricki. "Hearing that you were going to put a stop to all this nonsense took a big load off her mind, although I think that's a lot easier said than done. She wasn't exaggerating much when she said it was turning into a lynch mob."

"Which I'm sure is the reason Jules put in that call to Clay." Ricki drummed her fingers against the countertop. "So the gossip mill knew Sam was an impostor, which was out before we left town. But they don't know his real name? No one mentioned Malone's name?"

"Not that I know of. It also got out that the body was stolen," Dan said. "Marcie forgot to mention it, but I overheard that one."

"You're kidding." Ricki's eyes widened. "That was only known by a very small group, none of which can I see breaking their promise to keep it quiet."

"Maybe they aren't aware that they did let it out," Dan suggested. "A note in a chart, or a piece of conversation overheard, could have triggered that piece of gossip."

"So one of the group got careless within hours of making that promise, and it got all over town in a day?" Ricki shook her head. "I'm not buying it."

"Me either," Dan admitted. "What else struck you as odd?"

"How did the mob, as you called it, know that Preston Malone was a murderer, but not know his name? Marcie said outright that one caller claimed that the fake Sam had murdered so many people. Not one, but so many. Now how could they know that unless they also knew what happened during the robbery? And if they knew about the robbery, they would have to have known Malone's name."

"Maybe calling him a murderer was just a lucky fluke," Dan pointed out. "You know, someone said 'I'll bet he murdered people too', and someone else heard that and added it to their story until it became a truth as far as the mob was concerned." He nodded and reached for Marcie's coffee mug and took a sip. "It's happened that way often enough. A more vicious variation of the telephone game."

"Then Kentucky was a lucky guess too?" Ricki snorted. "A murderer who lived in Kentucky?"

"I saw Pete in the lobby manning the phone. Maybe he overheard Clay making your travel arrangements," Dan said.

"That would make sense, except we didn't decide to make the trip until we'd left the station and were back here. There was no way Pete could have overheard us. And Clay didn't tell either deputy exactly where he was going, just that he'd be out of town for a few days. Add to that the fact that Clay didn't make the travel arrangements. Finn did though the Bureau. No one else in town had any knowledge of our destination either."

Dan took another sip of cold coffee, then made a face. He made a move to get up from the stool but Ricki waved him back down again.

"I'll make it." At his pained look, she jerked her head toward the single-cup coffee maker sitting on the back counter, next to the stove. "In the machine." She reached into her pocket and withdrew the letter that Hailey had given her. "I got this from Hailey Dickson. She was Malone's girlfriend in Kentucky."

Dan's mouth dropped open. "You found her? So we won't have to go through all those old phone records Hamilton obtained for the case?"

Ricki's mouth formed into a half smile. "Thanks for the reminder. I'll put in my report that it helped verify her identity and her story." She set the letter on the island's top and slid it across to him. "I'll make the coffee while you read it."

"Okay." Dan picked up the letter and slowly looked over the front of the envelope. "Postmark is stamped Omaha, Nebraska." He looked up. "That's not Kentucky."

"No, it's not." Ricki dumped a cup of water into the coffee machine's well, then plucked a pod from the rack next to it and dropped it into the slot. "He took off with no warning, telling her he had to go see an old army friend who was sick and might not make it."

"Is that so?" His interest clearly piqued, Dan slid the single sheet of paper out of the envelope and carefully unfolded it. He didn't take his eyes away from the paper when Ricki set a mug of coffee in front of him, just murmured his thanks as he absently lifted the cup and took a quick sip.

Ricki made a second cup for herself, then turned and leaned against the counter next to the stove, waiting for Dan to finish. By the time he slowly refolded the letter and put it back inside the envelope, he could have read it three or four times. When he remained silent, she grew impatient. "Well? What do you think?"

"That he wasn't going back to Kentucky." Dan shot her a questioning look. "And he wrote this three years ago. Isn't that about the same time he showed up here?" When Ricki nodded, he stared at the letter he still held in his hands. "Do you have any brilliant thoughts on what the significance is of the magpie he mentioned?"

"Something that has a significance to Preston Malone." Ricki carried her coffee to the island and leaned over. Still holding her steaming mug, she rested her forearms on the smooth top of the counter. "That's what I thought it meant too. That Malone was referring to something. And that's the way Hailey described it. That her boyfriend had lost a magpie, which was a bird, or some kind of object." She waved her mug in the general direction of the letter. "But when I read it again, I noticed a minor difference between what I was thinking and what Malone actually wrote."

"Which was?" Dan asked.

"He didn't write that he'd lost 'a magpie'. He wrote that he'd lost 'Magpie', no 'a' in front of it, and he used a capital *M*. The way you write a person's name." She could almost see the lightbulb come on in Dan's head. "I think he was writing about someone, not something." She pushed away from the counter and began to pace. "Did you know Malone had a nickname? It was Buzzfeed."

Dan made a low grunting noise deep in his throat. "Yeah. I read it in the FBI notes, and that fits. He was an ace at communications equipment."

"Uh-huh," Ricki agreed, still slowly pacing across the kitchen floor. "A name he acquired during his time in the service. And he said he was going to see an old army buddy, who he then referred to as Magpie. A nickname that buddy of his most likely picked up in the army, too. Something that would fit him."

"Ah." Dan frowned at the letter. "A magpie is a bird. So maybe this guy was a pilot?" His frown deepened when Ricki snorted a quick laugh. "What? City boy here."

"But after the CIA you were a park ranger before you transferred into the ISB." Ricki grinned. "You had to have learned something about wildlife."

"I was assigned to Independence Square in the middle of Philadelphia. No magpies, that I recall," Dan said. "But I do know magpies are birds, so I assume they can fly."

Ricki rolled her eyes, but her smile stayed for another moment before gradually fading away. "Yeah. They can fly. But I don't think that's why Malone's buddy earned that name. Magpies are well known to clean up all kinds of bits and pieces, and mostly leftover kills, or bugs and ticks. In other words, they're scavengers."

"Okay. What else about . . ." Dan trailed off and his jaw dropped open. "Scavengers? Exactly the way Marcie described her brother?"

"That's right. I'm betting Preston went to Omaha to see his old army buddy, Sam Parkman."

Chapter Twenty-One

"What's this about Malone visiting Sam Parkman?" Clay asked. He'd opened the front door just in time to hear Ricki's pronouncement. He shoved the door closed with one arm, then stood a foot away from it, a frown on his face.

Ricki stopped pacing and set her coffee mug on the counter before walking over to give him a quick kiss. When she stepped back, her gaze roamed over his face. Her fiancé looked as if he'd reached the limit of his patience. "Do you want coffee or would you rather have a beer?"

"Beer. And I'll get it." He stepped around her and stalked over to the refrigerator. Grabbing a beer, he twisted off the top and took a long swallow before carrying it back to the island and pinning his gaze on Dan. "I feel like I've been sucked into an alternate universe. If you have some theory to explain the whole town falling into a cesspool of conspiracy theories over dead guys and nonexistent evidence, I'd sure like to hear it."

Dan nodded. "I mentioned to Ricki that if we were in my

old universe, this would be called a deliberate flood of misinformation to get everyone riled up."

"To what end?" Clay shot out. "It's hard to believe this whole whisper campaign wasn't cooked up by some annoying gossip. Like Pete." He stopped to take another sip of his beer and followed it with a deep breath. "It's damn destructive."

"And can get that way fast in a place the size of the Bay," Dan said. "Marcie has been hounded for the last twenty-four hours with people wanting to know where you were, and where Ricki and Anchorman were. She got asked why the FBI was in town, and if Cheron was hiding critical evidence in her lab at your request. Then there was the very popular speculation that you, Ricki, and Finn were conspiring to keep everyone in the dark about the fake Sam's real background."

"Which you'll be interested to know includes him being a murderer with multiple victims," Ricki put in, drawing Clay's gaze to her. "And being from Kentucky."

His eyebrows snapped together. "From Kentucky?" He turned his stare back to Dan. "Someone told Marcie that the fake Sam was from Kentucky?"

"Yep." Dan's mouth thinned out into a hard, flat line. "She made a quick trip to the grocery mart where she literally got backed into a corner by a group. One of them threw out that whole 'murderer from Kentucky' thing, but she was in so much shock over being confronted by people she'd considered friends, she doesn't remember exactly who." Deep lines settled across his forehead. "And that was the last time she ventured outside the house, other than to come over here. So the gossip is not only out of control, but it's keeping her a prisoner in her own home." He stared back at Clay. "This whole sequence of events is the perfect display of a mob mentality."

"Meaning what?" Clay demanded.

"That it can be manipulated," Dan stated. "The CIA trains

you to look for that kind of thing, especially in the more volatile regions of the world, where manipulating the mob can overthrow a government."

"Or gets the city council upset enough they fire the police chief?" Clay asked dryly.

Ricki felt a sudden burst of outrage, as her nerves sizzled all the way up her arms. "The council told you that?"

"Not yet." Clay shrugged. "But I got a couple of concerned phone calls, and I'm sensing they could definitely be pushed in that direction." He rubbed a hand across the back of his neck. "Maybe that's the end game here. Someone wants me fired."

"And wouldn't that be a handy way to stop the investigation into Malone's murder?" Ricki muttered under her breath.

Dan looked out the front window and studied a point in the distance. "Whatever that end game is, Clay, you can bet it's hidden somewhere in all the rumors. That's how it works. Kind of like flooding the airwaves, so the real message never gets heard."

"Well if that's how it works, then no one has reported hearing that the police chief should be fired," Ricki said firmly. "So it has to be something else. Like diverting the police chief from investigating Preston Malone's murder. Which would make the most likely suspect behind all of this one of the three men who pulled off that robbery seven years ago. Which is now down to two, and possibly one, if Sam Parkman is dead."

"Why one of those guys?" Clay asked. "It could be some sick piece of shit who simply enjoys creating chaos."

"Maybe," Ricki said, immediately drawing a scowl from Clay. "But that would leave out Pete. He enjoys the gossip, but he isn't a sick piece of shit. And who else would know that the fake Sam was from Kentucky and had murdered more than one person?"

Clay was about to take a drink of his beer, but his hand

froze in midair. "Hang on. If someone did deliberately start this flood of misdirection, as Dan has called it, then he would have to be here in the Bay. So if that same person is one of the three robbers, then you're saying it proves that Preston Malone's killer is still here?"

"There were three men who pulled off that robbery. Besides Malone, we don't know who the other two are, but they sure know each other," Ricki stated. "At least one of them killed Malone and has the only motive to stop this investigation. And yeah. I think he's still here, and has been for a while." She turned at the sudden ruckus being put up by Corby, a sure sign that someone was coming down the driveway. The last thing she wanted right now was a friendly neighbor knocking on the door with a lot of not-so-friendly questions.

She stood in front of the wide picture window, with Clay at her side. Both of them relaxed when Corby abruptly finished barking and sat down on the gravel drive, his body on full alert. A second later, Anchorman's big black truck came around the last curve, closely followed by a sedan with a large swath of paint scraped off the driver's side.

Anchorman jumped out of his vehicle and slammed the door before immediately heading to the cabin, while Finn exited the sedan, then walked around the front to open the passenger side door for Kate. Corby trotted along beside Anchorman and happily dashed into the cabin as soon as the door was opened.

The determined dog made a straight line toward his food dish while Anchorman walked to the refrigerator and helped himself to a beer. "I called Cheron and told her to come over when she was through testing some evidence for a cold case file sent up from Seattle."

Ricki's eyes narrowed. Given the mood of the town, she wasn't liking that too much. "Is she alone in the lab?"

The diner's cook and part owner sent her an annoyed look. "If she was going to be in the place alone, I would be looking over her shoulder, standing guard. But there's an officer from the Tacoma PD hanging out in the lobby, waiting for the test results."

When Kate stepped inside with Finn, she smiled at her brother and winked at Ricki.

"I don't know how your day has been going," the willowy blonde said with a cheerful note in her voice. "But ours has been filled with cold shoulders and weird stares." She tilted her head toward Finn. "Mostly directed at Special Agent Fionn Sullivan." She laughed. "I don't think anyone has noticed I'm even around, they're so busy glaring at him."

"Could have been worse," Anchorman said. "I was minding my own business doing a supply inventory at the diner when Minnie Cuthry strolled right in and gave me a thirty-minute earful about how I should not be part of the disgraceful cover-up. Since I couldn't get a sensible word out of the woman, I more or less politely showed her the door."

"Oh?" Kate's amusement shone in her eyes. "How did you do that?"

The big Marine shrugged and waved his bottle of beer in the air. "It's not that hard. I opened the door and shoved her out. Worked like a charm." He grinned at Ricki. "But you might not be getting any invitations to look at rentals for a while." He sighed. "Pete came by too. He wanted to know if I'd heard the latest rumors." Anchorman shook his head in disgust. "It's all anyone wants to talk about. The grand conspiracy of covering up a murder and burying evidence." He nodded at Clay. "Cheron explained it to me when I called her as soon as we hit town."

Clay ran a distracted hand over the top of his head, causing strands of hair to spike out in opposing directions. "I tried to track Pete down as a place to start in pinpointing the source of all these rumors, but couldn't get hold of him. I got the impression that the old busybody doesn't want to talk to me."

Dan suddenly slapped an open palm against his forehead, drawing everyone's attention. He gave Ricki an apologetic look. "I almost forgot. I fielded some of those calls coming in to Marcie's phone, and one of them was from a woman named Wanda Simms." He frowned at the low groan from Ricki. "I guess you know her?"

"Everyone who grew up in the Bay knows Wanda," Ricki said. And if they knew what was good for them, they'd make a point of staying on her better side.

If Pete was the king of gossip in Brewer, then Wanda was the undisputed queen of the entire area where she was born and had lived her whole life. That meant her influence was felt all the way from Massey at the top of Dabob Bay, back down to Olympia, seventy-five miles to the south.

Wanda's sources of information about anything and everything that happened in the Bay and beyond were a mystery and known only to her. And the sources were not only very deep and thorough, but generally accurate as well. The queen of gossip made sure of that. "Wanda wanted to talk to Marcie? Did she mention why?" Ricki asked.

"Nope," Dan said. "All she wanted was for Marcie to get a message to you to call her as soon as you could."

Genuinely puzzled, Ricki's boot tapped the floor. "And she still didn't say why?"

"No. I asked for her number and she laughed." Dan shrugged. "She said you already had it, and probably on speed dial."

"Not hardly," Ricki said in a dry voice. "But I'll give her a call." She walked over and stood next to Clay. "Since we can't stop the wagging tongues, we need to talk about what set them off in the first place. Or more accurately, who did?" She quickly stepped through the conversation between herself and Dan, starting with his theory about the wave of gossip being a deliberate misdirection to cause a distraction for some unknown reason, and ending with the conclusion that Preston Malone's old army buddy, also known as Magpie, was actually the real Sam Parkman.

Finn looked around the room. "Speaking of Marcie and her brother, where is she?"

"Upstairs, resting," Dan said quietly.

The FBI agent cast a look at the stairs before nodding. "Okay. Since it can't cause her any more pain, I'll point out that Malone told his girlfriend that he was going to see an army buddy that he didn't think was going to make it. If that was a genuine statement, and not just something he said as an excuse to get away from his girlfriend, then there's a strong possibility that Sam Parkman is dead."

"I don't think it was an excuse to dump Hailey. Malone wrote another letter to Hailey just last year, letting her know they wouldn't have to wait much longer, and promising her a good life," Ricki pointed out.

"Doesn't sound like a woman Malone wanted to put in his rear-view mirror," Anchorman said. "And that brings us back to the possibility that Marcie's brother is dead."

"Which would make a bizarre kind of sense," Finn cut in. "Malone goes to see Parkman, who is dying. Parkman passes away, and Malone, somehow knowing the FBI is hot on his trail and needing a place to hide, steps into Sam's old life here in Brewer." He tapped a finger against his chin. "But if Sam died three years ago, then it had to have been the third partner who discovered where Malone was hiding out and came here to shoot him."

"He didn't need to come here," Ricki said with a glance at

Clay, who nodded back. "I think he's been here all along." When Finn gaped at her, she stuck her hands into the back pockets of her jeans and shrugged. "Marcie said that Malone, posing as Sam, knew all about me. Now the real Sam might have told Malone about me, because he grew up in the Bay and so did I. But he also knew about Clay and Anchorman." She looked over at them. "You both arrived in the Bay long after Sam Parkman had disappeared. Which means Malone couldn't have been told about them by Marcie's brother, and some stranger, who blew into town just to shoot Malone and then blew out again, wouldn't have known about any of us. Especially not the kind of details to convince Marcie he was her long-lost brother."

Clay pushed his bottle of beer to the side to rest his forearms on the counter, clasping his hands in front of him. "There's a strong chance that whoever started this misdirection campaign Dan has spotted is that third man." When Finn frowned, Clay took a deep breath. "Just as importantly, he's made a mistake. One of the local gossips told Marcie that the fake Sam was a murderer from Kentucky. Now, outside of this room, how many people actually knew that Preston Malone had ties with Kentucky? Especially when he used an alias the whole time he was there?"

"The partner in crime he thought he could trust," Ricki said. "The guy behind getting this whole misdirection fiasco kicked off and who then put out too much information." Ricki's gaze was sober as she looked at the faces around the room. "He was careful not to mention Malone's real name, but let it slip that he was from Kentucky. That was a mistake. And oddly out of character for a man who's been careful enough to make off with two million dollars and then hide it and himself for seven years."

"Got any ideas on that?" Anchorman asked. "Because if

that's supposed to help us find this guy, I still don't know where to look. If he's really been hiding in plain sight around here for years, none of us has ever spotted him."

"I agree with Ricki, it's a strange mistake. But what's really bothering me is if he and Malone have both been living in the Bay for a long time, why kill Malone now?" Clay looked at Ricki, his face grim. "It's the timing of the shooting that makes me think there's something behind it besides greed. From what Malone was telling his girlfriend back in Kentucky about only having another year to wait, they already had a successful system in place to periodically move the money out of the country. So why not get rid of Malone six months ago? Or a year ago? Why now?" Clay straightened up before answering his own question. "Malone must have done something that made him a liability."

"Enough to kill him in broad daylight?" Finn protested. "That would do nothing but draw attention, especially to the fake Sam, and the real possibility his true identity would surface. Which it did."

"But that should have been a minimal risk," Ricki argued. "Because everyone in town, including his own sister, knew who Sam Parkman was. Or thought they did. Why would the authorities go to the trouble of taking fingerprints or dental records to positively ID him when a family member and half the town could do it?"

"Okay. I'm following," Finn declared. "So your target is dead, and should be safely buried under his fake identity. Then you hear through the local grapevine that the body in the morgue." He held up a quick hand when Ricki opened her mouth. "Or in this case the town's clinic, isn't the real Sam Parkman after all. So how do you keep the local law enforcement" --he swung a dramatic arm toward Clay-- "from discovering who the dead guy really is?" He beat two fingers of each hand against the island's countertop in a simulated drum roll. "You steal the body, of course."

Yeah, of course, Ricki thought. A scene played out in her head, and she narrowed her eyes in silent concentration to keep it in focus.

"You all look like you could use a break." Kate's calm voice quietly cut into the silence that had descended on the room. "How about if I call your favorite pizza place and put in an order?" She lowered her voice to a loud whisper. "And I'll pick it up so no one will be the wiser that the conspirators are holding a secret meeting here." She laughed. "And that it requires pizza."

Anchorman smiled at her. "Sounds good. I'll write down what everybody likes, then put in a call to Cheron to find out when she's going to make it out here."

"You write and I'll call Cheron," Kate offered. She produced her cell phone and walked out to the porch to make her call away from the sudden burst of noise as everyone else made sure Anchorman got the toppings right. When she came back inside, Kate smiled at Clay. "Ryan said to tell you that things seem to be calming down a bit. Apparently your big, bad self simply being back in town has helped a lot."

"Funny," Clay said. "Why were you talking to my junior deputy?"

"Because he's the deputy on call today and picked up when I called the station. Cheron wasn't answering, so I thought I'd ask whoever was on call to run over to her lab and tell her to get hold of her boyfriend and put in her pizza order. Luckily, he wasn't far from Cheron's lab and said he'd get right over there."

"Good idea." Anchorman grinned. "She gets all caught up in her work and doesn't hear the phone." He looked down at the list he'd made on a piece of paper Ricki had pulled out from a kitchen drawer. "So what would the beautiful Kate like on her pizza?"

"Watch yourself," Finn warned, with a good-natured wink at Kate. "This one is taken."

"So am I," Anchorman declared. "That doesn't make Kate any less beautiful."

Ricki only half listened to the teasing banter as she looked up at Clay. "What do you think?"

"I think I want to talk to Mr. Kroker at Hanover Industries about the spies he had hanging around town. We didn't spot them, so it's possible that third partner didn't either. Maybe they saw something useful. Or," he paused, a pained look on his face, "we're way off about the third partner kicking the rumor mill into overdrive, and those guys did it. The fact is, they also knew that the FBI had traced Preston Malone to Kentucky, so I think the coincidence of their presence here and the sudden shitstorm of bogus rumors needs to be cleared up."

"You're right," Ricki agreed. "While you check into that, I think I'll pay Wanda Simms a visit."

Clay's cell rang, and he glanced at the display and smiled. "Ryan," he announced before pressing the connect button. "What did Dr. Garrison have to say about pizza?" Clay asked without any preamble, then abruptly went silent. In the blink of an eye, his expression went stony as his gaze took on the flat, hard look of a cop. "Hang on. Slow down, Ryan. Yeah, I heard what you said. Did you call an ambulance?"

Within a heartbeat, there was a loud thump of heavy boots hitting the ground, then running across the wood of the cabin's floor. Ricki barely had time to step around Clay before the front door banged against its frame as it was thrown open.

She sprinted across the small open space, reaching the door just in time to see Anchorman's back as he leaped off the porch and raced to his truck. By the time she'd also jumped down the porch's two steps, the Marine's big truck was spinning around in the small cleared-out space in front of her cabin, barely missing Clay's SUV and Finn's sedan as it made a tight turn, spitting gravel in a wide arc before it took off down the driveway like a bolt of lightning. When Clay came running past her, he didn't stop to explain what Ryan had told him. He simply grabbed her hand and pulled her along toward his SUV.

Not wasting her breath or any time by asking a question, Ricki sprinted to the passenger side and threw herself onto the seat, buckling the seatbelt as Clay brought the heavy engine to life and took off after Anchorman.

"Ryan's out at the lab. The deputy from Tacoma is out cold, and Cheron was attacked. The ambulance is on its way."

Chapter Twenty-Two

Cheron's lab was on the other side of Brewer, closer to TK's clinic than it was to the cabin, but still only a five-minute drive away. Ricki braced her legs against the floorboard and held on to the door strap as the SUV sped down Main Street, its siren blaring and the headlights flashing. Tourists and locals alike popped out of shops and scrambled to the edge of the sidewalk, craning their necks to see what was going on.

When they reached the lab, the ambulance was already taking up the available space in the small parking lot, blocking in a white squad car displaying the blue lettering of the Tacoma Police Department on its side. Clay skidded the SUV to a stop at the edge of the street and Ricki jumped out of the passenger side just as a gurney was being rolled out of the lab.

Ricki kept running across the parking lot, even as her gaze flew to the patient's face. It only took a second to realize it wasn't Cheron lying on the gurney. The patient was an older man, with his eyes squeezed shut and his face as white as the sheet he was lying on.

TK walked beside him, holding up an IV bag as he barked orders to the young EMTs. "Careful when you load him up. No jostling. He's got a nasty crack on the back of his head."

"TK?" Clay called out, quickly covering the distance to the elderly doctor and his patient. "Who's hurt?"

"This man here," TK said without taking his eyes off his patient. "Deputy Donner with the Tacoma Police Department. No idea why he was here, and I don't care." He took a brief moment to give Clay a fierce look. "He's going to the clinic. We can take care of him there. Cheron is another matter. Dr. Torres is with her now. Go talk to him. See what he needs." He switched his glare to Ricki. "And do something with that cook of yours. He's getting in the way."

Without another word, TK grabbed the hand offered by one of the paramedics, who practically lifted the long-time doctor into the ambulance. Once TK was settled, the paramedic slammed the doors shut while his partner turned toward Clay. Ricki knew the young man. He was the same paramedic who had transported Malone after he'd been shot.

"An air ambulance has been called for Dr. Garrison. It's coming out of Port Orchard and should be here in thirty minutes. It will be landing at the clearing TK had built down the road from the clinic. We're going to unload the deputy at the clinic, then come right back for Dr. Garrison."

Clay nodded his thanks. "You'll have an escort there. We'll see to it. You take care of that deputy." He turned just as Ryan came out the front door of the lab and raced over to his boss. Before he opened his mouth, Clay pointed at the department's only cruiser, which was parked at the edge of the road, right in front of the SUV. "Get your butt in the car and follow that ambulance. Give it an escort to the clinic and then hightail it back here with it when they come to pick up the doctor and take her to the medevac point near the clinic." He leaned closer and stared into the young deputy's face. "Can you do that, Deputy Winters?"

"Yes, sir." Ryan swiveled on one heel and took off for his cruiser.

"He'll get it done," Clay stated, then strode toward the lab with Ricki right on his heels.

The small, deserted lobby echoed with the sounds coming through the open door leading into the main lab. Ricki walked in behind Clay, heading right to the back, where Anchorman and Dr. Torres were bent over Cheron. She was lying on the floor, looking like a rag doll who had suddenly collapsed into a lifeless sprawl. There was blood staining the collar and front of her plaid shirt, and ribbons of dark red running down the bib of her overalls. Anchorman was kneeling beside her, holding her limp hand as he watched the doctor carefully tape a bandage onto the right side of her forehead.

When Ricki got a look at Cheron's face, she barely stifled a sound of pure anguish. The doctor's glasses were missing and her eyes were shut. One of them was swollen to twice its normal size, and there were ugly bruises on both her cheeks that matched the angry-looking marks around her neck.

"Chief. Ricki," the doctor said without looking at them. "Now that you're here, I'm going to start this IV, if one of you would please hold the bag." He reached into a big two-tiered box filled with medical supplies and pulled out tubing and a large needle. "We've got the bleeding stopped," he said as he continued his preparations. "Once I have this IV going, I'll need to check for broken bones, then get her into a more comfortable position." Dr. Torres eyed the big man kneeling close to Cheron. "You'll need to move back, Mr. Beal." The way the doctor said it told Ricki it wasn't the first time he'd made that request and been ignored. When Anchorman didn't move this time either, the doctor looked up at Ricki.

She immediately laid a hand on the Marine's shoulder. "Come on, Anchorman. Cheron needs the doctor to see to her, and I need to get in there to hold that IV bag for him. Help her out. Let the doctor see to her." She leaned over his shoulder and reached out to curl her fingers around his forearm, putting her mouth close to his ear. "Step back. To help her, you need to step back."

When he shook his head, Clay's voice rang out in a sharp command. "Step back, Sergeant. Now."

The harsh order managed to snap through Anchorman's haze. He gently laid Cheron's hand down before slowly standing up. He backed up a step, seemingly completely unaware of pushing Ricki back with him. She did a quick move to the side to avoid his big boots, then angled her body in front of his to give herself a good position to grab the IV bag that Dr. Torres was holding out for her.

As she stood there, acting like a human pole, Torres continued to work, carefully feeling along Cheron's shoulder and limbs. Checking for any obvious signs of broken bones. "She has a bad head wound and we can't rule out internal injuries. She's going to need to see a trauma surgeon, and that means Harborview Medical Center in Seattle," he said in a matter-of-fact voice. "I've already sent a text to a friend of mine in Olympia. He has his helicopter license and has agreed to do a favor for Mr. Beal here." He cast a brief glance up at the tall man looming over him. "And fly him to the trauma center at Harborview Medical Center. He should only be a half hour behind Dr. Garrison."

"I'll get him to the landing spot we use for helicopters," Clay promised.

Ricki turned her head away from Cheron to look up at Anchorman. "Did you hear that? The doc has arranged a ride for you."

"I heard." Anchorman's words came out low and harsh, and his gaze never moved from Cheron's face.

Ricki sucked in a shallow breath. She'd never heard him use that voice before. Worried, she shot a questioning glance at Clay, who met it with a concerned look of his own. Even under the best of circumstances she and Clay together wouldn't be able to wrestle a furious Anchorman to the ground. And this was not the best of circumstances by a long shot. Several tense minutes passed with the only sound being the rustle of the doctor's lab coat as he moved around Cheron.

It seemed like an eternity before multiple sirens could be heard in the distance. They grew louder with each passing second until their blare was mingled with the crunch of tires rolling across gravel. Clay went out to meet the rig and its crew while Torres sat back on his heels. He put his stethoscope into his ears and carefully placed the flat edge on Cheron's chest.

When Clay came back in with the EMTs, he didn't hesitate to step right in front of Anchorman, putting his face a scant six inches away from the Marine's, effectively blocking his view of Cheron. "Ryan is waiting for you outside. He's going to run interference for the ambulance and take you to the airfield to make sure Cheron gets off safely and for you to wait for your ride." He moved his face an inch closer to Anchorman's. "Do you understand what I'm telling you? If you want to help her, this is how you can do it. Make sure she gets on that medevac chopper. That's what she needs the most right now."

Anchorman stared at him while Ricki held her breath. After a long, tense moment, he jerked his head into a nod, then took two steps back.

Cheron didn't move as she was loaded onto the gurney and wheeled into the parking lot with Dr. Torres on one side and Ricki on the other, still holding up the IV bag. When the two-man crew slid the gurney into the back of the ambulance, their patient let out a low moan before subsiding again into silence. The tiny sound of pain had Anchorman's face going from etched in granite to murderous.

As the gurney was being secured and Torres was climbing up behind it, the Marine reached into his pocket and tossed Ricki a set of keys. "See to my truck." He shifted his deadly stare to Clay, then raised his voice loud enough for Ryan, the doctor, and the two EMTs to hear him. "You put out a message for that asshole. There's nowhere on this earth he can hide. I'll find him." He turned and gestured at a frozen Ryan. "Let's go."

The deputy's wide eyes shot a look at Clay, who nodded back. Sucking in a breath, Ryan grabbed on to his hat and set off running after Anchorman. The ambulance followed a few seconds later, leaving Ricki and Clay alone in the parking lot, standing next to the abandoned Tacoma police cruiser.

"Shit," Clay said under his breath.

"I second that." Ricki reached over and touched the Glock securely nestled into her shoulder holster as her gaze carefully quartered the area. The lab was set back into the trees, and the densely forested surroundings had her wishing for her rifle with its high-powered sight.

"If he's still hanging out around here, we can't do anything about it," Clay said quietly. "Let's go in and poke around. The place looks like it was searched in a hurry, but I want to confirm that."

Ricki frowned. The mess in the lab had barely registered with her once she'd spotted Cheron. "Yeah. Let's do that." She took one last look at the closest stand of trees before following Clay back into the lab.

The shelves all along the back were empty, their contents strewn across the floor, along with shattered pieces of small equipment and broken glass from various containers for specimens. The place was in shambles, and Clay was right—it looked as if someone had been furiously searching the lab. Her forehead wrinkled as her eyebrows drew together. But looking for what?

Clay walked around a long table and crouched down on the other side of it. "Found some blood. Here on the edge of the table and on the floor."

Ricki walked over and knelt beside him. "Cheron had a gash on her head. It could have come from falling against the edge of the table." Her eyes narrowed as she stared at the blood smeared along the tile floor. "She fell while he was beating her, and it looks like she tried to crawl away."

"No question about the beating." Anger seeped into Clay's voice. "Cheron is what? A hundred and ten pounds soaking wet?" He got to his feet. "I wish she'd just told him where she was keeping whatever this jerk was looking for."

"Maybe she couldn't." Ricki took another long, slow look around the demolished lab.

"Because Cheron didn't have what he wanted," Clay stated, accurately reading her thoughts. His eyes cooled, turning a slate gray as he continued to look around. "I think you're right. The doctor is too practical to take that kind of beating. Especially since nothing in her lab would be worth dying for. If he wanted to know where she was storing something, she would have told him." He walked away a couple of steps, then turned back around to face Ricki. "And that brings up an interesting question."

"Which is?" Ricki asked.

Clay folded his arms over his chest and rocked back on his heels. "If the third partner in the robbery has been hiding out here in the Bay, then he had to have known about Anchorman and his relationship with Cheron."

Ricki briefly closed her eyes as she blew out a long breath. "Which would make assaulting Cheron a damn stupid thing to do." She nodded to herself, causing a strand of hair to break loose from her low ponytail. When it fell across her cheek, she impatiently pushed it away. "So either Mister Heavy Fists doesn't live in the Bay after all, or this," she swept an arm out to encompass the lab, "was due to something besides our robbery and that third partner. Like maybe whatever evidence that deputy from Tacoma was waiting on."

"I'll give Chief Davis a call and find out what case he sent over here that needed a deputy to wait for the results of whatever tests Cheron was running."

A dim bell rang in the back of Ricki's mind. Evidence. That's what Cheron's lab did. Process evidence. And that was the only thing here to find.

"Yeah," Clay continued. "I'd bet it's one hundred percent that whoever ambushed Cheron and that Tacoma deputy was looking for something she was working on."

"Or thought she was." Ricki's gaze slowly traveled across the room. "Dan said that the reason for the blast of misinformation going through the Bay like a wildfire was buried somewhere in the rumors." Her gaze returned to Clay. "Marcie said that she heard we were all going to Kentucky to gather evidence, which we would probably destroy." Ricki paused, her breath coming in slow increments as she heard Marcie's voice in her head. "Then she said that we might store it away in Dr. Garrison's lab." As Clay dropped his arms to his side, she nodded. "You mentioned a conspiracy about nonexistent evidence. The whole evidence thing keeps popping up from multiple sources. What if it got back to the third partner that we found evidence in Kentucky about Malone's murder?"

"Or that we already had it," Clay stated. He hooked his thumbs inside his belt and stared at the blood drying on the floor. "Remember that box Dan brought in from Malone's room at Marcie's place? I gave it to Jules to look over before he took it back to Marcie's. But if Pete saw him walk out with it, he might have assumed it was headed to this lab."

"Because this is where most of our evidence goes," Ricki finished.

"Besides Kroker and his Hanover goons, I think I'll put a bigger priority on tracking down Pete and having a little talk with him." His smile didn't reach his eyes. "Maybe send Jules out to his place and drag him down to the station."

"And I still want to have a chat with Wanda Simms," Ricki said.

"We." Clay quirked an eyebrow at Ricki's stare. "*We* are going to have a talk with Wanda. The new rule here is that we work in teams. This third partner has killed before, and now it's highly probable that he's attacked Cheron, so he's upping his game here in the Bay."

Ricki nodded her agreement. "All right, then. *We* are going to be interviewing Kroker and Pete and Wanda." She pulled her phone out of her jacket. "But my first call is going to Dan. I'll let him know what happened here and to keep his guard up and Marcie close by. I also want him to look for the real Sam Parkman somewhere in the vicinity of Omaha. We need to find out what happened to him to be sure we're looking for only one guy."

"You do that and I'll call Jules," Clay said. "Let him know he and Ryan need to patrol together. And I'll get in touch with Chief Davis in Tacoma. With his deputy being attacked, he might see his way clear to loaning us a couple of his guys to help with patrol for the next week, and after that, we'll see where we are."

"If he has some deputies with serious hunting experience, that would be a plus," Ricki said. She stared out the windows at the trees crowding in close and dwarfing the one-story building. "I have a feeling that will be a help."

"Will do." Clay took out his phone but only held it in his hand as he caught her gaze with his. "And tonight, you and I are going to sit down with Marcie and make a list of everyone you two can think of who's shown up in the Bay during the last seven years."

Chapter Twenty-Three

Ricki walked out of the lab, intending to take Anchorman's truck back to the cabin while Clay went to the clinic to check on the Tacoma deputy and call his chief from there.

"What's Merlin doing here?"

Clay's question pulled Ricki from her thoughts and had her scanning the parking lot. She spotted Merlin, dressed in cargo pants and a heavy sweater, with her shoulder-length hair pulled into a twist and anchored to the back of her head with a single chopstick. Lifting a hand in greeting, Ricki kept a close eye on the woman who was leaning against the front fender of Anchorman's truck.

"Hi." Ricki peered around, looking for Merlin's small pickup truck. "Where did you come from?"

"Town, actually. I was in my shop when I heard all the commotion and thought I'd come out and see what was going on." The solidly built brunette owned a small bookshop on one end of Main Street that was mostly stocked with local maps and guidebooks. "The ambulance was already here, so I parked down the road. I didn't want to get in the way but thought I would stick around in case you needed any help." She looked past Ricki toward the closed door to the lab. "Was that Dr. Garrison I saw being loaded into the ambulance?" At Ricki's abrupt nod, Merlin's eyes widened. "What happened?"

"We aren't sure yet," Clay answered smoothly. "You didn't happen to notice any other cars parked near yours, did you?"

Merlin shook her head. "Nope. Not a one. It was pretty quiet all morning until you came screaming through town with your siren blaring. The doctor wasn't shot, was she?"

Ricki lifted an eyebrow. "Now why would you think that?"

The brunette looked taken aback at Ricki's flat tone before quickly shrugging her shoulders. "Because the guy who turned out not to be Sam was shot, and it occurred to me this might be a repeat performance and maybe there's some connection between the two."

"Meaning?" Ricki asked.

A streak of red crept across Merlin's cheeks. "I don't know. It could be that the doctor isn't who she said she was either, and got shot for the same reason Sam did."

Clay lightly touched Ricki's arm, stalling the quick denial ready to leap out of her mouth. Firmly shutting it, she said nothing while Clay smiled at the former Army Ranger. "Different backgrounds. Dr. Garrison is well known in a field that would be impossible to bluff your way through. I wouldn't be too happy to hear that kind of garbage get spread around town."

Merlin gave him a tight smile that didn't quite reach her eyes. "Yeah. I guess that's true. It would be pretty hard to fake that kind of background." She straightened away from the truck. "Well, is there anything I can do? Maybe stand watch here, if that would help?"

"No need." Clay's voice was firm even as his polite smile stayed in place. "Jules is on his way."

"Okay." Merlin stuck her hands in her pockets and rolled her shoulders back. "Then I guess I'll take off." She cocked her head to the side. "You have my number if you need any extra eyes to take a shift here."

Oh yeah. I have your number all right, Ricki thought, even as she forced her mouth to curve into a smile while Clay thanked the woman for her offer. They both watched Merlin walk out of sight, then waited until they heard her truck start up. A few seconds later her blue pickup drove by, with Merlin waving out the open window.

Ricki glanced up at Clay. "Are you buying that story?"

He turned and stared at the empty road in front of the lab. "Only because I don't have a reason not to. Do you think Merlin is the third partner, and was skulking around in the woods, waiting for an opportunity to search the lab?"

Ricki considered it, then shrugged. "I don't know. I hear Army Rangers are pretty good at skulking around in the woods. And I don't know why she suddenly turned up here." She sighed and absently twisted the lock of hair hanging down in her face around one finger before shoving it behind her ear. "Is Jules really on his way here?"

"Yeah. I called him from the lobby. He's also going to contact Cheron's two assistants to find out if one of them has a key to lock the place up." He looked back at the rectangular-shaped building. "I didn't see any evidence of a break-in, so I'm guessing the attacker walked in the front door."

"There's a back door," Ricki said. "It leads into a hallway where there's a storage room and a couple of offices. Cheron uses one and her two staff members share the other." She frowned. "I got a grand tour before the lab officially opened for business."

"I should have checked back there." Clay shook his head. "It's been a long day."

Ricki had to agree with that. "It's hard to believe we were in Kentucky this morning."

"Early this morning." Clay looked over at the road, wearily nodding when the cruiser pulled into the small lot, with Ryan at the wheel and Jules riding shotgun. "It looks like our relief has arrived."

After a short wave aimed at the two deputies, Ricki held up the key fob to Anchorman's truck. "I'm going to head back to the cabin. Are you still intending to stop by the station?"

"Yeah. Then I'll be home to pick up a few things before going out again." When Ricki frowned, he leaned over and placed a quick kiss on her mouth. "I'll explain when I get back to the cabin. You're going straight home, aren't you? No stops in between?"

"No stops. I'm going to make an appointment with Wanda and start that list. I'll call in an order to Quick Pie if you'll pick it up on your way back from the station."

Clay grinned at her as he walked backwards a few steps. "Consider it done." He turned and strode over to where his deputies were waiting.

Making a mental note to put more meat than veggies on that pizza, Ricki walked over to Anchorman's truck and climbed into the driver's seat. She was glad for the heavily tinted windows as she passed through town. It spared her some curious stares she simply didn't want to deal with at that moment. When she pulled up to the cabin, Finn stepped out onto the small porch, closing the door behind him.

"How bad is the news?" he asked as she climbed the two steps to crowd next to him on the small porch.

"I wish I knew," Ricki said. "But she's on a medevac helicopter." She glanced at her watch. "They picked her up a few minutes ago, and Anchorman will be taking a helicopter ride right behind her, thanks to Dr. Torres."

The door to the cabin opened and Marcie stood on the threshold, her hands on her hips. "You two might as well come on in and tell all of us the news. And don't sugarcoat anything. We want the truth."

Ricki managed a weak smile for her friend. "I can do that." When Marcie stepped back, Ricki walked into her house, automatically leaning over to give Corby a good head scratch when he sidled up and bumped against her legs. "Cheron is on her way to Harborview Medical Center by helicopter," she said. "Anchorman is flying there, too, in a separate helicopter. Besides being able to confirm that she was alive when she left the lab, I don't know anything else."

"What happened? Did something blow up, or fall on her?" Marcie asked.

"No, nothing like that. Someone came into the lab and knocked out the deputy from Tacoma, then proceeded to beat Cheron," Ricki stated flatly, taking Marcie at her word about not sugarcoating anything. There was an immediate gasp from Kate as she flung a supporting arm around the shocked Marcie's shoulders. Finn's grim face matched Dan's, and she was sure her own looked exactly the same.

"Why?" Marcie croaked, sending a helpless look toward Dan. "Why would anyone do such a horrible thing to Cheron, of all people?"

"The lab was a mess," Ricki added. "It looked like it was searched by someone who was furious."

"What in the world does Cheron keep in that lab?" Kate asked. "We were just there, and I didn't see anything worth a beating."

"She keeps evidence," Finn said, his gaze on Ricki. "I don't suppose it could have been someone involved in that deputy's case? Or is she working on any high-profile crime-scene evidence at the moment?"

"I don't know," Ricki said. And that was the truth. She had no idea what Cheron had stored in her lab. "But it can't be ruled out. And neither can the possibility that the third robbery partner is here in the Bay and heard the gossip about evidence concerning Preston Malone being stored at the lab." She looked at Marcie, who blinked back at her. "You told me that someone had claimed we were collecting evidence to either be destroyed or stored in Cheron's lab."

Marcie walked over to the only couch in the small living space beyond the kitchen and sank onto it. "That's right. I heard that." Her eyes were as big as moons as she shook her head. "Look where all this nasty gossip got us. Cheron on her way to the hospital." She wrung her hands together as a single tear tracked down one cheek. "This is horrible. Just horrible." She raised watery eyes to Ricki. "What can we do?"

Ricki glanced at her watch. Hopefully Clay wouldn't be much longer. "First, we need fuel." She looked at Kate. "Can you call an order into Quick Pie for all of us? Clay is going to pick it up on his way here from the station."

"Can do," Kate said, then lifted an "okay" signal into the air when Ricki called out to load the pizzas with more meat than vegetables.

"What's Clay doing at the station?" Dan asked.

"He didn't say," Ricki replied. She walked over to the refrigerator and pulled out a bottle of orange juice. Having poured herself a large glass and downed a third of it, she turned back to face the waiting group. "But unlike at the lab, there is evidence on the Malone case stored there. In the small safe in Clay's office, so he could be there checking on it."

"Our pizza order will be ready in fifteen minutes," Kate announced.

Ricki nodded and took out her cell phone. She sent a quick text message to Clay, polished off the rest of her juice, then set the empty glass down in the sink. "There is something you can do, Marcie." She walked around the island and perched on the arm of the couch. "We need to make a list of anyone who's come to live in the Bay in the last seven years."

"Since the robbery?" Finn asked. "Then you're thinking Malone wasn't the only one who made his way here?"

"What *I'm* thinking is that Marcie can start her list in the car," Kate announced. She skirted Ricki and took a seat on the opposite side of the couch and leaned close to the waitress. "These three, plus Clay, are going to be insanely busy chasing down this mysterious third partner. We can't be much help here, but we can go and be with Cheron and Anchorman. I say we commandeer one of the cars and head for the hospital."

Marcie opened and closed her mouth several times before finally nodding. "I think that's a wonderful idea." She glanced at Dan. "You'll be in the thick of all this, too, and I don't want you worrying about me." Her voice grew stronger as she turned back to Kate. "Anchorman will need us. I say we go right now. We can pick up something to eat on the way there."

Kate immediately stood and held out her hand to pull Marcie to her feet. "Not a problem. I can call Quick Pie back and cut down on the order."

The older woman lifted a hand and wagged a finger back and forth. "Don't even think about it. If there's any left over, then Ricki and Clay can have it for another meal. Lord knows, there isn't much else in that refrigerator that's edible."

Finn held out a key fob. "Take the rental. I can drive Anchorman's truck until he gets back."

Kate walked over and gave him a deep kiss on the lips that had Dan looking up at the ceiling. "You can do that. Or Ricki can drive it, and you can take the limecicle." At Finn's sour look, she laughed. "I'll call you when we get settled." Stepping back, Kate inclined her head at Marcie. "Are you ready? We can go right from here."

"I might need to stop and get my toothbrush and a change of clothes," Marcie protested.

Kate hooked an arm through hers and started for the door. "No worries. That's what department stores are for, and lucky for both of us, I have as much money as Clay does." She leaned closer to Marcie's ear. "And that's quite a lot."

When the door closed behind them on Marcie's giggle, Ricki looked at Dan. "Kate will take care of her, and I think it will really help for Cheron to have a few friendly faces around."

"And to help keep Anchorman calm," Finn said in a dry voice. "He's got to be somewhere way beyond angry."

He's definitely that, Ricki thought, but she nodded at Dan. "I still need your help in tracking down the real Sam Parkman."

"How?" Finn asked. "The FBI never found him."

"The FBI didn't know he might have been one of the robbers, so they never looked for him," Ricki said. "You only went after the guy who belonged to those fingerprints from the captain's chair. And that was Preston Malone."

"I can find Parkman," Dan announced. "We have enough to start a search. We think he's the Magpie in Malone's letter that was posted from Omaha. Especially since that was Parkman's last duty station. If he was still in Omaha all those years after he left the service and disappeared, it's even money that he stayed in that area. Especially since it was where Malone went to meet him. Malone never strayed far from his last duty station, and it could be Sam never did either. At least it looks that way. And the longer he sat in one place, the easier it will be to find him."

"If he's like Malone, he'll probably be using an alias," Finn pointed out.

"Most likely with his actual birthdate," Dan countered. "And he's a trained mechanic. That's also a thread I can tug on." He walked over to a black backpack lying on the floor next to the small table Ricki used as a desk. Unzipping the large pocket, he pulled out a laptop. "I can get started tonight."

Finn nodded, then grinned as Clay walked in the door carrying three flat boxes that smelled like heaven. "Here, let me take those for you." When Clay handed over the pizza, Finn carried it the rest of the way to the kitchen.

"Everything is quiet at the station," Clay said in answer to the question in Ricki's eyes. "I have just enough time to eat and throw a few things together before I need to get back there." He gave a pointed look at the laptop Dan was holding. "I hope you can use that on the fly, because I'm short on bodies to help keep watch at a few places that might be targets."

Dan nodded and slipped the computer into the backpack while Finn opened the cupboards, looking for plates and glasses.

"What do you need us to do?" the FBI agent asked.

"Until we figure out what's going on, we work in pairs," Clay stated. "I've got both my deputies out at Cheron's lab, keeping watch tonight. I'm going to be at the station, and I need a couple of bodies to cover the clinic. Frank Davis, the chief in Tacoma, is going to send a couple of men over in the morning to help out on patrols for the next few days." He shot Ricki a knowing look. "They both have extensive experience hunting in the backcountry."

"That could come in handy," Ricki said, then held up her phone. "I'm going to call my Uncle Cy and ask him to spend the night at the station with you." When Clay frowned, Ricki's eyes narrowed. "You said we work in pairs. If you're going to stay at the station in case the third partner figures out that since the evidence we collected isn't at the lab, it must be there, then you need another body with you."

"Fine," Clay conceded. "My problem is that leaves you here alone." He looked around. "I thought Marcie could stay with Kate up at the hotel. Where are they?"

"On their way to Seattle," Ricki supplied. "To be with Cheron and Anchorman. And I already have a partner tonight." She pointed at Corby. At the sound of his name, the big dog lifted his head from his sprawled-out sleeping position under the front window. "Corby is a better alarm than any of us. If someone even walks up to the house, he'll let me know."

Clay was still frowning, but he reluctantly nodded. "Okay. That will have to do as a temporary fix." He walked over to the kitchen island and snagged a piece of pizza. "I need you to do something else," he said to Finn before taking a big bite of the cheesy slice.

"Shoot," Finn told him.

"I want to talk to Kroker, the guy who is currently heading up Hanover. Can you arrange that?"

"I can," Finn said. "Have you got a particular time and date in mind?"

"Tomorrow." Clay looked at Ricki. "Does that work for you?"

She nodded. "First thing in the morning, then we'll go and pay Wanda a visit."

Clay dropped a second piece of pizza onto a plate and carried it over to her. "Yeah. That's the plan."

Ricki smiled when he set the plate down in front of her. "It's always good to have a plan."

Chapter Twenty-Four

Ricki woke to a cold nose pressed to her chin and a pair of liquid-brown eyes staring her right in the face. She moved her head just enough to peer at the digital clock next to the bed. The glowing numbers said it was five minutes past six. She glared at her dog. "Seriously? You can't hold it until seven?" When he simply lowered his head and bumped it against her nose, she quickly pulled the covers up to form a flimsy barrier between them. "Hey. All right. I'm getting up." When there were no more assaults on her nose, she cautiously lowered the blanket and peeked over its edge. Corby had politely backed up and was now wearing his familiar patience-of-a-saint look as he waited for her to get out of bed.

With a resigned sigh, she swung her legs over the side and stepped onto the braided rug. Dropping to her knees, she reached underneath the bed, groping around for her slippers. Looking over her shoulder, her eyes narrowed on the big boxer. "You make off with my furry moccasin socks and then expect me to get up so you can go pee?"

When he only cocked his head to the side, she gave up with

a grumble and tiptoed over to the dresser. Pulling out a pair of thick socks, she hopped on one foot and then the other to pull them on before scooping up her phone and stomping her way to the stairs. Used to Corby's habits, she paused long enough for him to zoom past her before making the descent to the first floor.

She opened the front door, then closed her eyes and stood there yawning, waiting for the telltale click of four paws against a wood floor to let her know Corby had gone out to greet the day in typical doggie fashion. After a long moment of silence, she opened one eye. Instead of racing outside, the big dufus was standing in front of her, his food bowl in his mouth.

"If you think I dragged my butt out of a warm bed because you want an early breakfast, think again, bub." She pointed a finger at the open door. "Out."

Corby dropped his bowl with a loud clatter, then stuck his nose up in the air as he slowly passed her. Ricki firmly shut the door the minute he was over the threshold. "His highness can just go catch something if he wants to eat at this hour of the morning," she mumbled to herself.

She glanced at the stairs and considered going back to bed but decided a cup of hot coffee sounded better. It only took a few minutes to drop the pod into the machine and wait for coffee to appear in the cup she'd set under the filter. After a long, life-giving sip, she carried it to the island and made herself comfortable on a stool.

The cabin was quiet. Apparently Corby had taken up her suggestion and gone off to find his own food, leaving her with the silence and gentle sway of tree branches in the early morning breeze for company. She didn't mind the quiet, but she'd gotten used to Clay being around.

Thinking maybe she'd give him a call, she abandoned the idea as fast as it had popped into her head. If he was still asleep, she did not want to wake him up. He needed the rest. The previous day had been a long one for both of them, but Clay had taken the brunt of the vicious cycle of gossip, and dealing with a nervous city council. She was certain he would have preferred to be handed a double homicide to solve over either of those two problems.

With nothing else appealing coming to mind, Ricki went back upstairs and changed into her jogging clothes and running shoes. Tucking her phone, along with a set of keys, into a holder strapped to her upper arm, she left the cabin, locked the door behind her, and started out at a slow jog down her winding driveway. She was almost to the street when Corby emerged from the trees and joined her, happily trotting along as they made the turn toward downtown Brewer.

Main Street was empty at that hour. With the Sunny Side Up still closed, the early morning breakfast crowd had to either go to the St. Armand resort or stay home and settle for making their own eggs, toast, and coffee. She'd just passed the diner and was making her way toward the far side of town when her cell phone pinged with a message that also immediately appeared on her watch. Finn.

She stopped and retrieved her phone, simply because it was much easier to read, and pulled up the text. True to his word, Finn had arranged a call with Kroker. Seeing the appointed time, Ricki took another quick look at her watch. She had about an hour to get back home and set up her laptop to take the call. She sent an "okay" to the FBI agent, then jogged in place as she waited to hear that the time also worked for Clay. When he didn't answer her text, she sighed and tapped on his speed dial contact.

"Chief Thomas." His voice was layered with the graveled tone that told her he was still half asleep and had answered on automatic without even glancing at the screen.

"Hey. Sorry for the early morning tag, but Finn has set up that phone call with Kroker in an hour. Can you make it?"

"Hang on." She heard the slick rustle of nylon followed by a low murmured question answered in her uncle's deep voice. "Yeah. I can make it."

"Did you sleep in your jacket?"

"Had to go out twice last night, so it wasn't worth taking it off. I'll be home in no time." He went silent for a moment. "Is that a car I hear? Where are you?"

"Out on a run with Corby," she said. "But I'll be back home by the time you get there."

She heard a loud yawn and then a mumbled sound that might have been "goodbye" before the call went dead. Smiling, she tucked the phone back into the arm holder and started on the two miles back to the cabin, walking in the door ten minutes before the SUV came up the driveway. It was just enough time to feed Corby and have a cup of coffee waiting for Clay. She handed it to him as he stopped to drop a kiss on her cheek before heading toward the stairs.

"Shower," was all he said before disappearing. She made herself a fresh cup of coffee and set it on the island before going to her desk and gathering up her laptop. Carrying it back to the island under one arm, she set it near the plug and pushed the power button. Pulling up the app Finn had designated for the call, she considered her morning chores done and scrolled through the latest news feed on her phone while Corby inhaled his food.

Five minutes before the call was set to begin, Clay appeared in a fresh pair of jeans and a collared shirt with the police department's logo sewn onto the pocket.

Ricki smiled. "You look very official."

"I had to do something to compete with the thousand-dollar suit and silk tie that Kroker will undoubtedly be wearing." He made his way to the coffee maker, carrying his empty cup with him, and dropped in another pod.

Her smile turned into a wide grin. "Do you want me to buy you a tie for a wedding gift?"

He sat down next to her and positioned the laptop between them. "You can buy me anything you want as long as the wedding takes place sooner rather than later."

When the program she'd pulled up suddenly came to life, indicating a call was coming in, Ricki straightened on her stool and peered at the screen. A man with dark hair, piercing blue eyes, and a mustache came into view. Ricki gave a mental high-five to Clay when she spotted the perfectly tailored black suit and a tie the same blue as his eyes.

"Matlin Kroker. And I assume you are Chief Thomas and Special Agent James?" His voice was as rich and smooth as an excellent brandy.

"That's right, Mr. Kroker. We're investigating a homicide that happened in my town. The victim has been identified as Preston Malone, originally from Arkansas. But then, you already know that."

Kroker smiled, showing a perfect row of white teeth. "I do. And I understand you are aware that two Hanover employees were recently in your area, collecting information on Preston Malone." He paused and his smile faded. "The man took part in an operation that cost this company a great deal, and I'm not just talking about money, Chief Thomas."

"Two million dollars and five lives is what we were told," Clay said.

"Your information is correct. Those men were responsible for murdering our CEO and four other valued staff members before they completely vanished. At least until Malone suddenly shows up as a homicide victim. So I'm sure you can understand our interest in the matter, Chief."

"Your interest? Yes. Sending two undercover operatives to skulk around my town? Not so much." Clay didn't blink at the suddenly stoic expression on the other man's face.

"Skulk? An interesting word, and not one applicable to my men."

"Then there was some other reason they didn't stop by the station and introduce themselves?" Clay asked.

Kroker shrugged. "It was our understanding that you were out of town."

"My deputies weren't," Clay countered.

"An oversight, then," Kroker said smoothly. "Please accept my personal apologies. But I'm sure that's not the reason you requested this call."

Clay stared intently at the screen. "I'd like to know what they were doing here, Mr. Kroker. Malone was already dead. Were you thinking you'd find your missing two million? Or more accurately, the CIA's missing two million?"

Kroker's eyebrows lifted in surprise. "I'm impressed with your sources, Chief Thomas. But to answer your question, no. I'm assuming that the two million made its way to an offshore bank long ago. Our interests lie in finding the two men who were with Malone. We'd like to have a word or two with them."

"We're hoping to do the same."

The CEO slowly leaned forward. His blue eyes seemed to pierce right through the screen. "You know who they are." It was a statement, not a question. "I want names."

"We have a good idea," Clay responded without blinking an eye. "When we catch them, I'll send you a copy of the arrest report." He shifted slightly in his seat. "Now I have a question for you." When Kroker only inclined his head, Clay smiled. "Did your men tell anyone that Malone was a murderer who came from Kentucky?"

Not a muscle moved in Kroker's expression as he stared

back at Clay. After a few moments, he nodded. "Perhaps we could exchange information. I have something that might be of interest to you, and you have names that I want."

An entire minute dragged by as the two men stared each other down. Underneath the counter, Ricki nudged Clay's foot with the side of her boot. Kroker's sources inside the FBI were as good as their own direct line through Finn. He would find out about Malone and his charade soon enough. When Clay broke eye contact with Kroker to glance her way, she leaned close to him. "He's going to find out anyway. Let's get something for it."

Clay hesitated, then gave a slight, barely perceptible nod before facing the screen displaying Kroker's image. "We don't have solid proof of the identity of either of the other participants in that robbery seven years ago," Clay said evenly. "But we have a solid lead." When Kroker remained silent, Clay added a feral smile. "A lead we're certain is going to pan out."

"All right. That seems like a fair trade." Kroker reached an arm to his left, out of sight of the camera. When it came back into view, he was holding a file folder. "Curt Tandoon." He looked up from the folder and tilted his head to the side. "I see you are familiar with the gentleman?"

"We are," Ricki said. "He's a permanent resident here in the Bay. What's your association with Curt?"

"I wouldn't call it an association so much as a fortuitous encounter." Kroker set the open folder down in front of him. "Corporal Tandoon's tour in a combat zone was in the same unit as one of the men we sent to Washington to look into Preston Malone."

"Your man knew Curt?" Ricki asked.

"Not well enough to exchange Christmas cards, Agent James. But yes, he recognized Tandoon, and the corporal recognized him. They exchanged a few words, and agreed to meet again the next day, but, as you know, we received a strongly worded request from the FBI to withdraw our men, which we did."

"What few words did they exchange?" Clay snapped. "That we were in Kentucky?"

Kroker shifted in his chair. "I can't say it was specifically in the report, but it wouldn't surprise me if that was mentioned. It would have been a natural question to ask where three such visible members of the community had disappeared right after a shooting had occurred. It could have been answered in the pursuit of obtaining more information about Malone."

In other words, they spilled the beans, Ricki thought. At least it explained how everyone in town knew about the Kentucky connection. Curt Tandoon had thrown that one into the gossip firestorm. "And did Curt tell your men that Malone had been here impersonating Sam Parkman for three years?"

For the first time since his face had appeared on the screen, Kroker looked surprised. "The report I received stated that Malone was using the alias of Sam Parkman. It mentioned nothing about impersonating someone."

"What else did Curt tell his old acquaintance?" Ricki demanded, her voice now as sharp as Clay's had been.

Kroker's gaze narrowed as he considered his answer. "That he'd followed Malone on several occasions, looking for the communications setup he had bragged about to a mutual friend. According to our operative, the corporal heavily implied that he knew where it was and would share that information for a reasonable sum of money, which my men agreed to. Unfortunately, they had to bail out on the meet when the FBI demanded that they return to Dallas."

"Where?" Ricki wanted to know. "Where did Curt want them to meet?"

Kroker frowned as he picked up the folder again and

quickly scanned the page. "A specific address isn't listed, but the meet was set in a place called Massey." He looked up and straight into the screen. "I'm assuming you know where that is?" When Ricki nodded, he smiled. "It's now your turn. I need the name of your solid lead, Chief Thomas."

"Sam Parkman," Clay stated.

Kroker scowled into the screen. "That was Malone's alias, and we already know about Malone. I'm looking for the other two men."

Clay was shaking his head before Kroker finished. "It was Malone's alias, but it's exactly as Special Agent James said. Malone borrowed the name and stepped into the life of Sam Parkman. The real Parkman was an army vet, and we know Malone paid him a visit three years ago before he made his way here and completely disappeared from your radar. The two looked enough alike that Malone managed to pull off the switch, and we have to assume he did it with Parkman's blessing."

"And where is Mr. Parkman now?" Kroker asked.

"That's what we're tracking down. We should know where he is in the next few days," Ricki put in, mentally crossing her fingers. If Dan didn't come through, they would have no idea where the real Sam Parkman was. "And now that you have a name, I'm sure you'll do your best to do the same. If Hanover finds Parkman before we do, don't forget to give us a call."

Kroker's bland expression was back in place. "Of course. And the third man? Is he also close by?"

Clay hesitated again before finally nodding. "We think so, but we don't know where he is, or what name he's using. And I'm going to trust you not to pass that along to the CIA."

"That won't be a problem." Kroker closed the file and folded his hands on top of it. "Is there any other business we need to discuss?"

"Did your men talk to anyone else, or discuss anything else with Curt?" Clay asked.

The hint of urgency in Clay's voice sparked a real interest in Kroker's eyes. "I can check, but it's highly unlikely. According to the report they filed, besides a five-minute conversation with Corporal Tandoon, they didn't talk to any locals at all." His mouth flattened out. "Why do you ask?"

"A lot of misinformation has been making the rounds all over town," Clay stated. "Along with the false story that we brought back evidence from Kentucky. We think it was a smokescreen, possibly to cover an assault that happened recently. And I want to know the source of that information."

Kroker shook his head in denial. "As I've already stated, our men arrived the day you left town, and the Bureau ordered us to pull them out the next morning, which is exactly what we did. There wasn't enough time for them to track down anyone directly associated with Malone, much less talk to them." He frowned. "How many people knew Malone was impersonating this Sam Parkman?"

"Damn few," Clay said. "And no one who would talk about it. But word got out anyway. More because the Bay has a well-oiled gossip machine than anyone talking out of turn. It's a small place, Kroker. I know exactly who I can and cannot trust."

The dark-haired man with the polished voice smiled. "It sounds very different from Los Angeles."

Clay's eyes narrowed in response. "I guess you did your homework."

"Always," Kroker said, with no hesitation in his voice. "It's the way Hanover stays in business." He looked away for a moment. When his gaze returned to Clay, his poker face was back in place. "I had already been told that you had some trouble there last night. So it's true that Dr. Garrison was attacked in her own lab?"

"That's right," Clay said in a tight voice, not bothering to question where Kroker had got his information.

"And you believe it was in relation to Malone's murder, and not another case she was conducting some forensic work on?"

"We don't know for sure, but it's leaning in that direction."

"Which is why you think the third man is also living nearby."

It was another statement rather than a question, and Ricki couldn't help admiring the man's perception. Kroker was very, very good at what he did.

When Clay remained silent, Kroker nodded. "It sounds like you have your hands full. I know about that team you have there in the Bay." His gaze switched to Ricki. "And all of you are a force to be reckoned with. But if you need any additional resources, don't hesitate to call." He gave her a polite smile before it rapidly faded as he returned his attention to Clay. "So I'll wish you good hunting, Chief Thomas, and you as well, Agent James. I'll also leave you with a little advice. I have as much trust in my men as you do in your team. If you're looking for the source of that information about evidence found in Kentucky, I believe going fishing in a local pond is the right way to go." His smile was back, and this time it had a genuine look about it. "I intend to hold you to your promise of a copy of that arrest report." The screen went blank before a picture of a peaceful ocean danced across it.

Ricki let out a breath. Even behind a screen, the man was intimidating. She bit her lower lip as she stared at waves lapping gently against a shore of white sand. "What did you think?"

"I wouldn't want to go up against him in a chess match." Clay rubbed a hand across the back of his neck. "But I think he was telling the truth. It wasn't his guys. And his advice to look closer to home is right on target. It had to be someone who is tapped into life here in the Bay."

Since her gut was telling her the same thing, Ricki nodded. "Which leaves us with the third partner who's been living here, hiding in plain sight. Provided Sam Parkman has actually passed away, so we aren't looking for two men."

"A third partner who is at least partially responsible for five deaths, and the attack on Cheron," Clay said. "And the bastard is here somewhere. We just have to find him."

"Yeah." Ricki reached across the island and picked up a piece of paper she'd left there the night before. Setting it down in front of Clay, she tapped it with her index finger. "That's my list of everyone I could think of who arrived in the Bay sometime in the last seven years and is still here."

Clay looked down and smiled at the first two names on the list. "Clayton Thomas and Norman Beal."

When he pretended to scowl at her, she shrugged. "You said everyone."

"Curt Tandoon and Patricia Forker." He looked up from the list. "I knew Merlin wasn't a native. She showed up here after I did."

"She showed up about two years ago. Since we don't know who got here first, Malone or his partner, then those people needed to be included, too."

"But Curt?" Clay frowned. "You said he showed up ten years ago."

Ricki shook her head. "No. I was a few years off. After giving it some thought, I remembered that Curt walked into the Sunny Side Up not too long after I first opened the doors. It stuck in my mind because I served him his dinner, and he told me it was only his second day in town. So you and Curt both arrived about seven years ago. In fact, you've been here a few months longer than Curt."

"That timing is interesting." Clay picked up the list and continued to study it. "How complete do you think this is?"

"Not very," Ricki admitted. "People come, they stay, and I don't remember exactly when. Or even all of them, for that matter. But I know someone who can name everyone who has settled in the Bay within the last seven years." She glanced at the clock hanging over the sink. "And we're supposed to see her this afternoon."

"You're talking about Wanda Simms."

"None other," Ricki said with a grin. "We can ask her to make up her own list. I'm betting it will be twice as long as mine."

Clay looked at the column of names and winced. "Okay. It's a lot of people to check out, but at least it eliminates most of the town." He also stole a glance at the clock. "I need to get back to the station and touch base with my deputies as well as Finn and Dan. Chief Davis's two officers should also be showing up before noon." He reached over and ran a finger down Ricki's cheek. "What's on your agenda?"

"I'm going to hang out here with Corby for an hour or so and finish up some reports for my real, non-FBI day job. And I have to talk to Hamilton as well as send him those reports," Ricki said. "Then I think Corby and I will head over to the Sunny Side Up and get some work done so we can open up again." She sighed. Part of that work would be starting the search for a new part-time cook. Not a simple task with the limited labor pool available in the Bay. "Can you swing by there and pick me up for our date with Wanda?"

Clay nodded before his gaze drifted over to Corby napping under the window. "What about the big boy? Do we backtrack and drop him off here before going out to Wanda's place?"

Ricki shook her head. "No. He knows his way home, including which houses he can stop at and get a guaranteed treat along the way."

Clay laughed and slid off the stool. "Your dog is spoiled, James."

She couldn't argue with that.

Chapter Twenty-Five

Despite owning real estate all over the Bay, and in several areas beyond it, Wanda still lived in the small cottage her husband had brought her home to as his new bride over fifty years before. The house was covered in clapboard that was painted a fresh coat of white every two years, making it stand out from the rougher, natural-wood log cabins that were more favored in the area. Set at the end of a long dirt driveway, the cottage nestled itself comfortably in the middle of a tall stand of trees.

But Ricki knew the serene setting wasn't as isolated as it looked.

There were cameras mounted all the way up the drive, so Wanda could see who was coming to visit well before they landed in front of her tidy postage-stamp-sized yard. The advanced warning gave her the choice of whether or not she would answer the door.

Clay drove along the narrow two-lane road, passing several run-down shacks before Ricki pointed out the driveway leading

271

to the cottage. "This is pretty remote to know everything that's going on in town," he observed.

Ricki smiled. "And she doesn't come into town very often either. I've seen her at the Sunny Side Up maybe a half dozen times since it opened five years ago."

"But she still knows about everybody's business." Clay shook his head. "That's hard to believe."

"There's a saying in the Bay. If Wanda doesn't know about it, then it didn't happen."

"Yeah?" He rolled his eyes in disbelief. "Well, I guess we're about to put that one to the test."

When they pulled up next to the hedge covered in tiny pale pink flowers that bordered her lawn, Wanda was already standing on her porch, arranging chairs around a small table. She was almost as tall as Ricki, with layers of wrinkles criss-crossing her cheeks and neck—a result of spending a great deal of time in the sun despite living in the continually overcast Northwest. Her gray hair was pulled back from her face and coiled in her habitual small, tight bun at the nape of her neck. It was the only way she'd worn it since she was a teenager. Walking over to the railing surrounding the porch, she raised a hand in greeting as Ricki and Clay stepped out of the SUV. "Hello. I must say, I'm very disappointed in you two."

"I apologize, Wanda." Clay glanced at his watch. "I don't believe we're late, though."

"No, not in getting here for our appointment. I expected to have a wedding invitation by now." She tilted her chin down and looked at him over the edge of her wire-rimmed glasses. "I am certain you wouldn't be so foolish as to change your mind about marrying Richelle."

Clay grinned and wrapped an arm around Ricki's shoulders. "No, ma'am. Richelle here is the best thing that's ever come along in my life."

Wanda awarded him a beaming smile, clearly pleased with his answer. "He is a charming, handsome devil, Richelle," she said before looking over at Ricki. "You could do worse. Be sure to tell your mother I said that."

Ricki climbed the two steps leading up to the front porch and gave Wanda a hug. Besides her mom, Wanda was the only person who had ever called her Richelle. Just like the queen of the Bay had always referred to her dad as Thomas. Never Tom, or Einstein, which was the nickname everyone in town had used ever since he'd been a kid growing up there. "I'll tell her," Ricki promised. Her mom might not understand it, and certainly wouldn't remember Wanda, but the next time she went for a visit, she would tell her all the same.

"So, it's a beautiful spring day, and I made some lemonade for us to enjoy. I also brought out an extra chair." Wanda patted her hair into place before taking a seat in an elaborate wicker chair with flowers woven into the back. It looked more like a throne than a piece of furniture to keep on a porch. Once seated, she pointed at a metal folding chair. "That one's for you, Chief Thomas. And when we're through, you can fold it back up and set it next to the door."

The request didn't surprise Ricki. Wanda rarely entertained more than one guest at a time. And for good reason. Her guests were much more talkative if there was no one else there to overhear them, and as the grand keeper of all important and trivial activities in the Bay, Wanda made sure she provided a comfortable place to chat.

"Now then," she said, her brown eyes clear and sharp behind the lenses of her glasses. "We've covered the weather, so I think we should get right down to it." She lifted a finger and wagged it at Clay. "You are causing a disturbance in the Force."

Clay stared at her as if she was speaking a foreign language. "I'm sorry?"

Ricki lifted a hand to cover her smile as Wanda chuckled. "I'm a Star Wars fan. Surely you're aware of the Force?"

"Um." He looked to Ricki for help, but she was suddenly busy studying the scenery. "I've seen the movie," he said.

"Only one of them?" Wanda sighed as she handed him a glass of lemonade. "Now that is a crime. And I'm surprised that you aren't a bigger fan of the Force, Chief, seeing as you've had a decisive demonstration of it over the last few days."

"How is that?" Clay asked.

"The power behind idle talk can set you back on your heels if enough people tap into it and pass on the energy. Even when it's bad." She leaned back in her chair and used two fingers to rub the bridge of her nose. "This business with Dr. Garrison shows you how quickly destructive energy can get out of control." She dropped her hand and straightened her glasses so they once again sat squarely on her face. "I had already been at work trying to get to the bottom of things, even before that horrible attack. That's why I called and left that message for you."

Ricki leaned forward, her midnight-blue gaze concentrated on Wanda's face. "And what did you find at the bottom?" She gestured toward Clay without taking her eyes off Wanda. "We'd both like to know."

"All that talk that spread like wildfire came from a lot of different sources, and most of it had no basis in truth." She glanced from Ricki to Clay. "Most of it," she repeated. "I can say for a certainty that there is no conspiracy to keep the person who shot Sam Parkman from facing justice." Her mouth curved up with the hint of a smile. "Or whoever that poor man was. But I have to ask, Chief. When do you intend to bury the poor man? I'm assuming his body is being kept properly in that lab Dr. Garrison built?"

"What else do you have to tell us, Wanda?" Clay asked, ignoring her question.

The older woman's gaze sharpened, but she followed his lead and dropped the subject of the whereabouts of the victim's body. "I know that you all did indeed leave town, but for barely twenty-four hours. I don't know if you went to Kentucky or not, or if the man who had been passing himself off as Sam is from there. And I haven't been able to discover if he murdered anyone at all, much less several people. But I did find it strange that two mysterious men were in town poking around about Sam and the shooting while you were gone. And then up and disappeared the very next morning. Did you know about them?" She carefully studied Clay's face before settling more comfortably into her chair. "I see you did."

"Wanda," Ricki said quietly. "Did you hear anything about some evidence?"

"Which evidence?" Wanda demanded. "There's the cardboard box that Pete saw Dan Wilkes carry into the chief's office, only to have Jules Tucker carry it back out again. Then there's the evidence old TK was supposed to have collected from the body and sent over to Dr. Garrison's lab, but no one saw him actually do that. And neither did anyone see the evidence you supposedly brought back from Kentucky and also stashed away in the doctor's lab." She shook her head. "Small truths buried under layers of lies, and it's hard to know which is which."

"We're having the same problem sifting through it all," Ricki said. "And we need to get to the bottom of whoever is spreading all this nonsense before anyone else gets hurt."

Wanda reached over a hand covered in brown age spots and patted the one Ricki had lying along the armrest of her chair. "Everyone is feeding at this trough and spreading the nonsense whenever they can. She heard it from this person, who got it from so-and-so, who had lunch with another one. It's like a germ that spreads. Now I don't know who started what rumor, but I do know that when I ran a few of them back through that telephone line, they all seemed to have come out of the same spot."

"Which was?" Ricki asked, holding her breath.

"No one could remember exactly who they heard it from, but they knew where they were when they first heard it." Wanda indulged in a dramatic pause, smiling in satisfaction when her two-person audience moved to the edges of their seats. "They were all socializing with their friends and neighbors down at the VFW. It was the common thread between them that I found floating at the bottom of the gossip barrel. So that's where you need to start." She stood up and placed her hands behind her hips, stretching her back before waving toward the SUV.

"Now then, you'd better get to it. I heard Norman was fit to kill after the attack on the good doctor. You two need to get out there and put this whole murder investigation and the mystery of Sam Parkman, to bed, before that young man does something to ruin his life. I'm very fond of him, you know. And after I heard that Minnie Cuthry gave him an earful about conspiracies and whatever other nonsense popped into that silly head of hers, I summoned her here for a heart-to-heart talk. She's decided not to partake in any more gossip over this matter, and will be encouraging her friends to refrain as well. Pete also came to the same conclusion after our phone call." Wanda smiled at Ricki. "Like I said, I'm very fond of Norman, and you too, Richelle." She winked at Clay. "The jury is still out on you, Clayton Thomas, but I'm favoring that direction."

Clay stood up and politely nodded at her. "Thank you. I appreciate it." When Ricki got to her feet, he stepped back so she had room to pass him. "I guess we have our marching orders."

Ricki gave Wanda a last hug, then turned and trotted down the steps. She opened the car door before sending the older woman a final wave.

"Now remember, Richelle James," Wanda called out. "I expect to hear about a wedding date before the month is gone, or cut this one loose and find another."

Ricki's laughter echoed through the surrounding trees.

Chapter Twenty-Six

C lay navigated the SUV down the winding driveway. "I need to get back to the station and meet with those two deputies."

Ricki glanced at the clock built into the dashboard. Unlike the one in her limecicle jeep, this one actually worked. "There's no point in going to the VFW before seven tonight." She drummed three fingers against her knee. "How do you feel about making a trip up to Massey?"

"To look for that communication center that Curt mentioned to the Hanover guys?" When she nodded, he shook his head. "It's going to take more than an afternoon to search around all those weekender cabins up there."

Ricki curled her lips under as she considered the number of weekend cabins and fishing shacks up in Massey. "Maybe."

Clay smiled as he turned onto the narrow lane that led back to the main road. "I take it you have a better plan than a random search?"

She stared out at the passing scenery without really seeing

it. "It's a small town, Massey being the smallest one in the Bay. I think we can take advantage of that."

"How?"

"Tender Tankin." She caught his skeptical look and wiggled her eyebrows at him. "Is there a possibility you can spring Finn and Dan from guard duty so they can give us a hand?"

"Possibly," Clay confirmed. "But exactly what is a tender tankin? It sounds like some kind of fast food."

Ricki laughed before settling back in her seat with a satisfied nod. "Not a what, but a who. He worked the cruise lines for most of his adult life, and one of his jobs was to operate the tender." When he gave her a blank look, she smiled. "You know. That small boat that takes the cruise passengers to the shore when the port isn't big enough or deep enough for a huge ship to dock?"

"Okay," Clay said slowly. "And this helps us how?"

"Every morning Tender operates a small bait shop, set back in the trees from the others along the shoreline. I guess you'd call his shop sort of an area exclusive because he has the best bait from Port Orchard all the way down to Olympia, and he only sells to people he knows. Tender won't talk to anyone he refers to as a 'newcomer'. TK buys all his bait from him. But Dr. Torres and his partner have to take their business elsewhere because Tender considers them newcomers."

Clay's eyes lit up with amusement, but he still shook his head. "I'm not seeing how this helps."

"Simple," Ricki said. "This time of year, Tender spends most of his afternoons in a hammock in front of his place farther up the hill. From there, he has a great view of everything going on in Massey. Who comes, who goes, what direction they're headed in, and how long they're gone. He's like a breathing logbook for the town."

"I thought that was Wanda's job," Clay said with a snort. "How many town criers have we got?"

Ricki laughed. "Just Wanda and Pete, for the most part. Any tidbits that Tender picks up he passes along to Wanda. Otherwise, he keeps them to himself."

Clay shot her a curious look. "Why just Wanda? Does he consider Pete a newcomer?"

"Nope." Ricki grinned as she tucked a loose strand of hair behind one ear. "He just doesn't like Pete."

Clay chuckled as he negotiated the turn onto the highway leading to Edington and the police station. Once they were on their way, he cast a sideways look at Ricki. "Why doesn't this Tender person like Pete? He's harmless enough."

"Pete doesn't fish, and Wanda does. And every time she heads up to that part of the Bay, she drops in on Tender," Ricki said. "I also suspect she pays for his cell phone, which is another reason Pete is shut out." She winked at Clay. "But don't tell Pete that. He hasn't figured it out yet."

"The non-fishing group includes me," Clay said. "And I've never seen you with a fishing pole in your hand, either."

"No, I always preferred camping," she said cheerfully. "But my Uncle Cy loves to fish, and I used to go with him. Plus, I was born here. Don't worry. Tender will talk to me."

"Do you think he might have seen Curt lurking around Massey?"

"Or Preston Malone," Ricki pointed out. "I'm assuming Curt had a reason for thinking Malone had some kind of communication center up there, so I think we should try to retrace his steps. Hopefully with some help from Tender. But I'd ask him about Malone first. See if Tender had any interactions with him as his alter ego Sam Parkman. So how about it? Can you spare Finn and Dan?"

Clay nodded. "It's a good idea. If we find this communication center Curt was talking about, I'm not sure I'd know what kind of equipment we were looking at. But I'll bet Finn or Dan will."

"That's what I'm thinking too."

It was another fifteen minutes before they pulled up at the police station. A cruiser with blue lettering that matched the one driven by the deputy recovering in the town's clinic was in the parking lot.

Clay strode up to the station's double doors while Ricki deliberately lagged behind. This was police business, and she didn't want to get in the way. Instead of entering the lobby, she stood at the edge of the wide top landing and took out her phone and called Anchorman.

"Hey. How's the hunt going?" he asked the second he answered.

"It's going. We talked to the CEO of Hanover, and it turns out the two guys he sent are the ones who let the cat out of the bag about Malone's Kentucky connection."

"To who?" he demanded.

"Curt Tandoon. It seems one of the Hanover guys was in the same unit as Curt during an overseas deployment. Anyway, during their conversation, the information that we were in Kentucky pursuing a lead on Malone got out, although their boss stated that they never divulged Malone's name."

"What else did they tell Curt?"

Even though he couldn't see her, Ricki shrugged. "Not much. But Curt told them he was looking for a communication base of some sort that Malone had set up in Massey."

"Massey?" A loud sigh came through the speaker. "All those weekend places up there? That's like looking for a needle in a haystack."

"Uh-huh," she agreed. "Except I think he knew where it was, so we're going to take a run up there this afternoon. If we come up empty, we'll track Curt down during our visit to the VFW tonight and get more details out of him.

"We know two of the guys are vets, and we think the third one is too. And Wanda tracked down the source of the rumors as coming out of the VFW, although she couldn't pinpoint the exact person." When Anchorman didn't say anything, Ricki blew out a nervous breath. It was a bad sign when he went quiet. "Since Wanda got us that far, we'll be paying a visit to the post tonight and mingle in with the crowd to see what we can pick up."

"Cheron is being moved to a regular room in a few hours," Anchorman said in an abrupt change of subject. "I need to get her settled in."

Ricki frowned. "I talked to Marcie this morning. She said Cheron was being moved because she's improving?"

"She is," Anchorman said in response to her hanging question. "Better and faster than I had hoped. I just need to be sure she's settled in safe and comfortably in her room here. And I have a meet with a guy I know a little later."

"A meet?" She couldn't keep the suspicious note out of her voice. "For what?"

"It's just a meet, Ricki," he said quietly. "I'm in town, so I gave him a call. Look, I have to go. You let me know if you come across anything up there in Massey."

"Will do. Take care of Cheron."

"You can count on that," Anchorman said before he disconnected the call.

Ricki held her phone out in front of her and stared at it for a moment. A meet? *He's up to something*, she thought. But nothing came to her about just what that might be.

She was still thinking it over when Clay pushed through the doors, followed by two uniformed officers. "Everything is set up. We need to drop these guys off at the clinic and pick up

Finn and Dan." He turned and made quick introductions and then headed for the SUV. "They're going to follow in their squad car."

Ricki jogged over to the SUV and climbed into the front passenger seat. She buckled in while Clay said a few words to the Tacoma officers before getting behind the SUV's wheel and starting the engine. It only took ten minutes to get to the clinic, make the switch with Finn and Dan, and be on their way north toward Massey.

"Anything new?" Finn asked. "Because Dan has something big. But you two go first."

Ricki quickly recounted the conversation with the Hanover CEO, and then with Wanda.

"Not surprised about the VFW," Dan said. "I'm sure we're looking for another vet."

Ricki twisted around in her seat and peered at Dan. "You found a connection?" She frowned as her fellow ISB agent shook his head.

"Not yet," Dan said. "Or at least not directly. But I did find someone who might be able to make that connection for us."

Clay looked at him through the rearview mirror. "Don't keep us in suspense."

"You found Sam Parkman," Ricki blurted out. "The real Sam Parkman."

Dan drew in a sharp breath. "Not exactly. Well, I did, but that's not the big news."

"Parkman is dead," Finn stated flatly. "He died three years ago from cancer."

Ricki closed her eyes while Clay slapped a palm against the steering wheel. "Are you absolutely sure?" he asked.

Finn crossed his arms over his chest and nodded at Dan. "Tell them."

Dan opened his laptop and talked while he was booting it

up. "I had no luck with his birth name, but wasn't expecting to. It would have been very strange if Parkman had kept his legal name. But after some trial and error, I went to the digital archives of the local newspaper in Omaha, typed in the birthdate for a search, and came up with a short list of names. I thought he might have stuck with Malone's system and picked an alias with the same initials as his real name, but no luck there. One name did stand out to me though." He shrugged. "Well, the surname, anyway. It was Bannu."

Ricki's eyebrows winged upward. "Bannu? Why did that stand out?"

"I worked the Middle East desk for a while." Dan lifted his gaze to Ricki's and smiled. "Which meant learning the history of the area along with the current political environment. Bannu is from Egyptian mythology and has the same basic concept as the phoenix in Greek myths."

"The bird that rose from the ashes," Ricki said. "As in reinventing itself, so yeah, that fits."

"I pulled up the man's obituary. There was no picture associated with it, but it did mention that he passed away from cancer three years ago, after a long battle. It didn't mention any parents or siblings, but it did state that he owned a mechanic shop in Chalco, to the southwest of Omaha."

Clay let out a low whistle. "A mechanic shop? Sounds like you hit the jackpot."

"No doubt about it," Dan said. "The clincher was his full name was listed as Gary Bannu."

"His father's name." Ricki made a small sound in the back of her throat. "Marcie's father was Gary Parkman."

"Yeah. I thought 'bingo' when I read that," Dan stated. "Now, another kicker. Besides the mechanic's shop, he also had a list of survivors, which included a wife and three kids."

Ricki blinked. "You're joking?"

Dan shook his head. "Nope." He looked down and consulted the notes on his laptop. "Her name is LeeAnn Bannu, and we talked to her yesterday. She has quite a story to tell. When I told her that Malone had been shot, she wanted to talk to you personally, so I haven't heard everything she has to say. But I heard enough to know you are going to want to talk to this lady."

"Where and when?" was all Ricki asked.

"Tomorrow morning. She'll take an early lunch break from the café she works at there in Chalco, so that will be at eight thirty our time."

"I think we all want to hear what she has to say." Clay turned the SUV off the highway and onto the narrower two-lane road leading into Massey. "Okay, here we are. Now where should I go?"

"Down to the far end, past the wharf," Ricki directed. "Park anywhere because we'll need to walk from there."

The small town sat at the very tip of Dabob Bay, and boasted a single line of bait stands and fast-food hangouts along the shoreline. There was a wharf and boat-launching pad, and a cramped lot to park for the fishermen who came for the day, but the rest of the town was made up solely of compact cabins that dotted the landscape. They continued to pop up all the way along the slope of a small mountain directly behind the town, with a lighthouse perched near the top.

Ricki led the way up a narrow path that skirted the edge of a small bait shack that was closed up and had no name displayed on the outside.

"This is Tender's spot," she called over her shoulder to the group tramping along behind her. "His house is up there." She pointed to a lone building sitting on a cleared-off space about halfway up the hill.

She continued to climb, finally stopping at the edge of the

small clearing. There were spring flowers planted all around the border, with a rock pathway leading up to a tidy-looking house. The compact wooden structure had a low overhang above the front door and the two steps leading up to it. In the middle of the treeless space, that served as both a fire break and a front yard, was a large hammock, and to one side was a card table with four chairs around it.

When a head rose over the edge of the hammock, Ricki lifted a hand in greeting. "Hi, Tender. I was hoping to talk to you a bit."

The man with a mop of dark hair and deep brown eyes swung his legs over the side of the hammock and hopped to the ground. He wore a simple yellow shirt and white cotton pants, and on his feet were a pair of leather sandals. It was a look borrowed directly from a tourist hanging out on one of those cruise ships, or on a beach on a tropical island.

He waved a hand over his head, his huge smile displaying white teeth that were a contrast to the golden skin tone native to Pacific Islanders.

"Ricki James." He waved his arm again, then beckoned her forward.

"All three of you stay right here," she said to the men standing behind her before she went to join Tender.

Tender pointed to Clay, Finn, and Dan. "Who are they?"

She put her hands on her hips and shook her head at them. "Now, you know who Clay is. He's the police chief here in the Bay."

"I've heard that, but we've never met." Tender grinned and tilted his head toward the card table. He waited until Ricki took a seat, then selected one that allowed him to keep an eye on the men. "The chief doesn't fish. What about the other two?"

Ricki grinned. "I doubt it. Uncle Cy says 'hello', and so does Wanda. I was talking to her just this morning."

Tender's gaze widened in surprise. "She didn't send you here, did she? Because I don't know anything about all the craziness going on in town."

"Then you heard about Sam Parkman?" Ricki asked.

"I heard he was shot, and that he wasn't really Sam." Tender shook his head, sending his mop of hair flying in different directions. "Don't have much to say about that. I came to the Bay seventeen, maybe eighteen years ago now, but Sam Parkman had already left. So I never met him."

"He liked to fish," Ricki said.

The older man's face pulled down into a frown. "Then the man who was shot wasn't the real Sam, because he never went fishing. Not once. He sure never stopped by my bait shop, but then I wouldn't have served him. He was too new. But he never stopped by any of the shops that I saw."

Ricki immediately pounced on that. "But you saw him here in Massey?"

"Sure, sure." Tender rubbed his palms down the top of his thighs and back up again. "Every couple of weeks, maybe." He pointed toward the bottom of the hill. "Mostly in the early afternoon, you know, between lunch and dinner?"

She nodded. That made sense. After the lunch shift that Sam cooked for half the time, and before the dinner shift when Anchorman always manned the kitchen. "Did you notice where he went?"

"Walking," Tender said. He twisted in his chair and pointed to a path that came up from the road below and disappeared into the trees a hundred yards to the left of his house. "That path isn't used much."

Ricki leaned over in her chair and studied the dirt track. "I've been up there, but it was a long time ago. I remember a few places along the way, but not many."

"Three. There are three places up there," Tender claimed.

"At least that's all that are still standing. There used to be five, but one burned down, and the other one just fell down a few years back. All of them are more shacks than houses, and they're all owned by the same guy, I think. But I haven't seen him in a long time, so maybe he sold them." Tender shrugged. "I don't know."

"Anything else up there that Sam might have gone to see?" Ricki asked.

Tender laughed and slapped a hand against his knee. "Like what? There's no waterfall, or some scenic place. Too many trees in the way. The view is better from here. I figured he just liked to walk, or maybe he rented one of the places." Tender frowned, his forehead wrinkled in concentration. "Or maybe he just squatted in one of them. Usually he was just walking along, but sometimes I saw him carrying a bag." His eyes twinkled at Ricki. "You know, like a grocery bag? Maybe he liked cooking up there."

"Carrying something?" Ricki echoed. "Hmm. Well, maybe we should go take a look, in case he left something behind his family might want."

Tender's expression perked right up. "The guy who wasn't really Sam has a family?"

"We're still trying to figure that out," she replied smoothly. She looked off into the distance. "Do you know who Curt Tandoon is?"

"Yeah." Tender grinned as he bounced his head up and down. "He likes to fish. And he doesn't talk much, which is a good thing. Stopped by my shop a couple of times to see if he could get on my customer list." He winked at Ricki. "I always tell him I'm still thinking about it."

"Did you ever see him go up that path?"

The old cruise ship worker frowned as he lifted a hand and rubbed it across his chin. "I can't say. He's walked past the shop a couple of times in the last month or so. Mostly in the morning when I'm working. Didn't stop to talk, just kept on going. But I don't know if he took the path up the hill or kept going along the shore." He lowered his hand and gave her a curious look. "Why are you asking about Sam and Curt?"

Ricki smiled back at him. "You know how it goes, Tender, when someone gets themselves shot. We ask about everyone." She stood up and reached over to lay a hand on his shoulder. "Thank you. You've been a big help."

Tender's gaze shifted to the path, then drifted past the three waiting men before returning to Ricki. "Maybe you can stop by again and give me something to tell Wanda?"

"Maybe."

Chapter Twenty-Seven

Ricki led the way up the path, following the twists and turns as it gradually climbed the mountain. The first structure they came to was nothing but a pile of charred wood in the middle of a small clearing that was set off the path. She barely spared it a glance as she passed it, heading for the next spot. Tender had been right about what had been built up the deserted path. The second structure was little more than a shack, with several holes in the roof. It was barely big enough to store a minimal amount of camping gear.

Ten minutes later they came across the first real possibility. As Ricki approached the small run-down porch held up by a couple of sagging poles, she didn't see any signs of recent activity. The tattered curtains at the single window didn't show much of the dark interior, but it was enough to see the cobwebs crisscrossing the space.

"No one has been here for quite a while," she said, smiling when Clay tried the door and the handle came off in his hand.

"I'm going to agree with that." He tossed the handle over his shoulder. "Where to next?"

"We keep climbing." Straightening up, she returned to the path and continued walking. The day was unseasonably warm for the beginning of spring, so it wasn't long before she had shed her jacket, tying it around her waist.

"How's the next one looking?" Finn called out, sounding slightly out of breath.

"We'll know in a minute," Ricki replied. One last turn and another small building appeared in the trees. It was larger than the last one and looked much better kept on the outside. She stepped off the path and headed through the trees, her eyes on the ground. She didn't spot any fresh boot tracks but wasn't surprised given the heavy carpet of pine needles and constant spurt of rain over the previous few days.

Once she reached the covered porch, she saw several prints of dried mud on the floorboards. But more interesting was the brand-new lock on the door. While the door handle turned easily enough, the padlock kept the portal firmly in place. The curtains at the nearest window didn't offer much protection, but the black plastic cover over it certainly did.

"I think this is our spot. Spread out and check all the windows," she said before walking over to the second window, on the opposite side of the door.

"No window on this side or in the back that I can see," Finn yelled.

"No windows on this side either," Dan echoed.

Ricki glanced at Clay and lifted her shoulders. "You're the police chief. What do you want to do?"

Clay's response was to bend his arm and smash into one of the windows with his elbow. The crashing sound brought Finn and Dan back to the front of the shack at a dead run.

The former CIA agent skidded to a halt as he stared first at the glass scattered on the porch and then at Clay, who had calmly flipped the window lock. "Is this legal without a warrant?"

"Probably not." Clay pushed up the lower window frame and what was left of the glass. He shoved a long leg through the opening, then ducked and slid the rest of his body inside.

Ricki winked at Dan as she stepped past him and followed Clay into the interior of the cabin. Clay was already busy tearing down the black plastic from the other window, so Ricki turned around and did the same for the one they'd just come through. Tossing the plastic onto the ground, she took several steps forward, her gaze wandering across the space as Finn made his way through the broken frame, followed by Dan.

There were several tables pushed together so they lined three of the walls, creating one long counter space. In the center of the room were three rough-cut boards, held up by plastic crates. While Clay, Finn, and Dan walked around, looking at the parts that were strewn across the long table, Ricki went to the makeshift desk. There were several stacks of paper that looked like random pages printed from an online manual. She picked one up and frowned at the diagram.

"What is this?" she asked no one in particular. "It looks like he was building something.

Finn walked over and peered at the torn page. "Tracking device. I've seen these before. Even saw a couple of our guys building makeshift ones." He pointed to several bins on one of the tables. "Malone has the parts over there." He plucked a small plastic bag from one bin. "See this board? You can buy it online for twenty bucks. It has a processor with a built-in transmitter and an antenna. He's also got these batteries here for a power source." Finn picked up a miniature board and examined it. "This looks like a GPS tracker rather than Bluetooth."

"The difference being?" Clay asked.

"Range and mapping ability," Dan said. "The GPS transmitter has a much longer range. Basically unlimited if there aren't any major obstacles in the way." He looked at Clay and smiled. "Like mountains." He held up a plastic piece. "And here are the casings." He dropped the item back into its bin and looked at the parts scattered on the tables. "I agree. It looks like a GPS tracker rather than something with a Bluetooth chip."

"Okay. But why would he need so many?" Ricki asked. "He had a regular assembly line going."

"Battery life mostly," Finn said with a shrug. "They can last for a few weeks if they're transmitting continuously, or up to three or four months if they're only operating periodically."

Dan frowned. "As far as we know, the only thing that Malone had that was worth tracking was the money. But if the money is on the move, why did he sit here for three years?"

"Maybe to make sure the money doesn't actually move," Finn suggested. "Which would mean it's stashed someplace around the bay."

"Which also means they didn't move it offshore after all?" Clay shook his head. "Their greatest risk is having that money surface and then tracked back to them. The best case for the three that pulled this off is to get the money out of the country, in small increments that won't raise any red flags."

Ricki let the debate swirl around her as she studied the contents of the crudely constructed desk. On one corner was a folded piece of paper, held down by a flat rock. She moved the makeshift paperweight and picked up the notebook-sized paper. Carefully unfolding it, she stared down at the three sets of numbers written on it.

"Take a look at this."

Clay walked over to where she was standing and looked over her shoulder. "What are those?"

"GPS coordinates, city boy." She studied the numbers. "All

three have the same latitude and longitude numbers, but different minutes and seconds."

"Meaning they're close together?" Clay asked.

"That's right."

Finn came over and joined them, staring down at the paper in Ricki's hand. "So where is 47 degrees latitude and 122 degrees longitude?"

"Brewer, basically," Ricki said. "These precise locations are somewhere in the area."

"If I had my computer, there are a dozen programs that would pull up the locations with just the coordinates," Dan said. "You could do it on your phone, actually."

Clay glanced at his watch. "You and Finn can do that later. We still have to hike out of here and get some relief for my deputies." He ran a distracted hand through his hair. "We just don't have enough people to watch every place at once, so I'm going to have the Tacoma deputies stand guard at the clinic and leave Cheron's lab locked up. The odds are small that the third partner will be back there."

"Especially since Wanda put out that there was no evidence stored at the lab," Ricki said. "A point we can make very clear when we visit the VFW later on."

Finn looked over at the window with a look of distaste. "I suppose we're going to have to crawl out the same way we got in?"

"You guess right," Clay confirmed. "And after we get back to Brewer, you two head out and get something to eat and then some rest in a proper bed tonight. Ricki and I will cover the VFW, and we can all meet back at our place tomorrow morning for the call with LeeAnn Parkman."

It was another hour before they dropped Dan off at Marcie's place and then headed for the St. Armand Hotel. After they'd said goodbye to a tired-looking Finn, it was only a few more minutes before they pulled up to their cabin and an excited Corby. Ricki walked hand in hand with Clay up the steps and into the house on automatic. When Clay took her jacket from her hands and hung it up, she nodded an absent thanks, went to the refrigerator and pulled out a beer.

"It seems Marcie was right, and we'll be having leftover pizza, unless you want to stop by the Sunny Side Up and see what we can scrounge up," she said.

"Pizza is fine," Clay told her. "I'd appreciate one of those beers first though." When Ricki handed him a long-necked bottle, he patted the stool next to his. "Why don't you sit down for a few minutes and tell me what you're thinking so hard about?"

She slid onto the stool and took a long drink of her beer before setting the bottle on the counter. "Three partners, three GPS coordinates." She shifted her body around so she was facing Clay. "But there aren't three guys anymore. There's only been two since Parkman died, if we're assuming he was in on it."

"Which we are," Clay put in.

She nodded slowly. "All right. But with Malone dead, now there's only one."

"And if those trackers are wherever the money is stashed, then you can bet the last man standing has the receiver for that GPS signal," Clay said.

"And the only reason you'd need a signal is if it's somewhere that isn't easy to find." Ricki got out the paper and smoothed it on top of the counter. "These numbers mean it's west of Brewer and a little south. I'm guessing when Dan pulls this up, it will be close to the eastern boundary of the park."

"It bothers you that they might have hidden the stolen money in the park?" Clay asked.

"No. It bothers me that Malone was the communications

guy. He built the trackers. The third partner might have a receiver, but I'll bet he didn't know where that little assembly line was located, or he would have destroyed it after he killed Malone." When Clay frowned, she drew in a breath. "Finn said the trackers have a limited battery life. And the third partner wasn't the electronics guy. Malone was."

"Then he's going to have to grab the money and run before that signal dies." Clay crossed his arms over his chest. "So we could have anywhere from an hour to three months before the guy ups and disappears again."

Ricki sighed in exasperation. "Yeah. Something like that." She slid off the stool and went to the refrigerator and the left-over pizza. "We'd better eat and get over to the VFW. We need to cut this guy off before he turns into a rabbit." *As in going, going, gone,* she thought as she opened the fridge and grabbed the pizza box.

Chapter Twenty-Eight

The old house that served as the command post for the VFW was lit up like a beacon against the surrounding darkness created by tall trees, overcast skies, and no streetlights. Business was booming tonight, and the closest parking spot was two blocks away. Clay tucked the SUV on the dirt shoulder that ran alongside the pavement and joined Ricki on the sidewalk to head back to the post. It was a pleasant night, despite the clouds overhead that blocked out the moon.

The temperature wasn't warm, but it didn't have the bite of winter in it either, so Ricki left her jacket unbuttoned as she strolled along with a light breeze ruffling her hair and her hand tucked into Clay's.

"You know what would make this night perfect?" Clay asked.

She smiled. "If the third partner would jump up from his seat and say 'I did it, take me away'?"

He laughed and gave her hand a gentle squeeze. "Well, that too. But I was thinking if you had my wedding ring on your finger." He leaned over and dropped a kiss against her temple. "I'm not complaining about where we are. But I'm beginning to think between our family, friends, and chasing murder, there will never be enough time to make it happen."

"We don't need a lot of time," Ricki said. "Just cooperation."

"From what?"

"All those things you mentioned." Ricki sighed. The noise from the VFW reached out and slowly enveloped them. "But it's murder that has no respect for our plans." She pushed the sudden thought of her neglected wedding out of her mind as she pointed to the old house bursting with people. "It looks like we'll be wading through a full house tonight."

Clay's gaze pivoted to the post. "At least that gives us a better chance that the third partner will be present.

It took some time to get past the crowd lingering on the porch and make their way down the hall toward the great room in the back of the house. It was standing room only, with all the tables filled and the bodies packed in along the bar. Ricki wound her way through the maze, nodding when Clay touched her arm and then broke off in a different direction, heading for a table where Pete was holding court with Mike and four other guys.

At the bar, Ricki squeezed into a space, then turned to look out over the room.

"Looking for someone?"

She faced the bar again and smiled at Bill Langly. "No. Just looking."

"How's Dr. Garrison doing?" Bill asked. "We all heard someone did a number on her."

"Much better," Ricki said. "She's out of the ICU, which is a big step."

Frowning, she leaned forward and peered into the post

commander's face. "What's wrong with your eye?"

Bill put a hand over his right eye and blinked at her with his left. "I'm only operating with half my sight. I lost a contact this morning, and my spare set is at home."

"You don't have any glasses here that you can use in the meantime?" Ricki asked.

"And trade my macho look for a geeky one?" he joked. "Nah. I lost the last pair I had a few years ago and never bothered to get them replaced."

"Well, try not to pour the beer all over the floor." She turned her head when someone tapped her on the shoulder, then smiled at Clay. "How's Pete doing?"

"He's very sorry about any problems he caused by what he called 'misinterpreting Jules carrying a cardboard box out of the station.' And he's stopped taking calls or saying a word about the shooting or anything connected with it."

"I'd say Wanda is doing her job."

Bill lifted an eyebrow at Ricki. "What job is that?"

"It's not important," she said, raising her voice to be heard over the din. "I have a favor to ask, Bill."

The post commander brought a cloth out from under the bar and took a swipe at the counter in front of her. "Sure. What do you need?"

"A membership list."

Bill's eyebrows drew together at the request. "Can I ask why?"

"Just checking on a hunch." Ricki shrugged. "It's probably nothing, but I would really appreciate that list."

"All right." He said the words slowly, drawing them out. "Is there any other information you want on that list besides names?"

"The date each member joined the post would be great. Thanks."

"No problem. I'll drop it by your place in the morning." Bill looked past her and frowned. "You seem to be the center of someone's attention."

Ricki's gaze scanned the room, stopping when she spotted Merlin staring back at her from a table set squarely in the middle of the floor. Rory sat next to her, looking glum as he nursed a beer. She recognized the two other young men at the table as being part of the high school class that was a good five years behind hers. Ricki shifted onto a stool and slanted her head to the side when Merlin continued to stare, not breaking eye contact until the former Ranger finally looked away.

"Maybe we should go over and say hi to Merlin and Rory," Ricki told Clay.

"That would be nice," Bill said. He jerked his head toward the center table. "Rory got laid off today, so he could use some cheering up."

Ricki slid off the stool and stepped away from the bar. The small space she left was immediately filled with another body as she and Clay made their way to Merlin's table.

The retired Army Ranger looked up, annoyance showing all over her face. "Can we help you?"

"Just came to say hello," Clay stated, his voice friendly despite Merlin's surly look. When the two young men got to their feet and offered their chairs before wandering off, Clay thanked them and pulled out the nearest one for Ricki before taking his own seat.

"That's some very nice manners you have there, Chief," Merlin said. "Bet you don't pull out any chairs for your other deputies."

"She's not my deputy," Clay said in a mild tone. "She's a special agent and my fiancée, so I have no problem pulling out a chair for her, just like she has no problem shooting someone on my behalf."

"Really?" Merlin pointed her beer bottle at Ricki. "Shot anyone lately, Agent James?"

Ricki bared her teeth in a smile. "No. Have you?"

Merlin snorted and took a sip of her beer.

Ignoring her, Ricki smiled at Rory. "Bill said you were laid off today. I'm sorry to hear that."

The young man shrugged thin shoulders. "It's okay. I was already working short hours, so it didn't come as no surprise."

"Have any plans on what you'd like to do?" Clay asked. When Rory gave him a blank look, Clay cocked his head to the side. "Maybe you'd like to change careers? Do you like to cook?"

"I don't know." Rory's forehead wrinkled as he thought it over. "I'd sure like it if I didn't have to work out in the rain and snow anymore. And I'd much rather be around people. I did a lot of long solo drives in that truck to get to the job sites. Didn't care for that too much." He slowly nodded. "Yeah. All of that would be real nice." His mouth turned up into a smile. "I'll have to think on it some. I have a little money saved up, and summer is coming. Maybe I'll take some time and camp out in the park." He ducked his head before shooting Ricki a shy look. "I really like camping out in the park."

She grinned back at him. "I do too."

Merlin nudged his beer bottle with her own. "I thought you just said you wanted to spend more time around people. How are you going to do that if you're out camping alone in the park?"

"I don't know. Maybe you could come along?" he asked good-naturedly, then laughed at Merlin's sour look. "I know. You got enough of that roughing-it-in-the-woods stuff during your stint in the service. Maybe I'll tag along with the commander."

Ricki's smile faded just a little. "The commander? Are you talking about Bill?"

"Yeah. I do spend a lot of time camping in the park, and I've seen him up there hiking a few times."

"Why didn't you invite yourself along? He might have liked the company," Clay suggested.

Both Rory and Merlin shook their heads at the same time.

"No. You invite yourself along with your buds," Merlin explained. "Not with rank, and the commander was a captain in the army. So he'd have to do the inviting."

Curious, Ricki's boot tapped against the floor. "Even though you aren't in the military anymore?"

Merlin straightened in her chair and crossed her arms over her chest. "Rules are rules, whether you're still officially in uniform or not." She was back to giving Ricki the hard stare, but now she was including Clay in it as well. "And one of those rules is that the VFW is for vets. Like the name says, Veterans of Foreign Wars." Her lip curled up. "What foreign theater did either of you serve in again?"

Rory set his beer bottle down on the table with a thump and scowled at her. "That wasn't nice." In an instant, the scowl disappeared and his eyes grew wide as the whole room went silent.

When Merlin shrank back in her chair, Ricki looked over her shoulder to see what had caused the sudden change of atmosphere in the room. Anchorman stood in the doorway leading from the hall, his hands at his side as his gaze quartered the room before landing on Merlin.

Ignoring the sudden hush all around him, he strode across the room and stood next to Ricki. "Sorry I'm late. I'm sure you've been treated very well." He gave a glaring Merlin a hard stare. "As my guests."

"They don't need to be invited as guests," Bill called out

from behind the bar. "Clay and Ricki are welcome here any time."

There was a murmur of agreement before the noise level rose back to normal.

Anchorman pulled up a chair that had miraculously appeared, and sat down, propping one heavily booted ankle on top of the opposite knee. "Sorry. I didn't mean to interrupt. What are we talking about?"

"Um." Merlin looked at Rory, who only shrugged, and then over at Clay. "I was just getting ready to ask the chief how long you should wait before filing a missing person report."

Clay tapped a finger against the tabletop. "You know someone who's missing?"

Merlin slowly turned her beer bottle in a circle. "I think so. At least we haven't seen him in a few days, and that's kind of weird."

"Who are you talking about?" Clay asked.

"Curt Tandoon. I haven't seen him in a few days, and neither has Rory." She looked over at him for a confirming nod. "I went by Curt's place, but he wasn't home, so I left a note on his door. I still haven't heard from him."

"Was his truck at the house?" Ricki asked.

Merlin shook her head. "No. But I haven't seen it around either, and Curt never leaves the Bay."

"What are you talking about?" Rory's eyebrows came together in a puzzled look. "Curt's not missing. His truck's at my place because I gave him a ride to the airport. He went to Dallas."

Merlin's jaw dropped to her chest. "Dallas? What the hell for?"

Rory shrugged. "I don't know. He said something about looking up an old army buddy."

"You might have mentioned before I ran all over town

looking for him," Merlin groused.

Rory only shrugged. "you could have asked before trying to file a police report."

Clay intercepted Ricki's telling look and pushed back from the table. "It's been a long day, and I think we should call it a night."

Under the table, Ricki stomped a boot on Anchorman's foot before standing up. Getting the signal, the former Marine also stood and nodded at the other two, who were still seated.

"I'll call you tomorrow about our progress in locating Curt," Clay said before stepping aside to let Ricki pass.

She stuck her hands in her pockets and did a casual stroll toward the front hallway, casting a look over her shoulder to make sure Anchorman was following. Once they were outside in the fresh air again, she latched on to the Marine's arm and started tugging him along.

"I'm coming. What's the big hurry?" he complained.

As soon as they were out of earshot, she turned on him. "What are you doing here instead of hanging out at the hospital with Cheron?"

"She's fine," Anchorman said. "And she insisted I get back here to help. She doesn't trust Finn to have your backs."

Ricki put her hands on her hips as her boot did a rapid beat against the sidewalk. "And you thought that was enough to leave her there and come running back here?"

Now Anchorman's face scrunched up into a scowl. "I didn't leave her there all alone. Kate and Marcie are with her, and she has solid protection. The best thing I can do for her now is to catch the asshole who put his hands on her and make sure he can never do that again."

"Hang on there," Clay intervened. "We're out to catch this guy, not shoot him on sight."

"Did I say I was going to do that?" Anchorman tossed back.

"I'm your backup. That's how we work." He narrowed his eyes at Clay's skeptical look.

"What do you mean by solid protection?" Ricki demanded, drawing Anchorman's attention back to her. Understanding suddenly dawned as she stared at him. "That meet you had. You called in someone to stand guard."

"Two someones," he corrected. "They're old friends and reliable. They won't let anyone get past them."

Ricki waved a hand in the air. "Fine. Fine. We have a conference call in the morning at eight thirty with the real Sam Parkman's widow."

Anchorman's eyebrows shot all the way up his forehead. "Sam Parkman is dead?"

"Yeah," Ricki confirmed. "Dan tracked him down. He died of cancer three years ago, and his widow wants to talk to us."

"At your place?" When Ricki nodded, he did too. "I'll be there." He pointed in the opposite direction of the SUV. "I rented a car. It's parked down that way. I'll take a morning run tomorrow over to your place and pick up my truck then." He reached over and gave Ricki a brief hug, then nodded at Clay before he turned around and walked off toward his car.

Ricki watched until the dark swallowed him up, then grabbed Clay's hand. "Come on. Let's get home."

Clay didn't say anything until they were back in the SUV with the engine turned on to warm up the interior. "You didn't want to offer him a beer and some leftover pizza?"

She shook her head. "He needs some sleep, and we need to talk."

"About something you don't want him to hear?" When she sighed, Clay put the car into gear and pulled out onto the road. He didn't say anything until they walked into the cabin and were seated at the island, two bottles of beer in front of them. "Okay. What are we talking about?"

"Bill Langly," Ricki said in a flat voice. "He's our guy."

Clay whistled softly. "I thought you were leaning toward Merlin."

She shook her head as her eyes narrowed in thought. "No. She's too direct to pull off a charade for seven years. It's Langly." Anger crept along the nerves in her arms. At Langly for worming himself into the Bay, and at herself, for not recognizing him for what he was. A thief and a killer. "I should have seen it. When we got to the clinic after Malone was shot, he was already there. And had been inside with Nancy. We heard that a couple of times. So he easily could have overheard TK discovering that the Sam Parkman who was shot wasn't the real Sam."

Clay frowned. "Yeah. That's possible. And he's been here in the Bay long enough to feed Malone personal information about all of us."

"Which was a mistake," Ricki said. "He didn't realize that Sam hadn't known you or Anchorman."

"He was at the bar," Clay said slowly. "We told him the autopsy was going to be delayed until the morning. And that gave him time to steal the body to keep Malone from being identified."

"Except we didn't mention that Cheron had already taken the fingerprints." Ricki slid off her stool and paced to the far side of the kitchen. "He was at the Sunny Side Up that morning. I remember seeing him there. At least after the shooting. He could have gone around the back, shot Malone, and in the chaos just walked into the front of the diner and blended in with the rest of the crowd."

"Which would explain why we couldn't find a trace of the shooter," Clay said.

"And also explain how he knew there is a mat at the back door." At Clay's questioning look, she lifted her hand and jabbed a finger in the air toward the front window. "My jeep. When he moved my jeep, he said he'd leave the key under the mat at the back door. I should have picked up on that."

"He might have just assumed there was a mat at the back door of the diner," Clay pointed out. "It wouldn't be a far-fetched assumption."

"I should have still seen it." Ricki stopped and crossed her arms over her chest and glared at him. "Okay, then. He also lied to me. He told me he hadn't ever gone hiking or camping since he's been in the Bay. That he prefers to go fishing. But Rory said he's seen Bill hiking in the park." She walked over to the desk and picked up the piece of paper she'd taken from Malone's shack in Massey. "In the park, and very likely close to where these GPS coordinates are."

"Even if he fits our take on the third partner, it could still be a handful of other guys. We don't have any solid proof it was Bill Langly," Clay pointed out.

"Then let's hope we get it tomorrow from Sam's widow. This third partner is smart, and I'll bet a month's paycheck that he planned that robbery and handed out the orders to the other two. That's what an Army Captain would do." Ricki returned to the island and picked up her beer. "With any luck, LeeAnn Parkman will prove it."

"I'll toast to that." Clay picked up his beer and lifted it in a quick salute. "And to you for having the foresight not to talk this out in front of Anchorman. If he'd heard you say it was Langly, he would have been out of here and headed to the VFW with blood in his eyes before either one of us could catch him." He set the beer down without taking a drink then lifted the jacket he'd draped over the back of his chair and took his cell phone out of the pocket. "But proof or no proof, it wouldn't hurt to keep an eye on Langly. At least until after that phone call tomorrow morning."

Chapter Twenty-Nine

Ricki yawned. She'd tried to get some sleep, but had spent most of the night wide awake, staring at the ceiling and listening to Clay's even breathing next to her. When the first light of the morning sun had crept over the windowsill, she'd given up and quietly slipped out of bed and tiptoed downstairs.

Corby was waiting for her with his food dish in his mouth. She rolled her eyes but dutifully filled it, then let him outside. She'd enjoyed a quiet cup of coffee and had another one waiting for Clay when he came downstairs and she went back up to take a shower.

She was nursing a second cup of coffee and wishing she'd managed more sleep when Anchorman walked in the door, carrying a large brown paper bag in one hand and a gallon of milk in the other.

"I thought you could use something besides cold pizza." He set the bag down and smiled when Ricki made a face at him. "Since you both usually eat at the diner, cold pizza is about the only food you keep in the refrigerator." He lifted the jug of milk. "And you're probably close to being out of this."

Clay looked up from his phone. "No probably about it." He slid off the stool and took the jug from Anchorman, walking over to put it in the refrigerator just as a frantic burst of barking came from outside the cabin. "It sounds like Finn has arrived. If you're planning on making a much-appreciated breakfast, you'd better get started." He looked up at the clock. "The video call is set to happen in forty minutes."

"No problem. I kept it simple." Anchorman walked over to the stove. He set the grocery bag down on the counter, then bent over to grab a large frying pan from the lower storage drawer.

"Your truck keys are on the counter." Ricki watched him reach over and pocket them before raising her cup in greeting when Finn walked in the door, followed closely by Dan.

"Where do you want me to set up?" he asked. When Ricki pointed at the space next to her, he nodded and put the laptop there.

While her fellow ISB agent fussed with the device, Ricki checked her messages, sending a quick text response to a few, and deleting several others. She watched Clay from the corner of her eye as he stepped outside, then shifted her gaze to Anchorman, who was busy at the stove. Finn glanced at the closed front door, then sent Ricki a questioning look. She shook her head and went back to her phone.

When Clay gestured to her to join him on the porch, she picked up her coffee cup and strolled across the room, quietly opening and closing the door.

She went to stand next to Clay, who put an arm around her shoulders and turned them so their backs were to the front window.

"I can't get hold of Ryan. I'm going to wait another ten

minutes, and if he doesn't call back by then, I'll send Jules over to check on him."

Ricki frowned, not liking the sound of that. "Ryan is watching Langly?"

"Yeah. He relieved Jules at seven this morning."

"About an hour ago, and now he isn't answering his phone?" Ricki chewed her lower lip. Ryan was a good deputy, but he was new on the job and still learning.

"There could be all kinds of reasons, and he'll call back in a few minutes. We'll just wait it out. If he doesn't call, Jules will have to get out of bed and go check on him."

A sharp rap on the window had them both turning around at the same time. Anchorman pointed toward the kitchen island, where Finn and Dan were already digging in to heaping plates of food.

Clay tucked his phone into the pocket of his jeans. "We have about fifteen minutes to eat before the phone call. Hopefully that will tell us if we need to worry any more about Langly."

Since there wasn't anything else she could do at the moment about the absent Ryan, Ricki went back inside and sat down to eat her food. She got through half her plateful before pushing it aside.

"I'll finish it later," she announced while pulling the laptop closer.

She studied the screen, locating the icon for the video chat, causing Dan to quickly hop off his stool and move to stand next to her. "I'll get us in. Hang on."

While he tapped a few keys, Ricki looked over at Finn and Anchorman. "We don't want to spook Mrs. Parkman with a lot of unfamiliar faces, so it might be best if you two stayed out of sight."

"No problem. We can stand on the other side of the

counter," Finn said before shoveling the last of his scrambled eggs into his mouth. Still chewing, he eyed Anchorman. "Why do these taste so much better than I've ever had anywhere else? Do you put something wonky in them?"

Anchorman frowned. "Wonky? What the hell does that mean?"

Ricki lifted a hand before they got into a loud debate. "Shh. Someone is logging in to the call."

A few seconds later a woman's face appeared on the screen. Thin features with prominent cheekbones and dark, tired eyes stared back at Dan.

"Good morning, Mrs. Bannu," he said. "It's good to see you. I have Chief Clayton Thomas, and Special Agent Ricki James here with me." He stepped back and angled the laptop so the camera picked up both Ricki and Clay. "As I explained to you during our phone call yesterday, they know quite a bit about Preston Malone's murder and can shed some light on any questions you have." He turned his head and looked at Ricki and Clay. "Agent James, Chief, this is LeeAnn Bannu. Sam Parkman's wife."

"We're very glad to be talking to you, Mrs. Bannu," Clay said. "Agent Wilkes informed us that you wanted to talk to us about Mr. Malone's murder."

"It sounds strange to be called the wife of someone you've never heard of. I've always been Gary's wife. I'm still trying to get my head around my husband having a another life he never breathed a word about." LeeAnn rubbed her fingers against the bangs that covered her forehead. Thick brown hair reached past her shoulders, stopping short of the nametag that was pinned to her shirt. "I only have a thirty-minute break for my lunch." Her voice was soft, with the flat accent of the Midwest running through it. Her mouth pulled up into a sad-looking smile. "And I've never heard Preston called a mister anything.

He's always been Buzzfeed. Agent Wilkes said that you don't know who killed him?"

"No, ma'am, we don't." Clay's gaze softened with sympathy. "If you were close, I'm sorry for your loss, and I understand your husband has also passed away?"

"Yes." She sighed raggedly. "Gary's been gone three years and I still have a hard time believing it. It's almost nine years to the day that we got his diagnosis, and he went into treatment right away. It helped some. At least for a while. Then he couldn't fight it anymore." She looked away from the screen. "That's when Buzzfeed came to see him. There at the end. Then he stayed on for the service. But he disappeared the next day, and I didn't hear from him again until last month." Her gaze returned to the screen. "That's when the package came."

"What package was that?" Clay asked.

"Money. And a note that said 'more is coming.' I had my suspicions who had sent it but wasn't sure until Agent Wilkes called." LeeAnn took a long breath. "It was a lot of money, Chief Thomas. Almost one hundred thousand dollars. I'd never seen so much money in my whole life. And I knew Buzzfeed had sent it."

Clay shifted on his stool to lean in closer. "What made you think it might have come from Buzzfeed?"

"Because after Gary passed, he told me to sit tight, that he would be sure I got Gary's share. That he'd be sending it for me and the kids, but it would take some time. When years went by and I didn't hear from him, I forgot all about it. Until that package arrived in the mail from a private courier service. They sent me a notice and I had to stay home that day to sign for it. It was wrapped in tinfoil, and I couldn't believe it when I peeled the foil away. A stack of money." She bowed her head and said in a small voice, "Gary's share, I guess."

"Is that the last time you talked to Malone, Mrs. Bannu?" Ricki asked. "Right after your husband passed away?"

"Yes. Like I said, he told me he'd be sure I got Gary's share, then he said something about rank not having all the privileges. He gave me a hug and walked off, and that was the last time I ever talked to him or heard from him, until the money was delivered to my house."

Ricki cast a quick glance at Anchorman. His eyes had narrowed, and he'd taken a wider stance as he stared intently at the back of the laptop. "Rank has its privileges" was a common saying among officers in the military, and the former Marine would know that.

"I thought I'd be hearing from someone about that money," LeeAnn said. "So I wasn't too surprised when Agent Wilkes called out of the blue. And I was sure it was about the money when I heard there was a police chief from Washington who wanted to talk to me. The mailing slip attached to the package said it was from Seattle." She hesitated, then squared her shoulders and lifted her chin. "Gary and Buzzfeed stole that money seven years ago, didn't they?"

Clay sat back, a frown on his face. "What makes you think it was seven years ago?"

LeeAnn shrugged. "The only time Gary left home and I didn't go with him was for three days, seven years ago. He was in the middle of his second round of chemotherapy, and he said he had to get some specialized tests down in Kansas City, and he wanted me to stay home with the kids." Her voice dropped to a whisper. "I remember because we had a fight about it, but he wouldn't let me come. So I stayed home." She brushed a tear away from her cheek. "That was the last fight we ever had."

"I'm sorry," Ricki said softly. "I know this is hard for you."

LeeAnn closed her eyes as she visibly struggled for control. "It is. And I considered not talking to you at all. But I've known since it got here that the money was stolen. Agent Wilkes told me it was a robbery in Dallas, and five men were killed. So I wanted a chance to tell you that neither my Gary nor Buzzfeed would have killed anyone like that. And they couldn't have planned a robbery at our local bank, much less in Dallas."

There was a drawn-out silence before Clay said, "We don't think so either, Mrs. Bannu. There were three men reported as having been in the getaway van. We're still looking for the third."

"And this third man was in the army with Gary and Buzzfeed, wasn't he?" LeeAnn nodded, her eyes clear again as she stared straight into the screen. "During Buzzfeed's last visit, he had a couple of private talks with Gary, but I left the door open a crack so I could listen." She sighed. "I thought I might hear something about me, or the kids, or the business. And Gary did talk about us some, but then I heard Buzzfeed say something about the money. And how the Fort Riley guys really managed to pull it off. Then Gary said that he wasn't going to live to enjoy it, but wanted to be sure his share went to me and the kids and hoped everything worked out, so they didn't have to leave anything behind. Then Buzzfeed made some comment about how the big dog wouldn't leave a dime in the road if there was a semitruck about to hit him, so Gary shouldn't have any worries about that."

"The Fort Riley guys," Clay repeated slowly. "You heard him mention Fort Riley?"

"Yes. Plain as day," LeeAnn said. "So after I was done talking with Agent Wilkes, I went up to the attic. That's where I'm storing most of Gary's things, including an old cardboard box with pictures. There were a lot of photos of some forests and lakes that you'd never see around here. I didn't even know Gary had those pictures. I found the box in the back of a cupboard in his workshop. When I first found it, I looked through them all, but I wasn't in a good way back then, so I didn't really know what I was looking at besides a lot of green trees and some lakes. But after I talked to Agent Wilkes, I remembered there was something else mixed in with all that scenery." She leaned down and picked up a purse that was the size of a small trunk and set it on her lap. She rummaged around in it for a moment, then drew out a large photo. After setting the purse back down on the floor, she slowly turned the picture around to face the screen. The black-and-white photo was slightly yellowed from age and showed a row of seven guys, dressed in fatigues and standing at attention. "I know Fort Riley is an army base in Kansas. I looked it up when I found this picture again. Gary never talked about his past. He always said he'd lost his soul when he served in a combat zone." A single tear trailed down LeeAnne's cheek. "Gary hated killing. He felt awful if he stepped on a bug." She looked down and sighed. "I guess the only way he got past it was to walk away from everything, including his family. So I figure this is the only picture of his life before we met."

Not the only picture, Ricki thought. She'd bet that the photos of forest and lakes had been part of his former life too.

"Anyway," LeeAnn went on. "I figure if it was the guys from Fort Riley, then I thought maybe the man who planned that robbery and shot all those people was in this picture. So I scanned it last night and can send it to you, if you want to get a closer look at it."

"I'd like that very much," Clay said, looking over at Dan.

"I'm texting you my email right now, Mrs. Bannu," Dan said. "If you could forward that photo, I'll wait to be sure it comes through."

"I sent it to my phone, so I'll do that right now." She reached down again and came up with a cell phone.

A few seconds later she looked up, just before Dan's phone

pinged. He quickly tapped some keys, then smiled. "I've got it. Thank you."

"I haven't spent any of that money," LeeAnn said. "I thought if no one asked, I would keep it as sort of a college fund for my three boys." Her chin quivered before she drew in a deep breath. "I guess we'll have to find another way for all that now."

Ricki sent a questioning look toward Finn, who shrugged and lifted his hands into the air, palms up.

"We'll be in touch to let you know of any developments in the case," Clay said. "Thank you again for all your help."

"You're welcome, Chief. I hope you catch the guy who shot Buzzfeed. He wasn't a bad man. Just easily led, that's all." With a nod, LeeAnn disconnected the call.

Dan pulled the laptop toward him and opened the attachments to the email from LeeAnn. When a picture came up on the screen, he glanced at Ricki. "Can you get your laptop and open up the second attachment to the email? I think I know what it is."

Ricki walked over to the far side of the living room and scooped up her laptop. She carried it back to the island and set it down next to Dan's. It only took a moment for her to open her email and click on the second attachment. It was a list of names, arranged horizontally.

"That's what I thought. She also sent us a scan of the back of the picture."

"Magpie," Ricki read, then glanced over at Dan's screen. "According to this list, that would be the second guy on the left. And the guy standing in back would be a Major Byers." Her gaze ran across the names, stopping at one. "Hang on. The guy on the far left." She looked back at Dan's screen. "Can you enlarge the picture so we can get a better look at him?"

When Dan complied, she and Clay both leaned in closer.

"Well, I'll be damned," Clay said under his breath.

"Yeah," Ricki said. "He's listed on the back as 'Cap'. Take away the glasses and give him a bald head and beard? And we're looking at a younger version of Captain Bill Langly."

There was a crash, and a loud "shit" from Finn. Ricki looked over just in time to see the FBI agent land face down on the counter as Anchorman ran out the front door.

Ricki took off after him, with Clay right behind her. She'd almost reached the hood of Anchorman's truck when he threw it into reverse and shot down the driveway, a plume of gravel spewing from beneath the tires. Swearing under her breath, she switched directions and headed for the SUV.

Clay scrambled behind the wheel and started the engine just as Finn dived into the back seat. "What the hell is going on? And why did that moron shove me into the counter? I've got crumbs and bits of egg all over the front of my shirt."

"You're not dying, Finn. Buckle up," Ricki called as Clay flipped on the siren. "We're trying to keep Anchorman from committing murder."

"Again? It's getting to be a habit," Finn grumbled as he fought to snap his seatbelt into place against the careening movements of the car.

"Do you know where you're going?" Ricki shouted at Clay over the racket from the siren.

"Yep. The always helpful Langly had me over for a beer not too long after I came to the Bay." He scowled through the windshield. "Checking out the local cop, I guess."

"Who the hell is Langly?" Finn demanded.

"The commander of the local VFW," Clay growled. "And the guy my deputy is supposed to be watching." He took a hand off the wheel just long enough to wave it at Ricki. "Call Jules. He only lives two blocks from Langly. Tell him to get over there and check on Ryan."

While Ricki relayed the message, Clay stepped on the gas. It took less than five minutes to race down Main Street and turn onto the first street bordering the outskirts of the town. They reached the tidy log cabin and skidded to a stop next to Anchorman's truck.

"Back here," Jules called out.

Ricki and Clay followed the sound of his voice around to the side, where Anchorman was kneeling over an unconscious Ryan. Clay immediately dropped to his knees on the other side, just as his deputy let out a long, low moan.

"I think he'll be okay," Anchorman said. "He took a hard knock on his head, though."

"I've called an ambulance and checked through the house," Jules volunteered. "Langly isn't there." He reached into his shirt pocket and pulled out a grubby-looking piece of paper. "found this on the laundry room floor. It looks like a work schedule from the Sunny Side Up." He unfolded it and held it out to Clay. "I figure it belonged to Sam because the day he was sot, Anchorman's name is crossed off and he wrote his own in." When Clay took it, Jules gave a nod. "Langly must have thought Anchorman wasn't coming in that day. It was bad luck for him that he was there, and so were you and Ricki."

"Yeah. That was bad luck." Clay tucked the note into his pocket. "How did you get into the house?"

Jules coughed then looked up at the sky.

"Someone kicked the door in," Anchorman said. He glanced at the street as the ambulance pulled up.

While the EMTs worked on Ryan, with Jules keeping a close eye on them, Ricki, Clay, Finn, and Anchorman moved off to the side.

"Where do you think the bastard would run to?" Anchorman snapped at Finn. "You guys must know something about him."

Finn crossed his arms over his chest and glared back at the Marine. "We don't know much, since we didn't know who the bastard was until thirty minutes ago." He looked at Clay. "My guess is that he'll head for the border."

Ricki's boot was tapping as she slowly looked at the house where Langly had lived for six years, then focused on Finn. "No. Not yet," she said slowly. "How much money did you say they would need to move every year to slowly get the two million out?"

"About three hundred thousand, a little less," Finn said. "Which is probably all they had left to move since we're six months shy of being seven full years since the robbery."

"Yeah. And remember what Malone told his dying friend?" Ricki asked.

"She said something about the big dog not leaving a dime on the road," Finn said.

"Yeah," Anchorman agreed with a nod. "She said he wouldn't leave it even if a semitruck was bearing down on him."

"Well, shit," Clay and Finn said in unison.

"That's right. He's going after the money." Ricki's smile was grim. "And we know exactly where it is."

Chapter Thirty

Clay wheeled around and strode over to where Jules was standing, his hands in his pockets as he watched the EMTs load Ryan into the ambulance. Ricki kept an eye on them as she lifted her phone to her ear, willing Dan to pick up, and hoping he was still at the cabin.

"Hey, Ricki. Is Langly under arrest?" Dan asked the minute he came on the line.

"He's on the run. Are you still at the cabin?"

"Yes. Why?"

Ricki breathed a sigh of relief. Every minute counted, and it saved time if he was there. "I need you to pinpoint the exact location of those GPS coordinates. The paper listing them is in my jacket."

"I can do that." There was the sound of footsteps. "I can create an electronic map you can pull up on your phone."

"No, that won't work," she said, her mind racing to put the pieces in place. "Those coordinates are in the park, and if Langly is headed there, accessing the internet and anything in the cloud is not going to be an option. Next to my desk is a bookcase. On the second shelf is a folder with maps of the park."

"Paper maps?" Dan's voice sounded pained, but once again there was the sound of him walking across the wood floors.

"Get the ones that work, pinpoint those GPS locations, and then use the copy function on my printer to make half a dozen." She watched Jules take off for his squad car as Clay headed back her way, then slapped her free hand over her ear not attached to the phone as the ambulance siren snapped on. "And do it in a hurry," she shouted above the noise. "We'll be there in five minutes."

Still holding her phone, she pivoted on her heels and broke into a flat-out run toward the SUV. Finn and Anchorman charged after her, with Clay not far behind.

No one said anything as Clay executed a U-turn with tires squealing. He flipped on the siren as they raced back through town, reaching the cabin in the five minutes Ricki had promised Dan, with them all popping out of the car like corks from a bottle once it had skidded to a stop. As they piled into the house, Ricki spotted Dan standing over the printer.

He lifted his hand in the air and put his thumb and index finger together, signaling an okay.

Leaving him to finish the task, Ricki walked over to the gun cabinet, ignoring the hopeful Corby with his bowl in his mouth. The minute she took out a rifle, the big boxer mix dropped his bowl with a clatter and went to stand by the front door.

"I don't think you'll be going along this time, big boy," Anchorman said with a head pat before passing the dog to help Ricki with the rifles.

"My boots are all lined up in the bottom of my closet," Clay told Finn. "Go find something that's fit for hiking."

Finn didn't argue, but took the stairs two at a time, disappearing into the hallway leading toward the bedrooms.

Clay caught the rifle Anchorman tossed him and automatically checked the chamber. "Jules is leading those two deputies from Tacoma over here. They brought their rifles with them." He leaned the empty gun against the side of the island. "He also said Ryan came around before they loaded him into the ambulance, and he said the last thing he remembers is looking at his watch at seven thirty. So he was only on his surveillance shift for half an hour before he was knocked out cold. He also wanted to know if anyone saw Scout running down the road. He thinks in all the confusion, he ran off. I told Jules to go get the deputies and report with them here, and we'll worry about the dog later."

Ricki's head immediately came up. "Scout?" Jules was right. She hadn't heard the usual ruckus Langly's German shepherd put up whenever anyone who he couldn't see approached. Frowning, she handed boxes of shells to Anchorman.

"I take it Langly wasn't at his house, and you think he's going to pick up the money?" Dan frowned. "He has most of it. Why wouldn't he just keep on running?"

"Because escaping through the park is a brilliant idea," Ricki said. "There's a maze of intersecting trails that lead to different exit points. It would be next to impossible to track a person or to cover all the escape routes."

Dan looked around when Finn came bounding down the stairs and said, "If you think he's gone into the park, how do the four of you propose to track him down?"

"He doesn't know we have those coordinates," Ricki stated, setting her rifle next to Clay's. "Is that the map?" She pointed at the stack of papers Dan was carrying.

"This is it." He laid the stack on the island's counter, then plucked one sheet off the top and moved the rest aside. As the other occupants in the room crowded around him, Dan smoothed the paper out and pointed to a row of three bright red Xs inked onto the map, lined up along the same trail that ended at a small lake. "There."

Ricki bent over and studied the lines and symbols running across the map, showing the trails and campsites located within the boundaries of the park. "It looks like he's divided the money between three spots on the Cedar Lake Way Trail. What are they? A half mile apart?"

"About that," Dan replied.

"How far in?" Clay asked.

"He probably went in at Dosewallips, and took that up to the Gray Wolf River Trail, so I'd say about twelve miles in once you get to the Elkhorn Campground." She pointed to the image of a small tent. "Which is there." She squinted at the small track that led from the Dosewallips River north toward the Xs that Dan had marked on the map. "He can come in off this trail, and then keep going north toward Gray Wolf." Her finger followed the faint track on the map. "And see here? He can take off on one of three forks in the trail, depending on how much of a hurry he's in."

"Well, someone knocked that deputy out, so we have to assume it was Langly," Finn said. "He knows we suspect him."

"And what he'll be expecting is for us to shut down all the roads leading out of the Bay. As far as he knows, there isn't any reason for us to assume he's gone into the park," Clay stated. "Which means he'll have made some attempt to hide his car. I'll have Jules look around the area near the trailhead while we hike in. Maybe he can spot it."

Anchorman checked his watch. "It's going on ten now. If he took off just after seven, he's got a three-hour head start on us. We need to get moving."

Ricki straightened and plucked up three copies of the map before turning to face Clay. "You're right. A three-hour start will put him halfway up the trail. He's going to have to stop and get the money, and we can save some time by going cross-country off Gray Wolf Trail toward the lake and coming up on him from the south, which he won't expect."

Clay nodded and gestured for Finn to move closer. "Take a look at the map. When the deputies get here, you need to hike in and cut off the escape route coming back to his car." He glanced at Ricki. "Where would he do that?"

"Here." She pointed at the spot, leaving her finger in place as Finn bent over double to read the small print identifying the trails. "That's where the Gray Wolf River Trail intersects with the Dosewallips."

"You and the two Tacoma deputies stay glued to that spot," Clay told the FBI agent. "If Langly comes back down that way, don't let him get past you."

Finn nodded. "He won't." He looked at Anchorman and then Ricki. "I'll see you in a few hours. Remember, this guy has already killed six people that we know of. Don't do anything stupid out there."

Anchorman didn't smile, but jerked his head in a curt nod and headed for the door. Clay picked up his rifle and followed him out, while Ricki smiled at Finn. "Don't you do anything stupid either."

He gave her a quick salute. "You can count on that." His grin quickly faded. "Good hunting, Special Agent James."

Ricki picked up her rifle and went out the door, closing it in the face of a disappointed Corby.

The ride to Dosewallips Road and the trailhead was made in silence. As soon as the SUV rolled to a stop in the primitive dirt lot, Ricki exited the car and slipped her arm through the shoulder strap of her rifle. She settled it comfortably on her back, then dropped a bagful of shells that Anchorman was holding out into her jacket pocket.

Within two minutes of reaching the trailhead, they were passing the road's washout and making quick time across the state land toward the border of Olympic National Park. A small sign marked the trail's entry into the park, and they continued, walking through the new growth of light and dark greens that said spring had finally arrived.

Ricki barely noticed the lush scenery all around, or the tall trees towering over her, their tops swaying in the breeze. As they made it past the walk-in campground, the skies overhead darkened. And by the time they had covered the six miles to the intersection point with the Gray Wolf River Trail, it was a sure thing that they'd be hunting for Langly in the rain.

They navigated their way through a series of switchbacks, making the twists and turns without slowing their pace until they reached the spot where the trail crossed the Gray Wolf River.

"We go cross-country from here," Ricki said, taking out her GPS compass.

She stepped off the trail and kept going, listening to the comforting sound of the solid bootsteps behind her. Taking a northwest angle that would bring them close to the first GPS coordinates, they slowed to a crawl as they neared the spot until Ricki completely stopped, holding up an arm to signal to the two men who immediately spread out on either side of her. She consulted the map, then pointed to a spot slightly off to her right.

They moved forward together, watching through the trees in front of them. They were only a few feet away from where her compass said the coordinate point was, when Anchorman's arm shot up. He pointed at the ground and waved Clay and Ricki over before squatting.

When Ricki reached him, she stared at the drag marks left

by a small log that had been moved, and the hollowed-out area it had been covering.

"Looks like he's been here," Clay said in an undertone.

Ricki nodded and glanced around, her head cocked to the side as she listened for any sound that was out of place. Nothing. She looked at the map and the compass, orienting herself to the next set of coordinates before moving out again. Still paralleling the trail, they were just over the halfway mark back to the bigger Gray Wolf Trail when she abruptly came to a stop.

There was a sound coming through the trees, and not one she had expected to hear. As it rapidly grew louder, she stuffed the map and compass into her jacket pocket. "Shit. That's a dog barking. He brought Scout."

She started running toward the sound, her rifle in one hand, Clay and Anchorman taking off after her. Dodging through the trees and wiping the rain out of her eyes, she followed the noise, slowing down when she spotted a black-and-tan body streaking through the forest ahead of her, splatters of water coming off its back with every step.

"Damn dog," Anchorman muttered just as a shot rang out.

Scout's barking immediately changed from excitement to fear as he ran that much harder toward them. They fanned out again and moved steadily through the trees. Ricki had lifted her rifle into firing position against her shoulder and was scanning the area in front of her through its scope. A slight movement had her adjusting her aim and firing in one smooth motion. It set off the sound of someone crashing through the forest, stepping on downed branches with a series of loud cracks. A moment later there was a flash of bright light overhead, followed by the loud crack of thunder as the skies opened up.

"Damn dog," Anchorman said again, this time louder as Scout stopped his terrified dash by running into the Marine's legs.

Leaving him to deal with Scout, Ricki and Clay kept moving forward, picking up their pace as they crossed the trail. With no choice but to give chase, they kept going until a bullet pinging off a tree less than a foot to Ricki's left had them diving for the ground. She rolled to the right, coming up behind a large boulder as Clay continued to return fire. Crawling her way to the other side of the boulder, she peeked around the edge.

And spotted Langly. He was far enough away she couldn't see him clearly, but there was definitely a man behind a tree farther up the trail. The slight rise in the ground gave him an advantage, and he was concentrating on Clay.

Keeping her eye on him, she got to her feet, then bent in a low crouch and sprinted from behind the boulder, making it to a tree with a wide solid trunk before a flurry of bullets came her way. She stayed pinned against the tree, waiting for Clay to make his move. When he did, Langly switched his shooting direction back toward him, and Ricki made another dash, widening the distance between herself and Clay as they worked in tandem to swing around Langly on both sides.

On her fourth dash, Langly was ready. Ricki dived behind a tree just as the shot rang out, thudding into the trunk and spraying her face with chips of bark. She squinted against the dust, lifting her rifle and getting a clear look at him through her scope.

"You can't get away, Bill," she called. "That money isn't worth dying for, is it?"

"Why not?" He followed the question with a short laugh. "Everyone else died for it. Why not me?"

Ricki tightened her finger on the trigger, then blinked when she heard a deep voice.

"Have it your way. Happy to accommodate you." Anchorman stepped away from a tree barely six feet from Bill

Langly, his rifle aimed right at the man's head. "The good news for you is that you don't have to worry about any pesky wounds, because I'm not going to miss."

Ricki let out her breath and slowly stood up as Clay appeared on the opposite side of the trail.

"Set the rifle down, Langly," Clay told him. "Carefully. Set it down very carefully, then lace your fingers behind your neck."

Langly stared at him until Anchorman stepped forward and put the barrel of his rifle against the post commander's head. Then he slowly lowered his rifle and set it on the ground. "You aren't going to let this sniper kill me, are you, Chief? How would that sit with your conscience?"

"It might give me a few bad nights," Clay said as he moved forward and picked up the rifle. "But he's got good reason to do it."

Langly's shoulders tensed as Anchorman poked him with his rifle. "It wasn't personal. She had evidence in that lab that I needed to destroy, and she wouldn't tell me where it was."

"There wasn't any evidence there, so you beat her for nothing," Ricki said, the heat in her voice hot enough to melt rock. "Why did you kill Malone?"

Langly shrugged. "The order was no contact. No contact for seven years until we could get all the money out. I knew the CIA could trace those bills. That's why I issued that no contact order. And Malone broke it. He sent Magpie's wife one hundred thousand of our money. And he told me he didn't care about obeying the order. It had been long enough. But a soldier doesn't disobey orders, whether he likes them or not." He turned his head slightly to look at Anchorman from the corner of his eye. "You should understand that better than anyone."

Anchorman's response was to give the man another poke in

the back with the barrel of his rifle. Hard enough to send Langley stumbling and then sinking to his knees.

Rick walked around to stand in front of him. Waiting until Langly looked up at her. "You stole Malone's body from the clinic," Ricki said. "Where is it?"

Langly's lips twitched. "Loose a body, did you?" Beneath his beard his mouth curled into a smile. "I'm thinking no body, no crime, so good luck finding it."

"We'll have plenty of time to look. The FBI is searching the records of commercial airlines that flew in and out of the Dallas airport. They'll put you in Dallas at the time of the robbery." She pointed to an backpack lying next to a tree. "And I wonder if we'll find some of that money right over there?"

"There's an FBI agent waiting for you," Clay stated. "And you'll get a chance to help the CIA trace all that money, and maybe you can make a deal for better accommodations than an isolation cell at one of their supermax prisons if you cough up the name of your information source inside the Bureau." He moved the barrel of his rifle up and down. "Get up and turn around." When Langly had complied, Clay slipped some zip-tie handcuffs onto his wrists.

"We can walk him back along the trail. It's a longer hike, but easier than going back cross-country," Ricki said. She pointed north. "That way. It will cross the Gray Wolf River Trail in another mile or so."

Clay prodded Langly forward. "If you even twitch in the wrong direction, I'm going to let Anchorman shoot you. And it won't bother my conscience at all."

As they moved off, Ricki prepared to follow, then frowned when Anchorman stayed where he was, an annoyed look on his face as rain drizzled off his forehead and down his face.

"He'll end up in a federal prison for the rest of his life," she said. "That's going to have to be good enough."

"Yeah, I know that." Anchorman shouldered his rifle, then lifted his jacket and pointed at his waist. "I used my belt to tie Scout up to a small tree. I have to go back and get him before he breaks loose, or something around here eats him. Damn dog." He glanced over at the backpack. "no one's counted that yet, have they?"

"Nope," Ricki said. "it's a shame that whatever is in there will go back to the CIA."

Anchorman gave her a speculative look. "Yeah. I think it would be safer in a bank in Nebraska."

She shrugged. "I have no idea what bank the CIA uses." She let out a huge sigh. "That pack looks heavy."

The retired Marine grinned. "I'll carry it, and hand it over to Finn after I rescue Scout. Can I borrow that GPS compass you always carry around?"

Without a word, Ricki handed it over then shook her head at his wide grin. When he did an about face and marched off, her laughter followed him as he disappeared into the trees. She was still laughing when she caught up with Clay and Langly. Giving Clay a quick kiss on the cheek, she moved in front and led the way back down the trail. They were all soaking wet, and she was sure it would take a week to dry out her boots, but they'd got the job done. So right at that moment, rain and all, life was good.

Epilogue

Ricki stepped out of the limecicle and slowly walked up the cement steps leading into the flat one-story building that looked like a giant spider sprawled in the middle of a green space. She crossed the faded tile floor, buffed to a dull shine with several coats of wax that had her high heels sticking to it with every step. A long oak counter reached across the back of the lobby, and was manned by a young man and older woman, both of them in white scrubs.

Ricki smiled at the young man but turned toward the older woman, standing patiently in front of her until she looked up.

"Well, now, Ricki James, I wasn't entirely sure you were going to make it." Liddy Stoltz lowered her chin and peered at Ricki over the top of her glasses, held to her nose by a chain that looped around the back of her neck. She'd been the head nurse at the Golden West Home in Tacoma for as long as Ricki's mom had been there.

"It's not something I'd ever miss," Ricki said. "At least not if I ever wanted to show my face in town again."

After giving the brief instruction to "mind the lobby" to the young man sitting next to her, Nurse Stoltz pushed away from the desk and stood up.

"Everything is ready. Just come this way and we'll get you started." She led the way down the main hallway, stopping at a pair of double doors. "I assume you have no regrets about this?"

"No," Ricki said with a smile. "Not a one."

"All right." The usually stoic nurse gifted her with a wide smile. "Then I'll just say that you look beautiful." She cleared her throat and reached over to knock on the door. "I'll leave you to it. I'm sure all the residents will enjoy the cake you had sent over."

When the doors opened, Marcie and Kate greeted her with smiles and watery eyes.

The waitress threw her arms around Ricki in a fierce hug. "I can't believe this is happening. I am so very, very happy for you."

When Marcie stepped back with a loud sniff, Kate took her place. Settling for a quick kiss on the cheek, she handed Ricki a bouquet of vibrant wildflowers. "Straight from the park, just like you wanted."

Ricki smiled her thanks and looked down the short aisle of the chapel used by the residents of the rest home. Her mother was sitting quietly in a wheelchair next to the end of the front pew, with her Uncle Cy right next to her. Behind them was Finn, dressed in a black suit and light blue shirt with a matching paisley tie, which was a big contrast to Ricki's ex-husband, Bear, decked out in his usual outfit of jeans and a flannel shirt. On the other side of the aisle sat Seattle's district attorney, Andre Hudson, and his wife Lydia, who had an arm around Cheron's thin shoulders.

Moisture gathered at the corner of Ricki's eyes as she took in the small group before her gaze lifted to the three men standing at the front. Anchorman looked as imposing as ever in his dress uniform. When he winked at her, she beamed back at him before her gaze moved to the tall, thin figure of her teenage son, Eddie. He looked so much like her father that it brought a tear to her eye until she saw the horrified expression on his face.

Laughing, she shook her head at him, then fixed her gaze on Clay. He was always handsome, but today she didn't notice. All she saw was the love in his eyes as she drifted down the aisle. She stopped by the wheelchair and sank down until she was at eye level with her mom.

Reaching her arms around frail shoulders, she gently put her cheek against her mother's and closed her eyes, remembering the hugs and love Miriam McCormick had given her only daughter over the years.

"I found him, Mom," she whispered. "I found my Einstein." Her eyes opened in shock when she felt a hand lightly brush down her thick fall of dark hair. When she pulled back, for a moment, she could see the mom she remembered looking back at her.

Rising to her feet, Ricki turned and walked to Clay, a smile on her lips and tears in her eyes. In a few weeks they'd have the big party to celebrate the marriage the whole Bay had been waiting for, but right now she had everyone here that she loved the most and that was more than enough.

It was perfect.

* * *

Thank you for reading Chasing Lies. The adventure continues in C.R. Chandler's latest series, Gin Reilly, An FBI Thriller. Gin has joined the newly formed Critical Crimes Unit within the FBI, and along with a new partner, Treynor Robard, a former Naval Rescue Pilot, she's soon deep into the case of a serial killer with a decade of bodies strewn behind him. And much to her horror, she also uncovers a family secret of her own —a legacy from her murderous father that's more spine chilling than anything she'd imagined.

Now on Amazon! Click Here for A Hard Truth

Author Notes

Thank you for reading Chasing Lies. I hope you'll enjoy Special Agent Gin Reilly's equal dedication in hunting down killers and bringing them to justice as she tries to unravel the truth behind an old family secret of her own. *A Hard Truth*, Book One in the Gin Reilly, An FBI Thriller series is available on Amazon. Click Here

You can follow C.R. Chandler, by subscribing to the author's free newsletter. In addition to receiving notifications to any upcoming books, you will also be able to download a free e-book from the popular Special Agent Ricki James series, and only available to anyone who signs up to receive the free Author's newsletter. To sign up today, click here:

Subscribe to Free Author Newsletter here!

Author Notes

I'm always interested in hearing opinions and suggestions from readers. If you like a particular character, or book, plot, setting (or if there is one you really didn't like!), I'd love to hear your thoughts. Or—if there's a national park you'd like to see in a book, or more of a favorite character or storyline—let me know. Interacting with readers on a one-on-one basis is one of the better parts of my day. (I will admit, I am not very good on the larger social media sites since I'm a little on the introverted side on those kind of stages. . . but I'm working on it). Drop me a line: Send an Email to CR Chandler

* * *

I do have a Facebook page if you'd like to drop by there as well —and maybe remind me I should be posting to it on a regular basis: https://www.facebook.com/crchandlerauthor/

And for those of you on BookBub, here is the link to follow me (and much appreciated!): https://www.bookbub.com/authors/c-r-chandler

To visit my website, click here: https://www.crchandlerbooks.com/

Made in United States
Troutdale, OR
06/23/2024

20763075R00189